VAMPIRE HUNTER D

OMNIBUS BOOK TWO

VAMPIRE HUNTER D

VOLUME 4
TALE OF THE DEAD TOWN

Written by

HIDEYUKI KIKUCHI

Illustrations by

YOSHITAKA AMANO

English translation by

KEVIN LEAHY

Dark Horse Books

Milwaukie

VAMPIRE HUNTER D

Journey by Night

I

On the Frontier, nothing was considered more dangerous than a journey by night.

Claiming the night was their world, the Nobility had once littered the globe with monsters and creatures of legend, as if to adorn the pitch-black with a touch of deadly beauty. Those same repugnant creatures ran rampant in the land of darkness to this very day. That was how the vampires bared their fangs at the human idea that held the light of day as the time for action and the dark of night for rest. The darkness of night was the greatest of truths, the vampires claimed, and the ruler of the world. *Farewell, white light of summer.*

That was why the night was filled with menace. The moans of dream demons lingered in the wind, and the darkness whispered the threats of dimension-ripping beasts. Just beyond the edge of the woods glowed eyes the color of jasper. So many eyes. Even well-armed troops sent into devastated sections of the Capital felt so relieved after they'd slipped through the blocks of dilapidated apartment complexes that they'd flop down right there on the road.

Out on the Frontier it was even worse. On the main roads, crude way stations had been built at intervals between one lodging place and the next. But, when the sun went down on one of the support roads linking the godforsaken villages, travelers were forced to defend themselves with nothing more than their own two hands and whatever weapons they could carry. There were only two beings that chose to travel by night. The Nobility. And dhampirs. Particularly if the dhampir was a Vampire Hunter.

Scattering a shower of moonlight far and wide, the shadowy form of a horse and rider climbed a desolate hill. The mount was just an average cyborg horse, but the features of the rider were as clean and clear as a jewel, like the strange beauty of the darkness and the moon crystallized. Every time the all-too-insistent wind touched him, it trembled with uncertainty, whirled, and headed off bearing a whole new air. Carrying a disquieting aura. His wide-brimmed traveler's hat, the ink-black cape and scarf darker than darkness, and the scabbard of the elegant longsword that adorned his back were all faded and worn enough to stir imaginings of the arduous times this traveler had seen.

The young traveler had his eyes closed, perhaps to avoid the wind-borne dust. His profile was so graceful it seemed the Master Craftsman in heaven above had made it His most exquisite work. The rider appeared to be thoroughly exhausted and immersed in a lonely sleep. Sleep—for him it was a mere break in the battle, but a far cry from peace of mind.

Something else mixed with the groaning of the wind. The traveler's eyes opened. A lurid light coursed into them, then quickly faded. His horse never broke its pace. A little over ten seconds was all they needed to reach the summit of the hill. Now the other sounds were clear. The crack of a gun and howls of wild beasts.

The traveler looked down at the plain below, spying a mid-sized motor home that was under attack. Several lesser dragons were prowling around it—more "children of the night" sown by the Nobility. Ordinarily, their kind dwelt in swamplands farther to the south, but occasionally problems with the weather controllers would send packs of dragons north. The migration of dangerous species was a serious problem on the Frontier.

The motor home was already half-wrecked. Holes had been ripped in the roofs of both the cab and the living quarters, and the lesser dragons kept sticking their heads in. The situation was clear just from the smoking scraps of wood, the sleeping bags, and a pair of partially eaten and barely recognizable human bodies lying in front of the motor home. Due to circumstances beyond their control—most likely something to do with their propulsion system—the family had been forced to camp out instead of sleeping in their vehicle like they should. But words couldn't begin to describe how foolhardy they'd been to expect one little campfire to keep the creatures that prowled the night at bay. There were three sleeping bags. But there weren't enough corpses to account for everyone.

Once again a gunshot rang out, a streak of orange from a window in the living quarters split the darkness, and one of the dragons reeled back as the spot between its eyes exploded. For someone foolish enough to camp out at night, the shooter seemed well informed and incredibly skilled with a gun. People who lived up north had usually never heard where to aim a kill shot on southern creatures like these lesser dragons. But a solution to that puzzle soon presented itself. There was a large magneto-bike parked beside the vehicle. Someone was pitching in to rescue them.

The rider tugged on the reins of his cyborg horse. Shaking off the moonlight that encrusted its body like so much dust, the horse suddenly began its descent. Galloping down the steep slope with the sort of speed normally reserved for level ground, the mount left a gale in its wake as it closed on the lesser dragons.

Noticing the headlong charge by this new foe, a dragon to the rear of the pack turned, and the horse and rider slipped by its side like a black wind. Bright blood didn't spout from between the creature's eyes until the horse had come to a sudden halt and the traveler had dismounted with a flourish of his cape. The way he walked toward the creatures—with their colossal maws gaping and rows of bloody teeth bared—seemed leisurely at first glance, but in due time showed the swiftness of a swallow in flight. All around the young man in black there was the sound of steel meeting steel time and time again. Unable to pull apart the jagged teeth they'd just brought together, each and every one of the lesser dragons around him collapsed in a bloody spray as gashes opened between their eyes. And the dragon leaping at him from the motor home's roof was no exception.

The young man's gorgeous countenance seemed weary of the cries of the dying creatures, but his expression didn't change in the slightest, and, without even glancing at the two mangled bodies, he returned his longsword to its sheath and headed back to his cyborg horse. As if to say he'd just done this on a lark, as if to suggest he didn't give a thought to the well-being of any survivors, he turned his back on this death-shrouded world and tightened his grip on the reins.

"Hey, wait a minute," a masculine voice called out in a some-what agitated manner. The young man stopped and turned around. The vehicle's door opened and a bearded man in a leather vest appeared. In his right hand he held a single-shot armor-piercing rifle. A machete was tucked through his belt. With the grim countenance he sported, he'd have looked more natural holding the latter instead of a gun. "Not that I don't appreciate your help, bucko, but there's no account for you just turning and making tracks like that now. Come here for a minute."

"There's only one survivor," the young man said. "And it's a child, so you should be able to handle it alone."

A tinge of surprise flooded the other man's hirsute face. "How did you . . . ? Ah, you saw the sleeping bags. Now wait just a minute, bucko. The atomic reactor has a cracked heat exchanger and the whole motor home's lousy with radiation now. That's why the family went outside in the first place. The kid got a pretty good dose."

"Hurry up and take care of it then."

"The supplies I'm packing won't cut it. A town doctor's gotta see to this. Where are you headed, buddy? The Zemeckis rendezvous point?"

"That's right," the young man in black replied.

"Hold on. Just hold everything. I know the roads around here like the back of my hand."

"So do I." The young man turned away from the biker once again. Then he stopped. As he turned back, his eyes were eternally cold and dark.

The child was standing behind the biker. Her black hair would've hung past her waist if it hadn't been tied back by a rainbow-hued ribbon. The rough cotton shirt and long skirt did little to hide her age, or the swell of her full bosom. The girl was a beauty, around seventeen or eighteen years old. As she gazed at the young man, a curious hue of emotion filled her eyes. There was something in the gorgeous features of the youth that could make her forget the heart-rending loss of her family as well as the very real danger of losing her own life. Extending her hand, she was just about to say something when she crumpled to the ground face down.

"What did I tell you—she's hurt bad! She's not gonna last till dawn. That's why I need your help."

The youth wheeled his horse around without a word. "Which one of us will carry her?" he asked.

"Yours truly, of course. Getting you to help so far has been like pulling teeth, so I'll be damned if I'm gonna let you do the fun part."

The man got a leather belt off his bike and came back, then put the young woman on his back and cleverly secured her to himself. "Hands off," the man said, glaring at the youth in black as he straddled his magneto-bike. The girl fit perfectly into the seat behind him. It looked like quite a cozy arrangement. "Okay, here I go. Follow me." The man grabbed the handlebars, but before twisting the grip starter, he turned and said, "That's right— I didn't introduce myself, did I? I'm John M. Brasselli Pluto VIII."

"D."

"That's a good name you got there. Just don't go looking to shorten mine for something a little easier to say. When you call me, I'll thank you kindly to do it by my full name. John M. Brasselli Pluto VIII, okay?" But, while the man was driving his point home, D was looking to the skies. "What is it?" the biker asked.

"Things out there have caught the scent of blood and are on their way."

The black creatures framed against the moon were growing closer. A flock of avian predators. And lupine howls could be heard in the wind.

†

Expectations to the contrary, no threat materialized to hamper the party's progress. They rode for about three hours. When the hazy mountains far across the plain began to fill their field of view and take on a touch of reality, John M. Brasselli Pluto VIII turned his sharp gaze to D, who rode alongside him. "If we go to the foot of that there mountain, the town should be by. What business you got with them anyway, bucko?" he asked. When D made no answer he added, "Damn, playing the tough guy again I see. I bet you're used to just standing there doing the strong, silent type routine and getting all the ladies, chum. You're good at what you do, I'll give you that—just don't count on that always doing the trick for you. Sooner or later, it's always some straight-shooter like me that ends up the center of attention."

D looked ahead without saying a word.

"Aw, you're no fun," the biker said. "I'm gonna gun it the rest of the way."

"Hold it."

Pluto VIII went pale for a minute at the sharp command, but, in what was probably a show of false courage, he gave the grip starter a good twist. Uranium fuel sent pale flames spouting from the boosters, and the bike shot off in a cloud of dust. It stopped almost as quickly. The engine was still shuddering away, but the wheels were just kicking up sand. In the dazzling moonlight, his atomic-powered bike was not only refusing to budge an inch despite its five-thousand-horsepower output, it was actually sinking into the ground. "Dammit all," he hissed, "a sand viper!"

The creature in question was a colossal serpent that lived deep in the earth, and, although no one had ever seen the entire body of one, they were said to grow upwards of twenty miles long. Frighteningly enough, though the creatures were said to live their entire lives without ever moving a fraction of an inch, some believed they used high-frequency vibrations to create fragile layers of earth and sand in thousands of places on the surface so they might feed on those unfortunate enough to stumble into one of their traps. These layers moved relentlessly downward, becoming a kind of quicksand. Due to the startling motion the sands displayed, those who set foot into them would never make it out again. To get some idea of how tenacious the jaws of this dirt-and-sand trap were, one had only to watch how the five thousand horses in that atomic engine strained themselves to no avail. For all the bike's struggling, its wheels had already sunk halfway into the sand.

"Hey, don't just stand there watching, stone face. If you've got a drop of human blood in your veins, help me out here!" Pluto VIII shouted fervently. His words must've done the trick because D grabbed a thin coil of rope off the back of his saddle and dismounted. "If you screw this up, the rope'll get pulled down, too. So make your throw count," the man squawked, and then his eyes went wide. The gorgeous young man didn't throw him the rope. Keeping it in hand, he started to calmly walk into the quicksand. Pluto VIII opened his mouth to howl some new curse at the youth, but it just hung open—and for good reason.

The young man in black had started to stride elegantly over deadly jaws that would wolf down any creature they could find. His black raiment danced in the wind, the moonlight ricocheting off it as flecks of silver. He almost looked like the Grim Reaper coming in the guise of aid, but ready to wrap a black cord around the neck of those reaching out to him for succor.

The rope flew through the air. Excitedly grabbing hold of the end of it, Pluto VIII tied it around his bike's handlebars. The rest of the coiled rope still in hand, D went back to solid ground and climbed onto his cyborg horse without saying a word.

"Alright! Now on the count of—" Pluto never got to finish what he was saying as his bike was tugged forward. "Hey! Give me a second. Let me give it some gas, too," he started to say, but he only had a moment to tighten his grip on the throttle before the bike and its two riders were free of the living sands and its tires were resting once more on solid ground.

"Bucko, what the hell are you anyway?" Pluto VIII asked the mounted youth, with a shocked look on his face. "We'd be lucky to get away from a sand viper with a tractor pulling us, never mind a cyborg horse. And here you go and yank us out without even working up a sweat . . . I thought you was a mite too good-looking, but you're not human after all, are you?" Smacking his hands together, he exclaimed, "I've got it—you're a dhampir!"

D didn't move. His eternally cold gaze was fixed on the moonlit reaches of the darkness, as if seeking a safe path.

"But you don't have anything to worry about," the biker added. "My motto is 'Keep an open mind.' It don't matter if the folks around me have red skin or green—I don't discriminate. So long as they don't do wrong by yours truly, that is. Naturally, that includes dhampirs, too." Pluto VIII's voice had the ring of unquestionable sincerity to it.

Suddenly, without glancing at the biker who seemed ready to burst with the milk of human kindness, D asked in a low voice, "Are you ready?"

"For what?" Pluto VIII must've caught something in the Hunter's disinterested tone because his eyes went to D, then instantly swept around to the left and right, to the fore and rear. Aside from the piece of land the three of them were on, little black holes were forming all over the place. As sand coursed down into them the way it does into an antlion pit, the funnel-shaped holes quickly grew larger until one touched another, encircling the trio like the footprints of some unseen giant.

II

Son of a bitch . . . Don't seem like this freakin' sand viper aims to let us out of here alive," Pluto VIII said, the laughter strong in his voice. Sometimes a bit of cheer came to him in the midst of utter despair, but that had nothing to do with Pluto VIII's laugh, still full of confidence and hope.

But how on earth could they get themselves out of this mess? It didn't look like even D, with all his awesome skill, could get out of these preposterously large antlion pits. Especially since he wasn't alone. His traveling companion had a young woman strapped to his back, and, since she was suffering from extreme radiation poisoning, time was of the essence.

"Hey, what do we do?" Pluto VIII asked, looking extremely interested in the answer.

"Close your eyes and duck!" came the harsh reply.

Pluto VIII didn't have the faintest idea what was going on, but the instant he complied the whole world filled with white light. Under the pillar of light stretching down to the bottom of the colossal funnel, grains of sand grew super-hot, bubbled, and cooled almost instantly into a glassy plain reflecting the moon. The pillar of light silently stretched to the sky time and again, and, as D squinted ever so slightly at this mixing of light and darkness, his face was at times starkly lit, at other times deep in shadow. It seemed to go on for ages, but it couldn't have taken more than a few seconds. Aside from the dim, white depressions gleaming like water, the moonlit plain was just as it'd been before—deathly still.

"Looks like an atomic blast blew the hell out the sand viper holes— melted 'em and turned 'em to glass. Who the hell could've done that?" Pluto VIII asked, and then he once again followed D's gaze. He might've been well informed, but a gasp of wonder escaped from him nonetheless.

A black shadow that seemed both circular and oblong clung to the central part of the distant mountain range. It wasn't on the mountain's rocky walls. The shadowy shape was crossing the mountain peaks. Not only that, but, as it slowly moved forward, it was clearly coming lower as well. Taking the distance into consideration, it must've been moving at a speed of twelve or thirteen miles per hour at least. It was round, and about two miles in diameter.

"So, we have them to thank then?" Pluto VIII asked.

D gave a negligible nod. "Good thing there's still a mobile town around equipped with a Prometheus cannon. Incredible marksmanship, too. Our saviors got here right on schedule."

"Well, thank heaven for that. I just hope the mayor ain't the kind of guy who'll expect us to return the favor. Let's go," said the biker. "I don't feel like waiting around for the town to get here!"

The bike's boosters roared and the thud of iron-shod hooves on earth echoed across the plain. After they'd run at full speed for a good ten minutes, the huge black shape floated up over the crest of a hill before them like a cloud. The bottom was covered with spheres constructed of iron and wood, as well as with pipes. The white smoke erupting from the latter indicated that compressed air was one of the types of energy driving the cloud forward. And yet, how much thrust would be necessary just to move this thing an inch? After all, this massive structure that made the earth tremble as it came over the slope and slowly slid down it was a whole town. Even knowing that, even seeing it up close, it was no easy task to comprehend something so awesome. The town must've covered more than two square miles. On top of a massive circular base some thirty feet high, buildings of wood, plastic, and iron were clustered together. Between them ran streets, some straight and orderly, others twisting and capricious. At the edge of the densely packed buildings there was a small park and a cluster of tombstones that marked the cemetery.

Of course, in addition to the residential sector, there was everything you'd find in an ordinary village or town—a hospital, a sheriff's office, a jail, and a fire station. In the park, live trees swayed with the wind.

Startlingly enough, the base that supported this colossal establishment and was indispensable in its smooth movement hovered some three feet off the ground. That wasn't something just compressed-air jets or rocket engines could manage. No doubt power produced by the atomic reactor inside the base was run through a subatomic particle-converter and changed to antigravity energy. Still, to keep the structure a good three feet off the ground, there had to be some secret to the output of their atomic reactor or the capacity of their converters.

The base loomed blackly before the two men, and the mechanical whoosh blew closer and closer. A blinding light flashed down on the trio of travelers from a platform near the iron inlay on the top edge of the base. A voice boomed over the speakers. "What do you folks want?"

Pluto VIII pulled the microphone from his bike to his mouth and answered, "We're travelers. And we got an injured person here. We'd like to have a doctor take a look at 'er. Would you let us in?"

There was silence. The searchlight continued to shine on the pair. Well-concealed guns, no doubt, had them locked in their crosshairs. After a while, there was a reply. "No can do. We're not taking on any new blood. The town's population is already thirty percent over what our resources can support. Find yourselves another town or village. The closest one's twelve and a half miles from here—a place by the name of Hahiko."

"You've gotta be yanking my chain!" Pluto VIII growled, pounding a fist against his handlebars. "Who the hell's talking about twelve and a half miles?! Look, this girl I've got on my back's been doused real bad with radiation. She couldn't make it another hundred yards, let alone twelve and a half miles. What are you, the freaking Nobility?!"

"Nothing you can say's gonna make any difference," the voice said coldly. "These orders come from the mayor. On top of that, the girl is part of the Knight family—Lori's her name. Two and a half months back they left town, so we're not about to let one of them back in now."

"I don't give a rat's ass about that. We got a girl in the prime of her life about to die. What, don't any of you have kids?"

The voice fell silent again. When another announcement rang out, it was a different person's voice. "We're set to roll," the new speaker said, "so clear the way!" And then, sounding somewhat agitated, he added, "Hey, young fellah—you wouldn't happen to be named D, would you?"

The youth nodded slightly.

"Oh, you should've said so in the first place. I'm the one who sent for you. Mayor Ming's the name. Just a second and we'll let you on board."

Machinery groaned, the iron door rose upward, and a boarding ramp started to glide out.

D said softly, "I've got some companions."

"Companions?!" Mayor Ming's voice quavered. "I'd always heard you were the most aloof, independent Hunter on earth. Just when did you get these companions?"

"Earlier."

"Earlier? You mean those two?"

"Do you see anyone else?" the Hunter asked.

"No—it's just . . . "

"I've fought side by side with them. That's the only reason I have. But if you have no business with me, I'll be on my way."

"W . . . wait a minute." The mayor's tone shifted from vacillating to determined. "We can't afford to lose you. I'll make a special exception for them. Come aboard."

The earth shook as the broad boarding-ramp hit the ground. Once the travelers were on, along with the bike and the cyborg horse, the ramp began to rise once again.

"The nerve of these people and their overblown escalator," Pluto VIII carped.

As soon as the ramp had retracted into the town's base, an iron door shut behind them and the two men found themselves in a vast chamber that reeked of oil. A number of armed men in the prime of life and a gray-haired old man stood there. The latter was more muscular in build than the men who surrounded him. Mayor Ming, no doubt. He may have had trouble walking, as he carried a steel cane in his right hand. "Glad you could make it," he said. "I'm Ming."

"Introductions can wait," Pluto VIII bellowed. "Where's the doctor?"

The mayor gave a nod, and two men stepped forward and unstrapped the girl—Lori—from the biker's back. "I imagine your companion's more interested in eating than hearing us talk business," the mayor said, signaling the other men with his eyes.

"Damn straight—you read my mind. Well, I'm off then, D. See you later."

When Pluto VIII had disappeared through a side door following his guides at his own leisurely pace, the mayor led D to a passage-way that continued up to the next level. The whistling of the wind seemed to know no end. All around them, ash-colored scenery rolled by. Forests and mountains. The town was moving across Innocent Prairie, the second of the Frontier's great plains. Whipping the Hunter's pitch-black cape and tossing his long, black hair, the wind blurred the wilds around them like a distant watercolor scene.

"How do you like the view?" Mayor Ming made a wave of one arm as if mowing down the far reaches of the plain. "Majestic, isn't it?" he said. Perhaps he'd taken the lack of expression on the young man staring off into the darkness as an expression of wonder. "The town maintains a cruising speed of twelve miles per hour. She can climb any mountain range or cliff, so long as it's less than a sixty-degree incline. Of course, we can only do that when we give the engines a blanket infusion of antigravity energy. This is how we always guarantee our five hundred residents a safe and comfortable journey."

"A comfortable journey, you say?" D muttered, but his words might not have reached the mayor's ears. "That's fine, as long as wherever you're headed is safe and comfortable, too. What do you want with me?"

The Hunter's hair flew in the wind that howled across the darkened sky. They were standing on an observation platform set at the very front of the town. If this had been a ship, it would've been the bow—or perhaps the prow. Jutting as it did from the top of the town's base, it seemed like it'd be the perfect spot to experience wind and rain and all the varied aspects of the changing seasons.

"Don't you care how that girl Lori's doing?" the mayor asked, ignoring D's inquiry.

"Stick to business."

"Hmm. A man who can slice a laser beam in two, who's discarded all human emotion . . . You're just like the stories make you out to be. I don't care how thick the Noble blood runs in you dhampirs, you could stand to act a tad more human."

D turned to leave.

"Come now. Don't go yet. Aren't you the hasty one," the mayor called, not seeming particularly overanxious. "There's only one reason anyone ever calls a Vampire Hunter—and that's for killing Nobility."

D turned back.

"When I let that man on two hundred years ago, I never in my wildest dreams would've thought something like this could happen," the mayor muttered. "That was the biggest mistake of my life."

D brushed his billowing hair back with his left hand.

"He was standing at the foot of the Great Northern Mountains, all alone. When we had him in the spotlight, he looked like the very darkness condensed. Now as a rule this town doesn't take on folks we just meet along the way, but it might've been the way he looked that stopped us dead in our tracks. There was a deep, dark look to his eyes. Come to think of it, he looked a lot like you."

The wind filled the sudden gap in conversation. After a pause, the mayor continued. "As soon as he was aboard, he came up here to the deck and looked out at the nocturnal wilds and rugged chain of mountains for the longest time. And then he calmly turned to me and said, 'Choose from the townsfolk five men and five women of surpassing strength and intellect, that they may join me in my travels.' Of course, I had to chuckle at that. At which point he laughed like thunder and said, 'Agree to my offer, and your people will know a thousand years of glory. Refuse, and this town will be cursed for all eternity to wander the deadly wilds,'" said the mayor, breaking off there. Pitch-black fatigue clung to his powerful and strangely smooth face. "Then he was gone. A touch of anxiety filled my heart, but nothing happened to the town after that. The next two hundred years weren't exactly one continuous stretch of peace and prosperity, but now I think I can safely say they were times of pure bliss. Now that the dark days are upon us. If this town is indeed under a curse as he decreed, we shall never be graced with glory or prosperity again."

Perhaps the reason the mayor had invited the Vampire Hunter up onto the deck was to show him the deadly wilds of their destiny.

"Come with me," Mayor Ming said. "I'll show you the real problem at hand."

A girl lay on a simple bed. Even without seeing her paraffin-pale skin or the wounds at the base of her throat, it was clear she was a victim of the Nobility. The most unsettling thing about her was her eyes—she had them trained on the ceiling, but they still had the spark of life.

"This is my daughter Laura. She's almost eighteen," said the mayor.

D didn't move, but remained looking down at the pale throat against the pillow.

"Three weeks ago she started acting strangely," said Mayor Ming. "I picked up on it when she said she thought she was coming down with a cold and started wearing a scarf. I never would've dreamed it could happen. It's just impossible we'd have a Noble in our town of all places."

"Has she been bitten again since then?"

At D's icy words, the distraught mayor nodded his head. "Twice. Both at night. We had one of our fighting men watching over her each time, but both times they were asleep before they knew it. Laura keeps losing more and more blood, but we've seen hide nor hair of the Nobility."

"You've done checks, haven't you?"

"Five times—and thorough ones at that. Everyone in town can walk in the light of day."

But D knew that such a test wasn't proof-positive that one of the townspeople wasn't a vampire. "We'll run another check later," D said, "but tonight I'll stay with her."

A shade of relief found its way into the mayor's steely expression. Though the man had lived more than two centuries, apparently, at heart, he was just like any other father. "I'd appreciate that. Can I get you anything?"

"I'm fine," D replied.

"If I may be so bold, could I say something?" The firm tone reminded the mayor and Hunter there was someone else present. A young physician stood by the door with his arms folded. Making no effort to conceal the anger in his face, he glared at D.

"Pardon me, Dr. Tsurugi. You have some objection to all this?" the mayor said, bowing to the young man who'd interrupted them. The doctor had been introduced to D when the mayor brought the Hunter to his daughter's room. He was a young circuit doctor who traveled from village to village out on the Frontier. Like D, he had black hair and dark eyes, and there didn't appear to be much difference in their ages. But, of course, as a dhampir D's age wasn't exactly clear, so external appearances were useless for comparisons.

The young physician shook his intelligent yet still somewhat innocent face from side to side. "No, I have no objection. Since there's nothing more I can do for her as a physician, I'll entrust the next step to this Hunter. However—"

"Yes?" said the mayor.

"I would like to keep watch over Ms. Laura with him. I realize I might sound out of line here, but I believe it's part of my duty as her physician."

Mayor Ming pensively tapped the handle of his cane against his forehead. While he probably considered the young physician's request perfectly natural, he also must've wished Dr. Tsurugi had never suggested such a troubling arrangement.

Before the mayor could turn to the Hunter, D replied, "If my opponent can't escape, there'll be a fight. I won't be able to keep you out of harm's way."

"I can look out for myself."

"Even if it means you might get bitten by one of them?" asked the Hunter.

Anyone who lived on the Frontier understood the implication of those words, and for a heartbeat the hot-blooded doctor's expression stiffened with fear, but then he replied firmly, "That's a chance I'm willing to take." His eyes seemed to blaze with intensity as he glared at D.

"Not a chance," D said, impassively.

"But, why the—I mean, why not? I said quite clearly I was prepared to—"

"If by some chance something were to happen to you, it would turn the whole town against me."

"But that's just . . . " Dr. Tsurugi started to say. His face was flushed with crimson anger, but he bit his lip and choked back any further contentions.

"Well, then, I'd like you both to step outside now. I have some questions for the girl," D said coolly, looking to the door. That was the signal for them to leave. There was something about the young man that could destroy any will to resist they still had.

As the mayor and Dr. Tsurugi turned to leave, the wooden door in front of them creaked open.

"Hey, how are you doing, tough guy?" someone said in a cheery voice. The face that poked into the room belonged to none other than John M. Brasselli Pluto VIII.

"How did you get here?" the mayor asked sharply.

"I, er . . . I'm terribly sorry, sir," said one of the townsfolk behind the biker—apparently a guard. "You wouldn't believe how stubborn this guy is, and he's strong as an ox."

"Don't have a fit now, old-timer," Pluto VIII said, smiling amiably. "I figured D'd probably be at your place. And it's not like there's anyone in town who doesn't know where the mayor lives. Anyhow—D, I found out how the girl's doing. That's what I came to tell you."

"I already told him some time ago," Dr. Tsurugi said with disdain. "He learned about her condition while you were busy eating."

"What the hell?! Am I the last one to know or something?!" Pluto VIII scratched wildly at a beard that looked as dense as the jungle when seen from the air. "Okay, no big deal. C'mon, D! Let's go pay her a visit."

"You do it."

As the gorgeous young man leaned over the bed just as indifferent as he was before, Pluto VIII asked him, "What gives, bucko? You risk your life saving a young lady and then you don't even wanna see if she's getting better? What, is the mayor's daughter so all-fired important?"

"This is business."

Pluto VIII had no way of knowing that it was nothing short of a miracle for D to answer such a contentious question. With an indignant look on his face matching that of the nearby physician, the biker pushed his way through the doorway. "Damn, I don't believe your nerve," he cursed. Spittle flew from his lips. "Do you *really* know how she's doing? She's got level three radiation poisoning to her speech center, and just as much damage to her sense of hearing to boot. And neither of them can be fixed. She's got some slight burns on her skin, too, but supplies of artificial skin are limited and, since it's not life-threatening, they'll leave her the way she is. How's that strike you? She's at the tender age where girls look up at the stars and weep, and now she's gonna have to carry the memory of watching her folks get eaten alive, her body is dotted with burns, and to top everything off she can't freakin' talk or hear no more."

More than the tragic details of what was essentially the utter ruin of that young woman, it was Pluto VIII's righteous indignation that made the mayor and Dr. Tsurugi lower their eyes.

D quietly replied, "I listened to what you had to say. Now get out."

III

Once the clamorous Pluto VIII had been pulled away from the room by the mayor and four guards, D looked down at Laura's face. Vacant as her gaze was, her eyes were still invested with a strange vitality, and they suddenly came into focus. The cohesive will she'd kept hidden tinged her eyes red. The will of a Noble. A breath howled out of her mouth. Like the corrupting winds gusting through the gates of Hell.

"What did you come here for?" she asked. Her eyes practically dripped venom as they stabbed back at D's. Laura's lips warped. Something could be seen glistening between her lips and overly active tongue. Canine teeth. Once again Laura said, "What are you here for?"

"Who defiled you?" asked D.

"Defiled me?" The girl's lips twisted into a grin. "To keep feeling the pleasure I've known, I wish I could be defiled night and day. What are you? I know you're not just an ordinary traveler. We don't get many folks around here who use words like defile."

"What time will he be here?"

"Well, now . . . Suppose you ask him yourself?" Her pleased expression suddenly stiffened. All the evil and rapture was stripped away like a thin veneer, and for a brief moment an innocent expression befitting a slumbering girl of eighteen skimmed across her face. Then, once again her features became as expressionless as paraffin. Dawn had come at last to the Great Northern Plains.

D raised his left hand and placed it on the young woman's forehead. "Exactly who or what attacked you?"

Consciousness returned to her cadaverous face. "I don't . . . know. Eyes, two red eyes . . . getting closer . . . but it's . . . "

"Is it someone from town?" asked D.

"I don't know . . . "

"When were you attacked?"

"Three weeks ago . . . in the park . . . " Laura answered slowly. "It was pitch black . . . Just those burning eyes . . . "

"When will he come next?"

"Oh . . . tonight . . . tonight . . . " Laura's body snapped tight, like a giant steel spring had suddenly formed inside her. The blankets flew off her with the force of it. She let out what sounded like a death rattle, the tongue lolled out of her mouth, and then her body began to rise in the most fascinating way. This paranormal phenomenon often occurred when a victim's dependency to the Nobility was pitted against some power bent on destroying that bond. Hunters frequently had an opportunity to observe this behavior, so D's expression didn't change a whit. But then, this young man's expression probably wouldn't show shock in a million years.

"Looks like that's all we'll be getting," said a hoarse voice that came from between the young woman's brow and the hand that rested against it. "The girl doesn't know anything aside from what she's told us. Guess we'll have to ask her little friend after all."

When the Hunter's hand was removed, Laura crashed back down onto the bed. Waiting until light as blue as water speared in through the window, D left the room. The mayor was waiting for him outside.

"Learned something in there, did you?" said Mayor Ming. He demonstrated the mentality of those who lived out on the Frontier by not asking the Hunter if he could save her or not.

The fact of the matter was, when a vampire with a victim in the works learned that a Hunter had come for him or her, they'd make themselves scarce unless the victim was especially dear to them. After that, it was all just a matter of time. The future of that victim might vary depending on how many times he or she'd been bitten, and how much blood had been taken. There were some who could go on to live a normal life even after five fateful visits to their bedroom—though they usually became social outcasts. But there were also some young ladies whose skin turned to pale paraffin from a single cursed kiss, and they'd lie in bed forever waiting for their caller to come again, never aging another day. And then one day a victim's gray-haired grandchildren and great-grandchildren would suddenly see her limbs shrivel like an old mummy's and know that somewhere out in the wide world the accursed Noble had finally met his fate. The question was, just how long would that take? How many living dead were still out there, sustained by nothing but moonlight, hiding in the corner of some rotting, dusty ruin, their kith and kin all long since dead? Time wasn't on the side of those who walked in the light of day.

"Tonight, we'll be having a visitor," D told the mayor.

"Oh, well that's just—"

"Is your daughter the only victim?"

The mayor nodded. "So far. But as long as whoever did this is still out there, that number could swell until it includes every one of us."

"I'd like you to prepare something for me," D said as he looked to the blue sky beyond the window.

"Just name it. If it's a room you need, we've already prepared your accommodations."

"No, I'd like a map of your town and data on all the residents," said D. "Also, I need to know everywhere the town has gone since it started its journey, and what destinations are set for the future."

"Understood," said the mayor.

"Where will my quarters be?"

"I'll show you the way."

"No need to do that," the Hunter replied.

"It's a single family house near the park. A bit old, perhaps, but it's made of wood. It's located . . ." After the mayor finished relating the directions, he pushed down on the grip of his cane with both hands and muttered, "It'd be nice if we could get this all settled tonight."

"Where was your daughter attacked?" D asked.

"In a vacant house over by the park. Didn't find anything there when we checked it out, though. It's not far from the house we have for you, either."

D asked for the location, and the mayor gave it to him.

Then D went outside. The wind had died down. Only its whistling remained. There must've been a device somewhere in town for projecting a shield over the entire structure. The town's defenses against the harsh forces of nature were indeed perfect. Blue light made the Hunter stand out starkly as he went down the street. The shadow he cast on the ground was faint. That was a dhampir's lot. There was no sign of the living in the residential sector. For the tranquil hours of night, people became like breathing corpses.

Up ahead, the Hunter could see a tiny point of light. A bit of warmth beckoning to the dawn's first light. A hospital. D walked past it without saying a word. He didn't seem to be looking at the signs that marked each street. His pace was like the wind.

After about twenty minutes he was out of the residential section, and he stopped just as the trees of the park came into view. To his right was a row of half-cylindrical buildings—one of them was his destination. That was where young Laura had been attacked. The mayor had told him all of the buildings were vacant. At first, that'd only been true for the building in question, but, after the incident involving Laura, the families living nearby had requested other quarters and moved out. Dilapidation was already creeping up on the structures.

The house on the end was the only one shut tight by poles and locks. The fact that it'd been sealed with heavy poles instead of ordinary planks made it clear how panicked the people were. And there were five locks on the door—all electronic.

D reached for the locks. The pendant at his breast gave off a blue light, and, at the mere touch of his pale fingertips, the locks dropped to his feet. His fingers closed on the poles, which had been fixed in a gigantic X. The poles of unmilled wood were over eight inches in diameter and had been riveted in place. D's hand wouldn't wrap even halfway around one. It didn't look like there'd be any way for him to get a good grip on them. But his fingertips sank into the bark. His left hand tore both poles free with one tug.

Pushing his way past a door that'd lost its paint in the same crisscrossing shape, D headed inside. A stench pervaded the place. It was the kind of stink that called to mind colors—colors beyond counting. And each of them painted its own repulsive image. As if something ominous beyond telling was drifting through the dilapidated house.

Though the windows were all boarded up, D casually advanced down the dark hallway, coming to the room where they'd found Laura. As the mayor had said, they'd performed an exhaustive search, and anything that wasn't nailed down had been taken out of the room. There were no tables, chairs, or doors here. D's unconcerned eyes moved ever so slightly as he stood in the center of the room.

He stepped out into the hall without making a sound. At the end of another hall that ran perpendicular to the first he could see the door to the next room. A shadow tumbled through the doorway. It was like a stain of indeterminate shape. Its contours shifted like seaweed underwater, and the center of it eddied. Then it stood up. A pair of legs were visible. A head and torso were vaguely discernible. It was a human wrapped in some kind of protective membrane. What on earth was it doing here?

D advanced slowly.

The stain didn't move. Its hands and feet changed shape from one moment to the next, yet their respective functions remained clear.

"What are you?" D asked softly. Though his tone was quiet, it had a ring to it that made it clear his questions weren't to be left unanswered, much less ignored. "What are you doing here? Answer me."

Swaying, the stain charged at him. It was a narrow hallway. D had no way of avoiding it. His right hand went for the longsword on his back—and dead ahead of him, his foe waved its arm. A black disk zipped toward D's face.

Narrowly ducking his head, D drew his longsword. Seeming to have some special insight into the situation, the Hunter didn't use his unsheathed weapon to parry the disk, but slashed with the blade from ground to sky. His foe had already halted its charge, and now a terrific white light flashed through its crotch. From the bottom up, his foe was bisected. And yet, aside from a slight ripple that ran through its whole body, the shifting shadow was unchanged. An indescribable sound echoed behind it. Regardless, D advanced.

Without making a sound, the shadow backed against the wall. It certainly seemed just like a real shadow, because its clearly three-dimensional form abruptly lost its depth and became perfectly flat before being completely and silently absorbed by the wall. D stood before the wall without saying a word. The gray surface of the tensile plastic was glowing faintly. That was the aftereffect of molecular intangibility—the ability to pass through walls without resistance. The process of altering cellular structure and passing through the molecules of some barrier caused subtle changes in radioactive isotopes. That same ability had probably allowed the shadow to evade the blow from D's sword.

Doing an about-face, D ran his eyes across either side of the hallway. The disk had vanished. There were no signs it'd hit anything, either.

D pushed open the same door the shadow had come from. It appeared to be a laboratory that'd been sealed in faint darkness. The walls were covered with all sorts of medicines, and the lab table bolted to the floor was covered with burn marks and was heavily discolored by stains. He noticed signs that some sort of mechanical device had been removed.

D came to a halt in the center of the room. There were shields over the windows. What kind of experiments had been performed here in the darkness, sealed away from the light? There was something extremely tragic about the place.

This was where the intruder had come from. Had it been living in here? Or had it slipped in before D arrived, searching for something? Probably the latter. In which case, it would be relatively easy to discover who it was. Five hundred people lived in this town. Finding the intruder among that many people wouldn't be impossible.

D went outside. There was something in this house. But he couldn't put his finger on what exactly it was. The sunlight gracing the world grew whiter. D came to a halt at the door. A black cloud was moving down the street. A mass of people. A mob. It almost looked like every person in town was there. The intense hostility and fear in their eyes made it plain they were fully aware of D's true nature.

D calmly made his way to the street. A black wall of a man suddenly loomed before him. He must've been about six foot eight and weighed around three hundred and thirty pounds. The giant had pectorals so wide and thick they looked like scales off a greater fire dragon. Leaving about three feet between them, D looked up at the man.

"Hey—you're a dhampir, ain't you?" The giant's deep voice was soaked with vermilion menace.

D didn't answer him.

Something flowed across the man's features like water. A frightened hue. He'd looked into D's eyes. Ten seconds or so passed before he managed to squeeze out another word. "Seeing as how the mayor called you to his house, there ain't much we can do about you. But this here's a town for clean-living folk. We don't want no Noble half-breed hanging around, okay?"

The heads of those around him moved in unison. Nodding their agreement. There were men and women there, and even children.

"There's Nobility here. Or someone who serves them," D said softly. "The next family attacked might be yours."

"If it comes to that, we'll take care of it ourselves," said the giant. "We don't need no help from the Nobility's side."

Nodding faintly, D took a step. That alone was enough to part the fearful crowd. The giant and the others moved back like the outgoing tide.

"Wait just a damn minute!" Embarrassed perhaps to be afraid, the giant unleashed a tone that had a fierceness born of hysteria. "I'm gonna pound the shit out of you now, buster."

While he said this, the giant slipped on a pair of black leather gloves. The backs of them looked like plain leather, but the palms were covered with thin, flexible metal fibers. When the giant smacked his hands together, it set off clusters of purple sparks that stretched out like coral branches. People backed away speechless. Electromagnetic gloves like these were used by huntsmen. The highest setting on them was fifty thousand volts. Capable of killing a mid-sized fire dragon, they were lethal weapons to be sure.

"What are you, scumbag—half human? Or is it a third?" the giant sneered. "Whatever the hell it is, you're just lucky you're sort of like us. Now say your prayers that the only part of you I burn to a crisp is your filthy Noble blood." Purple sparks dyed his rampaging self-confidence a grotesque hue.

D started to walk away, oblivious to the giant's threats. The giant ran at him, right hand raised and ready for action. D's movements and his expression were unchanged. Like shadows that'd never known the light.

A sharp glint of light burned through the air. The giant shook his hand in pain. Sparks leapt wildly from his palm, and then a slim scalpel fell to the ground.

"What the hell are you doing?!" The giant's enraged outburst went past D and straight on down the street. Coming toward them with determined strides, his lab coat crisp and white, was none other than Dr. Tsurugi. "Oh, it's you, Doc," the big man said. "What the hell are you trying to do?" Though he tried his best to sound threatening, there was no doubt the giant had the recognizable threat of the physician's scalpel-throwing to thank for the slight tremble in his voice.

Coming to a stop in front of the crowd, Dr. Tsurugi said sharply, "Would you knock it off? This man is a guest of the mayor. Instead of trying to chase him off, you should be working with him to find the Nobility. Mr. Berg!" An elderly man, older than anyone else there, seemed shaken by the physician's call. "You were right here—why didn't you put a stop to this? If we lose our Hunter, it stands to reason the Nobility will remain at large. As you'll recall, all *our* searches have ended in failure."

"I, er . . . yeah, I thought so, too. It's just . . . " Berg stammered ashamedly. "Well, if he was a regular Hunter it'd be one thing. But him being a dhampir and all, I knew they wouldn't go for it. You know, the women and children been scared stiff since they heard the rumors he was here."

"And they can get by with just a good scare—a Noble will do far worse to them, I assure you," Dr. Tsurugi said grimly.

"B . . . but, Doc," a middle-aged woman cradling a baby stammered, "they say dhampirs do it, too. I hear when they're thirsty, they drink the blood of people they're working for . . . "

"Damned if that ain't the truth," the giant bellowed. "See, it ain't like we got no grounds for complaining. The whole damn town may be on the move, but information still gets in. Y'all remember what happened in Peamond, right?"

That was the name of a village where half the townsfolk had died of blood loss in a single night. Descending from the Nobility, dhampirs had a will of iron, but on occasion their spirit could succumb to the sweet siren call of blood. The man who'd been hired in Peamond found the black bonds of blood he'd tried so long to keep in check stirred anew by the beauty of the mayor's daughter, and then the Hunter himself became one of those he hunted. Before the inhabitants of the village got together and held him down long enough to drive a stake through his heart, the toll of victims had reached twenty-four.

"That's the grandfather of all exceptions." There was no vacillation whatsoever in Dr. Tsurugi's tone. "I happen to have the latest statistics. The proportion of dhampirs who've caused that sort of tragedy while on the job is no more than one twenty- thousandth of a percent."

"And what proof do we have that this ain't gonna be one of those cases?!" the giant shouted. "We sure as hell don't wanna wind up that fucking one twenty-thousandth of a percent. Ain't that right, folks?"

A number of voices rose in agreement.

"Come to think of it, Doc, you ain't from around here, neither. What's the story? You covering for him because you outsiders gotta stick together or something? I bet that's it—the two of you dirty dogs been in cahoots all along, ain't you?!"

All expression faded from Dr. Tsurugi's face. He stepped forward, saying, "You wanna do this with those gloves on? Or are you gonna take them off?"

The giant face twisted. And formed a smile. "Oh, this'll be good," he said, switching off the gloves and pulling them from his hands. From the expression on his face, you'd think he was the luckiest man on earth. The way the physician had nailed him with a scalpel earlier was pretty impressive, but aside from that he was only about five foot eight and tipped the scales at around a hundred and thirty-five pounds. The giant had strangled a bear before, so, when it came down to bare-knuckle brawling, he was supremely confident in his powerful arms.

"You sure you wanna do that, Conroy?" Berg asked, hustling in front of the giant to stop him. "What do you reckon they'll do to you if you bust up our doctor? You won't get no slap on the wrist, that's for damn sure!"

"So what—they'll give me a few lashes and shock me a couple of times? Hell, I'm used to it. Tell you what—I'll leave the doc's head and hands in one piece when I bust him up." Roughly shoving Berg out of the way, the giant stepped forward.

As the young physician also took a step forward, D called out from behind him, "Why don't you call it quits? This started out as my fight, after all."

"Well, it's mine now, so I'll thank you to just stand back and watch."

The air whistled. It could've been Conroy letting out his breath, or the whine of his punch ripping through the wind. Dr. Tsurugi jumped to the side to dodge a right hook as big and hard as a rock. As if the breeze from the punch had whisked him away. The young physician had both hands up in front of his chest in lightly clenched fists. How many of the people there noticed the calluses covering his knuckles, though? Narrowly avoiding the uppercut the giant threw as his second punch, Dr. Tsurugi let his left hand race into action. The path it traveled was a straight line.

To Conroy, it looked like everything past the physician's wrist had vanished. He felt three quick impacts on his solar plexus. The first two punches he took in stride, but the third one did the trick. He tried to exhale, but his wind caught in his throat. The physician's blows had a power behind them one would never imagine from his unassuming frame.

A bolt of beige lightning shot out at the giant's wobbling legs. No one there had ever seen such footwork. The physician's leg limned an elegant arc that struck the back of Conroy's knee, and the giant flopped to the ground with an earthshaking thud. Straight, thrusting punches from the waist and circular kicks—there'd been no hesitation in the chain of mysterious attacks, and how powerful they were soon became apparent as Conroy quickly started to get back up. As soon as the giant tried to put any weight on his left knee, he howled in pain and fell on his side.

"Probably won't be able to stand for the rest of the day," the young physician said, looking around at the chalk-white faces of the people as if nothing had happened. "Just goes to show it doesn't pay to go around whipping up mobs. All of you move along now. Back to your homes."

"Yeah, but, Doc," a man with a long, gourd-shaped face said as he pointed to Conroy, "who's gonna see to his wounds?"

"I'll have a look at him," Dr. Tsurugi said with resignation. "Bring him by the hospital some time. Just don't do it for about three days or so. Looks like it'll take him that long to cool down. But from here on out, there's a damn good chance I'll refuse to treat anyone who raises a hand to the Hunter here, so keep that in mind. Okay, move along now." After he'd seen to it that the people dispersed and Conroy had been carried away, Dr. Tsurugi turned to face D.

"That's a remarkable skill you have," the Hunter said. "I recall seeing it in the East a long time ago. What is it?"

"It's called karate. My grandfather taught it to me. But I'm surprised you'd put up with so much provocation."

"I didn't have to. You put an end to it. Maybe you did it to keep me from having to hurt any of the locals . . . Whatever the reason, you helped me out."

"No, I didn't." There was mysterious light in the physician's eyes as he shook his head. While you couldn't really call it amity, it wasn't hostility or enmity, either. You might call it a kind of tenacity.

And then D asked him, "Have we met somewhere before?"

"No, never," the physician said, shaking his head. "As I told you, I'm a circuit doctor. In my rounds out on the Frontier, I've heard quite a few stories about you."

The physician looked like he had more to say, but D interrupted him, asking, "Who used to live in that abandoned house?"

The physician's eyes went wide. "You mean to tell me you didn't know before you went in? The house belongs to Lori Knight—the girl you rescued."

Destination Unknown

CHAPTER 2

I

The girl was sitting up in bed. She looked like a snow-capped doll—the plaster for removing radioisotopes that covered her limbs was called snow parts. Glowing faintly in the evening from the radiation it'd drawn from her body, it hid the soul-chilling tragedy that'd befallen her beneath the beauty of new-fallen snow.

"There's no immediate threat to her life. I believe you heard all about her condition from Pluto VIII."

D met the physician's words with silence. The girl—Lori—was reflected in the Hunter's eyes, but what deeper emotions the sight of her stirred in D's psyche even Dr. Tsurugi couldn't tell. Or maybe it didn't stir anything at all. The physician thought that'd be entirely appropriate for the young man.

They were in one of the rooms in the hospital that stood near the center of the residential sector. Dr. Tsurugi and a middle-aged nurse lived there and treated every imaginable ailment, dealing with everything from the common cold to installing cyborg parts. His skill at being able to handle such a wide range of health problems made him a qualified, and accomplished, circuit doctor.

"Could I put some questions to her in writing?"

D's query put Dr. Tsurugi's head at a troubled tilt. "Perhaps for a short time," he said reluctantly. "It's just . . ."

D waited for his explanation.

"I'd like you to refrain from asking her any questions that may likely prove shocking. We're dealing with a young lady who's been seriously wounded both physically and psychologically. She's already well aware of what the future holds for her."

"How old is she?"

"Seventeen."

D nodded.

The physician looked rather concerned, but he soon walked over to Lori's bedside, took the memo pad and electromagnetic pen from beside her pillow, and jotted something down. An introduction for D, no doubt. Her white shoulders shook a bit, her downturned face shifted slightly toward D—then stopped. D watched expressionlessly as her face turned down again and her lily-white fingers took the electromagnetic pen from the physician. The pen moved with short, powerful strokes. Like it was fighting something off. Tearing off the page, the physician stood up straight and handed the message to D. In beautiful, precise penmanship it read, *Thank you so much.*

Returning the sheet to the physician, D settled himself into the chair beside Lori's bed without saying a word. The blue eyes peeking out from under her various white wrappings suddenly opened wide. The girl turned her face away. Quickly bringing it back, she cast her gaze downward. From her reaction, she apparently recognized D.

The physician got another pen and notepad and handed them to D. The Hunter's hand quickly went into action. *There's someone in your house,* he wrote. *Were there any strange occurrences there before?*

Lori stared at the page he'd given her. And continued to do so for a long time. It seemed like nearly ten minutes passed before she shook her head from side to side.

Once again D's hand scrawled a few words. *Do you know what your father's experiments involved?*

Again, she shook her head.

D readied his pen once more.

Lori shook her head. Over and over she shook it. Her shoulders began to quake, too. Bits of healing plaster fell from her like snow-flakes. Dr. Tsurugi held her shoulders steady. Still, Lori tried to go on shaking her head.

"Kindly leave. Hurry!" the physician said to D. The door swung open and the nurse rushed in.

Getting to his feet, D asked, "Where's Pluto VIII staying?"

"As I recall, he's in P9 in the special residential district. It's right by the law enforcement bureau," the physician called out, but his words merely echoed off the closed door and died away.

†

Exiting the hospital, D walked down the street. Despite the sudden madness they'd witnessed in Lori, his eyes were as cold and clear as ever. Any human emotion would've seemed like a blemish when it showed in the young man's eyes.

Though plenty of people were coming and going on the street, the path directly ahead of D was completely unobstructed. Every last person in his way stepped aside. They didn't do this out of the superstitious, ingrained distaste they had for those who dwelled outside their society, but because of the young man's good looks and the aura about him. Everyone knew. They also knew that not everyone out on the street was necessarily human.

And yet, there was a hint of intoxication in the eyes of all as they gazed at D. His gorgeous features made them shudder with something other than fear, and not only the women but even the men felt a sort of sexual excitement when they saw him. Most of the people wore work clothes and carried farm implements. Working the earth wasn't quite the same in a sector of a moving town, but people went about the business of living as best they could. They labored. On the far side of the park lay farms and fields, as well as a sprawling industrial sector.

D soon found the law enforcement bureau. Despite the grandiose name, it was no different from the sheriff's office you'd find in any town this size. The group of blue buildings across the street made up the special residential district. A pair of three-story buildings that looked like hotels—that was all there was to the district. As D came to the door, a cheerful voice shouted to him from across the street. On turning, the Hunter found Pluto VIII trotting his way. Both his hands were covered by a riot of colors—flowers.

"Hey, what are you doing, stud?" The biker wore a personable smile that made his hostility back at the mayor's house seem long forgotten. Once he'd reached D, he looked all around them. "They're mighty unfriendly in this town," he groused. "I heard there ain't a single florist anywhere. Someone said there was a flower garden, so I went to have a look-see, and they tell me out there they don't sell to outsiders. Well, that ain't so rare in itself, but I tell 'em, 'Dammit, I wanna take them to a sick friend,' and still they wouldn't give me the okay." He was truly indignant about this. Foam flying from his mouth, he added, "Hell, I told 'em the flowers were for Lori. I say, 'She used to live here just like the rest of you, right? I don't care if her family decided to leave; it ain't like she came back here because she wanted to. She lost her mother and father, and got hurt real bad herself, and only came back to try and save her life.' Son of a bitch—they still told me I couldn't have 'em. Said that once you leave town, you're an outsider."

To his snarling companion, D said softly, "So, how did you get those flowers then?"

"Well, er—you know. Anyway, I was pretty pissed off at the time."

"That's not exactly new territory for you, though."

"Yeah, you could say that," Pluto VIII confessed easily. It was frightening how quickly his mood could change. "Oh, well, not much I can do now. Anyway—did you have business with me?"

"I want to ask you something."

"Is that a fact? Well, let's not stand around here jawing. There's a bar around the corner. What do you say to having a drink while we talk?"

Laughing, he added, "Don't think they serve human blood, though." Knowing exactly who he was saying this to, his joke might've had deadly repercussions, but D didn't seem to mind. He followed Pluto VIII.

†

The bar was packed. Work in town must've been done in shifts. As the two of them entered, all chatter in the watering hole stopped dead. The eyes of the bartender and the men around the various tables focused on the pair.

"Excuse me! Coming through! Pardon me!" Pluto VIII called out amiably as they slipped between the crowded tables, finally seating themselves at an empty one in the back. In a terribly gruff voice he shouted, "Hey, I'd like a bitter beer. That, and a—" Turning to D, he asked in a completely baffled manner, "What'll you have?"

"Nothing."

"Dope, you can't just walk into a bar and order nothing—you're a nuisance." Yelling, "He'll have the same," to the bartender, Pluto VIII turned to D again. "So, what's this business you have with me?"

"I went into a certain house earlier," D said. "There was someone strange inside. Wasn't you, was it?"

"What do you mean?"

"I don't think anyone from town would be rooting through the house at this late date. And the only ones here from somewhere else are you and me."

Pluto VIII leaned back and laughed heartily. Those seated around them flinched and gave him startled looks. "Hate to disappoint you, but it wasn't me. Hell, even if it was me, you think I'd just come right out and say so?"

"Why are you here? Seems someone like you would be better off leaving town."

"I'd tend to agree with you," Pluto VIII conceded easily. "But it ain't that simple. Why, compared to the world down there, this place is like heaven. If you got money to spend, you can buy just about anything, and you can get by without messing around with any of the Nobility's deadly little pals. I tell you, I plan to stick around until they toss me out on my ear."

"You couldn't buy flowers," D reminded him.

"Yeah, but that don't change much." But, just as his confident smile spread across his gruff face, a number of people piled in through the bar door. A gray-haired crone was at the fore, and behind her three powerful-looking young men. All four were pale with anger.

D's eyes dropped to the bouquet on the table, and he said, "You stole those, didn't you?"

"No, I'm renting them, you big dope. I just didn't leave a deposit for them."

The whole bar started to buzz with chatter, and a bunch of people gathered around D and Pluto VIII's table. "There he is. There's the no-good flower thief. I'm sure of it," the crone shrieked, her bony finger aimed at Pluto VIII's face.

"Now that ain't a very nice thing to say," Pluto VIII said, knitting his brow. "I'm just borrowing these to take 'em to a sick friend, okay? What could make a flower happier than that?"

"The hell you say!" The crone's hairline and the corners of her eyes rose with her tone. "Do you have any idea how much back-breaking toil it takes to grow a single flower in this town? Of course you don't! You're a dirty, rotten thief!"

"He sure is," another person surrounding the table chimed in. "And thieves gotta pay a price. Let's step outside."

"Nothing doing," Pluto VIII laughed mockingly. "What'll you do if I don't go?"

"Then we'll have no choice but to use force."

The biker's confident laughter flew in the faces of the tense men. "Do you folks know who the hell I am? I'm the one and only John M. Brasselli Pluto VIII, known far and wide across the Frontier."

Silence.

"What, you bastards never heard of me?" Pluto VIII said with a scowl. "Well, at any rate, I bet you know my friend here. The most handsome cuss on the Frontier, a first-rate slayer of Nobility, an apostle of the dream demons, and all the beauty of the darkness in human form—I give you the Vampire Hunter D!"

Every face around them went pale. Even those of the men in the very back of the bar.

"Hell of a reputation he's got, eh?" Pluto VIII chortled. Looking around at the men who were now still and pale as corpses, he asked, "Still want us to step outside? My buddy can split a laser beam in two."

"For your information, this doesn't concern me at all," said D, his gazed fixed on the same spot on the table the whole time.

"What do you mean?" Pluto VIII said, bugging his eyes. "Oh, you're cold-blooded. Aren't we buddies? Don't listen to him, guys," Pluto VIII laughed. "He was only joking."

"Go outside if you want. But leave me out of this," said the Hunter.

"I don't believe you!" Pluto VIII rose indignantly. "Did you forget about the beer I just bought you?"

"Sorry, sir, about that," someone called from behind the bar, "we just ran out of your beer."

"God damn it all, this just ain't my day!" Pluto VIII cursed.

"Quit your bellyaching and step outside already," said one of the men surrounding him. "Stealing flowers is stealing all the same, and a thief's still gotta pay the price."

"Oh, really? And what did you have in mind?"

"A thousand lashes with the electron whip, or thirty days hard labor."

"Don't care much for either. Well, I'll go out with you anyway." Giving D a look that could kill, Pluto VIII didn't seem terribly afraid as he followed the men out. Still, it wasn't the fight headed outside that every eye in the place was following—their eyes were riveted to the handsome young man who remained at the table.

Four men escorted Pluto VIII outside. Two of them were in their thirties, while the other two were younger. They must've been around twenty years old. As was normal for laborers on the Frontier, the mass of their muscles was evident even through their rough apparel. Every one of them stood over six feet tall. Pluto VIII, on the other hand, was five foot four. The biker was just as big through the chest and shoulders, but, in a bare-knuckle brawl, he'd be at an overwhelming disadvantage.

Snapping his fingers, Pluto VIII asked, "Okay, who wants to be first?"

"Don't go looking to get yourself hurt any worse than need be," said the man who seemed to be their leader. "Just come along quietly to the law enforcement bureau and take your pick of the two punishments. Then this'll all be over."

Pluto VIII chuckled. "Not a chance." His face brimmed with self-confidence. Beneath the beard that hid his mouth, his deep red tongue was licking his lips. "If there's one thing I can't stand, it's assholes who get all tough when the numbers are on their side. See, I'm more of a loner. So don't just stand there acting scary. Hurry up and come get a piece of me!"

Even before he had time to realize the last bit had been a challenge, the young man on the left took a swing at Pluto VIII. He didn't say a word, didn't even exhale. He must've been a first-rate brawler. Just as the two figures were about to make contact, Pluto VIII backed away without moving a muscle. Still swinging his right hand down as hard as he could, the young man had no time to compensate and hit the ground shoulder first. What the hell happened? The perfect timing of the biker's defense against the attack almost made it look like the two of them were in collusion.

"Okay, next!" said the broadly smirking Pluto VIII. He didn't look the least bit perturbed. In fact, he seemed to be enjoying the brawl. Whatever weird trick he had up his sleeve, it made Dr. Tsurugi's martial arts seem commonplace by comparison.

The remaining trio of opponents were united by disquiet.

"What's the problem? I'll take the three of you at once. Look . . ." Both hands hanging down by his sides so he was left wide open, Pluto VIII lifted his chin to them as if begging them to punch it.

Howling curses, the two men in their thirties rushed him—one from the front, the other from behind. Trusting the abdominal muscles they'd hardened with a deep breath to protect them from any odd attack by Pluto VIII, the men had their arms spread wide to smash the little guy like a bug. It was a plan of attack that made it plain they had little regard for someone of his small stature. In a moment it became clear that was a mistake. As the two men came together to crush him, there was no trace of Pluto VIII there, and, the instant his form came back to earth some ten feet away, his massive assailants fell face first with a force that shook the ground. What the diminutive man had accomplished in this battle in the chill sunlight was nothing short of miraculous.

Nimbly, Pluto VIII turned around. The face of the one young adversary who remained was right before him. And it was more bloodless now than when he'd heard D's name mentioned before. "You coming to get some? How 'bout it, sonny?"

The only reply the young man had for that affable query was a dash in the opposite direction.

Watching the young tough run away without so much as a glance behind him, Pluto VIII's gaze was unexpectedly warm, and then his eyes shifted to the entrance to the bar. "What do you think of that? Am I faster than that sword of yours?" His tone was so steeped in self-confidence it made the sunlight pale by comparison, but D's only reply was a dark silence. "Well, then, I'm off to see a certain little lady next. You coming with me?"

Giving no answer, D turned away.

"Buddy, I don't care how damn good-looking you are, you gotta get a bit more sociable. I tell you, women these days are interested in what's inside a man." Cackling in a way that made it clear he was pleased with himself, even Pluto VIII couldn't be sure if his words had reached the black-clad figure whose back was now dwindling in the distance.

II

Afew minutes later, Mayor Ming was greeting a visitor in black.

"Why didn't you tell me about the house?"

The mayor recoiled from the serene tone in spite of himself. "What house?"

"Where they found your daughter. It seems it was the home of the girl who's in the hospital—Lori."

"That's right," the mayor said casually. "I didn't divulge that particular information because I didn't think it particularly vital. Did something happen?"

"I don't know exactly what happened, but someone was in there. I believe they were looking for something."

"What kind of character was it?" The mayor's eyes glittered with curiosity.

"There's no point getting into it. Have any of the townspeople shown any particular interest in that house?"

"Can't see how they could. The place is supposed to be locked up tight as a drum."

"Do you know of anyone in town with a talent for molecular intangibility?" asked D.

The mayor didn't answer.

"What was Lori Knight's family researching there?"

"He was merely . . . " the mayor began to say, but then he grew silent. A thin breath whispered from his lips. "For the longest time the Knights' experiments were the source of some concern for folks around town. Not their results, per se. It was simply that no one could grasp what they might be doing in there. As you're no doubt aware, in a town like this it's impossible to try and do anything without somebody finding out about it. At times, individual egos have been known to endanger the way of life for entire communities. I personally called on them more than a few times, but Franz—the girl's father—always maintained they were simple experiments in chemistry."

The mayor's face wore a heavy shade of fatigue. Saying not a word, D continued gazing out the window. As far as the eye could see, the brown plains bent away from them. The town's cruising speed, it seemed, was far from leisurely.

"If only I'd taken notice sooner . . ." the mayor continued. His voice was leaden. "Mr. and Mrs. Knight were the town's foremost chemists. It was only Mr. Knight's intellect that saved us from famine fifteen years back, or averted the thunder-beast attacks in the nick of time a mere four years ago. If not for him, a good seventy percent of the town would've gone to their reward. I thought we could overlook their somewhat unconventional hobby, and the townsfolk seemed to feel the same way. That was a mistake. And then one day, he suddenly decided to leave town . . . Yes, it was just about two months ago. I tried my best to dissuade him, but his resolve was strong as steel. I can still recall the look on his face. He looked like flames were ready to shoot out of his eyes. I suppose whatever he discovered here in town could've served him quite well in a life in the accursed world below. He could've very easily come up with something useful like that. And I had no choice but to let them off. Of course, I didn't neglect to make it perfectly clear they'd never again be allowed back in town. And that's all there was to it."

"I don't think it was," D said, as if conversing with the wind. "There was something in their house that bordered on utter ruin. Anyone would notice it. Where did you dispose of the things that were in the house?"

"There wasn't anything like that," the mayor said, fairly spitting the words. "The only really unsettling stuff was some odd-looking bottles of medicine and two or three contraptions it looked like he'd thrown together, and we wasted no time in destroying those. But the rest of the drugs and machinery were sent over to other labs or factories that could make use of them. There wasn't anything out of the ordinary at all."

"Who did the actual work?"

"Folks from all over town pitched in. Just check the names and you'll see."

"You mean to tell me you weren't involved?"

The mayor shook his head. "No. I give the orders around here. I was right there when it came time to board the place up."

D said nothing, but gazed at the mayor. His eyes were dark beyond imagining, and clearer than words could say. "I'll need a list of everyone involved in the project. I want to ask them about something."

"Why? Do you think I'm lying?" the mayor asked, not seeming the least bit angry.

"Anyone can lie," D replied.

"I suppose you've got a point there. Just give me a second. I'll make you a copy."

The mayor used the intercom on his desk to give the command to the listing computer, and in fewer than five seconds the mayor handed D a sheet of paper. The names and addresses of nearly twenty men were recorded on the list. Putting the paper in his coat pocket, D went back outside without making a sound.

†

The old room felt dirty. Aside from the industrial facilities, this place had more working machinery than anyplace else in the whole town, and after nuclear energy had been produced the waste was promptly processed and dispelled as a harmless dust. Despite that, the room did indeed look somewhat soot-stained.

A black figure crept over to the control panel that regulated the trio of nuclear reactors. Because this section provided energy for all the town's needs, it was protected by three Dewar walls each six feet thick. All activity in the building was monitored by the computer. Nevertheless, the shadowy figure stood suspiciously before the controls, unnoticed by the electronic eyes and unrecorded in their memories. A black hand entirely befitting the dark figure reached out and began flicking off lights on the panel—something that never should've been allowed.

†

In the depths of the swirling chaos, red spots began to form. A few of these spots quickly fused into one, and from a spot it grew to a stain, and from the stain a net formed. Within the scarlet was her father's face. His expression was oddly calm. Blue light danced about him. The light was as bright as lightning, but at the same time it also looked somewhat like coral. Her father looked up from the table. Several seconds later, an elated hue spread across his emaciated features. Her father's lips moved. "I've done it," he said. "I've finally done it."

The next thing she knew, her mother and father were wandering about in the wilderness. In the distance, the wind howled. It was a cold wind, as chilly as a fog. On the desolate plain before her there was nothing to see but clouds and sky. The clouds eddied, and the wind alone blew against her. And then that wind formed a face by her. One she felt she might've seen before, and yet at the same time she also felt she'd never seen. And there wasn't just one face. There was another, and this one was familiar. Its lips parted to speak. "Stay. Just stay here." As she and her family moved across the biting, wind-blasted wilderness, she got the feeling that the voice echoed after them for an eternity.

Exactly where her father and mother were trying to go she didn't know. At times, her mother looked back over her shoulder anxiously. While she realized they'd see nothing but desolate plains out there, her mother seemed to be afraid of something gaining on them. What made the girl uneasy was the unfamiliar face that hung in the heavens. Its eyes focused not on her father or mother but on herself— this the girl knew with every fiber of her being. The wind and bits of sand noisily struck the girl's face.

†

D was in the park. Sitting on a bench, he watched the water leaping in the fountain before him. As always, his thoughts were a mystery.

A black shadow suddenly fell across his profile.

"Hey, are you D . . . ?" someone asked in a deep voice.

D didn't answer. It was almost as if he'd expected the question. The man standing by the end of the bench was a giant who seemed to stretch to the clouds. Not six or seven feet tall, but closer to ten. With a frame like a massive boulder with logs sunk in it for limbs, his shadow easily covered D and stretched to the base of the fountain several yards away. On the chest of his blue shirt there was a tiny, sharp gleam of light.

Apparently not taking very kindly to being ignored, the giant continued, "I'm Sheriff Hutton. Keeping the folks here in town safe from unsavory outsiders is what I do. And it don't matter whether you're the mayor's guest or not, that won't get you no slack from me. You wanna stay in town, you'd best mark your time peaceably and not go looking to stir up any trouble. See, if you put in three days on the job and have nothing to show for it, even the mayor will give up. I'm gonna be the one who goes looking for *your stinking kin*. I'll find 'im and drive a stake through his heart all proper-like. Being sheriff, I don't much cotton to them ignoring me and calling in a punk kid like you."

Hutton had a deadly piece of hardware by his right side—a rocket launcher that seemed to consist of seven barrels banded together. A piece of heavy machinery like that could blow away a large beast or even a small building with one shot. And stuck through his belt was a huge broadsword. Even without seeing his weapons, the average person needed only a glance at the size of their owner to start quaking in their boots. With just one look at the sheriff, some folks might even confess to crimes they hadn't even committed.

"I wanna know if you'll promise me something," the sheriff said. "Just tell me you'll leave town without doing anything. Don't worry—I'll tell the mayor you did your darnedest to take care of business. You follow me?"

There was no answer. The only thing about D that stirred was his hair, brushed by the wind. Vermilion started to tinge Sheriff Hutton's face. Slowly, he backed away. The business end of the rocket launcher he still had tucked under his arm jerked up. All seven barrels glared blackly at D.

"Don't think I'll give you any warning." The slight metallic click was the sound of the safety being disengaged. "I only give you the hint once. Ignoring it is the same as crossing me. And it wouldn't do the town a bit of good to let a fool like that go on living," the sheriff said, his voice cheery and his face bright.

An icy tone mixed with the wind. "You were one of the people who investigated the Knight house, weren't you? What was in there?"

"What the hell are you yammering about?!" the sheriff said, his voice taut, but he didn't do anything. He didn't even move the finger he had wrapped around the rocket launcher's trigger.

"Answer me," the voice said again. The Hunter's eyes were still trained on the white pillar of water spraying upward, making it difficult to say just who was grilling whom in this bizarre scene. Neither of the two moved, but in the space between them an invisible but nonetheless fierce battle was unfolding.

Strength surged into the sheriff's trigger finger. His weapon had been set to discharge all seven projectiles at once. In a matter of seconds, the bench and the young man sitting on it would be reduced to ash by a thirty-thousand-degree conflagration.

The faint sound of a siren pulled the weapon's muzzle from its target. Looking unexpectedly relieved, the sheriff's long face turned upward. Something more than just clouds resided in the azure sky. "Looks like the bastards have come for us. Damn, you're lucky. The next time I catch you alone, you'll wish to hell you'd left town when you had the chance."

The sheriff kept his eyes on the sky as he walked off, but D didn't give the lawman so much as a glance. When the Hunter finally did raise his face, the flapping shapes coming down from above could clearly be made out as birds. A siren stuttered to life like a suffocating person gasping for air. People bolted into the residential sector, stumbling along in their haste. D stood up.

A flock of predatory birds was on the attack. Ordinarily, these vicious monsters flew at altitudes of six thousand feet or more, and fed on the air beasts and flying jellyfish that lived at that height, but, when food became scarce, they'd come closer to earth. The larger ones had wingspans of over sixty feet. They could even carry off a giant cyclops. But the most frightening thing about them was that they didn't act alone, but rather always attacked in flocks of dozens. To their starving eyes, the moving town must've looked like one tremendous meal for the taking.

In the distance, the chatter of what sounded like machine-gun fire started. Streaks of flame rose to meet the approaching shapes. A black curtain swiftly fell over the streets. Around D, the stand of trees bent backward from the intense pressure of the wind.

Giving a stomach-churning caw, a bird with a wingspan of over fifteen feet swooped down like it was going to land right on top of D. Resembling a short horn, its beak was filled with nail-like teeth. Between wings beating incessantly with gale-force winds, clawed feet were visible. Three digits as thick as tree roots went for D, hoping to catch him in their iron grip.

Silvery light flashed out. Though the Hunter's blade only seemed to paint a single arc, the colossal bird's wings were both cut down the middle, and fresh blood gushed from the creature's throat. The water spouting from the fountain was instantly dyed red. As D leapt away from the massive beast's falling corpse, other talons reached for him. Leaving only the crunch of severed bone in his wake, he slashed a gigantic leg off at the root.

A shrill scream filled the air. D turned around. Under a slowly rising pair of wings some fifteen feet away he saw a desperately struggling figure. It was a little girl in a long skirt. D ran directly under her and her captor. His left hand went into action. Leaving

a white trail in its wake, the needle he hurled pierced the colossal bird at the base of its throat. Giving a shriek, the creature stopped flapping its wings and began losing altitude at an alarming rate.

A second later, D's expression changed. In an instant everything around him was black, as a hitherto unseen bird of prey with an enormous sixty-five-foot wingspan swooped down on the bird that had the girl, sank its claws into the base of the other bird's back, and started to rise again. The monstrous bird flapped its wings, and a tremendous shock wave hit the ground. Trees snapped, and the fountain's geyser blew horizontally. One after another, the window-panes of every house around the park shattered.

The hem of D's coat shielded his face. Was that all it took to negate the gale-force winds coming off the monstrous bird? Though the winds buffeted him, D's posture didn't change in the least as he stood his ground. When the avian monstrosity lifted its wings a second time, D kicked off the ground with incredible force. Flying almost straight up, he rose over fifteen feet. His extended left hand latched onto the ankle of the massive bird the other was carrying. Having taken a deadly blow to a vital spot, the lower bird was already dead. And the girl it had captured had fainted. Using his left hand as a fulcrum, D swung his body like a pendulum. In midair his coat opened and, adjusting for wind resistance, D sailed skillfully onto the back of the larger bird. The avian monstrosity roared. The harsh cry was not that of a bird, but of a vicious carnivore.

Holding his sword-point down, D raised the weapon high above his head. All at once, the wings of the monstrous bird swept back. Quivering, they gave off intense vibrational waves. The bird-like monstrosity's back became semitransparent. The agony of having a needle driven through each and every cell in his body assailed the Hunter. D's brow knit ever so slightly. That was his only reaction. The longsword he swiftly brought down pierced the monstrous bird right through the medulla oblongata.

A howl of pain shook the sky, and, when it ended, the breakup began. The creature's death throes must've turned the vibrations against its own anatomy, because every last feather came out of its wings, and its skin and flesh cracked like drying clay. In the blink of an eye, the monstrous bird of prey was reduced to numerous chunks of meat spread across the sky.

All this took place at an altitude of six hundred and fifty feet. Together, D and the little girl fell from the sky.

†

All told, it took the town two hours to fight off the birds of prey. Afterward, traces of the battle remained. Bright blood ran down the streets, several buildings had their roofs blown away by the wind pressure, and a boy who'd picked up a still-hot antiaircraft shell cried out in pain. The faces of the people were unexpectedly bright. There had been no fatalities. Hardly anyone had been wounded, either. A few people had received minor cuts from glass blown out of the windows, but that was the extent of the injuries. What's more, the food situation in town had started to show signs of improvement.

The smaller birds of prey were being loaded onto carts and hauled away, while men with axes and chainsaws gathered around the gigantic carcasses that filled the streets. The whine of motors mixed with sounds of meat and bones being severed, and here and there the stench of blood pervaded the town. In less than thirty minutes a huge bird with a thirty-foot wingspan could be stripped down to the point it was no longer recognizable. After all, man-eating birds were delicious, even to the very people they'd intended to eat.

The town was bustling with activity. Carts were laden with piles of meat, viscera, feathers, and bones to be hauled away. All of them would be sent to the factories for chemical processing, with some of the meat being preserved and sent to warehouses for storage. The rest would circulate to the butcher shops and turn up on dinner tables this very night. In the factories waited men with various skills at their disposal. Spears could be made from some of the bones, tendons and viscera could be used for bowstrings, and the rest of the skeleton would be pulverized to make a paste to be delivered to the hospital. Even the sharp fangs could be turned into accessories. And the blood had its uses as well—trace amounts of it would probably be mixed in juice or in their nightly drinks at the bar. The blood of birds of prey had been proven to have an invigorating effect on humans.

Among all of the bustling activity, a mother suddenly noticed her daughter was missing. Seeing her dashing all over town like a woman possessed as she called out the girl's name, other folks finally realized they hadn't seen the woman's only child anywhere. As someone tried to soothe the half-crazed mother, one of her friends answered that her daughter had been seen headed for the park. There was every reason to suspect the girl might've met her end at the talons of the colossal birds.

Several people started to dash down the street, but quickly stopped in their tracks. From the opposite direction came a beautiful yet foreboding young man. By his side was a slight figure. The woman called out the little girl's name and ran to her. As the mother and child shared a tearful embrace, D turned and walked away without giving them so much as a glance. Where was he going?

After the mother had brushed the little girl's hair away from her neck and confirmed there wasn't a mark on her, a relieved smile swept over her face.

"Didn't do nothing funny to you, now, did he?" said one man. "He's a dhampir, you know." Everyone muttered their shared sentiments at that.

"He saved me," the little girl mumbled.

"Saved you? From what?"

"A bird got me . . . Carried me way up into the sky . . . "

"You're talking nonsense. Nothing like that fell in the park."

"But it's true," the little girl said absentmindedly. "We were falling from the sky. And then he saved me . . . He really did save me."

The eyes of the townsfolk sought the young Hunter. But they could no longer find the faintest trace of him on the noisy street.

The Townsfolk

CHAPTER 3

I

Night fell and the clouds appeared, swirling shapes borne by the wind. The light of the moon was snuffed out.

This day—or to be more precise, this evening—was entirely without precedent for the town. Ordinarily, the streets would've been filled with merrymakers. Unwinding after a hard day's work, men with flushed faces would be arguing in bars where the lights burned all night and the hum of the electric organ never faded. Women would be harping about their daily toils while children dashed through the streets with newly acquired fireworks in hand. But tonight, shutters were lowered before the bar doors, and the wind alone danced through the streets. From time to time someone passed by, but they were volunteer deputies with deathly grim faces. The windows of every home were shut tight, and men ranged with weapons and sharpened stakes. For what was probably the first time ever, this town had to deal with the sort of rampaging demon all too familiar to those in the world below.

†

As soon as Laura had fallen asleep, the mayor called for D. "Now it's up to you." And saying only this, he left.

Putting the armchair they'd provided him against the wall, D sat down to wait. It was eleven o'clock at night. One of the most common times for the Nobility to pay a call. The young lady in bed breathed easily as she slept. But, though her breathing sounded serene enough, D heard another sound over it. Her breaths were just a bit longer and deeper than those of ordinary people. When she exhaled, her breathing sounded more like a sigh.

If the Noble who'd attacked the girl lived only by night, then the chances were extremely good that he wasn't aware D was here. No matter who was guarding the young lady, they'd certainly be no match for the power of a Noble. That was exactly the sort of self-confidence that led to mistakes. And all Vampire Hunters found that sense of security the key to destroying the Nobility.

An hour passed, and then two, without anything out of the ordinary. Both D and the girl seemed like statues, motionless. D had his eyes open.

At one o'clock Morning, there was a rapping sound outside the window. Laura's eyes snapped open. An evil grin of delight rose on her lips, and red light shone from her freshly opened eyes. As if checking just how they'd left her, she looked up above her, then to either side. When her eyes found D, they stopped dead. *Damned interloper*, they seemed to say.

Those who'd known the rapture in their blood didn't flee from it—rather, they were doomed to drown in it. Regardless of what she made of the Vampire Hunter sitting there with his eyes closed, after watching him for a while Laura turned her gaze beyond the window. "Who's there?" she asked coyly. She put the question to the pitch-black space.

Faint laughter came from the darkness. A voice that only the closest of human ears would hear said, "I'm coming in."

"You can't," she whispered back. "There's a Hunter in here."

"I don't have to fear the likes of him. Not even your father can touch me now."

"But he's not like other people," Laura said softly. "There's something different about him."

"Don't be ridiculous."

Something that looked like a black stain started flowing in through the window while the girl watched. Before Laura's very eyes it gathered on the floor, took human shape, and became an actual person of flesh and blood. This vampire was gifted with one of the powers of legend—that of entering rooms as a fog. The sight of him there, in an orange T-shirt and wrinkled jeans, would've made the bulk of the Nobility grimace. Still young, he was a powerfully built man. Yet his whole body was subtly distorted, looking like a human figure molded by the hands of a child . . .

Looking first at Laura, the vampire shifted his gaze to D. Sleeping, perhaps, D kept his face down and didn't move at all. The vampire's eyes began to glitter wildly. Red light tinged D's form a crimson hue. Soon, the light faded again.

"That'll keep him asleep," the intruder said. "Just as it did with the others. He won't even remember me."

"Oh, please hurry. Come to me . . . " Laura writhed beneath the blankets. "I want your kiss. I—I need . . . "

"I know." The vampire's lips twisted into a grin. Though his teeth were dirty and crooked, his canines were particularly impressive. They slanted forward. When he slowly bent over the girl, whose eyes were shut in rapture, the air in the room grew unspeakably cold. And the chill emanated from one point in particular. The intruder looked over his shoulder in disbelief. "You dirty bastard," he growled. "You mean to tell me my gaze didn't work on you?"

D got to his feet without saying a word.

Just as he was about to launch himself at the Hunter, the intruder stiffened. His already pale face lost even more color. D's aura had just hit him. *If I move, I'm as good as dead*, he thought.

"Any more of your kind around? Before you answer that, you'd better tell me your name," D commanded him softly. Calm as his voice was, it had a ring of steel to it that said no resistance would be tolerated. "Answer me. What's your name? Are you the only one?"

"No, I'm not . . . " the intruder replied.

"How many others are there?"

"One."

"What's your name, and what's theirs?"

The intruder began to tremble. Every inch of him shook, as if he were struggling against the threat that ensnared him.

"You don't have to tell me," D said. "If I check you against the resident lists, I should find out who you are. Step outside."

The man nodded. Slowly he made his way to the door to the front hall. D followed behind him. Something caught lightly at the Hunter's coat. Laura's pale hand. Most likely the action was merely a reflex, and not some effort to save the intruder. However, D's attention was diverted for a split second, and the spell he had over the other man broke. The intruder's body lost its shape. Wasting no time, the fog rushed for the door's keyhole like a black cloud and poured through it in a single stream.

D's right hand went into action. A flash as bright as the moon arced over his right shoulder, and the intruder who was supposedly safely on the other side of the door gave a scream of agonizing death. D's expression actually changed. Quickly opening the door, he peered beyond it—into the mayor's living room.

Before him was the intruder, now leaning backward. A sharp wooden tip poked from the left side of his back. From the waist down, the man remained in his fog-like condition. With a deep groan, the intruder fell to the floor, both hands clutching his own throat. It seemed that the fog was probably his true form after all. His fallen body soon covered itself in a black hue and curled up on the floor with a rustling sound.

"What do you think you're doing?" D's quiet tone harbored an unearthly air.

"Nothing, I was just . . . " Dr. Tsurugi stammered, shaking his head. "I heard a strange sound and I froze in my tracks, trying to figure out what I should do, when all of a sudden . . . My eyes met his, and then I just panicked and ran him through."

Not saying a word, D merely gazed at bits of fog spreading across the floor and the stake dripping with black blood. "How did you get in here?" the Hunter finally asked. His voice was far more terrifying than any heated tone could've been.

"I snuck in," said Dr. Tsurugi, giving the sack over his shoulder a pat. There was a loud clatter that suggested it contained a hammer and stakes. "But everything's taken care of now, right?"

"It seems we face two foes." Heedless of the changes those words wrought on the physician's expression, the Hunter continued. "One may be gone now, but we don't know the whereabouts of the other. Are you sure there haven't been any other victims? None at all?"

Dr. Tsurugi nodded.

"The girl's probably back to normal," said D. "Go check on her."

"Sure," the young physician replied, and he was just about to nod his head. Then his eyes halted at the legs of the corpse that'd been reduced to dust. There was a gap of a fraction of an inch just below the knees. "It almost looks like . . . You cut him, didn't you?"

Giving no reply, D squatted down by the dusty remains. Once he was sure Dr. Tsurugi had gone through the door, the Hunter stretched his left hand over the dust. "How about it?" he asked.

"Oh, this is a tough one," a hoarse voice said in reply. "The memory's been completely erased from the cells. But then, I guess you already know this guy wasn't made to serve any Noble." Was the voice suggesting, then, that this vampire had just spontaneously generated?

Not surprised in the least, D nodded. "But those who aren't Nobility don't just turn into Nobles on their own."

"Then that'd mean someone had to make him that way," the voice suggested. "What we've got here is an imitation vampire. The question is, who made it?"

D didn't reply.

"Come to think of it, they did say something about letting someone into town two centuries ago. Could be him again . . . " the hoarse voice mused. "Still, it's all very strange. From what the mayor's said, and from the way the locals have been acting, it doesn't seem like there's been a ruckus over vampires before. So, these characters suddenly show up two hundred years after the fact? There's no way their strange visitor could still be in town after all this time. What do you think?"

Straightening up, D headed for the mayor's room. "There's another one out there," he said. "That's all I know."

When the Hunter knocked on his door, the mayor stuck his head out like he'd been waiting for him to come. "What is it?" he asked.

"He's been taken care of."

"My daughter's been saved?"

"Ask the doctor about that."

Just as the mayor's dazed face turned toward his daughter's bedroom, Dr. Tsurugi appeared. Seeing the mayor, he gave a satisfied smile. The mayor's shoulders dropped and a deep sigh escaped from him. "Can I see her?"

Not saying a word, D stepped aside. The mayor disappeared into his daughter's bedroom.

"Remarkable, isn't it?" As D was headed for the front door, the odd remark followed him. It was neither praising nor sarcastic, but the tone of it was nearly a challenge. "This thing had everyone quaking in their boots, but you come here and things get taken care of in no time flat . . . Although it was yours truly that put the fateful stake through his heart."

"Yes, it was." D turned around.

A strangely firm resolve, or something like it, graced the young physician's face. It was an unusual emotion, one no one had ever directed toward D.

The mayor quickly came back out of his daughter's room. A smile spread across his face, and he declared, "The wounds on her throat have vanished, and she's sleeping peacefully. And all thanks to you, D!"

"If you'll pardon me saying so, I was actually the one who finished him off."

Looking dumbfounded, the mayor turned from D to Dr. Tsurugi and back again.

"The doctor's right," D told him. "I was no use at all."

"Don't be ridiculous," Dr. Tsurugi countered vehemently. "Mayor, this gentleman not only prevented the sneaking vampire from laying a finger on your daughter, but also succeeded in driving him from her room. I merely happened to be in the right place at the right time. If any reward is to be paid, we'll split it."

"You're welcome to it," D said, sounding somewhat surprised. His tone was strangely agreeable. Perhaps he was taken aback by events.

"I'd like you to come to my room," the mayor said with a smile. "You'll be given your remuneration. We'll put you up wherever you like in town. Why, if you should decide to stay on permanently with us, that'd be fine, too."

"Can't do that just yet." In the present mood of jubilant confidence, the Hunter's words hung like icicles. "There's still another one out there."

"What?" the mayor began to say, but his mouth merely hung open. "Impossible!"

"No. He said there were two of them. I don't think he was lying."

"But—" the mayor sputtered, "You see, up till now there haven't been any victims aside from my Laura."

D turned to the physician. Gathering the drift of his question from that look alone, the physician shook his head. "No one's come to my hospital secretly for treatment."

"When was the town's last regular medical exam?"

"A week ago. There were some colds and minor chronic conditions, but there wasn't anyone out of the ordinary. No one skipped the medical exams. I can guarantee that."

"The last time his daughter was attacked was three days ago. How about since then?"

"I can't vouch for anyone after that."

Letting out a deep sigh, the mayor brought his fist to his forehead. "A fine mess we have here. One problem solved, and another arises to take its place. Now we hear our town—a town our foes in the outside world can't even get into—has been invaded by not one but *two* filthy freaks."

"Only two if we're lucky," Dr. Tsurugi said, his expression greatly changed. "You just happened to find out about your daughter, but there may well be other victims who've been bitten without anyone noticing. They might not yet have turned into vampires. In some cases, their families may keep them hidden, too."

"Exactly," D said with a nod.

While humans feared the Nobility to their very marrow, the love they felt for their own flesh and blood sometimes prevailed over their terror when a member of their family became one of the undead. Many were the families who'd watch their child growing thinner and paler each night and think it better to hide them in some back room of the house rather than have them run out of the village. That was usually the case when a whole family became dark disciples of the vampires. Love thinks little of courting death. When the fangs of the very child they'd risked their life to defend coldly pressed against their carotid artery, was it a feeling of remorse that skimmed through the mother or father's heart? Or was it satisfaction?

"I suppose it would be best if we didn't inform anyone that one vampire's been destroyed?" said the mayor.

Both D and Dr. Tsurugi nodded.

"This may sound a bit odd," the physician began, "but you'll have to keep Laura from leaving the house. We want folks in town to believe this incident hasn't been resolved—because, in fact, it hasn't been. Mr. D and I can handle the search."

D donned an unusual expression. The man in the white lab coat seemed intent on running the show. The problem was, he really didn't look like the pushy type. It was almost as if D's presence brought it out in him.

"Actually," the mayor began, craning his neck uncomfortably, "that's a job for the law enforcement bureau. I'll have to let them know about this."

"As they haven't been able to accomplish anything to date," D replied, "I don't imagine they'll be of much more use in the future. Leave everything to me. And talk some sense into the good doctor, too."

"Understood. Dr. Tsurugi, I'd like you to remain silent regarding this incident, and keep out of the investigation. Those are my orders as mayor."

"But—" Dr. Tsurugi began indignantly before restraining himself. "Very well, sir. As disappointing as it may be, I'll refrain from joining Mr. D in his work. And now, if you'll excuse me." Bidding them adieu in a loud voice, the young physician squared his sturdy shoulders and disappeared into the darkness outside.

"Another one?" the mayor mumbled, sounding very weary.

"Another one—and we have to wait until he claims another victim," D muttered. "The doctor must've seen the vampire's face. He didn't say anything in particular about it, though."

"You mean as to whether or not it was someone from town?"

Ignoring the question, D said, "When's the last time you had a death or a missing person?"

Squinting, the mayor replied, "Last death would be two years ago, missing person would go three or four months back. Exact cause isn't known, but most likely they got drunk and fell off the town. I'll make you a list of names and addresses."

D nodded.

II

The next morning, there was a rap at the door of D's assigned lodgings that created quite a racket.

"It's open," a low voice responded, but whoever knocked made no attempt to open to the door. "What is it?" the Hunter asked.

"Um, it's the mayor and Dr. Tsurugi. They want you to come right away. Someone's sick. Come to the A Block of the industrial sector." After these fear-filled words, there was the sound of furtive footsteps fading away.

Rising from his simple bed of hay without a word, D made his necessary preparations. Of course, those preparations consisted simply of strapping his longsword to his back.

†

The sun was already high. People on the street watched in terror as D walked by, his stride smooth as the wind. The industrial sector was on the edge of town. It consisted of three colossal blocks of buildings in a row. Aside from the actual energy used to keep the town in flight, everything they needed for their day-to-day existence was produced in the industrial blocks. It was the town's lifeline, so to speak.

Without needing to see the A Block markings on the doors, D was guided there by the otherworldly atmosphere. A few people were standing at the entrance to a semi-cylindrical dome. The mayor and doctor were among them. And, of course, the sheriff, with the silver rocket-launcher tucked under his arm. Some men, perhaps deputies, were pushing back a wall of people to keep them from getting any closer. As D approached, the mass of humanity parted smoothly, making a path for him. Gazes brimming with fatigue, astonishment, and hatred greeted the Hunter.

At the mayor's feet lay a man. A white waterproof sheet shrouded him. Keeping his silence, D went down on one knee and lifted the sheet. Under it was a middle-aged man, around forty years old. Eyes thrown wide open and lips zipped tight, his features were a detailed testament to a moment so horrifying he couldn't even scream.

"What's the story?" D asked quietly.

"Like you need me to tell you," the sheriff replied snidely. "There ain't a damn drop of blood left in his body. One of your pals must've sucked him dry."

"That doesn't seem to be what happened," D said, turning to Dr. Tsurugi.

The physician nodded. "Indeed, all the blood's missing from this body. However, there are no signs of a bite."

"Check 'im good enough and you'll find a bite, all right," said the sheriff. "At any rate, we've got another victim now. If you keep relying on some clown we don't know from a hole in the ground, we're gonna have a few more on our hands, too. Mayor, I think it's high time you let my office handle this. You leave it to us. Inside of seventy-two hours we'll smoke that freak out and get rid of anyone who's been bitten."

Mayor Ming's face was warped with anguish.

"Though the symptoms are the same," D said, "this isn't the work of the Nobility, or even of one of their victims. You won't find a mark on him. My guess is . . . "

Dr. Tsurugi was already nodding in agreement. "This could very well be some new kind of illness."

"What?! Now I know you two bastards have gotta be in cahoots!" the sheriff bellowed.

"I'd like another three days," said D. "If I haven't found your foe by then, I'll leave town."

"You've gotta be out of your fucking—"

"Good enough," said the mayor, cutting off the sheriff. "For the next three days, the search for the vampire is entirely in the hands of Mr. D. Sheriff, you're not to interfere with him in any way at all."

Though his whole face flushed vermilion, the sheriff held his tongue.

"A wise course of action," Dr. Tsurugi said, his back to the gigantic lawman.

"You little bastard . . . " the sheriff growled, latching onto the physician's shoulder with his meaty fingers. And then something wrapped around the lawman's wrist. The mayor's arm.

"Sheriff," the mayor said to the face of naked ferocity that greeted him. Just one word. The vermilion hue of excitement faded from the sheriff's face in a matter of seconds.

"Okay. You're the mayor. What you say, goes. But he only gets three days. And during that time, he ain't gonna get a bit of help from us. He'll have to do all the questioning and all the investigating all by his lonesome. And I'll tell you one thing—this here town's pretty damn big." And then he left, with his men following close behind.

"Well, then, about this body . . ." Dr. Tsurugi said, rubbing his eyelid. "Should we bring it to the morgue, or back to the hospital? Personally, I'd love a chance to dissect it. He didn't have any family, correct?"

The mayor nodded.

"Then we'll bring it back to the hospital for the time being. We can't discount the possibility this is some sort of illness."

On orders from the mayor, two of the townsfolk were selected and, one at each end of a stretcher, they loaded the body onto the back of the hospital motorcycle parked nearby.

"Well, then, I'll be running on ahead."

The young physician departed, leaving only the growl of an engine in his wake. That left only D and the mayor. A forceful wind gusted around the two of them. Perhaps it was a gale that blew from the light into darkness. Or maybe it was something else.

"What is it?" the mayor said succinctly. "You think it could be an illness?"

D didn't answer him. This was probably the first time he'd found a corpse that'd been drained of blood but didn't have a mark on it. "I don't know for sure. We need Dr. Tsurugi to hurry with that analysis. Depending on how this plays out, it may become necessary for him to come up with a vaccine. If that's the case, he will need to do it quickly."

"Then you do think it's a disease after all . . . " Beads of greasy sweat blossomed across the mayor's brow.

†

Sitting in a block of sunlight spearing through her window, the girl pondered the fate that lay ahead of her. She couldn't speak or hear. Dr. Tsurugi had given her the truth quite plainly. And she felt like she'd plunged straight into hell. She would be forced to live in a world stripped of all sound, where she couldn't convey a single thought unless she had a pen in her hand. The physician had tried to console her by saying that she wouldn't be left with any scars from the radiation poisoning, but what would that matter?

How old am I, again? The girl tried doing the math once more. *Seventeen.* At that age, her whole life was still ahead of her. And it'd all been wiped out. When she'd first found out what'd happened, she couldn't think of anything at all. She just wanted to die. And then *he* had come. The beautiful face of the man they said had saved her was lodged in her brain. Entirely too gorgeous and completely noncommittal. *He saved me,* the girl thought, obsessed with the notion. *Oh, I hope he comes to see me again. Just one more time.*

A number of sounds passed right by the girl. The footsteps of the physician and nurse as they went down the corridor. The creaking of the gurney bearing what looked to be a dead body. A voice filled with revulsion. Sounds from things like the generator and an electric saw passed right through the thin walls, stirring the girl's hair. Perhaps you could say she was lucky not to have to hear any of that.

So, what happens next? This thought alone continued to occupy the girl's mind. Before she knew it, the light outside her window had taken an azure tint. She had no idea whether the doctor and nurse were in the next room or not. Once the light was gone, she'd be separated from them by an eternal gulf.

Just then, she saw a figure reflected in the door across from her. As she watched, something like a black stain appeared in one part of the glass, soon spreading across its entirety like a flower opening its petals in a time-lapse film. Before the girl's very eyes, the stain quickly became a black mass of sorts, its contours shifting faintly as it approached her bed. The girl inched back in spite of herself. She was just about to press the emergency call button when a black hand deftly reached over and snatched it away.

Well, can you understand what I'm saying?

Piercing thoughts crept into her head. The girl's eyes went wide with astonishment.

Don't be so surprised. It's called telepathy. With it, a person can make their thoughts understood without ever speaking. Even a young lady with no voice. Would you care to try it?

The girl nodded. She moved her head so vigorously it almost looked like some sort of exercise.

Okay, I'll show you how to do it. But in return, there's something I want to ask you. Will you answer me?

The girl nodded. As her eyes gazed at the unsettling black mass, they seemed to cling to it for dear life.

I understand certain experiments were conducted at your house. The voice rang through her head, and it was accompanied by a delightful stimulation. *The secret of that research is hidden somewhere in your house. Tell me where. No, you don't need to say it. Think it.*

The girl shut her eyes. Gathering up all she remembered of the life they'd once lived, she began searching for some concrete example of the experiments her father had undertaken. Coming away empty-handed, the girl conveyed that result.

That can't be! The shadowy figure's thoughts were like flames. *Your father was involved in forbidden experiments. And only he was able to make them succeed. Answer me. You must remember!*

The question burned in the girl's brain like molten steel. Her whole body trembling, she collapsed on the bed. At that moment, the door opened. The shadowy figure seemed to look that way.

"What the hell are you?" Dr. Tsurugi shouted, his words spreading across the room like a wildfire.

The shadow turned to face the physician without making a sound. Perhaps it was his youth, or maybe he was just reckless, but the physician spread his arms wide and tried to grab hold of the shadowy figure. His hands sank into the intruder's form. Not just that—the shadow actually passed right through the physician's body. Molecular intangibility was at work.

"Hey," Dr. Tsurugi shouted as he raced to Lori's side, though he had no idea what was going on. "Are you okay?" he asked.

Managing to follow the movement of his lips, Lori nodded in reply.

Noticing the pale blue phosphorescence of his own limbs, the physician pulled back in surprise. That was the aftereffect of the molecular intangibility. "Looks like I'll have to take something for radiation, too," the physician said absentmindedly, smiling at Lori.

But in her mind, the shadow's thoughts still pulsed. *You can use telepathy, too*, the shadow had said.

†

The body of the deceased citizen was to be buried in the town's cemetery. According to the autopsy, death had resulted from massive and rapid loss of blood—that was all they could tell. The corpse had been checked from the top of its head to the tips of its toes, but, aside from a few minor abrasions, there wasn't any sign of the fateful wound. As they carried the coffin with the man's corpse to the cemetery, everyone thought the same thing. *When the sun goes down, he's gonna get up.* After the undertaker's secondhand robots had finished digging the hole, the corpse was laid to rest. The soil was shoveled back in, and the undertaker—who doubled as a reverend—intoned several words of prayer. And with that, the man was firmly laid to rest with the past.

Soon after, the sun went down. Not a single person remained around this desolate patch of earth, but then a woman of about thirty came with a hurried gait. She was the wife of the man who ran the general store. But there was something strange about the way she walked. It looked like she was being called forward, and didn't care for it one bit. As the woman moved forward, she threw her head back, dug her heels in, and was tugged along.

Presently, she stood before the fresh grave. Brushing her cheek against the mounded dirt so it rustled against her skin, she then got to her feet again. Hunching over, with a frightened expression and a chilling grin, she began digging into the fresh grave. With every movement of her hands, a vast quantity of earth was thrown behind her. In no time she had made a small mountain of dirt. Even though the soil was loose from the recent burial, the sheer volume of it was extraordinary.

When the lid of the wooden box could be seen at the bottom of the hole, the woman's lips twisted in an expression of sheer delight. What a blackly evil smile it was. The hole was ten feet deep. The woman stared at the box. The sun had already sunk beyond the edge of the plains. Nothing but the white street lights threw any illumination on the woman's deeds.

Slowly the coffin began to rise. As if pushed up by the earth itself it ascended, not the least bit unsteady as it approached the lip of the hole. Anxiety and rapture intertwined in the woman's countenance.

Rising clean out of the grave, the coffin stopped level with the woman's chin. The lid of the box opened from the inside, pushed open by a pale hand. With the same gingerly pace at which the box had risen from the grave, the dead man sat up. Still seated in the coffin, he turned to the woman and smirked. Pearly canines jutted from his mouth. His eyes gave off a red glow. With a look from him, the woman was completely stripped of her freedom. She smiled back at him. With strangely stiff movements, the man climbed down to the ground. The coffin stayed right where it was.

The man came closer. Saying nothing, the woman waited. For the first time it dawned on her that in life this man had been in love with her. There was a short, soft whistle, and at that point something stuck in the nape of the man's neck. A thin needle of unfinished wood.

"Sorry to say this, but that's as far as you go," a low voice said. To the man's right there was a rustling of tree branches. The man was at a loss for words. "And since you've risen again, I take it you know what the person who did this to you looks like. Tell me."

Even if the man had wanted to answer, he was still pierced through the throat. Needle stuck in his neck, the man leapt back a good six feet, and at the same time the woman crumpled to the ground.

"You must be destroyed," D said coldly. "But before you go, you should leave the world of daylight something. How about it?"

The man reached for the end of the needle with his right hand. He had no difficulty pulling out the wooden shaft D had hurled at him. A stream of blood squirted from the wound. The man pursed his lips.

D raised his left hand. Holding it flat and straight like a knife, he moved forward. The red stream that issued from the man's mouth was split down the middle by the edge of the Hunter's hand, and both halves vanished in the darkness. But D sensed white smoke rising from the ground where the man's blood had fallen.

"Quite a strange power you have there," the Hunter remarked. "But now the end is at hand." Not giving the man a second chance to purse his lips, D covered him completely with his coat. The moment it opened again, the man fell to the ground unconscious as if jerked down by ropes. Looking down at the man, D said softly, "I've taken care of him. Come out now."

"Thanks a bunch." There was the sound of branches shaking in a thicket some fifteen or twenty feet away, and then a fairly limber figure appeared. "So, you've got a trick that can knock a Noble's underling out in one shot? When you've got a little time to kill, I'd love to see how you do that." Punctuating his last comment with a burst of cackling laughter was none other than John M. Brasselli Pluto VIII.

"Why are you out here?" D asked.

"Aw, don't get all tough with me, partner." Pluto VIII smiled at the Hunter, his expression intimating they'd been friends for ages. "I knew he was bound to come back to life, so I was just waiting around for it. I tell you, that was a hell of a fight you gave that critter. I'm impressed. Very impressed!"

"What are you after?" D asked softly.

"Not a thing," Pluto VIII replied, shaking his head in earnest. If he was tortured to the point where he could no longer speak, he could probably get by on that gesture alone.

"It doesn't matter. Just stay out of the way."

"Yes, sir." It was hard to tell just what was going through Pluto VIII's head, but for some reason he gave the Hunter a round of applause, then said, "By the way, were you by any chance planning on taking this creep back with you and making 'im spill his guts?"

"What are you talking about?"

"It's pretty obvious, ain't it? You aim to find out just who went and made this character like this. After all, he lost all that blood but doesn't have a scratch on him. How weird is that?! You've gotta look into what's causing this."

"You're exactly right." Easily carrying the fanged man on one shoulder and the unconscious woman on the other, D turned away.

"Hey, hold on! Wait just a minute," Pluto VIII cried out excitedly, scampering after the Hunter. "Let me carry the lady. I tell you, I can't believe how tough it is trying to crack the gals in this here town. I can talk myself blue in the face, but they won't give me the time of day. I should take this opportunity to make a reputation for myself."

While it wasn't quite clear whether the Hunter was dumbfounded or not, as D stood there Pluto VIII basically pried the woman away from him and cradled her body in his arms. "Buddy, do you seriously think this character is just gonna tell you everything? I mean, after all, he's a freaking vampire!"

D said nothing.

"I'll let you in on a little secret. I can get him to spill his guts for you. I'll let you ask him whatever you want, just let me get some questions in, too."

D stopped in his tracks. As he slowly turned, Pluto VIII must've sensed something in the Hunter's face, and, giving a cry of surprise, the biker leapt back a good ten feet. "Didn't I tell you not to look at me all serious like that? Just thinking about that mug of yours gives me a powerful urge to jerk off, you know. At this rate, I'm liable to fall in love with you if you don't watch it."

"Just what are you up to?"

"Not a blessed thing."

"Should I talk to the mayor and have him toss you out of town?"

"Won't do you a bit of good," Pluto VIII chortled. "I figured you might try something like that, so I found myself a new hideout. Besides, you can't even find where the vampire's holed up. You know, I wouldn't be a bit surprised if you wound up with another one on your hands." What Pluto VIII said was right on the mark. "So, what'll it be? Stop looking so grim and make up your mind already."

"Okay," D said softly with a nod.

†

Where Pluto VIII finally led D was to an abandoned boarding-house next to C Block in the industrial sector. "What do you think? Pretty great, huh? Got myself three rooms here. Can cook up my grub wherever I please. You're looking at the lord of the manor," Pluto VIII said pompously. "It don't matter to me if you tell anyone else where to find me. Given five minutes, I can move myself into another hideout, you know. I'm a slipperier eel than any vampire."

"What are you really after?" asked D.

"Who do you think you're dealing with here?" Pluto VIII said, settling himself into a plastic chair. He invited D to do the same, but the Hunter wouldn't sit down. The woman from the general store had been left lying next to a street that saw a lot of pedestrian traffic in a place where someone was sure to find her right away. Anyone summoned by a vampire's power, as she had been, wouldn't remember a single thing that had happened while under the vampire's spell. Pluto VIII had set the unconscious vampire down on a large bed of rather simple tastes. Fingering the fiend's extended canine teeth with morbid curiosity, he said,

"Well, now. Let's see if we can't get him to answer two or three questions. Okay, now watch closely."

Saying that, he clambered onto the bed and over to where he'd put the vampire, then laid down on his back right next to the other man. D saw him squeeze down on the vampire's hand. Pluto VIII closed his eyes. As he did so, all trace of expression vanished from his face. At the same time, the vampire began to tremble all over and his eyes opened wide.

"Pretty slick, eh?" the vampire said in Pluto VIII's voice. While the face was still clearly that of a farmhand, the expression had taken on an indefinable fullness, and through the eyes and mouth it bore a distinct likeness to Pluto VIII. This little stub of a man actually had the ability to possess other bodies. "Damn, it's cold," he groaned. "Inside this guy's head and all through his body it's just one great big winter wonderland. On the other hand, being in here I know everything he's thinking. Now, according to him, he got turned into a vampire by . . . wow, by no one at all. All of a sudden he got cold and fell to the ground in front of that factory. And that's about the size of it, it seems. Ain't that the damnedest thing!"

"Is the illness contagious?"

To D's question, Pluto VIII replied, "I don't know. What I can tell you is he's got a powerful thirst for blood. That's it." Suddenly Pluto VIII's voice became muddled. Malevolence flooded into his normally amiable expression. His face now that of a demon, he leapt to his feet. The human who'd possessed this vampire had been overthrown with remarkable ease. Imitation vampire or not, the mental powers that condition endowed the victim with were certainly formidable. Slowly, the demon headed toward D—and then he suddenly grinned from ear to ear, just like Pluto VIII. "Sorry about that," he laughed in the biker's voice. "Didn't mean to alarm you—not that you budged an inch. Well, I guess that's D for you. So, that's the only question you've got?"

"No, I have another. What in the world were they researching in that house?"

"Can't say," Pluto VIII replied indifferently. "He's probably got the information, but everything related to it is in a fog. Guess that means no answer."

Nothing from D.

"Looks like our plan has run awry."

D gave a slight nod.

One of the paranormal phenomena that often linked the bloodsucker to its prey was a transference of memories. Often the memories of a vampire were copied into the brain of his or her victim. In most cases what was transferred was only a small portion of vampire's recollections, but there were some victims who wound up with all of a Noble's memories. By sending his consciousness into the other man's body, Pluto VIII had hoped to access any memories that might've belonged to whoever made him.

Not saying a word, D slung the undead body over his shoulder.

"Hey, what're you doing?!" the corpse—or rather, Pluto VIII—shouted.

"If we're through with him, I have to get him back in his grave. If you want to get out of him, better be quick about it."

"What a selfish little ingrate you are," the man sneered, and then all stiffness left his body. At the same instant, Pluto VIII's body got up from where it'd been lying on the bed. "I'll have you know it takes a good deal of mental preparation to leap from one body to another. Oh, I think I'm gonna be sick—"

D left the biker's room without making a sound.

†

As it moved forward, the town seemed to be glaring down at the brown plains. A group of shepherds and merchants looked up at it enviously and waved. Offering them nothing in return, the town continued its remorseless advance. But one had to wonder if it was actually making any progress. The town went on diligently, headed straight for the sun as it shone down with a strangely spiteful hue.

†

The next day, D called on the twenty or so men listed on the mayor's sheet as being involved in boarding up the Knight family's home. All of them gave him the same reply. No one had seen or heard anything strange while they were moving things out of the house. The mysteries of that abode remained shrouded in fog. As D was getting ready to call on the last person on the list, Sheriff Hutton, someone behind him called out his name. It was Dr. Tsurugi. Turning around, D asked, "How did it go?"

"His condition remains unchanged. I wasn't able to learn anything from the corpse." He was referring to the man who'd risen from his grave the previous night. D had carried the body Pluto VIII had occupied to Dr. Tsurugi and had him subject it to a second medical examination. "It's certainly my opinion this was caused by some sort of viral infection, but at the moment I can't seem to put my finger on the culprit."

"There'll be trouble if you can't." That was all D said.

Realizing just what kind of trouble the Hunter was talking about, Dr. Tsurugi used the back of his hand to wipe away the sweat he'd just realized was pouring from him. Cold sweat.

"I'll see you later," D said, turning his back.

"Wait a minute," the physician called out to him.

"What is it?"

The young physician shyly scratched at his head, which seemed to be a habit with him. "If you don't mind, do you think you could pay a visit with me? To Lori Knight, I mean. She's been acting a bit strangely."

"Strangely?"

"Yes. Ever since she was attacked by this weird, shadowy character yesterday, her behavior's been rather unusual."

"My going to see her wouldn't change anything."

"Well, by not going you certainly won't do her any good."

"Then you'll have to wait until I've taken care of one bit of business," D said, and began to walk away. Twisting and turning through a number of streets and back alleys, he arrived at the law enforcement bureau. Pushing his way through a cracked glass door patched together with strips of heavy tape, he made his way inside.

Sitting behind his desk with his feet up while he joked with a couple of his deputies, the giant developed a sudden twitch in his face as soon as he caught sight of D. "What brings you here?" he asked. "You still got two days left. Don't tell me you want off already?"

"I have business with you," D said plainly. "Could I speak to you in private?"

Struck perhaps by the Hunter's chilling aura, the two deputies quickly got to their feet, but the sheriff pushed them back down with hands the size of catcher's mitts. "Wait just a cotton-picking minute, boys. This here's the law enforcement bureau. We don't take orders from no outsider. Least of all from a stinking Vampire Hunter. You're not going anywhere. You'll sit right here with me and hear what he's got to say, you savvy? So, how's that by you?" The last remark was aimed at D.

D nodded. "Doesn't matter to me. I just have one question for you. When you were boarding up the Knight house, did you see anything?"

"What do you mean by 'anything'?" The sheriff laughed, showing a lot of yellow teeth.

"Were there any unusual items? Strange drugs, papers with formulas or equations? Special creatures? Anything like that."

The sheriff snorted loudly, "Of course there wasn't a damn thing like that."

"Then I have another question for you. Why did the Knight family leave town?"

"You might wanna ask the mayor that."

"Did the whole town drive them away, or—"

"Or what?"

"Or were they glad to leave? Which was it?"

"You come here looking to start trouble, buster?!" Sheriff Hutton snarled. The two deputies braced themselves for action. The sheriff started to rise from his oversized chair. His rear was only about an inch out of the chair when he stopped dead in his tracks. D was standing right in front of him. He was just standing there, an unearthly aura radiating from every inch of his body. That alone kept not only the sheriff but his two deputies as well from moving a muscle.

"Answer me straight," said D.

"You—you gotta be fuckin' kidding me," the sheriff blustered, but his voice quivered nevertheless.

"In that case, you leave me no choice."

Raising his left hand, D pressed it against the sheriff's forehead. The same vacuous expression seen on a mental defective spread across the sheriff's face. Eyes covered with a semitransparent film and drool coursing from the corner of his mouth, the lawman stared vacantly into space.

"Why did the family leave town?"

A reply wasn't soon in coming. No doubt a battle was raging in the sheriff's mind, a battle between his own ego and D's words. The only question was how it all would end.

"That family . . . was doing freaky experiments . . . Don't know all the particulars . . . " The words were clearly being torn from the sheriff. And it went without saying the power of D's left hand was to blame.

"You knew that, and still you did nothing?" the Hunter asked.

"Wanted to . . . but then . . . mayor stopped me."

"The mayor?" D's eyes shone. "Why would he do that?"

"Don't know . . . But I had official orders . . . Wasn't supposed to do anything . . . about that family . . . ever . . . Seems the sheriff before me . . . had the same orders."

"How long had it been going on?"

"From way back . . . Roughly two hundred years . . . "

According to what the mayor had said, that was right around the time the eerie stranger had come on board.

"And their strange experiments had been going on all that time?"

"I . . . I wouldn't know . . . "

"Was the Knight family run out of town, or did they leave of their own accord?"

"They . . . ran away . . . "

"Ran away?"

"Night before they run off . . . mayor gave me orders . . . I went to their house . . . Knights were there . . . Arrested 'em on the spot . . . just like the mayor told me to . . . Threw 'em . . . in jail . . . Daughter was with them, of course . . . Mayor never did tell me . . . why we had to do that . . . Just said they'd committed a serious offense . . . against the whole town . . . and that was all."

"I see."

The "offense," then, was experiments the Knight family had been conducting for generations. But what reason would the mayor—who'd always supported the Knights—have for ordering their arrest? And what could they have told the mayor?

"How did Mr. and Mrs. Knight seem?"

"I don't know . . . They weren't scared . . . at all . . . The two of them . . . looked to be giving some serious thought to something . . . What it was . . . I don't know."

"How did they get away?"

"The next day . . . I go for a look . . . and the cell wall . . . was melted away. Mr. Knight was a chemist . . . Figure he had something hidden on him . . . Acid or something . . . "

"I'll be seeing you again." D's hand came away from the sheriff.

It wasn't until the hem of the Hunter's black coat was well out the door that the sheriff and his two men collapsed into their chairs as if utterly exhausted.

†

Dr. Tsurugi was waiting for D. "I realize you must be busy, but I'd really like for you to come with me," he said.

D nodded. "I said I would. Let's go."

The two of them set off for the hospital.

"Quiet town," said D.

"I guess it is, at that. The sheriff and mayor probably have a pretty easy time keeping the peace. They don't get strangers coming in and causing trouble. And the townsfolk are all well-behaved types who follow the rules. Every so often someone gets a little rough, but no one's any rougher than the sheriff."

A smile formed on D's lips. "Except for you," he said.

Dr. Tsurugi didn't say anything, but he gave a great big grin. Quickly looking to D again, he asked, "How long will you be in town?"

"If I was done, I could leave tomorrow." And then, in a rare move for the Hunter, he asked in return, "How about you?"

"Well, my contract is for a full year. But I suppose I'll be getting off before then."

"Wouldn't it cause problems if their doctor were to leave town?"

"Nothing they couldn't solve by finding another physician," Dr. Tsurugi replied.

"Are you bored?"

"Don't be ridiculous. You wouldn't think it to look at me, but I studied a bit of psychology. And from a psychological standpoint, you couldn't find a more intriguing place. By their very nature, towns on the Frontier must exercise rather rigid controls in order to protect themselves from enemies without, but here they've taken it to the furthest extreme. Where do you think this town is headed?"

D gave no reply.

"Actually, they wander the earth far and wide with no goal at all."

"People down on the ground don't have a goal, either. Humans, Nobility—all of creation is that way," D said.

"Yes, but in a village, people come in. In towns, people leave. Here, there's neither. Do you have any idea how much time and energy the people of this town invest to come up with drugs that combat the problems caused by inbreeding? In my humble opinion, the only folks in town in their right mind were the Knights."

"Do you know anything about them?" the Hunter asked.

"Unfortunately, no."

"I suppose this place might not suit you. You like traveling then, do you?"

The young physician nodded. It was a deep, hearty nod. His dark eyes sparkled. "Yes. I've met all kinds of people. You might say I became a doctor because I like to travel. The Frontier's not completely hopeless. No matter what they've been dealt there, everybody's giving life all they've got. I bet the same is true for the remaining Nobility. And I just want to help folks do that."

Saying nothing, D continued walking. But in his eyes was something that looked incredibly like a bit of warmth. The young physician failed to notice how his words had brought about a minor miracle.

"You're a dhampir, correct? Been traveling long?"

"A bit longer than you," D replied

"I'll be like you before too long," the physician said in a fervent tone. "I suppose I'll get as experienced as you are. Along the way, I'll learn how to ride and how to use a sword."

Though the young doctor's words sounded almost like a challenge, D remained silent.

Presently, the pair arrived at the hospital. The nurse walked just ahead of them, escorting them to the sickroom. Over the course of the ten feet or so they had to go, the nurse nearly crashed into a table, almost put her hand through a window pane, and had to be caught by the physician after tripping over the threshold . . . All because she could do nothing but look at D.

Some pink discoloration remained on Lori's skin. That was the extent of her injuries. Apparently the plasters for drawing the radioisotopes from her body were no longer necessary, as all her

bandages had been removed. Now the girl was wearing blue pajamas and sitting up in bed.

After a bit, Dr. Tsurugi took the memo pad in hand and wrote, *How are you feeling?* He handed it to her. He did so because D hadn't bothered to say anything at all.

Scanning the note, Lori nodded. Fidgeting, she adjusted the collar of her pajamas and tugged down the sleeves. She seemed embarrassed to have anyone see the marks her radiation poisoning had left.

Mr. D came to see you, the physician scribbled on the memo pad. *He wants you to get well soon.*

D picked up the pen. On seeing what he wrote on the memo, Dr. Tsurugi's eyes bulged out: *Why did your parents leave town?*

"Wait just one minute," the physician snarled. "This young lady's still a patient undergoing treatment. I didn't bring you here for this. I wanted you to help bring a little life back into her. Most patients need cheering up more than anything. Especially a girl her age."

"And I came here because I have questions," D replied.

"I can't believe your nerve. I never should've brought you here."

"You can cheer her up any time. But my work won't wait."

The physician held his tongue.

D continued, "One of the Nobility has been created through means that are still unclear. If that number is allowed to swell to a hundred, we'll be powerless to stop them. It's my job to get rid of him. But if I had to take out every person in town, that'd be a bit too much of a workload."

"This is insane," the physician said with a mournful sigh.

D turned to face Lori. Silently, he awaited her reply.

Memories flickered in Lori's mind. This was the same question the shadowy figure had put to her the night before. No one cared about her at all. Her parents' experiments were the only thing on anyone's mind. Choking the rage that'd risen to her throat back down again, Lori raised her face. The Hunter's visage greeted her. Cold and veiled in an unearthly aura, his dashing countenance seemed sad nonetheless. The anger vanished from Lori's heart.

Putting her left hand over her right so the scars on the back of it couldn't be seen, Lori slowly scratched away with the pen.

I don't know. On our last night in town, as I was walking past the lab, I heard my father tell my mother, "This is going to change the world." Right after that, the two of them headed out somewhere, and while I was sleeping the law came and hauled us off to jail.

"Change it how, I wonder?" Dr. Tsurugi mused. Not saying a word, D looked over his shoulder. Over to the next room. The operating room. The room that had a corpse strapped to the table. The physician's complexion turned the color of clay. "You couldn't possibly mean—"

"I don't know," D said. "But you'd best leave."

"What on earth do you mean?"

"You're better off not knowing."

"You must be joking, after all I've gone through." Dr. Tsurugi added petulantly, "Need I remind you that I was the one who destroyed the vampire last night?"

"I'll see you later."

"But, I—" The physician was about to say something, but he bit his lip. Indignant, he left Lori's sickroom.

D's right hand went into action. *Aside from your family, who went into the lab the most?*

After pausing for a moment, Lori wrote, *Mayor Ming.*

Shining Serpent Pass

CHAPTER 4

I

The following incident took place shortly before D visited the hospital. Taking advantage of her employer's departure for a town meeting, the mayor's maid Nell snuck into the garden. Checking to see that no one else was around, she called out, "Ben!" Her muscular paramour from the cleaners didn't answer. Knitting her brow dubiously, Nell headed over to the base of the massive peach tree that always served as the site of their trysts.

"Boo!" Ben shouted, suddenly poking his head out from behind the tree.

"Oh, Ben, don't scare me like that!" Though relief spread through her heart, an odd sense of incongruity started to gnaw at Nell. Ben didn't quite seem like himself. Sure, his face and his build were the same as ever, but there was something strange about him. Was that an annoying little smirk on his lips?

"What's wrong, Nell? Do I have something stuck on my face or something?" he asked. He sounded just like Ben, too.

Nell shook her head. "It's nothing."

"Oh, really? Then how about a kiss?"

And with that he took Nell in his arms before she could resist and his lips met hers. For a few seconds the two of them stood fused together like a lone pillar by their firm embrace, but soon the strength fled Ben's body. Limp as a wet noodle, he quickly collapsed among the roots of the tree.

Sparing not a glance to the lover who'd so suddenly lost consciousness, Nell scanned her surroundings. Her countenance remained as sensuous as ever, but there was something inexplicably strange about her expression.

"When I saw the young buck here slipping into the mayor's backyard, I had a hunch about what he was up to—and it paid off," Nell said, adding, "I should give this little lady a piece of my mind for screwing around while she's on the clock. Of course, it made my job that much easier, so I'll let it go this time. Lover boy's gonna be out for a while—I'm gonna have to borrow your body, missy."

And then, after dragging her boyfriend's limp form into the cover of the bushes, Nell reclaimed her prim demeanor and returned to the house with a light gait.

On entering the house, Nell quickly locked each and every door. She stood in the middle of the living room with a pensive expression that suggested she was lost in deep thought or grim recollection. But soon she opened her eyes and gave a satisfied nod. "Oh, I see now—there's still another vamp around. And where they're covering this up and making like the girl's not better yet . . . That'd be a D plan, I bet," she laughed.

While the voice was Nell's, the manner was unmistakably that of Pluto VIII. But the real question was, what did he hope to accomplish by inhabiting her boyfriend, then leaping from him to her and rifling through her memories?

"Nothing at all out of the ordinary around the house, she thinks. Hold everything—she's been told not to go into the cellar without asking permission. Bingo! Then I say we go have us a permission-free peek."

Walking softly so Laura wouldn't hear her from the bedroom where she remained in hiding, Nell headed for the cellar door with a shameless grin. It wasn't locked. Pushing the door open, she found a wooden staircase that sank down into the darkness.

Muttering, "Eww, creepy," with unabashed interest, Nell gathered up the hem of her long skirt and slowly stepped into the dark.

Power lines and hot water pipes coming all the way from the industrial sector ran the length and breadth of the ceiling. From the center of the cellar, with its walls lined with wooden crates and jugs of fuel, Nell surveyed her surroundings with a deeply suspicious gaze.

"Well, nothing out of the ordinary here," said the maid. "Now, then, what was the focus of Miss Nell's suspicions . . . " Her eyes, now charged with an eerie gleam, crept along the walls, floor, and ceiling in rapid succession. Before long, they stopped again at her own feet. Coarsely muttering, "Damn, I just don't get it," Nell folded her arms in deliberation. "Any way you slice it, it's just a plain old cellar."

Her eyes began to creep all over the place again, but this time they were infused with an even more tenacious glint. "If I were hiding a switch in the cellar, I'd put it somewhere no one could find it, I reckon."

And, saying that, Nell headed to a corner stacked with empty boxes. "No, I wouldn't—I'd do the exact opposite. The best place a person can hide is in a crowd. And if you had a switch you didn't want anyone to notice, you'd put it where anyone could see it."

Swishing the hem of her skirt, Nell headed over to the control box high on the wall. "As our Miss Nell recalls, she heard strange voices and the creak of gears around here. Meaning . . ." Her sharp eyes stared at a row of nearly a dozen levers. "Maybe it's this one, the least grimy of the lot . . . " Grabbing one in the middle of the row, Nell gave it a twist to the right. With a harsh creaking, just as the maid recalled, there was the sound of gears meshing.

"Whoa!"

As Nell cried out, her body swung about in a circle. To be more precise, she was turned completely around when the spot she was standing on pivoted away easily and revealed a circular hole. A wooden ladder stretched down into a darkness far deeper than the gloom of the cellar.

"So, this must be what made our Miss Nell so suspicious. Don't worry, dear. Uncle Pluto will find the answers for you now," she chortled.

Eyes glittering wildly, Nell went over to the ladder. Checking that no one else was around, she headed down into the new, lower cellar. The ladder was sturdy enough, but the smoothness of the rungs clearly suggested someone had been making frequent use of it for decades now. Fifty rungs down, she reached the bottom.

"Let's see. A switch, a switch . . ." Groping in the dark, her hand soon struck a wall. Finding a small switch, she flicked it on.

A feeble light swelled in the darkness. There lay an area so vast it almost seemed as if the whole town would fit inside it. In the very center of that chamber rested a lone box of an unmistakable nature. Though its surface was free of ornamentation, it was clearly a coffin.

Anxiously muttering, "It's still morning," to herself, Nell started walking toward the coffin. "Hard to believe the mayor of all people would be keeping a monster in his cellar."

As she reached for the coffin's lid without hesitating, someone grabbed Nell by the hair. She started to scream, but, before she could finish, her neck was slashed wide open. Bright blood splashed across the floor.

And, at that very instant, there was a most bizarre incident in another part of town. A short while earlier, a carpenter had discovered a squat man sleeping in the woods. Or at least he'd decided the man was sleeping after checking him for a pulse, but, by the time several other townsfolk and the people from the law enforcement bureau had arrived, his opinion had changed. He now believed it to be a corpse. After all, while the man's heart was still beating, he wasn't breathing at all. When it became known the body was that of the outsider who'd accompanied the gorgeous Vampire Hunter, the site was surrounded by a squawking throng.

"Why on earth—?"

"Went and killed himself. Must've wanted to get even with us for not making him feel welcome in town."

"And I keep telling you even though I seen him mixing it up with the locals in my saloon, he just didn't seem the type to do himself in."

"Heart's beating but he ain't breathing none," one of the onlookers noted. "What good can come of that, I ask you?"

"Good question," said someone from the law enforcement bureau. "At any rate, we'll have to put him out of his misery, right?"

"Right you are," said one of the townsfolk with a nod. "Good riddance, I say. Finish him off!"

"Will do," one of the lawmen said. Drawing an enormous automatic handgun from his holster, he pointed it at Pluto VIII's head. The surrounding mob hustled back out of range. And then, just as the public servant was about to pull the trigger, the man leapt up, fresh as a daisy. With a startled cry, the lawman flinched away.

"You damn idiots! I ain't on display here!" the squat sleeper bellowed. Looking around contemptuously and seeing how the crowd of townsfolk watched him from a safe distance, he spat, "You people are pathetic. You don't have the faintest clue what kind of crazy shit your trusty leader keeps for a pet, but you'll stand around and watch someone who collapsed in the street get their brains blown out."

Needless to say, the foul-tempered man was Pluto VIII, having returned to his own body the instant his host Nell was slain.

†

Shortly after D watched Lori write the mayor's name, the Hunter left the hospital. Dr. Tsurugi requested that he stay and talk with the girl a while longer, but D replied that business came first. Stepping out the door, D was surrounded by three figures. Sheriff Hutton and two deputies—the very same people he'd gone to see at the law enforcement bureau earlier. All of them were wearing gun belts.

"Figured you'd be here, creep," the sheriff snarled, rocket launcher in one hand. The other two held shotguns at the ready.

Seeing their weapons leveled at his heart, D asked, "You have some business with me?" His tone was languid. He was standing in full sunlight. For a creature like a dhampir, descending in part from the Nobility, the conditions couldn't be worse for doing battle.

"You wanna know if we got business? What did you think, we came here to take you out for a drink?" said one of the deputies. "For a freakin' outsider, you got some nerve. I don't care if you're a dhampir or whatever the hell you are—you're out of line. We're gonna give you a nice, long lesson in what happens when you threaten the sheriff in this town."

"I've got a full day tomorrow before my time's up. Can't this wait until then?"

"Are you nuts?! We let a little bastard like you take care of our trouble here, and me and my boys won't look like we're worth our pay no more." Gouts of flame seemed to shoot from Sheriff Hutton's eyes. His rocket launcher was set to discharge all its chambers in a single shot. He had only to push the button, and seven pencil missiles would blast the beautiful Hunter into unrecognizable scraps.

Seeing that a fight was unavoidable, D asked softly, "Are we going to do this here?"

"Now, that's what I like to hear. I'm impressed you ain't trying to make a run for it. Of course, we're still gonna make you pay for coming off so damn tough," the older of the two deputies muttered, swinging the end of his shotgun to indicate an alley that was dark even by daylight.

Meeting the flames of hatred focused on him like a blowtorch with his ever-frosty demeanor, D asked, "Ready to make your move?"

"You first."

Each standing ten feet away, the two deputies braced their shotguns. They'd taken up positions they calculated to be well beyond the reach of D's longsword. No matter what move he might try to make, their shotguns should prove faster than his sword. Their guns already had the first shell in the chamber. The tension was rising by the second.

A lone invader ivy bush grew from the ground by D's feet. Because it had an amazing knack for propagation, exterminating this weed was of the utmost importance, but efforts toward that end never went well. Every time someone thought they had it beat, it would put forth a new shoot within three days, if even part of its fine root structure remained, and it took less than three weeks for it to reach maturity. Though it had no blossoms, it displayed the greatest determination to live and had spread everywhere from the colder regions to the greener belts. D's right hand reached for one of its branches. It was a graceful movement that kept the tense lawmen from putting any more pressure on their trigger fingers. Effortlessly snapping the plant off at its root, D waved it at the men like a great green wad of cotton candy. "Come on."

"You got it!" they shouted, squeezing the triggers with the brute strength their delight lent them. With the gravest of roars, each weapon released three dozen pellets—seventy-two balls of shot loosed in a sheath of flame at D's chest. One can't help but wonder if the two men saw the flash of green that seemed to sweep the hot lead away a split second before it was due to strike. Tiny lead balls plunked down on the crushed stone road, and the two deputies felt the chill of the blade sinking into their skulls. Surely neither of them would've believed he could use the invader ivy leaves and branches to knock the flying buckshot out of the air.

Still brandishing his bloodstained sword, D said to the rocket-launcher-packing giant, "Come on."

The giant trembled. The murderous implement under his arm had become a mere chunk of iron that offered no security at all. What guarantee did he have that a man who could knock buckshot out of the air with a branch couldn't turn his own missiles back on him? Imagining himself caught in a burning white flash that would reduce him to bloody chunks sailing through the air, the sheriff grew pale.

"How about it?" the Hunter said. "You've already got your weapon out."

Hutton had no choice but to go through with it. But no matter what weapon he had, he didn't think it would save him from the Hunter's sword. The sheriff felt the Grim Reaper brushing the nape of his neck.

At that moment, Dr. Tsurugi came running into the alley in great haste. Instantly realizing what was going on, he stepped between the two of them and turned to D. "Please, just stop," the physician said. "There's been entirely too much killing already. If you kill the sheriff, then you really will have to leave here. Even the mayor couldn't do anything about it."

D's hand went into action, easily shoving the physician aside. The fight had already begun, and D's sword had been drawn. It wouldn't be going back in its sheath until it'd tasted the blood of all who made themselves his foe.

The sheriff's Adam's apple bobbed as he swallowed loudly. For the first time, it dawned on him just who he'd chosen to go up against.

The stir of excited voices suddenly hung in the air over town. "Sheriff! Sheriff!" a voice cried, and there was the sound of approaching footsteps.

"You're a lucky man." Giving a light wave of his right hand that threw every last drop of gore from his blade to the ground, D walked right by the frozen sheriff's side. He simply left, as if saying he was finished with the lawman. And in the Hunter's place, a deputy came running into the alley. Seeing the carnage, he froze in his tracks.

"Wha—what do you want?!" the sheriff stammered.

No sooner had he asked the question than the ground shook terribly. No earthquake could even begin to compare to this. It felt like the earth itself had shifted nearly ninety degrees. Panic swept over the people. The crying of children echoed from more than one home.

"What on earth's going on?" This time it was the physician who shouted the question.

"It's Magnetic Storm Pass."

"That's impossible. We're not supposed to be headed south-southwest!"

"Yeah? Well, we are!"

Frightened screams and angry shouts bounced across the shifting earth as it continued to rock wildly. Ahead of the moving town, the entrance to a narrow pass formed by the slopes of a pair of mountains was visible, and a purple cloud could be seen masking that entrance. That magnetic field would wreak havoc with anything electronic, and the town was headed straight for it.

So, what exactly was the Magnetic Storm Pass? Simply put, it was another slice of insanity spawned by a dispute between Nobles. At the end of an interminable battle over the borders of their domain, one Noble faction had set various offensive and defensive devices along the perimeter of what they held was their land. They built a spatial distortion that could pack infinity into a finite area and swallow any invaders. They made visible light into a weapon that could slice through the solid steel hull of a flying battleship. They constructed illusion projectors that not only made people see things, but could even convince them they were part of an entirely different ecosystem. And finally, they created a magnetic storm with the power to disrupt the electrical systems of any machine. Though the Nobility that created these defenses were dying out, the weapons, fed by nuclear power sources, continued to terrorize humanity. And it was one such deadly device that had its lair in the very pass the town was now rushing toward.

"That's odd . . . the warnings aren't sounding."

"Warnings be damned. There's no way in hell our route should be taking us through there!" a voice bellowed angrily out on streets where darkness and light intermingled seductively.

Purple bolts of lightning zipped down the lightning rods. The string of small explosions that could be heard were most likely from circuit breakers that could no longer bear the load. Now, blackness claimed the heavens and earth, and tendrils of light like colossal serpents surrounded the entire town. Factory shutters rattled down noisily, and the radiating fins spread wide on the electrical discharge towers. Energy absorption rods began extending from the ship's sides.

"What's wrong with the navigational computers?" shouted someone in the underground control room.

"There's nothing wrong with the computers," another voice replied shrilly.

"But we're way off course!"

"Someone put in bad data, I tell you!"

"Damn it! Who in blazes could've done that?!"

†

Grains of sand and small pebbles struck D and Dr. Tsurugi's cheeks.

"This doesn't look good. Doctor, you'd better hurry home."

"Come to mention it, so should you," the young physician replied. "It's a long way back to my quarters."

"I'll walk you there."

D looked at the physician's face. And then he casually started to walk away. Dr. Tsurugi followed right behind him.

Lightning raced across the earth. Thin, wriggling threads of it. Spraying sand, flinging stones, the lightning wrapped around a gatepost and gave off a shower of sparks. The dazzling display of light made D look like white-hot metal. Along the town's sides, the energy absorption rods were also catching the lightning. It would be sent to the nuclear reactors via transformers. Tasting untold bounty for the first time in ages, the reactors showed their satisfaction with their rising, pale blue flames.

D continued silently down the street. Serpents of light raced all around him, raising their heads menacingly at the hem of his coat and spitting fire.

"I'm going back," the physician said from behind him. "Not because I'm getting scared or anything. Oh, I'm scared, all right. But I realized at present we really can't afford to have me getting hurt."

D nodded.

Bowing and excusing himself, the physician did an about-face. Just above him, there was a flash of silvery light. A bolt of lightning that was about to strike his head was split in half, and the fragments twitched on the ground. Completely oblivious to what had happened, Dr. Tsurugi raced off.

Again the town shook. A phosphorescent flash engulfed an electrical discharge tower, and flames shot from its base. Flashes of electricity zipped from the ground in the industrial sector. The energy absorption circuits had surpassed their capacity. Absorption and discharge—both methods had reached their limits.

D had noticed that the town's course had changed. There was no way a navigation system governed by a number of computers working in concert would plot a course that took them right through the middle of a magnetic storm. Some outside agent had adjusted it. But why? Where on earth were they taking the town? Those were questions best put to the mayor.

D stopped in his tracks. A man staggered from the path that ran beside a house. He was clutching at his throat. This was no victim of electrocution. D's eyes glittered at the sight of his oddly pale skin. Turning around, D went to cross the street. The man collapsed on the spot.

An especially massive electricity snake wriggled down the street. D sprinted. The shining serpent sank into the man's midsection. Black smoke rose from him, and the stench of burning flesh pervaded the area. His charred corpse rolled into the street.

Lightning coursed at D from all sides, only to be sundered by silvery flashes.

As D was about to take a step forward, the smoking black mass suddenly moved. Bracing himself with his arms, he slowly raised his torso. Needless to say, his hair and clothes were singed, and his face was burnt to a crisp. Bits of sizzled cloth and hair rained down on the road. The man was getting up.

There weren't many creatures that could be jolted with fifty thousand volts and not be the worse for wear. The Nobility was one of them. It seemed this man was infected with the disease.

A red cavity opened in the lower half of the blackened face. His mouth. That alone was as red as ever, as if to offer some contrast to his pearly white fangs. How does a person charred to a crisp get to their feet? Burnt body framed with white light, he slowly began walking toward D. Smoke wafted from his limbs. Probing bolts of lightning crackled from his singed flesh.

D didn't move a muscle. A blackened hand reached for him. A second before it closed on the Hunter's throat, the hand swept away in an elegant arc and then fell back to earth. D seemed to listen for the *thunk* of it hitting the ground.

The charred human form began to lose its thickness, turning into a pile of dust. In the blink of an eye, the gusting winds had scattered the remains far and wide. This was the second case of the vampire infection. However, simply just because a person had turned into a vampire didn't necessarily mean they would crumble like ash when true death claimed them. The degree of corruption their body manifested depended entirely on how long it'd been since they'd been made a servant of the Nobility. A person who'd spent three days in their service would leave a rotting corpse. Given two weeks, the flesh would melt from their bones. If more than a year had passed, then they might be reduced to dust. In death alone they would be bound by the same rules as the living. What'd just occurred to the corpse of this vampirized individual simply wasn't possible. Or was this a case where his transformation into one of the Nobility had long been concealed? No, that wasn't possible, either. This was an entirely new disease. Perhaps it should've been called Nobilitation Syndrome.

D turned his back on the remains and started to walk away. But the question remained: where was he headed?

II

The town's ability to insulate itself from the storm had reached its limits. Breakers in four of the five electrical discharge towers had burnt out from the overload, and the remaining tower was down to fifty percent effectiveness.

"Nuclear reactor number one—energy level at fifty-two percent over normal capacity."

"Number two is fifty-seven percent over. She's got all she can handle."

"Number three is sixty-nine percent over—well into the danger zone. Danger! Danger! Danger!"

"Navigational control room, how many minutes more until we're clear of the magnetic storm?" Mayor Ming asked.

"We can't be certain. According to our data, this magnetic belt is approximately 2.95 miles wide. At our present speed, that'd be 5 minutes, 19.6 seconds."

"Report what degree of danger the town would face in that five minutes if we were to shut down energy absorption for one, two, or all three of our reactor towers."

"If all three towers are shut down—town will be destroyed in 2 minutes and 22 seconds. Two towers—town will be destroyed in 3 minutes and 5.4 seconds. One tower—town will be destroyed in 5 minutes and 21.3 seconds."

"Keep only the number one reactor in operation. Increase cruising speed to twenty-five miles per hour."

"That's insane. The outer shell will suddenly be taking three times as much voltage—it'll blow the reactor!"

"I realize it's crazy," the mayor said. "But we can't do a damn thing unless we get clear of this storm!"

"Roger that."

The instant the other two nuclear reactors stopped absorbing power, the remaining energy turned at once on the number one reactor, snapping at it like the fangs of a crazed beast. Fire shot from the energy flow control system and five of the safeties, and the now unbalanced flames of nuclear fusion quickly drove the needle toward the danger zone. In no time at all, pale blue flames had burst through the bottom plates of the town and were shooting wildly into the air.

†

Wracked by the powerful shocks, Lori gave a silent scream and clung desperately to her bed. Dr. Tsurugi ran to her. Shouting Lori's name, he threw himself at her and pulled her tight to him. Lori clung to his warm chest. The physician's heart kept pounding wildly. *He's just as scared as I am*, Lori thought. For the first time, she found herself feeling something other than curiosity toward the young doctor.

†

Ahead of the town, there wriggled a particularly large and fierce serpent of light. Lightning crackled from every inch of it, and when bolts from it brushed the craggy cliffs to either side of it, the surface was fused into glass or rained down on the town. Chunks of rock crashed through the roof of a house somewhere, and a woman could be heard screaming. A compressor in one of the factories took a hit as well, turning the braided steel air hose into a high-voltage cable that whipped into workers' bodies and scalded their faces. White light engulfed the town. Silicon polymer roofs were being blown off houses, and whole trees were being sucked up into the sky, roots and all. People scrambled into their basements for protection.

The fierce suction assailed D as well. His traveler's hat and the hem of his coat began to rise. Securing the hat's wide brim with his left hand, D drew his sword with his right. Turning the blade over, he drove it into the earth. Kneeling, he waited. Pebbles flew up, and roofing materials followed right after them.

†

The true mayhem was concentrated in the reactor and navigation control centers. A serpent of light that slipped in through a fresh hole in the wall thrashed ruthlessly through the bulkhead, flinging workers everywhere. The pungent odor of burnt flesh filled the air. Snagging a flying worker with one hand, the mayor slammed him back against the floor. The old man's strength was incredible. Raising his voice, he asked, "Can't correct our computers, am I right?"

"No, it's no use!"

"Then switch to manual controls!" Mayor Ming snapped back.

"Manual controls on these were scrapped over five hundred years ago."

The mayor's face took on the fierceness of a demon. Pulling the serpent of light that was devastating his surroundings to his chest, the mayor tore it apart with his bare hands. Black smoke rose from his hands and his torso. His hair stood on end, and lightning leapt around in his mouth. "Where the hell are we going?" he said. "Who's doing this, and where do they think they're taking my town?"

†

D heard the riot of life and death all around him. Kneeling, gripping the sword he'd driven into the earth, he looked like an obsidian statue. With all the elements howling furiously around him, he alone remained unaffected. Light filled the air above him. A serpentine form twice as thick as any man could get his arms around was dropping toward D, scorching the air molecules as it went. Here was the leader of this deadly swarm. Never breaking his pose, D flew backward. Passing him in midair, the serpent fell to the ground and broke in half before taking to the air once again.

†

The magnetic belt is pulling away from the town."

"Pull out of it at full speed."

As if in response to that joyful cry, blue-black space stretched across the forward view screen—a sky sealed in tranquil darkness, without a hint of blinding light. As if beaten off by the winds gusting against them, the lights coloring the town began to fall off behind them.

"We're clear!" someone shouted. Cheers suddenly filled the air.

†

When Sheriff Hutton called on Ming, some three hours had passed since the mayor had left one of the workers in charge of overseeing the removal of the radioactive waste. The sheriff found Ming settled into a chair in his private chambers. "How are the townsfolk?" the mayor asked in ill humor, his eyes shut.

"They're finally settling down. We're looking into the number of injured now," the sheriff said in a tone that sounded somewhat intrigued.

"Then, I gather there were no fatalities?"

"Yeah. Surprisingly few wounded, too. Hard to believe no one got electrocuted. Radiation poisoning's been pretty minor, to boot."

"We have that medicine I came up with forty years ago to thank for that. Anyway, what do you want?" The mayor opened his eyes. Somewhat reproachfully, he added, "You ought to still be out there."

"Actually, I've come to gab about old times with you," the sheriff said, smiling at him. The mayor had never seen him smirk like that. "You happen to remember Ende Remparts? He was a twelve-year-old kid."

The expression that formed on the mayor's face was that of an entirely different person. "Just what the hell do you think you're doing?!"

"Poor kid had a muscular disease they could've treated well enough in a town on the ground, but you hated the idea of anyone getting off. Told him the condition was untreatable, and he ended up offing himself as a result, didn't he?"

"Hey!"

"How about that time with Ebenezer Villzuya?" the sheriff continued, stroking the barrel of his rocket launcher. "That one I had a hand in. We were in the middle of a famine, and he stole a half-pound more synthetic butter than he was supposed to get. His kids were on the brink of starving. The rest of the town pretended not to notice. After all, no one else was half as bad off as his family. Why, even you were pretty easy on him at first. But in the end, you just couldn't find it in you to let the first man to break the rules in the town you made get away with it. So, this cuss here, who was just a deputy at the time, went in and gunned down his whole family, then made it look like suicide."

The mayor got up out of his chair and barked, "Who the hell are you?!"

"It's me. Take a good look now. I'm the one and only Sheriff Hutton. Given name: Bailey Hutton; height: nine feet nine inches; weight: five hundred thirty-five pounds; place of birth: three hundred thirty-fourth sector of the Eastern Frontier. I first came on board . . ."

A loud crack resounded at his jaw. The massive frame of five hundred and thirty-five pounds lurched backward and rolled on the floor. Dashing over, the mayor was just about to stomp his right foot down on the giant's throat when the barrel of the rocket launcher rose from the floor to stop him.

"Hey, now—cut that out. I don't care how tough you are. Seven blasts from this will send you straight to the hereafter," the sheriff said, rubbing his jaw as he got back up. He was like a walking mountain. If someone had opened the door just then, they wouldn't have seen anything besides his back. On the other hand, the mayor stood only five foot eight and weighed less than a hundred and fifty pounds. Though nutritional supplements might've helped to explain how he'd lived to be over two hundred, the punch he'd just delivered was beyond anything imaginable. "Ow, that smarts. You pack more of a wallop than I'd heard," the sheriff said as he nursed his jaw, but his voice was clearly that of another person.

"Oh, it's *you*? Got one hell of a strange power there," the mayor said, not seeming particularly upset as he went back to his chair. He must've figured that as long as he knew what and whom he was dealing with, he could do away with them whenever he pleased. "I thought you were a bit of a shady character from the moment I heard you were D's partner—and then you go off possessing our sheriff and stealing his memories. Well, what exactly do you intend to do next?"

"Nothing serious, really. Compared to what a heavyweight scoundrel like you gets away with, what I'm asking for is small potatoes."

"I see. And that would be?"

"I want what the Knights left you."

"Really?"

"I've been over every inch of that house, and I couldn't find a thing. From what they told me, it seems you wanted it, too. In which case, it's pretty obvious where it'd have to be now."

"Unfortunately, I don't know its location either." Sitting there in his chair, the mayor spread his hands in a display of innocence. "When I found out you tried to save them, I very much wanted to ask you exactly the same thing."

"I see. So, you were the one behind that whole little act about bringing me in for stealing some flowers?" the sheriff said in Pluto VIII's voice, grinning at him as the biker would. "Too bad about that. But, you see, I've got no proof what you're telling me is true. Worse yet, your town's got these vampires running around and no one knows when the hell they got on. *Got on* . . . " he snorted. "That's a laugh. Of course no one would know when. They've *been here* since the very beginning, after all."

The voice suddenly became that of the sheriff. "Six months back, on your orders, I snatched Dumper Griswell and Yan Will. Didn't have the foggiest notion what you intended to use them for, but no one in town was gonna miss a couple of worthless drunks. But with things as they are now, I kinda have to wonder—did them two maybe get themselves turned into vampires?"

"And just what would you do if they did?" the mayor said menacingly.

"Hey, now! I thought I told you not to move. Besides, trying to do anything to me won't accomplish anything. Your sheriff here's the one who'll take the lumps, while I'll just go back to my old body and slip into someone else. Hell, I could even use your own daughter . . . "

"And could you move into another body from the one you're in now?" the mayor asked.

"Yep."

"Hmm. Then maybe you ought to try possessing me. That way you'll know straight away whether I'm telling the truth or not."

"Wow, knock me over with a feather. Are you sure about this? I'll be privy to your every little secret."

"I don't mind a bit. After all, this way, you'll see it'd be in your interest to join forces with me for a little while."

"Join forces?"

"That's right. We're both after the same thing, but there are any number of ways it might be used."

"Ah, I see. So, as long as your use and mine don't conflict, we'd be fine. Good enough."

"What'll you do about the sheriff?"

"I'll screw with his brain a bit and leave him snoozing. Make sure no one comes in here for a while."

The mayor spoke into his intercom, saying something to the effect that no one was to be let into his chambers. He turned to face the sheriff. One of the giant's hands latched onto his deeply wrinkled wrist. Two seconds passed . . . then three . . . And then, with a crash that shook the whole room, five hundred and thirty-five pounds of lawman fell over like a tree. An expression of amazement that wasn't his at all quickly formed on the mayor's face as he sat there with his eyes shut.

"I . . . I can't believe that." The voice that slipped from his dry lips was choked with fear. Almost as if his own thoughts terrified him . . . "Who could do such an awful thing . . . And you still call yourself—or should I say myself—human?!"

Lori

CHAPTER 5

I

Though the crisis had passed, the town showed signs that it hadn't yet recovered from the tragedy. The owners of devastated houses didn't look very motivated to repair the damage as they sat around sulking, and their neighbors didn't seem at all inclined to help cheer them up. Every face wore a demented expression, and the people stood around like empty husks, or milled about in the streets aimlessly. It was almost as if the overwhelming disaster had stripped everything that mattered from them. But in the midst of the milling townsfolk, mixed with the chatter of the frantically scrambling relief party that answered directly to the mayor, a crisp and spirited young voice rang out. It was that of Dr. Tsurugi, working at the emergency medical facility that'd been established in front of the hospital. "Okay," he said, "I want you to form a single file—no pushing—and one by one, take a seat."

Once a patient was seated in the simple revolving chair, Dr. Tsurugi ran his hands over their clothed form and asked them a few questions. The palms of his gloves were imprinted with some kind of medical diagnostic program. The questions were to gauge the level of mental upheaval each patient had suffered.

"Okay—Point nine seven. A slight case of radiation poisoning. Mental balance is . . . no problem. Pick your medicine up over there. Okay, next!"

Only at the very end did a bit of honest emotion slip into the doctor's face, but shortly thereafter he reclaimed his beaming countenance. It was a sight to see him in action, working through the endless chain of patients at a rate of less than a minute each. However, the person by his side dispensing medicine wasn't the nurse. It was a lovely young lady of seventeen who couldn't compliment anyone or say a single word to comfort them, but who showed all the compassion she could muster in her large eyes as she quietly handed them their medicine. It was difficult to believe that, less than ten hours earlier, her whole body had been covered with plasters for removing radioactive contamination. It was Lori.

After seeing how terribly overburdened Dr. Tsurugi was, she'd volunteered to help out. Of course, the physician's situation hadn't been helped by the fact that his nurse had been horribly frightened and had yet to recover from her dementia. As Lori gazed at the townsfolk and the numb expressions they wore, there was sorrow in her eyes, but another, more invigorating feeling filled her slight frame. She'd lost the use of her voice and ears, but she had to go on living. The determination to do so burned strongly in her. However, on a more basic level, the girl was immensely pleased to be able to do something on her own.

Lori's smiling eyes were suddenly infused with an intense glimmer. A powerful figure in black was coming down the same street filled by the lines of townsfolk.

D stopped next to the physician. "Make it through okay?" he asked. From the Hunter's tone of voice it wasn't clear whether he was actually concerned or just being polite. And, of course, the sound of it didn't reach Lori's ears at all. Still, she got the feeling there was something beyond the usual severity in the gaze he cast on the physician and herself, and it made her heart leap.

"I muddled through somehow," Dr. Tsurugi replied. "How about you? I've heard dhampirs have a far greater tolerance for radiation than the average human—" The physician caught himself and quickly bit his lip. A few of the townspeople looked surprised by what they'd heard, but most showed no reaction at all. While the shock of the magnetic storm was to blame, the effect it'd had on the populace was just too great.

"Is the corpse inside?" the Hunter asked.

"Yes, he's still asleep. I don't know what you did to him, but it must've been incredible."

"I'd like a look at it."

"Fine. But I'd like something in return," the physician said, his hands never taking a break from examining patients.

"What's that?"

"Once you're done with that, I'd like you to help me out."

"There's nothing I could do," said D.

"If you've got arms and legs, we've got work for you."

"Okay, if I've got time." And with that uncharacteristic reply, D went through the door.

Lori's sorrowful gaze followed the Hunter. He hadn't so much as acknowledged her presence.

†

On entering the operating room, D took a portable atomic lamp off the shelf and switched it on. A pale flame blazed up around the wick. The body of the man lying on the operating table on the other side of the room was outlined in blue. Twisting the faucet to get the water running, D looked down at his left hand and said, "I've got some soil ready, too, but what would you like first?"

"Don't ask dumb questions," a voice quickly answered. At the same time, a human face complete with eyes and a nose mysteriously surfaced in the palm of the Hunter's hand. Forming a scowl, it said, "You're splitting hairs with all this talk about fire first or water first, when the truth is nothing's been all that tasty lately. After all, I'm the one who's gotta eat them. Oh, my—we've got a nuclear reactor today? That looks positively delicious. None of that alcohol lamp or dried werewolf dung, thank you. That stuff's the worst!"

Taking a handful of dirt from one of his coat's inner pockets, D put it beside the lamp. "Be quick about it," he said. "The corpse should be waking up soon."

"Hmph. Well if it does, you can just put it back to sleep again. Day in and day out, you're always pushing me around."

"Fire or water?" the Hunter asked.

"Hmm, I'll take the dirt."

D held his left hand over the blackish pile. There was the intense squeal of air being drawn in, and the clod of earth broke apart into a powder that was inhaled by the palm hanging over it.

"That tastes awful!" the voice said after sucking up every last grain of dirt. "This soil hasn't known the usual ups and downs, or been part of the natural circle of life, death, and rebirth. It doesn't take its life from the planet. It's just a decoration laid down over steel. You're not gonna be very satisfied with the kind of results you get by feeding me crap like this!"

Without saying a word, D held his left hand up to the atomic flames.

"Sheesh! You dolt. Water's supposed to be next," the voice squawked, but the Hunter didn't move a muscle. Further curses of "freak" and "sadist" soon died out, and the atomic light—as impossible as it sounds—quickly condensed into a single glowing stream that disappeared into D's hand. Or, to be more precise, into the tiny mouth that'd opened in the palm of his hand. And just how voracious was that mouth? Well, the ultracompact reactor the lamp was equipped with was supposed to be enough to power the atomic flame for more than a decade, but in less than two minutes its color faded, it flickered, and finally it went out.

D didn't so much as raise an eyebrow at that bizarre occurrence, but instead put this hand under the spigot in the sink, palm up now. A few minutes later, the voice sputtered, "That's enough," and as it did, D twisted the faucet to shut it off.

"How are you feeling?" D asked. His eyes remained trained on the corpse.

"Well, I'll get by. I suppose I'm a hell of a lot better than I was last night." Along with the words, a gout of flame roared from the palm of the Hunter's hand. In a mouth left pale blue by a few thousand degrees of heat, a red tongue flicked impassively, saying sharply, "So, what the heck do you want analyzed?"

Devoid of pity or any other deeper emotion, D brought his left hand over to the man on the operating table—and put it against his forehead. At that instant, the whole corpse stiffened and bent backward from the waist, like a bow. It snapped into the shape so fiercely that it wouldn't have been strange to hear his hipbones shattering. Countless red points began to form all over his body, along with specks of blood. Had this body, which had supposedly long since ceased to function, begun to have metabolic activity once again? The vivid red spots grew larger and larger, and in no time their surface tension broke and they began to course down the sides of the body, leaving disturbing trails on his flesh. When the first drop hit the operating table, a faint moan escaped from the corpse.

D had his eyes half-closed. What was his hand trying to do? What kind of analysis? What did he hope to learn from this corpse?

†

When the treatment of the townsfolk and the distribution of medicine had finally wound down, Lori quickly looked at the physician. Massaging his hands, Dr. Tsurugi nodded to her. The girl got up and went into the hospital. Talking pains not to tread too loudly, she peeked into the waiting room. There was nobody there. Was he in the office, or maybe the operating room? It had never even occurred to Lori that D's business there might be with a corpse. Once more, she stepped out into the hall. She decided to try the office.

A few inches away from her, the door to the operating room opened inward. A figure suddenly appeared. A man completely covered in blood.

Lori froze in her tracks, choking back a scream. The man suddenly collapsed in a heap. When Lori saw the other figure that stood behind him, she desperately tried to keep her knees from failing her. She didn't want him to see her do anything stupid. Having lost her voice and hearing, she was damned if she'd lose anything else now.

As the girl tried desperately to steady her footing, D watched her without saying a word. Waiting until she'd gotten her trembling under control, the Hunter grabbed the corpse by the neck and brought it back into the operating room. As they gazed at the blood spilled on the floor, his eyes held a dark tint.

By the time D went back out into the hall, Lori had returned to her senses. She'd always been a brave girl.

"You want something from me?" D asked. He said it out loud.

Lori tried desperately to follow the movements of his lips. Somehow, she managed to read them. She shook her head. She had no business with him. She just thought it would be nice to see him. That was all.

"While you may not be able to get back what you lost, you can learn something new in return," D remarked impassively, almost as if he didn't care what became of Lori. Not understanding exactly what'd been said to her, Lori pursed her lips with grim resolve and tried not to miss anything else. D said to her, "Come with me. We probably don't have much time."

And with that he walked out. Lori followed after him. A smile had risen to her lips. By watching D's cold profile, she understood what he was saying.

"Just where are you two going?" the physician called to them as they came out the front door.

"Where's the highest point in town?" the Hunter asked in return.

"That'd be the hill behind the factories. Why?"

Nodding with satisfaction, D began to walk away. As the two figures walked off down the street, the physician watched them coolly.

†

The damage to Chad Beckly's house had been relatively minor. Fastening a waterproof tarp over a couple of holes that falling rocks had left in the roof, he decided the repairs could wait for another day. They were a family of four. There was Chad, his wife Vera, and their two sons Luke and Simon. Chad's family was extremely concerned about the way he was acting. Ever since he'd come home from the navigational control room, his expression had been one of deep depression. Skipping dinner entirely, as soon as he'd put the sheet over the roof he'd gone straight to bed.

What was troubling Chad was where the town was headed. The new route that'd been programmed into the computers clearly had them headed right for some of the Nobility's ruins. They'd probably be there in less than two days. The question was, what was waiting for them there? Even the mayor said he didn't know. Legend alone had the answer. Graves. And not the kind of Noble resting place ornamented with elaborate crests and guarded by electronic devices. What slumbered there was . . .

Hauling his mind back from its slide into anxiety, Chad tried his best to get to sleep. The wind howled outside his window. Tomorrow, he'd have to get up before dawn and head back to the control room. What on earth was going to happen to the town? Chad's brain was burning with worry. Downstairs, his wife and children were still up and about. So much had happened, they probably couldn't get settled down to rest.

There was a slight sound . . . A rap at the door, perhaps? His wife walked around. The floorboards creaked. He'd have to speak to the mayor about getting them replaced. But who could be out at this hour? There was absolutely no way he was going back to the control room. Someone came in. The door was still open. There was the sound of something falling over. *Did the missus trip over that dang chair again?* he wondered. *Wait a minute—they didn't get back up.*

Footsteps crossed the living room and started up the stairs. Creaking all the while. Must be his wife. Out in the hall now. Still coming. Slowly. Coming this way. The footsteps stopped. Out in front of the boys' room.

Maybe I should go see who it is? he thought. *No, it's just the little woman, of course. Besides, I'm dog-tired.*

The door opened. *Aw, she shouldn't have gone and done that. Hey, that was a scream just now, wasn't it?* More thuds as things fell. Two of them. The door closed. The footsteps were coming closer. Slowly. No hurry . . . They stopped. In front of his bedroom. It couldn't be . . .

There was a knock on his door. Chad remained in bed. The knocking continued, then stopped for a bit—and started again.

Chad got out of bed. Step by step, each one feeling like it was sinking into the carpet, he headed for the door. He didn't want to go. He knew it was his wife outside the door. But what if it wasn't . . .

Right in front of the door, Chad paused for a moment. The knocking stopped. The doorknob clicked as it turned. Gently at first, then quickly . . .

With a tremendous snap, the doorknob, the plate around it, and the section of door they were attached to all vanished. There was a gaping hole now. And the door had swung open. Someone was standing there. It wasn't his wife.

A horrible choking sensation assailed Chad. He reached up to claw at his own throat, but before his hand got there his heart had stopped.

†

While it was indeed a hill, with a height of only about fifteen feet, it hardly had a commanding view. And yet, for one of the two it was surely more than adequate. After all, Lori wasn't alone, and by her side was a man the darkness suited more than anyone. Despite the moonlight, the plains they overlooked were as dark as anything imaginable, but the sky to the east was already laced with the first thin light of dawn. The wind pricked at Lori's cheeks. It was as cold and sharp as an awl. Lori gazed at D while D watched the eastern sky. Did those trapped in darkness hope for the light of dawn, too?

So, what had they come up here to do? D bent down by Lori's side and put one of the fingers of his left hand to the ground. Lori read the words he wrote in the sand. *I hear voices*, D had written. What voices was he talking about? The message seemed almost cruel.

Lori turned up the collar of her coat. The wind tossed her soft hair as it passed. *So cold*, she thought. *Maybe people weren't meant to live out in the wild.* After all, it was this cold even at daybreak.

The town was still moving. But going where? It had no destination. Where was it heading? Not even Lori had any idea what D was thinking about. While it was true she'd been raised in town, she'd also experienced life out in the wilderness. The wilds were just too terrible. The fear inspired by the monstrosities and vicious beasts the Nobility had loosed was still enough that the world would quake at dusk today.

Lori had wanted to go back to the town with all her heart. However, the paradise she'd wanted now seemed so hollow. Lori no longer had words or sounds, which was exactly why she could feel things so much more intensely . . . She thought of working reasonable hours, and having reasonable accommodations, food, and clothing, of having a life that was satisfactory, but not satisfying at the same time. The overwhelming sense of loss from the people after they'd made it through the magnetic storm only served to highlight her feelings. If she hadn't experienced life in the wilderness, she probably would've been just like the rest. Although she was far from conceited, Lori knew there was something wrong with the town as it was now. But, in her silent world of despair, did she have reason to be proud of being different from the rest? An inescapable sense of loneliness filled her little heart. While she had the feeling the world she was meant to live in was just around the next bend, for Lori that was a far-distant land. *If I get off this town, what'll happen then?* she wondered.

To the east, the edges of the mountains had begun to glitter with a rosy hue. Light slipped down the mountainside, becoming a torrent that flooded the plains, and in no time Lori's entire field of view was tinged in gold. She closed her eyes. Even with them closed, she could see. She saw the color of wind. And how the wind shined in its own way.

After a while, D opened his mouth. Lori tried to read his lips. She didn't catch it all. A bit more slowly, D repeated it. Finally she understood him.

Next time, come alone. That's what he was saying.

†

It was a little past six o'clock Morning when D called on the mayor. He found the mayor sleeping in his chair in his office. As a cold pain tightened his chest, the mayor jumped up and saw the Hunter standing by the door. Putting his hand to his throat and breathing a sigh, he asked, "How long have you been there?!"

D said nothing.

"So, it seems I have you to thank for scaring the daylights out of me . . . Just having a dhampir around seems to be enough to give folks nightmares."

"I'm here because I need to ask you something."

"Ah, yes, that's right . . . You were by a little earlier, weren't you? You'll have to excuse me. I was out at the time."

"It seems you had the Knights detained."

The Hunter's softly spoken words made Mayor Ming's eyes bulge. "Who told you that?"

"It doesn't matter. Why did you stop them? Why'd you have them thrown in jail?"

"Do I have to answer that? The only thing you're here to do is to kill our vampire."

"And what if someone manufactured that vampire?" D asked.

"What?!"

"What did the man who boarded your town two centuries ago have to say to you?"

The mayor greeted the question with silence.

"What did it involve?"

More silence. Beads of sweat appeared on the mayor's brow. "Just what I told you before," the mayor finally said.

His voice lacked strength of will, and D shattered it with his own soft tone. "What did the man who visited here two hundred years ago tell you? I can imagine what it was, but I won't mention it. However, it was the Knights who accomplished what your visitor hoped to do. But only after long years had passed. That's what you wanted. What did you want it for? Why did you have a falling-out with the Knights?"

Nothing from the mayor.

"After two centuries, vampires suddenly start showing up here, and yet we can't find the cause for it. There's no one here sucking people's blood and turning people into vampires. There's only one answer—they were manufactured. Made that way by somebody's special process." D's eyes looked like they could suck the soul from the mayor. "Made with the technique he gave to you, and you taught to the Knights. What was in their house?"

Bracing both hands on the head of his cane, the mayor hung his head. "Peace must be maintained in town for all time." A voice closer to a groan flowed from beneath the mayor's bowed head. "The conditions now are ideal. But we're still hounded by destruction and the creatures of nightmare. The mayor has a duty to protect the townsfolk."

"Peace and ideals," D muttered. Coming from his lips, the words lost all meaning and became mere sounds.

"This town is what the Frontier would be ideally." Saying this, the mayor lifted his face. It was warped. His lustrous skin had surely been artificially augmented. The ugly wrinkles that crept across his cheeks looked like furrows in a freshly plowed field. "To live serenely out in the untamed forces of nature without fear of the Nobility or their despicable ilk—that was the human ideal. When I formed this town and peopled it with a select few, I believed I'd gotten closer to that goal than anyone. But many threats still remained. It was still far from perfect . . . "

The mayor's finger pressed the top of his desk. Suddenly, D was in the middle of town. It was the residential section immediately after the magnetic storm. The images must've been shot with a holographic camera. The plastic roofs of many houses were melted, and the electrical discharge towers gave off pale smoke and spat sparks in their death throes. People with burns either hobbled along on their own or were held up by family as they tottered slowly down the street, most likely headed to the hospital. A little girl passed right through D's waist and disappeared into a back room. A fire engine ran over a sofa, then plowed through someone's front door. Fires were springing up everywhere. A middle-aged man grabbed an electrified handrail, lurching backward as purple light shot from him. It was a ghastly tableau.

"This is the town at its limits. A mere magnetic field can't even begin to compare to the other monstrosities the Nobility loosed on the world. Yet, if running into it wreaked this kind of havoc, then what the town considers ideal is still far shy of what I have in mind."

"And making those ideals a reality involves making sacrifices and taking certain steps, doesn't it?" the Hunter said. "Certain bloody steps, I'd say. What exactly did you ask the Knights to do?"

The mayor swallowed loudly. He didn't suppose D was going to leave now, and he wasn't the kind to be taken in by a lie. As Ming was about to slowly take a step, his foot froze in place. An unearthly aura was filling the room. *So this is what a dhampir can do?* he thought. *This is the man called D?* So terrified it wouldn't have been strange if his heart had stopped, too scared to even shake, the mayor gazed at the Hunter's gorgeous countenance.

"Answer me. What did you ask the Knights to do? What did they discover?"

"It was . . . " the mayor panted. An incredibly powerful essence threatened to crush his psyche. "It was . . . "

At that very moment, the intercom on the mayor's desk flashed red. With the series of short, tension-filled buzzes, D's unearthly aura dissipated almost immediately. Wiping at his greasy sweat, the mayor grabbed the intercom microphone. "What is it?"

"This is the navigational control room. We've got a lone flying object approaching from north-northwest at a range of forty miles. Speed is sixty miles per hour. The object is—roughly the same size as our town. We're trying to hail it, but haven't gotten an answer."

"I see. I'll be right there. Don't forget to prepare for a counterstrike, just in case." When he switched off the intercom, the mayor had a relieved look on his face. He felt more at ease having some unknown intruder threatening the town than he did sitting in the same room with the young Hunter. "Guess I'll be going, then," the mayor said without looking in D's direction. Just then the intercom buzzed loudly again. "What now?"

"The flying object has launched missiles. Three in all. They're approaching now—twenty seconds to impact."

"Get the barrier up!"

"It was damaged by the magnetic field—repairs are still under way."

"Begin firing antiballistic missiles and antiaircraft guns!" When the mayor raised his now pale face once again, he saw no trace of D.

†

The Grim Reaper was winging his way toward the town. A trio of long, thin reapers, actually, with sensors in their tips and flames gushing from the nozzles to their rear. Taking into account their own speed and that of the town, they were constantly adjusting their course to the target as they closed in on it at full speed.

†

At the sight of the Hunter in black who'd appeared without a sound, everyone in the energy output control room forgot their approaching death and stood in a daze.

"Where's the barrier projector?" D asked softly. Even knowing that death was drawing ever nearer, he still managed to maintain his detached tone of voice.

The eyes of all the workers focused on one corner in the back. D headed over to the silver cylinder. He was like a sprinting shadow. Saying not a word, the workers stepped to either side. In the gap they left was a gaping hole where a riot of pale blue electromagnetic waves danced chaotically. There was only one man who didn't leave his post. Welding gear in hand, his body unexpectedly flew backward into the room. Fire rose from the protective plates on his chest. He'd just taken a blast of electromagnetism. Silently, D stood between the man and the rough hole. His handsome face shone blue and cold.

"Don't bother. Can't turn off the electromagnetic wave output," the man shouted as he used his hand to beat out the flames on his chest. "There's a hundred thousand volts running through there. Without a protector on, we're talking instant death."

"Get in touch with the control room," D ordered the frozen workers. "When you need the barrier, I'll send the current through."

Asking no questions, and offering no arguments, the men nodded. One, who appeared to be in charge, brought his mouth over to the microphone on his shoulder, and had them patch him through to the navigational control room.

A slight tremor passed through the ship's hull. The anti-aircraft fire had started. While the town was equipped with antigravity generators and an electronic barrier, their armaments were incredibly primitive. Aside from the Prometheus cannon—which, in a cruel trick of fate, had been stripped down for inspection an hour earlier—they had only twenty high-angle machine cannons with a two-inch bore and thirty antiballistic missile launchers. Of course, they couldn't be expected to produce their own shells and missiles, so those were procured from flying merchants who specialized in dealing with floating cities like theirs. Even so, such merchants were few and far between, meeting the town only three times a year. If they ran out of goods they couldn't produce in the interim, a floating city had no choice but to find them on their own. Many of the battles between two floating cities had resulted from this mutual need. But the hostile actions of the unidentified flying object firing upon them were nothing short of indiscriminate slaughter.

Prismatic flames spread across the sky, and black smoke enveloped the area. To increase their destructive power, the shells for the machine cannons contained depleted uranium and were armed with proximity fuses. Even if they failed to score a direct hit, they would automatically detonate if their sensors detected a target within their destructive range. Each time the big guns fired, the whole town rocked wildly.

The incoming missiles displayed the most astounding behavior. Like sentient beings, they dodged shells and adjusted their speed as they rushed steadily closer. They seemed to be mocking the town.

Minute course adjustments were nearly impossible for the town's antiballistic missiles. Every one that'd been launched left an ineffectual trail of white through the empty sky as it disappeared.

A small, black shadow of death clung to the town. People looked out their windows at the three points of approaching light. On every face was a despondent expression. The thought of the fate those missiles held for them robbed them of their willpower. Long spared the threats of the world below, the fragility of their peace had been made evident by their enemy's attack.

Missiles closing—three seconds to impact!" came the bloodcurdling news from the microphone on the man's shoulder. All eyes were on D. The Hunter reached into the hole in the wall, and, grabbing a fistful of cables, he pulled down. From his shoulder to his wrist, pale blue electromagnetic waves clung to him like a spider's web, and white smoke rose from his body. His face didn't show the slightest hint of pain. His right hand went into action, pulling out the ends of the severed cords. Electromagnetic waves covered D entirely . . .

Perhaps it was the first time this young man had worn a color other than black. Using his body as a conductor, energy suddenly shot from the reactor to the barrier projector.

Richly colored blossoms opened near the town. Flames that could get as hot as fifty million degrees and a lethal dose of electromagnetic waves and radiation churned through the atmosphere, threatening to destroy the electronic wall that'd suddenly appeared.

The people saw the electromagnetic waves running from D's right hand to his left in reverse direction. D's eyes narrowed. The flow changed back again. The barrier didn't fade until the trio of blasts dissipated in the air.

II

Even after D had backed away, no cheer went up in the control room. What they'd just witnessed was so incredible it left them absolutely stunned with amazement. Their amazement, along with their overwhelming sense of relief, was enough to throw them into a state of dementia. The man before them—their savior—clearly couldn't be human. That's why he was so good-looking.

Lightly tossing his head, D shook off the white smoke still rising from his body.

"The flying object is closing," a somewhat listless voice announced through the microphone. The main craft still remained.

Braced, perhaps, for the next attack, D didn't move.

"It's closing on us—just a thousand yards off, nine hundred, seven hundred, six hundred . . . "

"It's gonna hit us . . . " someone muttered.

"We can't change our heading."

"We've had it now . . . "

A black wind fluttered by the men.

D exited the control room. Racing up the stairs, he charged across the street. The center of town was completely empty. With sunlight falling in a bright shower, the town was a picture of tranquility. A voice he knew cried out, and D looked over his shoulder. Lori and Dr. Tsurugi were dashing toward him. D didn't stop for them, but kept on running. Something became visible beyond the town's defensive walls. The form of their foe was clear now.

It seemed that floating cities of various kinds followed the same basic structure, and the shape flying toward them at high speed bore a strong resemblance to their own town. In fact, it was almost identical. The familiar rows of dwellings, the navigational control tower, and three-dimensional radar arrays all stood out in the sunlight. Perhaps the only point where the two towns differed was that all of the structures on the other town were reinforced with menacing armor plating. One look at the new town and its aim was apparent. The vessel was built to plunder.

Posing as an ordinary city, they might close in on their victims under a pretext of trade, then use their cannons to rob their prey of their defenses before sending armed troops to board. In other words, they were pirates of the sky. But, strangely enough, not only wasn't there a single person to be seen on the streets or in any of the ship's portholes, but no one was visible through the control room's window, either.

"That's odd—if this ship's here to loot us, they should be softening us up with their guns now," D heard the winded Dr. Tsurugi say from behind him. "But they're pulling alongside us instead. We'll have to fight them."

"What about the sheriff?" D asked, eying the pirate ship slowly circling them.

"He'll be here soon, I'm sure," the physician replied. "The real question is whether he'll be of any use or not."

"Why's that?"

"As you may already know, due to their overprotected state, people around here are incredibly susceptible to shock. The towns-folk here have had peace for too long. Fights and other disputes have always been the sort of things they could settle among themselves in their little town. Forget the fact they wouldn't know how to begin to deal with attackers from outside—the whole incident with the lightning has left the lot of them in a stupor."

"Then it's up to just the three of us."

A perplexed expression wafted over Dr. Tsurugi's face. "The three of us?" he muttered, paling instantly. "I can't believe you! You intend to have Lori fight? Why, she's just—"

"She has to live on her own." D's words had an edge like the wind.

After a bit of hemming and hawing, Dr. Tsurugi nodded. "You're right. That's what life on the Frontier is all about. But what'll we do?"

A sharp impact shook the ground they stood on. The enemy ship had finally pulled alongside the town.

D produced a memo pad from one of his coat's inner pockets. It was the same pad that'd been left out for Lori at the hospital. Eyes wide with astonishment, the physician wondered why he'd been carrying it around. Putting the tip of his forefinger in his mouth and nicking it open, D drew it across the memo pad. *Fight or die,* he wrote. *We want you with us.*

Us. That meant the three of them were going to fight together. Lori nodded fervently.

"But, what'll you have her do? She's an injured girl."

"Go to the weapons bunker and get us some arms. She'll carry the ammo and be in charge of reloading."

"Okay."

The two of them dashed away. D looked back at the blocks of buildings. As his companions' footsteps faded out, more rough footfalls arose to take their place. It was the mayor, the sheriff, and some of his men—four men in all. And the physician had said he didn't know if they'd be of any use . . .

There was another impact against their protective walls. From the deck of the pirate ship, several steel sheets extended toward the town. Hooks sank noisily into the top of the town's walls, and the sheriff and his companions unconsciously backed away. Every face was taut with fear. These men lived in a closed society where everyone understood just how tough they were supposed to be, but now that they faced invaders who wouldn't know the reputations they'd long relied on, they were reduced to cowards.

D's eyes narrowed ever so slightly. He waited, but what he waited for never appeared. Silence. . . Nothing happened. While the planks had been laid for plundering, not a single blood-crazed outlaw appeared.

"What the hell is this, then?" one of the lawmen said, sounding rather relieved. "Are they just fucking with us or what? Not one of them has shown himself."

"They'll come out any second," another one said, his voice on the verge of tears. "And when they do, they'll rip us to shreds with some god-awful weapons. Damn it! God damn it all! Why do we gotta go up against these damn freaks?!"

The sheriff roared, "Knock it off! You're turning my belly. We're here now, so there's no use bitching about it. We ain't letting a single one of them marauding motherhumpers into town."

Compared to his compatriots, Hutton was certainly brave. In the wake of that outburst, his cowardly deputies readied their shotguns again. And yet, still—nothing happened.

The mayor looked at D suspiciously. "Somehow, I don't think they're toying with us . . . "

No reply came from the Hunter, but his black coat zipped past the men's noses. D stood on the gangway bridging the two vessels. Black hair streaming in the wind, coat fluttering, he trained his gelid stare on the deck of the enemy ship. Suddenly, he advanced without making a sound.

The men looked at each other. They must've realized protecting the town was an unavoidable part of their duty, but the mayor stayed where he was, led by the sheriff, while the others struggled up the wall and began to cross the same gangway. Just as they finished crossing the ten-foot-long plank, two things made the men grow pale—a strange aura and a stench. The aura could only mean death. And the stench was that of death as well.

Just moments earlier this ominous vessel had them fearing for their very lives, but now the unsettling silence did even more to start these rough men shaking. There was no sign of D. The men hopped down onto the street. Right in front of them lay the residential sector. The layout itself wasn't all that different from their own town.

"Pete, you and Yan find the control room. I'm gonna check out this area."

"But, Sheriff—this place gives me the creeps . . . "

"You damn fool! The way things are going, there's probably nobody on this tub. Maybe they took to killing each other, or some kinda epidemic broke out, but for all we know everyone could be dead. Now think for a second what that'd mean."

Pete's face, sullen until now, suddenly shone. "Oh, I get you! This here was a marauder ship. Meaning there's probably a load of treasure here."

"Damn straight! We'll tell the ol' mayor the town could use some of their energy surplus or their navigational computer or something, but the most precious cargo we'll keep for ourselves."

"Damn, you're a shrewd one. No wonder you're sheriff. But what'll we do about the Hunter that went on ahead of us?"

"That's pretty obvious. Kill 'im," said the other man, Yan, but he didn't know what D was capable of. While he knew about how D had killed the two deputies, not having seen it with his own eyes meant he found the account impossible to believe. "Lucky for us, the bastard's all caught up in searching the ship. It's a perfect chance to blindside him. What the hell—we can always say some automated defenses got him."

"That's real good thinking," the sheriff responded, but his words sounded hollow. He knew, as only someone who'd had the tip of D's blade pressed against their throat could, what a dhampir was capable of. "But don't lay a hand on him, you follow me? We'll just take whatever we want. I know how tough he is. You lump him in with normal Hunters, and you'll be in for a world of hurt."

"Yeah, but—" Yan began.

"We'll come up with some way to get rid of him later. You savvy? No matter what happens, you don't lay a hand on him," the sheriff said sternly, adjusting his grip on the rocket launcher.

Parting company with Pete and Yan, the sheriff walked into the residential sector. Unconsciously, he sought a sound or anything else that would show some sign of life. Anything would do. Some hint of murderous intent rising from malicious thugs in hiding. The snarls of vicious beasts just waiting to cross the gangways with their masters and sink their fangs into the windpipes of helpless victims. The sound of a safety being disengaged on an automatic crossbow. Anything at all . . .

But there was nothing except the . . . howling of the wind. There was no sign of anyone on the roads, where the artificial sand had blown away, leaving the underlying dirt exposed. There were just lines of dead trees down either side of the street, their branches rattling dryly. Dust catching in his throat, the sheriff pressed a handkerchief to his mouth. His cough created an unsettling echo in the otherwise still air. The sheriff shuddered.

The sky was blue. His own shadow stretched long and wide across the ground. And yet, the giant was nearly paralyzed with fear. Here was a town. It had buildings. It shot missiles. It pulled alongside them, then laid gangways for boarding. And yet, there wasn't a single crewman. How terrifying was that?

As Hutton was about to set off to look for the home of the local mayor—or, rather, the commander of this pirate ship—the tip of his boot struck something hard. When his eyes casually dropped to the ground, they ended up bulging from their sockets. It was a single bare bone. Most likely it'd been there for quite some time, as it was dried out and had a thin brown patina to it. It was clearly a femur. Seeing the severed end of it, the sheriff's eyes went wider still. It was burnt. There were signs of carbonization. As he rubbed it with his finger, some of it fell away as powder. This hadn't been charred little by little at a low temperature, as would happen in a fire. It'd been exposed to a blast of ultrahigh heat. Probably a laser.

For the first time, the sheriff noticed the white things hap-hazardly scattered about the place. There was a skull. And a rib cage. And another denuded skull resting on a pile of rags. As his eyes squarely met the skull's empty sockets, cold sweat started soaking his broad back. Stirring his mind to keep it from freezing solid with fear, the sheriff headed over to a shack that appeared to be a bar and the intact skeleton lying in front of it. The steel arrow jutting from its forehead was a vivid testament to the tragedy that'd unfolded here. One of the skeleton's arms was outstretched, and tight in its bony grip was a gleaming black automatic handgun of vintage design. Prying the weapon from its fingers, he examined it. All the ammo had been expended—most likely the result of a long, deadly conflict. But what in the world could've caused the roughneck crew of a pirate ship to start killing each other?

Sensing something behind him, the sheriff turned his gigantic form with lightning speed. Standing stock-still in the face of the seven barrels of his missile launcher were Dr. Tsurugi and Lori. "Oh, it's just you two . . . " he sighed. Wiping the sweat from his brow, the sheriff lowered his weapon.

"What in blazes is going on with this ship? What happened here?" Even the voice of the hot-blooded physician trembled a bit.

Looking around at their ominous surroundings and the remains at their feet, Lori seemed anxious, too. However, unlike the physician or the sheriff, she was completely detached from the whole world of sound, and this actually served to mitigate the terror for her to some degree. She and Dr. Tsurugi each carried a shotgun.

"Just what you see. Looks to me like they just went off on a goddamn killing spree. From the shape of these bones, I'd wager it was quite some time ago. And it looks to me like not one of them made it out alive."

"Well, they launched missiles at us. And put down gangways. Is that the sort of thing a crewless ship does automatically? For starters, we don't even know why they fired the missiles. They might've been small scale, but they were still nukes. If they'd scored a hit, they'd have most likely knocked the town out of the sky with one shot."

"So, failing to shoot us down, they decided to close with us," the sheriff spat. He looked at the skeletal faces, and, an instant after relief swept over him, the urge to plunder filled his head. The presence of the doctor and Lori quickly became a hindrance to his plan. *They'll get theirs, too*, the lawman thought, a kind of madness suddenly at work in his mind. The barrel of the rocket launcher rose smoothly.

And that was when it happened. Screams echoed off in the distance. Two of them—Yan's and Pete's. Exchanging glances, the physician and sheriff started running as fast as they could toward the sound. The sheriff halted in front of the control center, where the iron door had fallen into the room. There was a blue tinge to the air, and the foul smell of burnt flesh hit his nose. Smoke was creeping out through the doorway. Someone was in there. *Don't tell me they went after D*, he thought.

Apparently realizing his duty as a lawman, the sheriff told Dr. Tsurugi, "You two stay right here." And then he slipped through the doorway alone. It didn't take long at all. At some point someone or something had utterly destroyed the control room, and on the floor lay a pair of charred corpses, one on top of the other. He didn't even have to look at them to know they were Pete and Yan's remains. An optical weapon with less output than a laser had burnt them to a crisp. Most likely it was a heat ray.

Shifting the rocket launcher to his left hand, the sheriff drew a huge explosive-firing handgun with his right. While its design closely resembled that of an old-fashioned revolver, it could hold thirty-six shots. The exploding rounds were powerful enough to drop a lesser dragon with one shot, or dispatch a medium-sized fire dragon with half a dozen. He couldn't very well start blasting away with his missiles indoors. Suddenly, a metallic sound reverberated from a pitch-black corner of the room. Looking over his shoulder, the instant Sheriff Hutton's eyes caught a semicircular shape, his handgun roared.

The deafening report of a weapon made Dr. Tsurugi tense up. Beyond the doorway, a red glow swelled momentarily, and an incredible shriek rang out. Lori clung to Dr. Tsurugi's arm, trembling. Though he'd told her to wait, the girl was determined to go with him. Apparently she could gather from the red light and Dr. Tsurugi's tension that something had happened. Slowly mouthing the words, "Wait here," Dr. Tsurugi pulled his arm free from her grasp.

Lori didn't disobey him. In her travels with her parents, she'd learned far too well what resulted when action was precipitated by curiosity or fear.

Laying both hands gently on the girl's shoulders, Dr. Tsurugi headed quickly for the doorway. His steps suddenly halted. With a strange sound, a dark figure appeared from the room. The doctor readied his shotgun. The first thing he saw was an arm-like protrusion that called to mind a thermal-ray cannon. Following that was the spherical body. And supporting that body from below were caterpillar treads like those of a tank.

"Get down!" the physician shouted as he shoved Lori out of the way, a wave of orange sailing right over him. The tremendous heat set the back of his white lab coat ablaze, and flames licked from his hair. Screaming, the physician writhed in pain. Cradling his head, he rolled his back against the ground in an effort to put out the fire.

Grabbing him by the scruff of the neck, Lori dove off to the side. A second heat shower narrowly missed the pair, striking the ground near where they lay. Without so much as looking at the physician's back, Lori shouldered the shotgun and pulled the trigger. The blast struck the dome-shaped torso, and the buckshot ricocheted off in all directions with a beautiful sound. Lori threw herself to the ground. There was no way to escape now.

The arm that was going to spray them with white-hot death, however, turned in the opposite direction along with the rest of its body. In the shadow of a building some fifteen feet away there suddenly stood a figure in black so beautiful and tragic it numbed even the electronic brain of this machine. Perhaps that was the reason why it was delayed a tenth of a second aligning the sights on its thermal-ray cannon.

Easily leaping over the shower of blistering heat his foe unleashed, D brought his longsword down, slicing the top of the machine's head into a half-moon shape.

Land of the Dead

CHAPTER 6

I

Sparks and electromagnetic waves shooting from the newly cut opening, the machine halted, and, in the very same instant, Lori threw herself on the physician. Rubbing against his body, she crushed out the still-smoldering fire. Giving off only bluish smoke now, Dr. Tsurugi moaned. Above her, the girl sensed someone moving. Lori looked up and moved her lips. *Hurry,* she mouthed. *We have to get him to the nurse quickly!*

"I should have a look at him first," D said slowly, and, helping Lori out of the way, he pulled off the physician's lab coat.

"I'm fine," the disheveled Dr. Tsurugi said as he tugged at his own hair. "It's not a serious burn. I can walk on my own. Kindly leave me be."

D stood up. Despite the other man's sharp tone, the Hunter didn't seem particularly angry. Without giving the physician another glance, he looked at Lori.

An awesome tempest of fear and self-loathing raged in the girl's eyes. *Didn't even try to help the doctor . . . I just . . . took the gun . . .*

"Well done," D said soberly. Of course, Lori had no idea how close to miraculous it was to hear those words coming from him. "If you hadn't taken that shot, the machine probably would've killed you both. You knew the doctor's burns weren't too bad."

But I . . .

"And when you took the shot, you even put yourself in front of the doctor," the Hunter continued. "Not many people would've done that."

The girl's eyes were gleaming. Only after D said those words did she realize just what she'd done.

"Yes, indeed," the physician said as his hand picked through the miserable remnants of his hair. "If you'd bothered with me, both of us would be checking into the hereafter. I owe you my life. Now, then—lead on. My nurse hasn't been any use since the magnetic storm. This time it'll be *my* turn to get looked at."

Lori nodded. The girl knew that she was needed now.

Just then, they noticed there was no sign of D. A few minutes later he reappeared from the door to the control room.

"What happened to the sheriff and his men?"

D simply shook his head.

"What the hell was that thing?" the physician muttered, his voice fraught with anger.

In reply, D merely said, "An internal defensive system for the ship, no doubt. It seems to be the only thing moving. The ship's crew died off three years ago."

"How do you know that?"

D pulled a yellowed ship's log from his coat. After the physician had run his eyes over the last page of it, ineffable shades of terror and misery colored his face . . . an expression that didn't fade for the longest time.

The crew of this pirate ship had grown weary of their aimless voyages. Though they freely sailed the skies, the floating cities and cargo-laden sailing vessels they preyed on were few and far between. What's more, when the pirate ship finally *did* get a chance to shine, all her opponents had either mounted heavy firepower or acquired three-dimensional radar and more powerful engines, making fight or flight the only viable solutions. The number of targets a pirate ship could go after had decidedly decreased. Apathy and ennui began to take over the ship, and before long many of the crew took their own lives, while the rest either started killing each other to stave off the boredom or grew sick and died. But the ion engines of the ship itself still ran, and could continue to do so until the end of time. Carrying nothing save a load of corpses, she continued her voyage across the boundless seas of fear.

"And the person who kept this log?"

"He was in his cabin," D said, "shot through the forehead."

"In that case, who in the world fired those missiles?"

"The computer must've been programmed to do that. Someone told it to go right on plundering even after they were all dead."

The physician shook his head in disgust. Looking at D, he asked, "And none of this bothers you? There's carnage all around us, and your expression says you don't feel a thing. What does it take to break that pretty face of yours? What could make you cry? Or make you laugh?"

"I've seen too much," D said dispassionately.

"Still—" the physician began to say, but then a mysterious light filled his eyes. "Okay, I understand about the missiles. But what about the gangways being sent over after they pulled alongside us? You mean to say that was programmed into their computers as well?"

"I don't know."

"I see. But . . . "

"Let's go."

D turned around. As the physician was about to ask him to wait, he heard a low groan beneath his feet. The ship was starting to move. "What in the name of—"

"It's setting off on another journey. A new voyage of plunder." D's voice trailed off into the distance.

The other two went after him. The whole ship was mired in an eeriness that staggered the imagination. Just as the three of them finished crossing the gangway, the pirate ship gradually began pulling away from the town.

"Where do you suppose she'll go?" asked Dr. Tsurugi.

Lori gazed at D. The same question swam in her innocent eyes.

Both of them had already noticed something—the dark destiny that hung over the pirate ship. Somewhere on it, something still survived: the will of the crew that'd grown tired, killed their compatriots out of that boredom, and ultimately programmed their computer with orders for indiscriminate destruction and marauding before they themselves disappeared. The ship would leave on another voyage. Without a destination, she was steered by a shapeless hand on a horrifying journey of nothing but murder and plunder.

D and his companions watched the ship's dwindling form for what seemed like ages.

"Mayor's not around, is he?" D said.

"Probably at home. It's kind of strange, though. Barring extraordinary circumstances, he's not really the type to sit on the sidelines in a situation like this . . . "

"You should send Lori back to the hospital. And don't forget to take those weapons. You should go back with her."

The physician scanned the area, a shaken look in his eyes. If a man who didn't run without good reason had turned tail, there could be only one explanation—something big had happened. Taking Lori by the hand as the girl wondered what was going on, Dr. Tsurugi walked off toward the hospital.

D headed straight for the mayor's house. Ming's daughter came out and told the Hunter her father was in the control room. Not even acknowledging the thick, syrupy gaze the young lady kept trained on him, D turned right around.

As the town slid into a calm afternoon, an unnatural atmosphere hung over everything. D alone understood. Only he saw the resemblance between the mood in town and the eerie atmosphere that hung over the pirate vessel.

As he slipped in through the control room door, a shadowy form blocked his field of view. Using just his left hand, D caught the man flying toward him like a rag doll. It was one of the men who worked in the control room. His lower jaw had been completely torn off, and bloodstains covered his chest like an apron. His eyes had rolled up in his head. Fear and massive shock had stopped his heart. It was the work of a monster, something beyond the human ken.

Gently setting the dead man down, D turned his gaze forward to the perpetrator. Weapon in hand, the mayor was frozen in place. In front of him stood another worker. Several corpses lay at the worker's feet. All of them had bulging eyes, and skin as pale as paraffin. There was no need to see the wound at the base of each neck.

The worker turned toward the Hunter. He was in his forties. According to the list the mayor had given D, his name was Gertz Diason.

"Careful, D! He's a vampire!" the mayor shouted.

The worker opened his mouth, displaying a pair of stark white fangs. Discarding the bloody lower jaw he had in his hand, he slowly walked toward D. He knew who the real foe was. His feet stopped moving. If the vampire knew who his enemy was, he also knew the extent of his enemy's power. Fear left a clear taint on his cruel face.

"When did he start acting strangely?" D asked. His tone was so tranquil in the face of this fearsome opponent that it absolutely beggared belief.

"Been like that ever since he got back a little while ago," the mayor replied. He was also rather composed. And not just because D was there. "About three hours ago, they let him go home for a nap. After he came back to the control room, it seems he attacked the nearest guy. When a second man went down, one of the workers came and got me."

"Where's the town going?" D asked, his question on an entirely different track.

The enemy snarled. Whipping up the air, he attacked D. It was an ill-conceived attempt. As he passed D's shadowy form, it became clear that the Hunter had his longsword in hand. The blade sank deep into the fiend's chest, and, as the menace dropped, the mayor let his shoulders fall.

"Is this the result of the Knights' experiments?" D asked softly. "Is this what you wanted to get your hands on? Is this the peace you idealized?"

"Stop it!" the mayor shouted. "The Knights succeeded in their experiments, I tell you. Right in that very house. I knew that much. What they produced was perfect. That's why I wanted their method! Because my own efforts turned out imperfect."

"You kept what you'd created alive, and hid it somewhere. Kept the failure your experiments had created, when the Knights had been successful."

A frightening silence descended. It was D who formed the silence, and D who broke it.

"What did you hope to accomplish by turning the people in your town into vampires? Did you want to make eternal travelers?"

The mayor's Adam's apple bobbed wildly.

II

Before they had made their way back to the hospital, Lori noticed that a ghastly atmosphere had shrouded the town. Someone was watching them, she felt, through the keyhole in a closed door, or through a crack in drawn blinds, or from a back alley entrance. Lori was going to latch onto Dr. Tsurugi's arm, but then thought better of it. He was the one who was really hurt here. This wasn't a matter of who was a man and who was a woman. Maybe she couldn't hear or speak, but the strong still had to take care of the weak. And neither strength nor weakness had anything to do with one's physical condition.

However, the road carried them back to the hospital without incident. Though the physician called out the nurse's name, there was no answer. "Looks like she's gone," he clucked. Then, flopping down into a rickety chair, he quickly grabbed a memo pad and handed it to Lori. *Stay in the hospital. You mustn't go outside. And don't forget that shotgun.*

Lori wrote a reply: *Okay, but you need to be taken care of first. Where's the medicine?*

Stored with the other drugs in the next room. You'll have to apply it to me.

Nodding, Lori straightened herself up. Her body brimmed with vitality. This was the joy of accomplishment. Leaning her shotgun against the wall, she hurried out of the examination room.

For a hospital that seemed so cramped, the drug storeroom alone was huge. This room held the keys to life for the whole town. Lori knew the name of the medicine she needed—after all, she was the daughter of two chemists. The various medicines were organized according to their usage. The jars she was looking for were stored next to the artificial-skin patches back on the farthest rack, stacked one shelf below the acid. Grabbing two jars and a heap of skin patches, Lori turned.

A woman in white was standing in front of her. It was the nurse. Her eyes were strangely red. Like she was angry.

I'm sorry, Lori mouthed slowly. As a nurse, the other woman would be used to things like that.

The woman's lips slowly twisted and formed a smile. From the corners of it, fangs peeked out.

Lori froze in her tracks.

The nurse's thick fingers latched onto the girl's frail shoulders. Lips that loosed the winds of hell slowly climbed up her throat.

Help me! Lori shouted. But no voice came from her. Of course it wouldn't. Though the girl struggled with all her might, the vampire's hands didn't budge. *Help me!* Lori screamed, not giving up. *Help! Please! Somebody, help me!*

They were cries no one could hear. The voice of despair, frail and futile. Lori knew at last she was truly alienated. Left in a world where she sought aid, but no one would come. She was its sole resident. The significance of the sunrise she'd watched with D was swept away with everything else. Fear of the unknown filled the girl's mind.

When the nurse pressed her lips against the nape of Lori's neck, the girl reached out with her left hand and grabbed a jar on the shelf above. She smacked it against the woman's face with all of her might, and the jar shattered. White smoke enveloped the fiend's hateful visage. The nurse reeled backward. Acid had gone into her eyes.

Knocking the nurse out of the way, Lori ran. A hand as cold as ice caught her ankle. The chill spread throughout her body, and Lori grew stiff. There was a strong tug on her leg. Pulling her back to the fallen fiend. Another pull. Her body slid across the floor. Something heavy clambered onto her back, and Lori tried to give a scream.

No one came. The doors were closed. Something as minor as the sound of a glass jar breaking wouldn't reach the examination room.

Lori was mired in despair. Then, the pressure of someone sitting on her back suddenly vanished. Something black was oozing through the middle of the door. As the blackness took human shape, Lori looked up at it with teary eyes.

How have you been? a cheerful voice said in her head. Today it sounded terribly bold.

You can understand me, right? You understand what I'm saying, Lori thought back. *Please, you've got to help me!*

Just leave it to me, the voice agreed readily.

The nurse pulled herself up. She burned with a demonic urge to fight this new foe. As she held her hands out in front of her chest, the fingers were spread for clawing. Like an animal the nurse pounced, but the black shadow went right through her. A black semicircle jutted from the white chest of her uniform. The nurse collapsed in a heap.

In no time, the semicircle had vanished. Lori couldn't begin to imagine what kind of physical properties the weapon must've possessed.

How about that? That's what happens when a monster or two crosses my path. You wanna learn how to do this stuff, too?

I do, Lori thought, wishing it with all her heart. Telepathy—a way to speak without using words. A flying disk that could kill a servant of the bloodsucking Nobility with one blow. Lori had to have these things.

Then we should be able to do something here. I need to ask one favor of you, if that's okay.

Just name it. I'll do whatever you want.

Lori's feverish, trembling thoughts were overlaid with a man's cold laughter. *Well, it's like this . . .*

†

A special kind of death was racing around town. Just now, it'd paid a visit to one house, and, after meeting it for just a few seconds' time, all five members of the family thudded to the floor. It couldn't drink their blood, and this displeased it. But it was fated not to drink the blood of its peers. You might say it was performing the same role as a kind of infectious germ.

Emanating from every inch of it were what could be called vampire bacteria. The bacteria entered into the unlucky people through their skin and then moved into their muscle cells, going all the way to the marrow of their bones. And then something else was born. Night's baleful energy sprang from the marrow of their bones, and their muscles grew ten times stronger. No matter how much damage the skin cells might take, they'd regenerate in a few seconds. Surpassing humanity in every respect, and terrifying them in every respect as well. All because of their lust for blood . . .

Less than five minutes after their visitor had left, the family members awoke. They felt the hunger. And there was another powerful urge as well. They had to make more of their kind. They'd been made to avoid competing with each other.

More of our kind—

Make more of our kind—

And then the family left their home behind, each member off to separately fulfill their common duty.

†

When D came to the hospital looking for Lori, he heard from a deathly pale Dr. Tsurugi how the girl had been attacked by the vampire nurse. The Hunter seemed to have only the slightest interest in the incident. "Was she okay?" he asked.

"More or less," Dr. Tsurugi replied.

And that was the end of it.

Gripping a memo pad and electromagnetic pen in her delicate hands, Lori wrote, *What can I do for you?*

D's well-formed lips began to move. "I want you to go to your old house."

Why?

"Your parents hid certain chemical and mathematical formulas somewhere in the house before they ran off. If we don't dispose of them once and for all, there's likely to be more trouble, and you've seen the abominable results of such experiments with your own eyes."

But I don't know anything!

"Was there any place in particular in the house where your parents often brought you?"

Yes, there was.

"That's what I need to know, and that's why you have to go with me."

Okay. Putting the pen down, Lori got up.

†

About the town—where do you think it's headed? Lori asked D as they walked along. Her lips merely shaped the words. She got no answer. Perhaps that was because it didn't matter.

Suddenly, D said, "Apparently a new destination's been programmed into the computers. That's where we're headed."

But where is that?

"Given our present course, a place where there's ruins and graves that belonged to the Nobility."

Why would we go to such a place?

"We'd have to ask whoever input the heading. Though I have a feeling I might know."

What do you mean by that?

This time D didn't answer her. The two of them entered the old Knight house.

"Now, then, if you could show me the place you mentioned," D said softly.

Lori nodded.

Not surprisingly, the first place they went was the laboratory, someplace that'd been searched thoroughly by both D and the black shadow.

My father was always tapping the top of that desk with his finger. He may have been hiding something.

D reached for the pressure-resistant desk crafted of mahogany. "Where did he hit it?"

Lori pointed at a certain section. Though the surface of the desk seemed perfectly normal, on closer inspection it appeared that just that one spot was a bit more faded than the rest.

D stroked the surface. "How about it?" he asked.

Although Lori couldn't hear what he'd said, her eyes were riveted to him. There was definitely something rising grotesquely from the palm of his left hand. It resembled a human face. Lori watched silently as its lips moved.

"Hmm. The surface has been finished with something to bring out the shine. But it's oddly light in the part she just pointed out. The problem doesn't seem to be the thickness of the coat, but rather the composition."

"Is the composition the same?"

"Nope."

"Okay. Stand back, please."

Lori backed away, just as she was told. After all, there was something she *had to do* to the young man.

D's longsword flashed out. The swipe of his steel was faster than any eye could follow. Cleanly sliced from the desk, the piece of wood in question landed in D's left hand. "Analyze it," D commanded.

"Damn, you're a regular slave driver," the mouth in his hand remarked with discontent.

D pressed the thin board into the palm of his hand. A second passed, then two, then three.

"Good enough," a cramped voice said, trickling out between the hand and the board.

D opened his hand. The face on his palm had been reduced to just a pair of lips. A red tongue hung from them. Apparently his left hand had analyzed the material by licking it, as evidenced by the fact the surface of the board was wet.

"The atomic arrangement of each element forms a single letter or digit in the formula. That's a real good hiding place. If any given element is too thick or too thin, the letter disappears."

"Yes, it certainly is clever. So—" D began to say, but, as he looked over his shoulder, a pale little hand slammed a wooden wedge into his chest. Staggering back, D thudded to the floor. Surely he never dreamed Lori would reach around from behind him to put a stake in him.

But, in fact, Lori hadn't driven a stake into him at all.

With the realization that D's body wasn't moving in the slightest, the girl's sweet countenance suddenly crumbled, and an indescribably crude smile surfaced in its place. The voice that came from her was that of a man. "Now that's the way you do it! That's one obstacle out of the way, I guess. I bet it never occurred to him I might slip into the little lady he trusted the most. No hard feelings, bucko. Everything in life just boils down to business."

When the girl smiled broadly once again, her expression was unmistakably that of John M. Brasselli Pluto VIII.

†

The town kept moving. D still lay on the floor with a stake through his heart. The mayor had come and was engaged in an uncharacteristically enthusiastic conversation with Lori, and somewhere in town Pluto VIII's body wasn't breathing at all, while his heart alone kept beating. Dr. Tsurugi knew none of this, but mantled as he was in a vague fear, he could do nothing but arm himself with a scalpel and a shotgun.

†

Those scattering the vampire plague were paying quiet calls on the houses in town, while those who had fallen waited impatiently for the sun to go down. And those intently watching the three-dimensional radar in the navigational control room discovered a vast expanse of ruins on the plateau some twenty miles ahead of them—and they were terribly shocked to find there was less than an eight-inch difference between the height of the plateau and their present altitude.

†

Okay, time to come up with a final price. How much are you offering, fancy pants?" Lori asked, her lovely lips twisting into a sneer. Needless to say, the falsetto voice belonged to Pluto VIII. "I've got the chemical formula and mathematical equations you need to become a Noble. You've gotta be willing to pay handsomely for that."

"Fine. Fifty million dalas."

"Don't make me laugh. We're not talking about a kid looking for his allowance here. With this, you'll be able to make people who can go about their lives just as they do now and only have to drink blood once or twice a month—you follow me? Naturally, they'd be able to walk in the light of day. They could fall into water without drowning. And they wouldn't need to eat. You could blast 'em with a rifle or laser or whatever and the damage still wouldn't kill 'em. Plus, their personality won't change at all. There's nothing but advantages to this, right? You don't go offering a lousy fifty million dalas for something like that."

"Make it five hundred million dalas, then," the mayor said, smiling broadly.

The offer had just grown tenfold, but Pluto VIII shook Lori's head from side to side. "Five hundred billion dalas—and not a bit less. After all, you're getting the secret to making supermen. And, as an added bonus, I already borrowed this little lady's body and got rid of the Vampire Hunter who was holding up the works. So you won't be getting any further discount from me. Hell, you want me to go tell everyone how you cut my throat wide open while I was in your maid's body? I hate to break it to you, but I can get into rotting corpses, too. I could work her vocal cords and have her testify if I had to."

After thinking a bit, the mayor nodded and said, "Okay. It's all for the good of my town. You'll get the price you named—five hundred billion dalas. But I'll need one thing to sweeten the deal."

"And what would that be?"

"In place of the Vampire Hunter you killed, I'll need you to take care of the last vampire plaguing us—he's one of my experiments gone wrong."

Pluto VIII said nothing.

"The man I let on board two hundred years ago gave me a certain chemical formula and a procedure for making humans into vampires. However, it proved too difficult for me to complete successfully. I had to wait two long centuries for a pair of geniuses like Mr. and Mrs. Knight to be born before my hopes could be realized. But then they ran out on me at the last minute. Didn't care for my orders that the fruits of their labor only be used on the residents of our town. They wanted to use it for the good of the whole world. The fools," Mayor Ming spat. "There's only a small handful of people who actually want to live in peace. Just try giving something like that to the world below. Before you knew it, they'd start murdering each other. Those who were going to live in peace would only wind up courting death. I conducted my own research without their assistance. Though two of my guinea pigs came extremely close to success, it was simply beyond my power to root out the vampire cruelty budding within them. And, unfortunately, both of them escaped.

One of them targeted my daughter to exact his revenge, but he was destroyed by the Vampire Hunter. The other one is still active—spreading the vampire bacteria within him everywhere he goes."

"That's rich," Lori—or rather, Pluto VIII—said, clutching *her* belly as he laughed. "Sounds to me like the situation is proceeding just like you hoped it would. Care to tell me why you want the vamp killed?"

"The cruelty of the Nobility is so great, it drives even *them* mad. I'm sure you're aware not only of what their kind did to us, but also how vicious the disputes were that raged between fellow Nobles. I want the life of the Nobility. However, at the same time, that life must be one of eternal peace."

"You're a greedy cuss, I'll grant you."

"Say what you will. It would be difficult for me to say the present strain of Nobilitation would suffice, no matter what we might try. You'll have to hurry and dispose of him before he turns every last person in town into an imitation vampire. And if you don't like that, then the whole deal is off."

"Okay," Lori/Pluto VIII said, nodding. "I'll drop your freak with one shot. Consider it as good as done."

The intercom buzzed loudly.

"What is it now?" the mayor fairly barked.

"The town is approaching a plateau. Preparations for landing have already begun."

"Aha," Pluto VIII said, eyes gleaming. "Then I guess this must be the destination that got fed into your computers. It should be kinda fun to try and figure out why he'd do that."

"If he input these coordinates, it's pretty obvious that once we get there he'll gain some advantage. Hurry up and get rid of him."

"Understood." Nodding his agreement, Pluto VIII got up. "You said there's already been some victims, right? That's just too damn funny. Let's hope some of them at least *wanted* to be vampires . . . "

†

Leaving the mayor's home, Pluto VIII felt an unspeakably weird aura envelope his borrowed body. Twilight was approaching. The aura wasn't particularly concerned with him individually—it filled the very air. A vast number of sources for the unsettling emanations were moving about nearby.

"Well, I'll be damned. The ol' mayor sure took his sweet time moving on this, and now it looks like we're talking about more than half the town—this place is a freaking undead paradise," Pluto VIII muttered, walking down the street on Lori's beautiful legs.

A presence soon stirred in his vicinity.

"Came to play, did you?" Pluto VIII muttered, and Lori stopped in her tracks.

In the feeble darkness stood a motionless figure with black gloves on. The weird atmosphere seemed to radiate most strongly from his body.

"I've been waiting for you," Pluto VIII laughed. "I don't know where the hell you're taking this town or even why, but it's all over now. I'll make quick work of you, then get off this ride—once I get what I've got coming, of course. The know-how that made you immortal should fetch me a nice price elsewhere, too. It's too bad you won't get to see your buddies multiply, but you'll have to get over that."

Though it was unclear how exactly Pluto VIII manipulated Lori's supposedly nonfunctioning vocal chords, he had her talking a blue streak. He then made a broad wave of his right hand in his foe's direction.

The instant it looked like the flash of black was going to buzz through the foe's heart, the vampire sailed silently over Pluto VIII's head. With a speed that staggered the imagination, the vampire launched a kick.

Evading the blow with unbelievable agility for a man in a young lady's body, Pluto VIII hurled his disk-shaped weapon with a scooping motion. The weapon's aim was true, and it quickly ripped the vampire open from crotch to chest and showered the road with bright blood.

"Got 'im!" Pluto VIII shouted through the beautiful girl's face.

It was only a second later that same face froze solid. The darkness behind where the fiend had collapsed had just sent forth a tall youth of unearthly beauty.

"No, not you . . . " Pluto VIII groaned. "It can't be . . . I mean, even a dhampir . . . You couldn't just take a stake through the heart . . . "

"Too bad." D's soft voice ripped Pluto VIII's heart from his chest. "Tell me what you discussed with the mayor."

Pluto VIII backed away. Though he was looking for a chance to run, he realized that would be impossible.

"The girl's parents told you something, didn't they?" D said, but Pluto VIII couldn't even tremble at his softly spoken words. "Probably where they hid the procedure and formula they'd perfected for making humans into Nobility. Why would they leave something like that here in town when they ran off? Answer me that."

"Because they were ready to die." Perhaps Pluto VIII had reconciled himself to the notion of fighting D, because his voice was incredibly calm. "Think about it. They'd always had an easy life, safe and secure in their little town. What could they do out on the Frontier? Even if they had the tools for it, they still didn't have the heart. And Mr. and Mrs. Knight knew it. But what the two of them accomplished was just too big for them to throw away. Maybe they wanted to help the future generations or something, but I'm sure the better part of it was due to the lust for fame. And, after some consideration, they couldn't think of anyplace safer to hide it than this town. Is that a heartbreaking tale or what? Dying like dogs, forgotten out in some far corner of the Frontier after all they did . . . So, you know, I figured I might as well use what they found to earn myself a little coin . . . "

"Did you kill the Knights?"

"What do you mean . . . ?" Pluto VIII's eyebrows rose. He looked ablaze with indignation.

Ever serene, D continued, "I don't think it likely a pair of chemists would fail to notice their trailer's nuclear reactor was malfunctioning. They went outside and got eaten. Now, no matter how sheltered those scientists might've been, there's no way they wouldn't have known how dangerous it was to go outside on the Frontier in the dead of night. Unless, of course, you promised them they'd be safe."

"Hey, wait just a minute there!" Pluto VIII protested, sticking out his right hand to stop that train of thought. "Not to toot my own horn or anything, but I saved the little lady."

"Yes, because I was there. Molecular intangibility lets you go right through radiation. You couldn't bring yourself to let the dragons eat her, but figured you could kill her easily enough inside the vehicle—and that's where you made your mistake."

"You're unbelievable. You're just a walking heap of suspicion." A smile zipped across the pretty young face Pluto VIII was using. A wicked grin he hadn't shown before. "Though you're right about some of that stuff. You know, when I first met you I got a real bad feeling, and it looks like I was right on the money."

"What was the mayor's aim?" D said, as if he hadn't heard a word of Pluto VIII's chilling admission. "To turn all the townspeople into Nobility—into vampires?"

For a brief instant, D's longsword danced out and split the twilight with stark, white flashes. A pair of figures who'd been closing on him from behind silently fell to the ground.

With that momentary weakening of D's uncanny aura, Pluto VIII was swallowed by the darkness. "It's too late, D," he called back. "Too late. These folks have all been infected by the mayor's failed experiment. And now they're just gonna keep on multiplying. This town is finished. Well, it's just what the mayor hoped would happen. Trying to turn human beings into perfect Nobles is just flat-out impossible."

He was probably right. The visitor two centuries ago, the mayor, the Knights—each of them probably had a dream. The town rode on a dream, was in fact made of dreams. And now the town was waking from that dream. Waking with the worst possible results.

"I didn't wanna have to throw down with you," Pluto VIII said, "but there's no way around it now. Let's do it. I'll see you again in hell, fates willing!"

The instant D realized the baneful air directed at him was melting into the darkness, he shut both eyes. His longsword went into action. It had no problem at all slicing the disk blade into pieces that scattered through the air.

D charged. Around him, the wind roared.

There was nothing Lori/Pluto VIII could do. D's fist sank into the girl's delicate solar plexus, but it swept right through her body as if her body was mist. Once again, the superhuman ability known as molecular intangibility had come into play. Lori's body had been transformed into a runny, shifting shadow.

D turned around. Like a tuft of grass fluttering in the breeze, the shadow billowed down the street and faded into the ground without a sound. Not bothering to watch the black tip of its head disappear, D looked instead into the distance, at the vast expanse of sky and earth.

The route some mysterious hand had put the cursed town on carried them now over ruins that stretched as far as the eye could see. Massive stone pillars, canopies, and streets stood naked and dejected in the lights shining from the belly of the flying town. Though it went without saying that all of these ancient constructs were cracked and crumbled and otherwise reduced to terrible rubble by the ravages of wind and time, for some reason this land had an even ghastlier atmosphere. Out on the Frontier, ruins that'd belonged to the Nobility weren't particularly rare. Nevertheless, this land didn't stir the deep feelings of loneliness usually associated with such sites. This place suggested only one thing—an unsettling evil. And D alone knew the form that evil would take.

From out of the shadows of meandering rows of stone pillars, shapes stirred as if they'd noticed the coming town—human shapes, moving as if enraged . . . or overjoyed.

"At last . . . we're here . . . " said a desperate sigh of a voice that made D turn. It was a dark, blood-spattered figure lying in the road a few yards away. Even after D saw that it was the same unnatural creature Pluto VIII's disk blade had bisected, his expression never changed.

"So, you were the one guiding the town?" He put the question to the corpse just as he would to any living person.

"That's right. Everyone in town has what it takes to become one . . . " he said, his voice weak, his breath ragged. By "one," he no doubt meant one of his kind. "This is where . . . all the failures meet. Not alive, but . . . unable to die. Cursed with an endless hunger, and a future without dreams . . . no place could be more fitting for the people of this town."

"Six more hours?" D muttered. That was how long it was until dawn. Such a short time for the tremendously long engagement that was about to begin.

"The failures number over five thousand . . . Will the living prevail, or will death sing its song of victory? No . . . It won't be either. That's what makes this the perfect fate." His final words mixing with laughter and a death rattle, the figure collapsed on the ground once more, never to move again.

Destruction echoed from somewhere in the distance. No doubt the vampirized townsfolk were attacking another house. Even if the law enforcement bureau had gone into action, with things this far along they wouldn't have been able to handle the situation. Besides, they'd probably already succumbed as well . . .

Glancing briefly down the road—in the direction of the hospital—D set off for the navigational control center. In no time at all he was there. About a dozen workers were thoroughly engrossed in inspecting their weapons. An extraordinary tension filled the room.

On seeing D, the mayor showed more relief than hostility. "I suppose I should thank you for coming," he said.

"Take a good look down there," D said softly. "This is the end of the road you started them on. Down there, five thousand things that couldn't become Nobility are waiting for five hundred living people. They think the residents of your town will make fitting companions."

"They were failures." The mayor looked tired. "But we were going to be a perfect new breed of humanity. A creature with the mind and heart of a human and the immortal flesh of a Noble, reveling in an eternal life free from the filth of the mortal world. I may have failed, but the Knights succeeded. And as soon as they did so, they tried to get out of town."

"The vampire who attacked your daughter was one you made, wasn't he?"

"That's right. I made two, and both of them escaped. One of them turned his fangs on my daughter, the other one is spreading his germs all over town now."

"Half the town's already been turned into vampires. If you want to hire me to do it, I'll take care of them." Despite the present situation, a Hunter was always a Hunter.

"Is this the end of everything, then?" The mayor put both fists to his forehead. And then, looking at D, he smiled with satisfaction. "No, not yet. So long as there are still decent folks in this town, my dream will never die."

Frigid light filled D's eyes. If one was mad for having a mad dream, then the mayor was already out of his mind.

Abruptly, the ground tilted forward. Some unsecured machinery crashed against the mayor's shoulder. No blood came from him, but blue lightning crackled out of the wound. He was a cyborg.

"Touchdown in seven seconds . . . " a technician clinging to a control panel exclaimed.

The town from the sky was descending to the earth it was never supposed to meet.

"Six seconds . . . "

In the ruins below, countless things were starting to stir.

They're here! They're here! More of our kind have come!

The grating sound of lids being pushed open on coffins of stone, wood, or steel, and the putrid stench. Pale hands protruded from the graves, and crimson eyes gazed out.

"Four seconds . . ."

As Lori headed for a dilapidated building, Dr. Tsurugi came running up behind her.

"Three seconds . . ."

The town was silent. As if no one had been there from the very start.

"Two seconds . . ."

A disk blade gleamed in Lori's right hand. It was actually a solidified chemical compound that would disappear once it'd served its purpose.

"Zero!"

Before the jolt threw the people into the air, the thunder of the impact shattered the windows of every house. Lori and the physician rolled across the ground. The shock wave became a heavy wind that blasted through the town, knocking houses at an angle and snapping off trees. Half of the townspeople were injured in some way or another. The other half were actually injured as well, but it didn't bother them.

"Engine nozzles have been damaged."

"We have cracking in the convection pipes."

Voices shot back and forth across the control room in confusion.

"How long will it take to input a new course and get airborne again?" the mayor asked.

"Four hours minimum."

"Do it in two."

"Roger."

D ran to the entrance. Warped by the impact, the iron door wouldn't budge an inch. D hit it with his shoulder. By the time the door hit the ground, sending scraps of metal flying every-where, D's form was already racing down the darkened streets.

†

With silent footsteps, death's countless shapes were closing in on the town. Scrawny hands imbued with the strength to snap trees in two reached for the entrance hatch on the bottom of the town's base. The air outside began to stir with the dim sound of them pounding away at the door with their fists.

"They're getting in!" a bloodstained controller cried out.

"Relax. Even with the strength of a Noble, they couldn't break through that hatch," the mayor said as he smeared repairing compound on his shoulder wound. "We just have to hold out for two hours. Hook some power lines into the outer walls and the barrier. Juice them to a hundred thousand volts."

"Roger!"

Soon, the whole town was enveloped in pale light. The front rank of vampires reeled backward, smoking and giving off sparks. All of them had their hair standing on end.

"We did it!" one of the operators shouted.

"It's no use. The voltage is too high," another worker muttered.

One after another the shadowy figures emerged from the darkness. From behind stone columns and under domes. Out of the very ground. New bodies piled on top of the charred ones. Fire burst from the new ones, too. Planting their feet on the shoulders of the ones below them, they put their hands to the outer wall and began to scale it.

"They should be dead . . . but they're climbing up it," someone said.

And to that, someone else replied, "The Nobility are immortal . . . "

"Raise the voltage!" the mayor ordered. "We'll burn them down to the marrow of their bones. Deputies and security, head outside and shoot any intruders. We can't let a single one get on board."

The light had lost its bluish tint and was now stark white. The figures scaling the outer wall crumbled like clay figures cracked by the hot sun.

"They're running! We're saved!" someone shouted jubilantly at the sight of the retreating figures on the control room's screens.

"Don't let your guard down. They still have time yet. They'll be back again for sure. And we can't count on the barrier. Get outside and start shooting." As the relief of the present crossed the mayor's face, so did the fears of the future.

†

D was out in the middle of the street. The glow of the barrier had vanished, and, aside from the lingering stench, the town was peaceful and quiet. The people were now either locked in their homes cowering from this new threat or out seeking the blood of others. It seemed the latter had all became one with the darkness while spreading their death.

Figures appeared in front of D, and behind him as well. Crimson eyes filled with an atrocious hunger, they edged closer. It seemed that almost everyone in town had been turned into a fiend. There wasn't anyone left for him to protect now . . . aside from two people.

Something flew past the Hunter with the speed of a swallow. D knocked several more away with his left hand, and all the rest sank into the chests of the approaching figures.

Cries of pain split the darkness. The missiles were wooden wedges from stake-firing guns. The men from the law enforcement bureau didn't have time to fire a second volley, as people pounced on them from the roofs of various houses.

D's longsword flashed out, and several figures who'd been run through the chest fell to the ground. All of them were townspeople.

"Can't hold them off any longer. Prepare to abandon ship," D ordered the frightened, faltering lawmen as he lowered his bloody blade.

"We can't do that. There are tons of them outside. Wherever we go, they'll kill us. We'll just have to wait for daybreak," one of them said in a hollow voice. The only emotion coloring it was a deep shade of despair.

"Then do what you like." D turned and left without another word.

The town would rot away silently, as if this had all been decided two centuries earlier. For the town's people, tomorrow would never come.

As D hurried down the street, a pale figure rushed at him from the right side. Without even turning to look that way, D simply swept his right hand horizontally. When the figure fell with fresh blood gushing from its chest, D recognized the face. It was the little girl he'd saved from the colossal birds. The fangs jutting from her mouth slowly vanished.

†

D walked on. Before he got to the hospital, he was attacked several times, and each time was but a single exchange. Once he'd killed one, there was no one willing to make a second attack. The unearthly aura around D cowed even the dead.

D came to a halt in front of the hospital. The white building was completely destroyed. If the two of them were still inside, even a miracle wouldn't be enough to save them. Gazing at the rubble for a while, D turned.

A shadowy figure stood there like darkness congealed. Under either arm he carried a body. Dr. Tsurugi and Lori. "They're both okay, D," Pluto VIII said. "But I don't think you'll be able to get them safely out of here the way things stand now—plus, we've got us a fight to finish!" And, with the last word, he let the two bodies fall to the ground.

D sprang instantaneously.

Pluto VIII's body transformed into a black stain, and two disks flew from him. There was a silvery flash of light. The disks ricocheted away.

Shrinking and shifting, the black stain returned to the form of Pluto VIII. A dark line ran down his forehead. "Thanks," he said. "Noticed I didn't have much time left, did you?"

Bright blood spilled from Pluto VIII's mouth, but it wasn't the result of any wound D had dealt him. Just as he/Lori had been about to kill Dr. Tsurugi, the jolt of the town landing had dealt a grievous wound to Pluto VIII's real body wherever he'd left it sleeping.

"There's one thing I have to tell you . . . " Pluto VIII groaned as he slowly sank to his knees. "I took her body against her wishes. Tried swaying her with offers of telepathy—but she fought me to the very end."

"I know," D said, nodding. "But I'm sure she was always grateful to you for saving her, too."

It was unclear whether D actually caught the smile chiseled into Pluto VIII's face at the moment of death.

D went over to where the two bodies lay. They both had a pulse. More surprisingly, some of their cuts had been crudely bandaged. Pluto VIII must've done it. He was a strange man.

Screams rose in the distance. Residents were being attacked by former residents, by neighbors who finally had a goal, thanks to this need to turn everyone into vampires.

D put his right hand on the physician's brow. His eyes opened immediately. As his dim gaze bounced from left to right, there was a glint of will in his eyes. Staring at D, after a moment he asked, "Did you save us?"

"Not me. Him."

A sorrowful gaze fell on the lifeless form. "I just can't figure that . . . " the physician muttered. "What about the town?"

"This town died a long time ago. Now true death has come for it. But I'll get you both out of here safely. Rest assured."

"I give up . . . " Dr. Tsurugi said. "You're just too much for me. I finally see why *she* felt the way she did."

"What are you talking about?" D asked.

The physician said the name of a village, and D's expression changed. It was as if he'd just been touched by a gentle breeze in midsummer. Several years earlier, he was in that village, locked in a fierce battle to the death with a vampire to protect a brother and sister who lived on a ranch on the outskirts of the small town.

"Are they both well?"

The physician nodded. "Extremely. The little guy helps his sister out like a grown man, and their ranch is even bigger now. I would've loved to stay there doing what I could for the rest of my days, but it seemed she had her heart set on somebody else." Finishing his inspection of Lori, the physician nodded with satisfaction and straightened himself up.

"Where do you think you're going?" the Hunter asked.

"You don't know how to work the exits on your own, do you? Let me help you."

"You're wounded."

"I couldn't win that girl's heart. At least let me do something that would've made her happy."

D looked straight into the other man's eyes and saw the perplexing emotions that swam there. "How long did you spend in that village?" he asked.

"Not long. Six months."

"The two of them were lucky to have you."

"Thank you." The physician's eyes glittered. A look of pride shone in them.

†

The barrier's voltage is dropping rapidly!"

As if in response to that last cry, shadowy figures that'd been headed away surged toward the town again.

"How goes inputting the course into the computers?" the mayor shouted.

"It's finished."

"Take her up then!"

"We don't have enough thrust, sir!"

"I don't care. Just do it!"

"Roger."

As pale figures cleared the outer wall, pouring down like an avalanche, the town escaped the bounds of earth. It bobbed up into the air as if that were its sole purpose. Still, a few shadowy figures came down the inner wall. The last thing they ever saw was a gorgeous young man who gave off the most unearthly air. Running every last intruder through the heart, D lowered his longsword and turned.

The mayor was standing there. "My journey has only just begun," he said. "As soon as the dawn comes, the vampires will be destroyed. I'm sure the remaining townsfolk and I will somehow manage to keep the town running."

"This is a dead town," D said quietly. "Where will you go? And for what purpose?"

The mayor laughed. It sounded ghastly. A figure leapt at him from behind, its fangs bared. The mayor's fingertips sank into its heart, and the figure fell at his feet. It was Laura.

Off in the distance, the wind howled. The dawn was still far off.

"There's a plain a dozen miles from here. You and your friends get off there." The very sound of the mayor's voice was dark and distant.

†

Saying not a word, the trio watched the departing town. Where would it go? No trace of the formula had been found on Pluto VIII's body . . . Where could he have hidden it? Would the mayor ever find it again?

D stroked the muzzle of his cyborg horse. It was one of three the mayor had left with them.

"What'll we do about the girl?" the physician said, believing Lori to still be asleep, but when he looked over his shoulder he found her awake.

Her eyes gazed across the plain at the blue dawn. Her pale finger moved across the sand. The two men read what she'd written. *I've heard the sound of the wind and the songs of the birds*, it said. So, that was the perspective the girl had after seeing life and death up close? As her long hair fluttered in the morning breeze, Lori's shadow was etched distinctly on the ground.

"A mile and a quarter ahead of us is a town. The two of you should go there together." Saying that, D got on his steed.

"Where will you go?"

Giving no reply, D advanced on his horse. Mount and rider quickly dwindled as they headed off, bound for the mountain ridges that grew bluer by the minute.

Postscript

This is my first new postscript for the English editions of my books. I'd like to thank my readers in America and elsewhere for supporting D for so long. Due, no doubt, to the two animated features, sales of the novels have been good, and the author is overjoyed. I can't sleep with my feet toward the anime directors. (According to Japanese custom, sleeping with your feet facing someone you are indebted to means you aren't grateful to them. Well, since I don't know where either of them lives, I may actually have my feet pointed toward them . . .)

I've loved horror and sci-fi since I was a kid, and I never missed one of these kinds of films when they were showing in my hometown (which was a desolate port town like Lovecraft's Innsmouth.) Even when I had a fever of about a hundred and four, I acted perfectly fine in front of my parents, and, once I was outside, I staggered over to the movie theater. (The film was *The Brides of Dracula*.) Hammer's *The Revenge of Frankenstein* was showing on the same bill with a rather erotic French film, and the woman at the ticket booth said to me, "For a kid, you've come to see a pretty lewd movie." But I pretended I didn't know what she was talking about and went right on in. Unfortunately, the erotic film proved more interesting. (Laughs.)

As I was born in 1949, what left the strongest impression on me were the Hammer horror films from England. In particular, I'll never forget the impact *Horror of Dracula* had on me when I saw it. Gripped by the fearsomeness of Count Dracula as portrayed by Christopher Lee, every night I slept with a cross fashioned from a pair of chopsticks by my pillow.

Mr. Lee and Peter Cushing, who played the part of Van Helsing, became my favorite stars. Though I never did get a chance to meet Mr. Cushing, about ten years ago I met Mr. Lee and got his autograph when he came to Japan for the Tokyo Fantastic Film Festival. Wow, was he huge! (I'm not quite five foot seven.)

But the first time I ever saw Dracula and Frankenstein, the Wolf Man, mad doctors, and the rest was in a horror/comedy production by Universal called *Abbott and Costello Meet Frankenstein*. Made in 1948, the film was screened in Japan in 1956.

All of the monsters who were to decide my future were in this one film. How lucky could you get? I think I was some-how fated to write about them. And the way I completely missed *Horror of Dracula* the first time it showed in my home-town but caught it when it came back for another showing a few years later was nothing short of miraculous. Once again, it was destiny.

This is how the hero known as Vampire Hunter D came to be. I was thirty-three when I gave life to him, and I continue writing about his adventures twenty-two years later. Not only in novels now, he's spread to animation and games, and plans for his Hollywood debut and an American comic version are progressing nicely. However, more than anything, it pleases me that the novels have found acceptance and an audience with you.

I'm quite proud of *Tale of the Dead Town* and the action I penned as D does battle with the Nobility against the wondrous backdrop of a floating city. Please sit back and enjoy it, just as you'd watch a scary, fun, and thrilling horror/action movie.

Until we meet again. From under distant Japanese skies, to all my readers abroad.

Hideyuki Kikuchi
October 14, 2005,
watching *Horror of Dracula*

VAMPIRE HUNTER D

VAMPIRE HUNTER D

VOLUME 5

THE STUFF OF DREAMS

Written by

HIDEYUKI KIKUCHI

Illustrations by

YOSHITAKA AMANO

English Translation by

KEVIN LEAHY

Dark Horse Books

Milwaukie

VAMPIRE HUNTER D

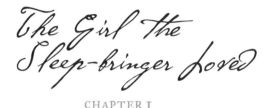

The Girl the Sleep-bringer Loved

I

The moon was out.
No matter how dangerous night on the Frontier had become, the clarity of the night itself never changed. Perhaps supernatural beasts and fiends alone had pleasant dreams . . .

But there was someone else here who might have them, too. Here, in the middle of a dense forest, he slept.

As if to prove that night on the Frontier was never silent, voices beyond numbering sang from the tops of the demon's scruff oaks or from the dense greenery of a thicket of sweet mario bushes.

Though the sleeper's dreams might be peaceful, the forest at night was home to hunger and evil. Spraying poison to seal their opponents' eyes, dungeon beetles were known to set upon their prey with sharp teeth no bigger than grains of sand. A swarm of them could take a fifteen-foot-long armored dragon and strip it to the bone in less than two minutes. Sometimes the black earth swelled up, and a mass of absorption worms burst out, crawling in all directions. Over a foot and a half long, the massive worms broke down soil with powerful molecular vibrations and absorbed it through the million mouths that graced the nucleus of each of their cells. Usually they'd latch onto a traveler's ankle first and melt the foot right off before pouncing on more vital locations like the head or the heart. How could anything escape them when their very touch ate through skin and bone alike?

Colors occurred in the darkness as well. Perhaps catching some odd little noise in the sound of the wind, the snowy white petals that opened gorgeously in the moonlight trembled ever so slightly as the flower sprayed out a pale purple mist, and, as the cloud drifted down to earth, tiny white figures floated down with it. Each of them carried a minute spear, and only those who'd made it through the forest alive knew that they were evil little sprites from within the flower, with poison sap made from petals.

And of all the blood-hued eyes glittering off in the darkness a little way off, and further back, and even deeper still, nothing was merely an innocent onlooker.

While everyone who went out on the Frontier might not know it, those who actually lived there realized the forests weren't a wise place to choose for a night of restful sleep. They were aware that the plaintive birdsong was actually the voice of a demon bird that muddled the senses, and that the gentle fog was in fact mist devils trying to sneak into their victims' bodies. If they absolutely had to sleep in the forest, people would keep a bow with an incendiary-tipped arrow in one hand, and shut their eyes only after zipping their asbestos sleeping bag up over their head. Sprite spears and the teeth of nocturnal insect predators couldn't penetrate a half-inch thickness of that cloth, and, if a traveler drank an antidote derived from the juice of hell berries, they didn't have to worry about demonic fogs, either. Their head, however, would be aching the next morning. If, by some chance, the attacks should persist, then the bow and arrow came into play.

However, the traveler now surrounded by all these weird creatures seemed completely ignorant of the threats the woods held. Lying on a bed of grass, the moonlight shone down on him like a spotlight. While his face couldn't be seen for the black, wide-brimmed traveler's hat that covered it, the deep-blue pendant that hung at his chest, the black long coat, the high leather boots with their silver spurs, and, more than anything, the elegant longsword leaning against his shoulder left no room for muddled conjecture or doubt. All those things were meant to adorn someone beautiful.

However, part of his description was still lacking. Watch. When the monstrous creatures blanketing the ground come within three feet of the traveler, they rub their paws and pincers and begin to twitch uncontrollably, as if checked by some unseen barrier. They know. They understand. Though the traveler sleeps, something emanates from his body—a ghastly aura declaring that any who challenge him will die. The creatures of the wild know what the young man actually is, and the part of his description that is absolutely indispensable: He is not of this world.

The young man in black went right on sleeping, almost as if the poisonous mists of the sleeper grass smelled to him like the sweetest perfume, as if the indignant snarls of the ungodly creatures sounded to his ears like the most soothing melody.

Consciousness suddenly spread through his body. His left hand took hold of his hat, and, as he sat up, he placed it back on his long black hair. And anything that looked upon him realized that unearthly beauty did indeed exist.

People called him D. Though his eyes had been closed in sleep up until this very moment, there wasn't even a tiny hint of torpor in them. His black, bottomless pupils reflected another figure in black standing about ten feet ahead of him. Well over six and a half feet tall, the massive form was like a block of granite.

A certain power buffeted D's face, an aura emanating from that colossal figure. An ordinary human would've been so psychically damaged by it that they'd spend the better part of a lifetime trying to recover.

In his left hand, the man held a bow, while his right hand clutched a number of arrows. When bow and arrow met in front of that massive chest, D's right hand went for the handle of his longsword. The elegant movement befitted the young man.

An arrow whined through the air. D stayed just where he was, but a flash of silver rushed from his sheath and limned a gorgeous arc. When the smooth cut of his blade met the missile's beautiful flight in a shower of sparks, D knew his foe's arrows were forged entirely from steel.

The fierce light that resided in his opponent's eyes looked like a silent shout. The instant their respective weapons had met, his arrow was split down the middle, and the halves sank deep into the ground.

D stood up. A flash of black ran through his left shoulder. The black giant had unleashed this arrow at the same time as his second shot. Perfectly timed and fired on an equally precise course, the arrow had deceived D until it pierced his shoulder.

However, the black shadow seemed shaken, and it fell back without a sound. He alone understood how incredibly agile D had been, using his shoulder to stop an arrow that should've gone right through his heart.

As his foe backed away, D readied himself. Making no attempt to remove the arrow, he gazed at the giant's face with eyes that were suspiciously tranquil. D was reflected in his opponent's eyes as well.

"Don't intend to tell me your name, do you?" D's first words also held the first hint of emotion he'd shown. An instant later, the hem of his coat spread in midair. The blade he brought down like a silvery serpent's fang rent nothing but cloth as the black figure leapt back another fifteen feet. As his foe hovered in midair, the *twang* of a bowstring rang out. With as mellifluous a sound as was ever heard, the long, thin silhouette of the Hunter's blade sprang up, and D kicked off the ground with all of his might.

His foe was already partially obscured by a grove a hundred yards ahead. The few hundredths of a second it'd taken him to draw back for his third shot had proved critical.

Still not bothering with the arrow in his left shoulder, D sprinted into action. Inheriting much of the Nobility's powerful musculature in their legs, dhampirs could dash a hundred yards in less than six seconds. With his speed, D covered the distance in under five seconds, and he showed no signs of slowing. However, the shadow had been lost in the darkness. Did D sense that the presence had abruptly vanished?

He kept on running, and, when he halted, it was in precisely the same spot where his foe had disappeared. D had noticed that the deep footprints that'd led him that far ended in the soft grass.

His opponent had vanished into the heavens or sunk into the earth—neither of which was especially uncommon in this world.

D stood still. Black steel jutting from his left shoulder and fresh blood dripping from the wound, D hadn't let his expression change one bit throughout the battle. But the reason he didn't extract the arrow wasn't because he didn't feel the pain of it, but rather because he simply wasn't going to give his foe an opportunity to catch him off-guard.

Frozen like a veritable statue, he broke his pose suddenly. Around him, everything was still and dark. The air of their deadly conflict must've stunned the supernatural creatures, because not a single peculiar growl or cry could be heard.

D's face turned, and his body began moving. There hadn't been any road there from the very start, just a bizarre progression of overlapping trees and bushes. Like an exquisite shadow, he moved ahead without hesitation, finding openings wherever he needed them. There was no telling if it would be a short hike or a long, hard trek. Night on the Frontier was a whole different world.

The wind bore a sound that was not its own whispers. Perhaps D had heard it even at the scene of the battle. Beyond the excited buzz of people and a light melody played by instruments of silver and gold, he could make out a faint glow.

The stately outline that towered protectively over the proceedings looked to be that of a chateau. As the Hunter walked closer, the outline gave way to rows of bright lights. Presently, D's way was barred by a gate in the huge iron fence before him. Not giving his surroundings a glance, D continued forward. Before his hands even touched it, the gate creaked open. Without a moment's delay, D stepped onto the property. Judging by the scale of the gate, this wasn't the main entrance.

Ahead of him was a stone veranda that gave off a shimmering light. The glow was not due to the light of the moon, but rather it radiated from the stones themselves. In the windows behind the veranda were countless human figures. Some laughed gaily. Some danced with elegance. The sharp swallowtails of men's formal attire flicked back and forth, and the hems of evening gowns swayed. The banquet at the mansion seemed to be at its height.

D's gaze fell to the steel jutting from his shoulder, and he took hold of it with his left hand. There was the sound of tearing flesh as he yanked the steel out, vermilion scraps of meat still clinging to it. As fresh blood gushed from the wound, D covered it with his left hand. It sounded like someone was drinking a glass of water. All the while D kept walking, climbing the stone steps of the veranda and then reaching for the doorknob. The bleeding from his shoulder hadn't stopped.

The doorknob was a blue jewel set in the middle of golden petals, and it turned readily in his well-formed hand.

D stood in a hall filled with blue light. One had to wonder if the young man realized that hue was not the white radiance he'd seen spilling from the windows. Perhaps the mansion was mocking D, because now only two figures danced in the room. The girl must've been around seventeen or eighteen. The fine shape of her limbs was every bit as glamorous as her dress, which seemed to be woven from obsidian thread, and each and every strand of the black hair that hung down to her waist glittered like a spun jewel. The light melody remained. Her partner in tails was also reflected in D's eyes. Still turned the other way, his face couldn't be seen.

D stepped further into the hall. It was clear the mansion had been meant to draw him there. If it had only two residents, one or both of them must've arranged this.

The girl stopped moving. The music ceased as well. As she stared at D, her eyes were filled with a mysterious gleam. "You're . . . ?" Her composed voice made the light flicker.

"I seem to have been invited here," D said as he looked at the back of the man who was still facing away from him. "By you? What's your business? Or where is he?"

"He?" The girl knit her thread-thin eyebrows.

"If you don't know who I'm referring to, perhaps that man does. Well?"

The man didn't move. Perhaps her partner was fashioned from bronze, and made solely to dance?

Asking nothing more, D plowed through the blue light to stand just behind the man. His left hand reached for the man's shoulder—and touched it. Slowly, the man turned around. Every detail of the girl's expression—which couldn't be neatly classified as either horror or delight—was etched into the corner of D's eye.

D opened his eyes. Blue light graced his surroundings. It was the pale glow of dawn, just before sunrise.

Slowly, D rose from his grassy resting place. Had it all been a dream? There was no wound to his left shoulder. Where he was now was the same spot where he'd gone to sleep. The cyborg horse that'd been absent from his dream stood by the tree trunk to which its reins were tied.

As the Hunter took the longsword and sheath in his left hand and slung it across his back, a hoarse and strangely earnest voice said, "No, sirree. That was too damn real for a plain old dream. Hell, it hurt *me*." The voice must've been referring to the steel arrow that'd penetrated the Hunter's left shoulder. "That mansion was calling you, sure enough. And if they called you, they must have business with you. Bet we'll be seeing them again real soon."

"You think so?" D said, speaking in the real world for the first time. "I saw him."

"Indeed," the voice agreed. But it sounded perplexed.

Setting the saddle he'd used for a pillow on his horse's back, D easily mounted his steed. The horse began walking in the blue light.

"How about that—it's the same!"

What the voice meant was this locale they'd never seen before bore a striking resemblance to the place in the dream, suggesting . . . that the source of the voice had the very same dream as D.

In a few minutes, the horse and rider arrived at an empty lot surrounded by a grove of sizable trees. This was where the mansion had been. A banquet in endless warm, blue light, light that spilled from the windows as men and women danced in formal wear, never seeing the dawn. Now, everything was hidden by the green leaves of vulgar spruces and the boughs of poison firs. Giving the landscape a disinterested glance, D wheeled his mount around. Beyond the forest, there should be a real village settled almost two hundred years ago.

Without looking back, the rider in black vanished into the depths of a grove riddled by the light of dawn, as if to say he'd already forgotten his dream.

II

D came to a halt in front of the gate to the village. Like any other village, it was surrounded by triple walls to keep out the Nobility and other foul creatures. The sight of verdigris-covered javelin-launchers and flamethrower nozzles poking out of those stockade fences was one to which most travelers would be accustomed. The same could be said for the trio of sturdy, well-armed men who appeared from the lookout hut next to the gate. The men signaled to D to stop. But one thing was different here—the expression these men wore. The looks of suspicion and distrust they usually trained on travelers had been replaced with a strange mix of confusion and fear . . . and a tinge of amity.

As one of them gazed somewhat embarrassedly at D on his horse, he asked, "You're a Hunter, ain't you? And not just any Hunter. You're a top-class Vampire Hunter. Isn't that right?"

"How did you know?" The soft sound of the man on horseback's voice cut through the three of them like a gust of wintry wind.

"Never mind," the man in the middle said, shaking his head and donning an ambiguous little smile as he turned back to the gate. Facing a hidden security camera, he raised his right hand. With the tortured squeal of gears and chains, the gate with its plank and iron covering swung inward.

"Get going. You're going in, right?" the first man asked.

Not saying a word, D put the heels of his boots to his horse's belly. As if blown out of the way by an unearthly wind gusting from the rider and his mount, the three men slipped off to either side, and D went into the village.

The wide main street ran straight from the gate into the village. To either side of it were rows of shops and homes. Again, this was a typical layout for a Frontier town. The kind of looks that'd greeted D outside the gate moments earlier met him again. People on the street stopped and focused stares of fear or confusion or affection on him, but it was the women whose gazes quickly turned to ones of rapture.

Ordinarily, women on the Frontier never let down their gruff and wary facade, even when the most handsome of men passed within inches of them. They were well aware that a pretty face didn't reflect the mind behind it. For all they knew, they might be the only one who saw him that way. What guarantee did they have that he wasn't, in fact, a poisonous crimson spider—a creature that not only had the power to hypnotize, but who could also give substance to hallucinations? Who could say for certain he hadn't been sent by bandits planning to burn the village to the ground and make off with all their money and their women? To crack the Frontier woman's hard-bitten demeanor took a beauty that was not of this world.

When he'd ridden halfway down the street—passing through odd looks and ecstatic gazes—a young woman's voice called out to his black-clad back, "Um, excuse me!" Her voice suited the morning.

D stopped. And he didn't move a muscle after that.

There was the sound of someone's short, quick steps on the raised wooden sidewalk off to D's left, a head of black hair slipped right by his side, and then the girl turned in front of him. A smile graced her face, which was fresh and rosy and bursting with youthfulness.

"You're a Vampire Hunter, aren't you?" The words were formed by lips painted a faint shade appropriate to her age. She was sixteen or seventeen—at the stage where she wanted people to look at her. Without waiting for an answer from D, she continued. "Well, if you are, please go out to the hospital on the edge of town. Sybille is in room seven."

D's expression shifted. Apparently, he'd recognized the girl, in her snowy white blouse and blue skirt with wine-red stripes, as someone worth talking to. "Have we met before?" he asked.

The girl's form tensed. D's tone was no different from what he'd used with the men out at the gate. It wouldn't be the least bit strange for it to leave a timid girl quaking. But this young lady just bobbed her head vigorously. "Yes. Only it—oh, just hurry!"

"Where did we meet?"

The girl smiled wryly. "You wouldn't believe me if I told you. It's better you hear it from someone upstanding, like a grown man, instead of from me. Hurry up and get to the hospital. The director will be so happy to see you."

It was a bizarre discussion. Although somewhat lacking in explanation, it was clear from the tone of the girl's voice that this was an urgent matter. What sort of conclusions were being drawn in the heart beneath that black raiment?

Asking nothing further, D resumed his advance. Once he was off the main street, the Frontier land rapidly grew more desolate. Almost all of the arable land had been bequeathed by the Nobility, given with the knowledge that fields which scarcely provided enough to survive were good insurance against insurrections. Of course, after the decline of the Nobility, there were some villages where crops and soil had been repeatedly improved, and, as a result of centuries of persistent toil, the townspeople had managed to make bountiful harvests a reality. But such successes never went any farther than the village level—they never spread across whole sectors. This desolate earth bore mute testimony to the fact there were only a dozen places on the entire Frontier that tasted such bounty, while elsewhere the battle against misery and poverty continued as it had for centuries.

But this community was actually one of those rare exceptions. As D's eyes ran along the edge of the village, he saw vast expanses of fragrant green forests and farmland, all of which seemed to be nestled between hills covered with neat orchards of verdant fruit trees. This village of five hundred harvested enough to feed nearly twenty times that number. Four times a year, when the entire village was done packing up their bounty, fifty massive transport vehicles hauled the town's excess food roughly sixty miles south to the freight station, where it was then shipped out to more impoverished villages on the Frontier or to the distant Capital. The reason homes and infrastructure in this village showed comparatively little wear was due to the income generated by their food surplus.

Following an asphalt-paved road for another five minutes, the Hunter saw a chalk-white structure atop a respectable-sized hill. The rather wide road forked off in several different directions before continuing up the slope. The flag that flew from the three-story building at the top of the hill had a five-pointed star on it—the mark of a hospital.

This must've been the place the girl had told him to go. But he'd never had any intention of doing what she asked . . .

The complete antithesis of the refreshing blue sky and greenery of morning, the black rider and horse reached the base of the hill at their own leisurely pace. Although the young rider didn't appear to pull back on the reins, his horse came to an immediate stop. Soon the beast changed direction, as if looking up at the hill, and they began to slowly ascend.

Twining the reins around a fence by the entrance, D went through the front door. The doors were all glass and were fully automated. As there probably wasn't a power station nearby, the doors must've run on the material fluid power that'd recently gained popularity.

But the village would have to be incredibly well-off if they could afford to use that recent innovation on something so trivial.

D went over to the information desk beside the door. The nurse behind the desk had a mindless gaze and a vacant expression on her face. Of course, the same went for the female patients and other nurses dotting the vast lobby. This was beyond the level of just feverish stargazes—they seemed like their very souls had been sucked out.

"I'd like to see the person in charge," D told the nurse in a low voice.

Reaching for a switch under the desk, the woman said, "He'll be right here," though it was nearly a moan. Her syrupy tone seemed to have an almost wanton ring to it.

"He needn't do that. I'll go to him."

"No," the nurse said, shaking her head, "he expressly told me to let him know the moment you came in."

"So, he knows me, then?"

"Yes. Actually, so do I . . . "

It'd happened again.

D looked at the nurse. The light of reason had already left her eyes. He turned to the far end of the lobby.

Just then, footsteps echoed from one of the numerous corridors, and a figure in white came running toward him. The figure became an old man with a white beard who crossed the lobby at a lively pace and halted in front of the Hunter. Gazing steadfastly at D, he moaned, "Oh, my!" By the look on his face, he wished he were a woman. "Looks like I'll have to move my female patients and nurses somewhere else. I'm Allen, the hospital director."

"Call me D," the Hunter said in his usual brusque manner. "So, do you know me, too?"

Director Allen nodded deeply. "Though I only just met you *last night*. Looks so good it even made a man like me lightheaded—not a chance I'd forget that. So, what brings you here?"

"A few minutes ago, a girl told me to come here."

"A girl?" the aged director asked. His expression grew contemplative, and he asked, "Was she about sixteen or seventeen, with black hair way down to her waist? Pretty as no one's business?"

"Yes."

"That'd be Nan. Not surprising, really. You're just the man for the job."

"How did you know I'd come?"

"That was the impression I got last night." As he finished speaking, the hospital director swallowed hard. D was calmly gazing at him. The black of his eyes, impossibly dark and deep, awakened fearful memories etched in the very genes of the director's cells. Small talk and jokes had no place in the world of this young man—this being. Director Allen did all he could to look away. Even when the young man's image was reduced to a reflection on the floor, the director was left with a fear as chill as winter in the core of his being.

"Please, come with me. This way." His tone bright for these last few words alone, Director Allen started retracing his earlier steps. Traveling down a number of white corridors, he led D to a sickroom. A vague air of secrecy hung over this part of the hospital. There wasn't a single sound. The room was surrounded by noise-dampening equipment that worked almost perfectly.

"So we don't wake the sleeping princess," the director explained as he opened the door, seeing that D had noticed the arrangements.

This place had turned its back on the light of day. In the feeble darkness of the spacious sickroom, the girl lay quietly in her bed. Her eyes were closed. Aside from the usual table, chairs, and cupboard, there wasn't any other furniture in the room. The windowpane behind the drawn curtains was opaque.

The dream last night, the watchmen at the gate, and the girl with the long hair—they all had to be part of a plan to lead D here. But toward what end?

The girl didn't seem to be breathing, but D stared down at her in pensive silence.

You should be out laughing in the sunshine.

"This is Sybille Schmitz—she's seventeen," the director said, hemming and hawing a bit when he came to her age.

"How many decades has she been like this?" D asked softly.

"Oh, so you could tell, then?" the hospital director said with admiration. The fact of the matter was she'd been that way for nearly thirty years. "One fall day, she was found lying out in the woods not far from the village. Right off we knew what'd been done to her. She had those two loathsome marks on the nape of her neck, after all. The whole village pitched in and we took turns watching her for three days without sleep so no one could get near her. In the end, the guilty party never did appear, but Sybille didn't wake up, either. She's been sleeping here in my hospital ever since. Our village was just about the only place that got along with the Nobility, so I don't see why something like this had to happen."

It was unclear if D was really listening to the man's weary voice. In this whole absurd business, D had confirmed only one thing as fact. A young lady dancing on and on with elegant steps in the blue light. People laughing merrily at a never-ending banquet. D turned to Director Allen. "How did you know I'd come?"

The hospital director had a look of resignation. "I had a dream about you last night," he replied more forcefully than necessary. He still hadn't fully escaped the mental doldrums the young man's gaze had put him in.

D didn't react at all.

"And not just me," Director Allen added. "Now, I didn't exactly go around checking or anything, but I'd wager the whole village did, too. Anyone who had that dream would understand."

"What kind of dream?"

"I don't remember anymore. But I knew you were going to come. You'd come to see Sybille."

Dreams again?

"Have there been any strange incidents in your village recently?"

The director shook his head. "Not only hasn't there been any problem with the Nobility, but we haven't had any crimes by outsiders or villagers, either. I imagine arguments and fisticuffs between those who've been hitting the bottle hardly qualify as the kind of incidents you're talking about."

Why, then, had the Hunter been summoned?

"What's supposed to happen after I get here—can you remember?"

The director shook his head. He almost looked relieved. It was as if he had the feeling that, if he became involved with this young man in any way, there'd be a terrible price to pay later.

D drifted toward the door. He didn't give another glance to the girl or the hospital director. He was about to leave. There was nothing here to hold a Vampire Hunter's interest.

Wanting to say something to him, the director realized he really had nothing to say. There were no words to address a shadow. When the door finally closed, the director wasn't completely sure that he'd actually met the young man.

On his way through the lobby to the exit, D passed a man. He was middle-aged and dressed in a cotton shirt and trousers and, while both garments were clean, they'd also been patched countless times. His rugged face had been carved by the brutal elements. Anyone could easily picture him out working the soil to earn his daily bread. With a weary expression, he quickly walked past D.

Slipping once more through the feverish gazes of the nurse and patients, D exited the lobby. Silently riding down the slope, he came to a little road. It wouldn't be much farther to the main road. But, just as he was going around a curve at the bottom of the hill, he found a dragon-drawn wagon coming from the opposite direction.

Not all of the supernatural creatures and demons the Nobility had unleashed were necessarily ferocious beasts. Though extremely rare, there were certain species, like sprites and smaller dragons, that humans could keep. Some of these creatures could howl for flames in freezing winter or summon the rains that were indispensable for raising produce, while others could replace machinery as a source of cheap labor. The beast before D now was a perfect example of the latter.

The dragon seemed to have sensed D even before it saw him. Its bronze flesh was covered with bumps that manifested its fear, and not even the whip of the farmer in the driver's seat could make it budge.

After lashing the beast a number of times, the farmer gave up, throwing down the whip and drawing the electronic spear from a holster beside his seat. As he hit the switch, it released a spring inside the handle. A three-foot-long spear suddenly teles-coped out to twice that size. At the same time, the battery kicked in and the steel tip gave off a pale blue glow.

The weapon was far more powerful than its appearance suggested—even if it didn't break the skin, the mere touch of it would deliver a jolt of fifty thousand volts. According to the *Complete Frontier Encyclopedia*, it was effective against all but the top fifty of the two hundred most vicious creatures in the midsize class. While jabbing a beast of burden in the haunches with it might be a bit rough, the technique certainly wasn't unheard of. The dragon's hindquarters were swollen with dark red wounds where it'd been stabbed before. Electromagnetic waves tinged the sunlight blue. The farmer's eyes bulged from their sockets, but the dragon didn't budge.

No amount of training could break a dragon's wild urges. Cyborg horses were something the dragons loved to prey on, but, even with one nearby, there wasn't the slightest glimmer of savagery in the beast's eyes. It remained transfixed, and tinged with fear. It couldn't pull away . . . It stood still as a statue, almost like a beautiful woman enthralled by a demon.

As D passed, the farmer clucked his tongue in disgust and pulled back his spear. Since his cart was so large, there were fewer than three feet left to squeeze by on the side of the road. The point of his spear swung around. An instant later, it was shooting out at full speed toward D's back.

III

The blue magnetic glow never would've suspected that at the very last second a flash of silver would drop down from above to challenge it. D's pose didn't change in the least as his right hand drew his blade and sent the front half of the spear sailing through the air.

Still leaning forward from his thrust, the farmer barely managed to pull himself straight. The farmer, after only a moment's pause, made a ferocious leap from the driver's seat. In midair, he drew the broadsword he wore through the back of his belt. When he brought the blade down with a wide stroke, a bloody mist danced out in the sunlight.

Looking only for an instant at the farmer who'd fallen to the ground with a black arrowhead poking out of the base of his neck, D turned his eyes to what he'd already computed to be the other end of that trajectory. There was only an expanse of blue sky . . . But the steel arrow stuck through the farmer's neck had flown from somewhere up there.

The stink of blood mixed with the almost stifling aroma of greenery in the air, and, as D sat motionless on his steed, the sunlight poured down on him. There wasn't a second attack.

Finally, D dropped his gaze to the farmer lying on the ground, just to be sure of something. The bloodstained arrow was the same deadly implement the man had used to attack him in his dream. Perhaps the arrow had flown *from* the world of dreams.

Putting his longsword back in its sheath, in a low voice D asked, "You saw what happened, didn't you?"

Behind him, someone seemed to be surprised. Just around the base of the hill, a slim figure sat astride a motorbike of some kind, rooted to the spot. The reason her long hair swayed was because her whole body was trembling.

"Uh, yes," she said, nodding slowly. It was the same young woman who'd told him to go to the hospital.

"Tell the sheriff exactly what you saw," D said tersely, giving a kick to the belly of his horse.

"Wait—you can't go. You have to talk to the sheriff," the girl cried passionately. "If you don't, the law will be after you until the whole situation gets sorted out. You plan on running the rest of your life? Don't worry. I saw the whole thing. And don't you wanna get to the bottom of this mystery? Find out why everyone dreamed about you?"

The cyborg horse stopped in its tracks.

"To be completely honest," the girl continued, "that wasn't the first time I'd seen your face, either. I've met you plenty of times. In my dreams. So I knew about you a long time before everyone else did. I knew you'd come for sure. That's why I came after you."

Up in the saddle, D turned and looked back at her.

Though the girl had no idea she'd just done the impossible, her eyes were gleaming. "Great. I'm glad you changed your mind. It might be my second time seeing you, but, anyway, nice to meet you. I'm Nan Lander."

"Call me D."

"Kind of a strange name, but I like it. It's like the wind." Though she'd intended that as a compliment, D was as uncongenial as ever, and, with a troubled expression, Nan said, "I'll hurry off and fetch the sheriff." And with that, she steered her motorbike back around the way she'd come.

Due to urgent business, the sheriff wasn't in, but a young deputy quickly wrapped up the inquiry. D was instructed not to leave town for the time being. The deputy said the farmer who'd been killed was named Tokoff, and he had lived on the outskirts of the village. He was a violent man prone to drunken rages, and they'd planned on bringing him in sooner or later, which explained why the matter of his death could be settled so easily. Even more fortunate was the fact that he didn't have any family.

"But for all that, he wasn't the kind of man to go around indiscriminately throwing spears at folks, either. If we didn't have Nan's word for it, your story would be mighty hard to believe. We're gonna have to check into your background a wee bit." The trepidation in the deputy's voice was due, no doubt, to the fact he'd already heard D's name. But that was probably also the reason why he'd accepted the surreal tale of Tokoff being slain by an arrow fired from nowhere at all after attacking the Hunter.

Nan said she'd show D the way to the hotel. The two of them were crossing the creaky floor on the way to the door when D asked in a low voice, "Did you dream about me, too?"

A few seconds later, the deputy replied, "Yep." But his voice just rebounded off the closed door.

With Nan at the fore, the two of them started walking down the street, D leading his horse while she pushed her bike. The wind, which had grown fiercer, threw up gritty clouds that sealed off the world with white.

"You . . . you didn't ask him anything at all about Tokoff," Nan said as she gazed at D with a mournful look in her eye. "Didn't ask the name of the man you killed, or his line of work, or if he had a family. Don't you care? Does it just not matter now that he's dead? You don't even wonder why he attacked you, do you? I can't see how you can live that way."

Perhaps it was her earnestness rather than her censure that moved D's lips. "You should think about something else," he said.

"I suppose you're right," Nan replied, letting the subject go with unexpected ease.

On the Frontier, it was taboo to show too much interest in travelers, or any concern for them. Perhaps it was the enthusiasm all too common in girls her age that made her forget for a brief instant the rule that'd been borne not out of courtesy, but from the very real need to prevent crimes against those who would bare their souls to strangers.

D halted. They were in front of a bar. It was just a little before twelve o'clock Noon. Beyond the batwing doors, women who looked to be housewives could be seen clustered around the tables.

Under extreme circumstances or in impoverished Frontier villages that lacked other recreation facilities, this one institution—the bar—often played a part in essentially everything the villagers did.

The bar served a number of purposes—a casino for the men, a coffee shop and chat room for housewives, and a reading room and a place to exchange information on fashion and discuss matters of the heart for young ladies. It wasn't even frowned on when the tiniest of tots tried their hand at gambling. For that reason, the bar was open all day long.

Nan watched with a hardened expression as D wrapped the reins around a fence in front of the building. "Aren't we going to your hotel to talk? I wouldn't mind. It's not like I wanna be a kid forever."

Giving her no reply, D stepped up onto the raised wooden sidewalk. He didn't even look at Nan.

The girl gnawed her lip. She wanted to look him square in the face so she could glare at him. All the anger she could muster was directed at his black-clad back, but the wind that came gusting by at that moment lifted the hem of his coat to deflect her rage. When she pushed her way through the doors a moment later, she found the figure in black was already seated at a table right by the counter.

From the far left corner of the bar, where all the housewives congregated, D was being bombarded with whispers and glances. Every gaze was strangely feverish, yet filled with fear at the same time. Everyone could tell. Everyone could see this young man belonged to another world.

Feeling a certain relief at D's choice of table, Nan took a seat directly across from him. Telling the sleepy-eyed bartender on the other side of the counter, "Paradigm cocktail, please," she looked at D.

"Shangri-La wine," was all D said, and the bartender gave a nod and turned around.

"You know, you're a strange one," Nan said, her tone oddly gloomy. "You can watch someone get killed without even raising an eyebrow, but you won't take a woman back to your room. On the other hand, you did get me a grownup seat here. Are all Vampire Hunters like you?"

"My line of work was in your dream, too?"

Nan nodded. "Even though you didn't come out and say it, I just knew. And I knew you'd come here, too. Though I didn't know exactly *when* it would be."

"You know why you had that dream?"

Nan shook her head. "Can anyone tell you why they dream what they do?" Quickly donning an earnest expression that suited a young lady, Nan added, "But I understand. I saw that you were just walking on and on in this blue light. Where you came from, where you were going—no, scratch the first part. I only knew where you were going. To see Sybille. And there's your answer."

Was she trying to suggest the sleeping girl had summoned him? Why would Sybille do that? And why had only Nan seen D over and over again? The mystery remained.

"Thirty years ago, she was bitten by a Noble. The doctor said it was only natural you'd tell me to go to the hospital. Why are you so concerned about her?"

"Why did Sybille call you here, for that matter? How come I'm the only one who's dreamed about you more than once? I'm going to be honest with you—I'm so scared, I can't stand it." There was a hint of urgency in Nan's voice. "No matter how scary a dream may be, you can forget it after you open your eyes. Real life is a lot more painful. But this time, I'm just as scared after I wake up. No, I'm even more scared . . . " Her voice failed.

The millions of words embedded in the silence that followed were shattered with D's next remark. "This village is the only place where humans and Nobility lived and worked together on equal terms," he said. "I hear they aren't around any more, but I'd like to know what it used to be like."

For a second, Nan focused a look of horrible anger at the Hunter's gorgeous face, and then she shook her head. "You won't get that from me. If that's what interests you, Old Mrs. Sheldon could tell you plenty."

"Where can I find her?"

"The western edge of the village. Just follow the orchards, and you'll find the place soon enough. Why? Is something going on?" Nan asked, leaning over the table.

"Hell, we'd like to know that, too!"

As the rough voice drifted across the bar, a number of figures spread out in the room, too. The batwing doors swung wildly, hinges creaking.

"Mr. Clements."

Nan's eyes reflected a man baring his teeth—a man who looked like a brick wall someone had dressed in a leather vest. It wasn't just the material forming the contours of the secondhand combat suit he wore that made him look more than six and a half feet tall—the massive frame of the man inside the combat suit was imposing in both size and shape.

A killing lust had taken over the bar. The housewives were a sickly hue as they got to their feet. In addition to the man called Clements, there were six others. All of them wore power-amplifying combat suits.

"Mr. Clements, we don't want any trouble here—" the bartender called out fretfully from behind the counter as he loaded glasses onto a tray.

"Go out back for a while, Jatko," the giant said in a weighty tone. There was a little gray mixed in his hair, but he looked like he could strangle a bear even without his combat suit. "Tally up yesterday's take or something. We'll pay you for anything that gets broken. Nan, you'd best run along, too. You start getting friendly with these drifter types, and you're not gonna be too popular around town."

"I can talk to whomever I please," Nan retorted, loudly enough for everyone to hear.

"Well, we'll discuss that matter later. Move it!" Clements tossed his jaw in Nan's direction, and a man to his left went into action. An arm empowered with hundreds of times its normal strength grabbed Nan by the shoulder.

Suddenly, her captor's face warped in pain. Oddly enough, neither the men there nor even Nan had noticed until now that D had stood up.

A black glove held the wrist of the man's combat suit. The man's body shook, but D didn't move in the slightest. It looked like his hand was just gently resting on the other man. But what was gentle for this young man was cause for others to shudder.

The Hunter moved his hand easily, and the arm of the combat suit went along with it as it limned a semicircle. "This young lady came in here with me," the Hunter said. "It would be best if she leaves with me, too." And then D calmly brought his hand down, and the sound of bones snapping echoed through the quiet bar.

Clements looked scornfully at his lackey, who'd fainted dead away from the pain. "Beat by a damn Hunter. That really makes me sick," he spat, gazing at D. "Stanley Clements is the name—I head up the local Vigilance Committee and breed guard beasts. I'm a big deal in these parts, if I do say so myself. You remember that when you tangle with me."

D was silent.

Perhaps mistaking silence for fright, Clements continued. "We hear tell you killed Tokoff. For a lousy drifter, you've got a lot of nerve laying a hand on a clean-living villager," Clements said, his voice brimming with confidence.

"That's not how it was, Mr. Clements. I saw the whole thing. And Bates agreed, too. He's not the one who shot that arrow, I tell you!"

Ignoring Nan's desperate explanation, Clements sneered, "I don't know what the hell that deputy told you, but you're gonna leave town quick. After we have a little fun with you, that is."

It seemed Nan had a good deal more courage than the average person. The girl reprovingly interjected the comment, "Orders from Mr. Bates are as good as orders from the sheriff. You know, you're all gonna catch hell when he gets back."

"Shut your hole, you little brat!" Clements barked as rage gave a vermilion tinge to his already demonic visage. "Go ahead and take 'im!"

With that command, three men in combat suits charged at D. They didn't give the slightest consideration to the fact that he had Nan with him.

No sooner had D pushed the girl away than he was swallowed by a wave of orange armor. Nan's eyes were open as wide as they could go. Look at that. Didn't all three Vigilance Committee members just sail through the air and slam against the floor with an enormous crash? Weren't they supposed to have the strength of five hundred men in that armor?

If by some chance there'd been a super-high-speed camera there to film this scene, it would've caught D as he slipped between the jumbled forms of the trio and twisted their wrists behind their backs with secret skill. The wrist and shoulder joints of every last man were shattered beyond repair. Of course, even a dhampir was no match for the strength of a combat suit. In addition to the ancient technique he used to turn his opponents' strength and speed against themselves, he must've called on all his inhuman strength. But executing those moves with absolute perfection was something this young man alone could've done.

"Well, ain't that something," Clements groaned, growing pale as he did so. But he hadn't yet lost the will to fight. He still had two lackeys left. Slowly, they inched forward.

It was then that a composed voice declared, "That'll be enough of that."

"Sheriff!" Nan shouted with delight. The men in orange stopped what they were doing and closed their eyes. The fight that'd burned in them like a madness left like a dream.

"Who started this, Nan?" asked the tall shadow standing in front of the doors.

"Mr. Clements."

"You've got it all wrong, Krutz," the giant growled, vehemently refuting the charge as he turned to the lawman. "You gonna believe this little bitch? I swear to hell, I've been true to my word to you."

"In that case, I want you to resign as head of the Vigilance Committee right this minute," the man in the topcoat said. The silver star on his chest reflected Clements's anger-twisted features.

"C'mon, Krutz, I was just—"

"Take your men and clear out of here. You should thank him for throwing your boys so neatly. Today you get off without paying any damages."

Hesitating a bit, the giant started to walk out with his head hung low. The other two men followed closely behind him, with their four injured cohorts leaning on their shoulders for support. They banged out through the doors without a parting remark.

"Welcome back, Sheriff," Nan said, joy and trust suffusing her countenance as she greeted him. "You take care of that case already?"

"No. Truth is, I was just on my way home now. Have a little work in the fields that needs doing, you know." The sheriff's stern visage smiled wryly, and then he nodded to D. "Just glad I was able to keep this acquaintance of yours out of trouble." To the Hunter, he added, "Though there could've been a hundred of them up against you and they still wouldn't have had a chance."

The first time D had seen this man, he probably hadn't realized the other man's position, as Krutz hadn't been wearing his badge then. His face—placid, yet imbued with strength and iron will—belonged to the man the Hunter had passed in the hall back at the hospital.

With a polite tip of the head to D, he said, "I heard about the situation from Bates. Though I need you to stick around for a while, I'd like you to keep out of trouble if you can. I'll put the word out, but every village has a couple of characters who like to beat up folks on the sly." And then, his magnificent facade broke a little as he added, "Of course, any cuss stupid enough to go after you won't live long enough to regret it."

Nan was watching D as if waiting for some favorable reply, but the Hunter was as emotionless as ever when he stated, "I have no business here in town. I'll thank you to be fast about confirming my identity."

"Already done," Sheriff Krutz said, as he watched D with a calm gaze. "You can't very well live on the Frontier without knowing the name of Vampire Hunter D. I've met folks you helped before. What do you suppose they had to say about you?"

The black shadow slipped between the sheriff and the girl without a sound. "I'll be in the hotel." That was all they heard him say through the batwing doors that swayed closed behind him.

"Wait," the sheriff said, his gnarled fingers catching hold of Nan's shoulder as she was about to go after the Hunter.

"But I have to talk to him. It's about my dreams."

"You think talking's gonna solve all this?"

Nan suddenly let her shoulders drop. Her obsessive gaze stayed trained on what lay beyond the door. The sunlight swayed languidly. It was afternoon light.

"You keep away from him, understand me?" Nan heard the sheriff say, though he sounded miles away. "That's one dangerous man. Getting close to him won't bring you nothing but misery . . . Particularly if you're a woman."

"You said you'd met people he'd helped, didn't you?" Nan said absentmindedly. "What did they have to say about him?"

The sheriff shook his head. It was ominously slow as it moved from side to side. "Not a thing. They'd all just keep quiet and stare out the door or down the road. That must've been the way he'd gone when he left. And it'll be the same when he leaves our village, too."

"When he leaves here . . . " Nan's eyes were dyed the same color as the sunlight.

The sheriff pondered the next thing she said for quite a while after that, but in the end he still didn't understand what she meant.

"Before he could leave, he had to come," Nan said. "Had to come here, to this village."

When the Dream Comes

CHAPTER 2

I

Leaving his cyborg horse at the hotel stable for inspection and repairs, the first thing D did when he got back to his room was draw the curtains. As a thin darkness claimed the room, the languor slowly wicked away from his body. Only those of Noble blood ever experienced such things. However, even a dhampir who'd inherited the better part of their Noble parent's strength and their human parent's tolerance for sunlight would be short of breath after half a day spent walking under a cloudy sky, and would need several hours in pitch darkness to relieve them of the fatigue that would accumulate in their flesh. After spending three hours out in the blazing sun, they'd need to sleep nearly half a day to recover. D, on the other hand, was no ordinary dhampir.

Descending as they did from the vampiric Nobility, all dhampirs took only what nutrients they needed to live rather than subsisting on solid food as humans did. Dropping a pair of dried blood plasma capsules into his palm from a case he kept in his saddlebags, D quickly swallowed them.

If some uninformed child had been there by his side, the Hunter's actions would've thrown the youngster into convulsions. Dried blood plasma was extremely hard to come by unless one went to questionable doctors who skirted the law or bought it on the black market. Purchasing of a jar of a thousand capsules would allow a dhampir to go a year without food. Given D's constitution, those two capsules would sustain him for at least a week, and possibly as long as two.

Settling into the room, D removed his longsword. Just as he was about to take his coat off, there was a knock at the door.

"Come in." Low as it was, the Hunter's voice traveled well. It had a chilling ring that would've brought the person in even if they'd knocked on the wrong door by mistake.

The door opened at once, and the hotel manager appeared with his gleaming bald pate. Staring down at the wooden platter he had in his left hand and the thick wad of bills resting on it, the man quickly turned his steady gaze in D's direction. "I finally managed to get your change," he said. "You know, it's been a good long time since anyone in town's seen a ten thousand dala bill. Had to go down to the saloon and borrow the difference."

Even after D had taken his change, the manager showed no sign of leaving.

"Sure does come as a shock, though," the bald man continued. "A dream is one thing, but I never thought I'd see a man with such good looks in the real world. What I wouldn't give to have even one hair like that on my head."

"Why are you letting me stay here?" D asked dispassionately, his left hand resting on the longsword.

Seeming a bit startled, the manager replied, "Why? Because you want to stay, I suppose. I'm running a business here. Oh, you mean because you're a dhampir? Put your mind at ease, friend. The owner of this establishment isn't as narrow-minded as all that."

Underlying their conversation was the fact that a dhampir who wasn't traveling with their employer wouldn't ordinarily be permitted to stay at a hotel unaccompanied. The reason really went without saying. In order to let a dhampir sleep under the same roof as ordinary people, a hotel needed a reasonable guarantee of reparations in the event that the dhampir started killing people in a blood craze.

This was why the people who hired the half-breeds were usually among the wealthiest individuals on the Frontier. While dhampirs disposed of the Nobility, only the very rich could afford to pay out the ensuing damages. In light of that, the actions of the hotel manager were so unusual that it was difficult to reduce them to human tolerance or generosity—even in a village where humans and Nobility had coexisted.

"And it seems you also put that Clements in his place, am I right?" the manager said, a smile beaming from his face. "That jerk acts all high and mighty just because he has some land. We've got ourselves a fine sheriff here, so he can't get too far out of line, but I've still had about all I can take of that bastard. Why, old Jatko said he'd never seen such a fine display of skill in all his years. He was a good ways past excited—almost in a trance." Perhaps noticing at that point that he'd been letting his mouth run, the manager held his tongue, coughed nervously, and made a show of fiddling with his bow tie with his thin fingers. "But please, watch out for yourself. For someone prone to flying off the handle like he is, you couldn't find a more vindictive bastard, either. He won't just let this sit. The sheriff's busy with his own work and can't be worrying about the town every minute of the day, so Clements might get away with something like throwing a bomb into your room here."

"I'll be careful."

"Please do. Well, I'll be off now. If you need anything, kindly press the buzzer."

Once the manager had gone, D stripped off his coat and took a seat on the sofa. There were a number of things he had to consider. The fact that everyone in the village dreamt of him could be attributed to the incredible power of the young lady who summoned him. It was a fairly common occurrence for those with certain mental powers to have an effect on people around them, so it wouldn't be that strange for the girl to draw others into her dream. Still, for what purpose had the girl called D there? What did she get out of the dance in the blue light? And another thing—the thug who'd attacked

D had been shot with a steel arrow that should've existed only in dreams. Was that supposed to mean the same man who'd shot D in his dream the night before didn't want the Hunter dead? No, his incredible shot in that dream had been charged with murderous intent. Then why had he helped D later? Or was it just a coincidence? There was only one way for him to shed some light on these matters.

D lay back against the sofa and closed his eyes. Dhampir or not, he still needed sleep. As fighting at night was unavoidable to curb the night-prowling Nobility, the daylight hours were naturally the time to rest. The superhuman biorhythms of the Nobility had their nadir at high noon, but were depressed for a good two hours both before and after that. Veteran Hunters usually arranged to dispatch their prey during that time frame, and if all went well they would ordinarily sleep after that until night fell. If they botched their assignment, the complete advantage they had over their foes would last only until the sun sank and the afterglow was gone. After that, they could either fight a battle that was already a foregone conclusion or hole up somewhere and wait for dawn. Either way, a Hunter didn't have any time to rest. That was why only the most outstanding individuals—only those who could survive under the most extreme conditions—were fit to be called Vampire Hunters.

At present, it was coming up on one o'clock Afternoon, the most suitable time for a dhampir to sleep. What would D dream about? What worlds awaited him, and who dwelt there? The calm breaths of slumber that soon trickled from the Hunter were far beyond the range of human hearing, and the room alone was privy to them.

†

Fog flowed around his ankles. The grove of trees that surrounded D had become as thin and flat as a paper silhouette. There was just enough breeze to carry the vapor. Every time he took a step, the fog was brushed out of his way. Suddenly D was greeted by an iron gate, which he recognized as that of the mansion.

He heard voices alive with laughter, plaintive dance music played by an orchestra, the chime of crystal-clear glasses meeting in midair, jokes rich with humor. He saw amber liquid being poured, shadowy forms of men and women meandering in the gardens. It seemed the party was taking place this evening as well. The question that remained was whether D was invited?

Slipping through the gates, D headed down a path through the elaborately landscaped gardens. He was just stepping onto the magnificent mansion's veranda when all the noise receded like the tide, leaving the Hunter surrounded by nothing but the embrace of the blue light. The slight sound at his feet as he walked was from a carpet of fallen leaves, now yellowed and tattered. It was not clear whether the countless cracks lacing the mansion walls caught D's attention or not as he entered the building.

Standing inside the mansion, a thin shadow flickered beyond the still blue light. It was Sybille.

Without a word, the young lady in the white dress and the Hunter in black faced each other. Distance no longer existed. At the same time, the few yards between them were infinite.

"What business do you have with me?" The blue light flickered before D's lips like an illusion as he spoke.

There was no answer. And yet, that somehow seemed appropriate for this girl. Sybille gently pushed a single lock of hair that had strayed across her brow back into place. A mysterious glimmer resided in her eyes—one that could be taken both as pleasure and as pain. Perhaps both were one and the same hue?

D turned his back and started to walk away. Seeing Sybille directly ahead of him again, he stopped in his tracks. Apparently, the door was behind him now. "So, you invite me here, but won't answer me or let me leave?" D muttered. "I can't stay around here forever. You may not wake from this dream, but I—"

Sybille nodded. "I know." Her voice seemed somehow feathery. "I simply had to have you come here. Please—you must help me."

"What can I do?"

Sybille fell silent.

"Then I suppose I can't do anything for you. I'm a Vampire Hunter. There's only one kind of job I perform." Once again, D turned sharply. The door was straight ahead of him and he began walking toward it, scattering blue light all around him.

"Please, wait."

Sybille's words halted his steps, but D didn't turn around.

"I know you're a Hunter. In which case, there's only one thing you could do for me. Put an end to him."

She hadn't said to kill him, she said *put an end to him*. This young lady knew her own fate and what the one who'd consigned her to it truly was. There was only one person she could mean by *him*.

"This is a dream world. I don't know if I can even find him, or if beating him here will put an end to him. And then—"

"And then—?" Sybille repeated after D, swallowing hard.

"What was it he wanted from you?" He stopped himself, asking the question not as a continuation of what he'd just been saying.

During the brief silence that followed, Sybille's expression stiffened. "You . . . you know him, don't you?" she stammered.

"Answer me. What was he after when he bit you?"

"Stop it!" Sybille cried, her whole body quaking. "Don't ask me such a horrid question."

"That's how this all started. That's why you called me here. I have no problem with doing away with him, but first you must answer me."

Sybille said nothing. Tears spilled from her eyes, but as she gazed at D, there wasn't a trace of hatred or resentment in them.

The black Hunter loomed with frosty indifference in the blue light. "Answer me," he repeated. Was this D's dream, or the world that Sybille controlled?

At the ice-cold query, the young lady's throat moved imperceptibly. "He wanted . . . the whole world to . . ."

An instant later, D unexpectedly faded away.

Sybille couldn't say another word. She grew as rigid as a stone statue, leaving only shimmering blue light at the end of her outstretched hand.

"He wanted . . . the whole world to . . ."

†

D awoke.

The opening of his eyes was nearly simultaneous with the twist of his body. There was the sound of shattering windowpanes and a black cylinder rolled to the center of the room, but only after D had leapt to one side. Most likely, it'd been propelled there by a grenade launcher mounted on a rifle.

The ceiling, walls, and floor all bulged out at once. The explosive energy from the special gunpowder packed in the cylinder ripped through what resistance the room offered in a thousandth of a second, and material from the hotel flew out of the building.

Several minutes later, the manager, fire extinguisher in hand, raced into a room that bore no resemblance to its former state. "What?!" he coughed, although his choice of words was a bit tame for the horrible spectacle that froze him in his tracks.

The ceiling and walls had been blown away so that beyond their shattered remains the fair afternoon sky could be seen. Somehow, the figure garbed in black stood aloof amidst the rubble. The manager surveyed the scene with utter amazement. There wasn't a single flame anywhere. Wisps of smoke rose from the few scraps of the curtains that remained, but the smoke was quite thin for a weapon that was supposed to produce a thick cloud of it, and the air was just as clear here as it was outside. It was almost as if something had swallowed it all.

"Damnation! What in the world happened here?!" the wide-eyed manager asked the Hunter. But he quickly added, "Oh, you don't have to say a word. I can see that someone lobbed a bomb in here.

What I want to know is what happened after that. Like, what happened to all the smoke and flames?"

"It seems retribution was swift." D glanced down at the wispy purple smoke coming from his long coat. No one would've thought its thin fabric could've protected him from the blast and flying fragments. "Thanks for the hospitality," D said as he held several gold coins out in front of the manager's face.

"I'm terribly sorry about this. We'd truly love to have you stay here, but this is likely to happen every night." And scratching his pate nervously, the manager took just a single coin, saying, "This will suffice."

"Go on and take the lot of them," the extended left hand said.

The manager gasped. Thinking he had just heard the words come from the Hunter's limb itself, his eyes fell reflexively, but by that time D's left hand had already dropped the remaining coins into the chest pocket of the bald man's shirt and settled back at his side.

"I can't believe the nerve of them, pulling something like this," the manager snarled. "Must be Clements's bunch. But this time he's bitten off more than he can chew. After all, you're a Vampire Hunter. You'll teach him a thing or two, won't you?"

Not saying a word, D walked over to the devastated door.

"Wh . . . where will you go, sir?"

"There's a windmill out by the hospital." Then, saying nothing more, the figure in black headed down the stairs.

II

As the sun sank, there was the sound of footsteps on dead leaves moving through the forest. It was Nan. The last few days seemed to be the worst for falling leaves, and every ten feet or so she had to bring her hand up to brush off bits of foliage that'd lodged in her hair. A nasty cold that'd been making the rounds the last couple of days put all the teachers out of commission and cancelled school as a result, so Nan's parents didn't object to her just hanging around.

But they most certainly wouldn't approve of her paying a call to the Vampire Hunter. Going there was a bit of an adventure for Nan.

For all intents and purposes, this visit was to talk about her own dreams and Sybille at greater length, and to resolve some of the mystery surrounding D. But while she had these thoughts in mind, her heart of hearts beat feverishly on account of what could only be described as the young Hunter's dazzling beauty. Nan had dreamt of him three days before the rest of the town. And from the first time she'd laid eyes on him, his solitary figure had been chiseled into her bosom with all the detail of the finest engraving. Gorgeous was the only way to describe the man. Nan was only eighteen years old, after all. And who could laugh at something that made a young lady's heart beat fast?

The windmill tower was suddenly visible in the golden glow of evening. The four massive blades cast a deep black cross of a shadow on the ground. Treading across a lawn that still retained some of its green, Nan headed for the living quarters that stood to the left of the tower. With its roof on the point of collapse, the rusted hub of the windmill blades and the walls with boards that looked like they'd fall off if someone breathed on them too hard, the structure was terribly dilapidated. A decade earlier, it had the most powerful generator in the area and was the village's main energy source before it was abandoned. All things considered, the village was lucky that monsters hadn't made it their home.

The door to the living quarters was open. A foul, musty stench assailed Nan's nostrils, and she used one hand to cover her nose and mouth. There were bedrooms to either side of the hall that ran straight from the entrance way. By all accounts, eight people had worked here around the clock. But D wasn't in any of those rooms.

Taking the semi-cylindrical passageway that connected the living quarters to the windmill, Nan entered the tower, where a thin darkness had congealed. A huge conical space greeted the girl. The distance from the ground to the uppermost reaches of the tower was easily fifty feet, and was split into three tiers. The first floor was intended for the power-generating facilities, but anything serviceable had been hauled off to the nuclear fusion power plant three miles away. All that remained now were a few pieces of machinery red with rust. That other power plant was out of service now, too.

The force of the gigantic rotating shaft and the rollers that relayed the blades' revolutions to the energy transformers would've been enough to inspire something akin to dread. The sunlight glittering off the shattered windowpanes was beginning to take a bluish tint. Cables that ran up to the ceiling hung like vines, and as Nan took a few steps forward in her search for D, her shoulder brushed against one, causing her heart to stop for a moment. If the generators had been operating as they used to, she would've been given a lethal jolt at best, or more likely burnt to a cinder. Slowly exhaling, Nan started walking again. Along the way, part of the floor she stepped on gave way and her right foot sank up to the ankle, leaving her ready to scream.

"I hate this place," Nan fumed quietly as she pulled her foot out. Just as she did so, something black cut across the circle of light ahead of her. It was the doorway to a passageway that ran around the hut. "D?" she cried out in a tone unavoidably tinged with reliance, but the shadowy figure didn't show even a moment's hesitation as it disappeared down the passageway.

Anxiety enveloped Nan. *Clements's bunch might be here*, she thought. She started running for all she was worth. The floor groaned, and dust flew up in a dingy curtain on her surroundings. She went out into the corridor, but the shadowy figure wasn't there. It had simply vanished, without the sound of footsteps or any sign it'd passed this way. Running to the stairs, Nan charged up the creaking wooden steps as fast as she could. The door to the second tier was right at the top of the stairs. Nan leapt through it—then stopped suddenly so that only her hair and the beads of sweat on her body still surged forward.

In the blue darkness stood a figure in black raiment. He seemed like he'd been standing there for ages. D.

Nan wanted to call out to him, but couldn't say a word. She'd already felt the ghastly aura emanating from his being. It was a call to battle.

The second tier was where adjustments were made to the windmill. A few dozen gears, both large and small, and a series of large energy rods ran across the room. The energy rods connected to the revolving shaft that went through the ceiling and ran all the way down to the floor, and they dispersed the excess energy generated by the wildly spinning shaft. There were hundreds of gears ranging in diameter from ten feet down to eight inches or so, and to keep them from interfering with human activity they were set on rods at least ten feet overhead or higher. Given the utterly chaotic way they were meshed horizontally, vertically, and diagonally, they would've been a disturbing sight to see back when they were in action.

While Nan was frozen in place, her eyes gazed at the thin darkness around D. There was nothing else there. All that was behind him was a worn-out locker with a toolbox beside it. Her vision grew blurry and she felt a sharp pain in her eye as a bead of sweat dripped into it.

Just as she shut her lids reflexively, a hard clang startled her out of her black field of view. Snapping her eyes open again with single-mindedness, Nan dimly viewed the collection of gears and rods, realizing that they were turning now. But how? At the same instant that she had a memory that the windmill controls had locked in place a decade earlier, D's shadowy figure began to move. The stub of the longsword over his shoulder grew to twice its previous size. Just as Nan realized the Hunter was drawing his blade, she felt the familiar sting that always accompanied a drop of sweat in her eye and her vision again blurred.

In darkness, Nan could only hear the sounds. A shudder ran through her soul. That noise just couldn't be right. It was definitely the creaking of gears, but even to a girl who knew nothing about technical things, it was clear from the sound that there was something wrong with the way they were running now. High and low, to her left and to her right, over her and under her. And along with the gears, there were indications the rods were moving differently, and the windmill's shaft spun as well. If Nan hadn't been troubled by her eyes, perhaps she would've noticed they were all moving in the opposite direction from normal. The windmill wasn't driving them. Instead, the rods and gears were turning the enormous upright shaft. And, although there was no way Nan could see them, the windmill blades remained wrapped in twilight, without the slightest tremor.

The question was, had D noticed that all this activity was trying to supply energy to something else?

There was the sound of hinges snapping, and the door to the locker fell to the floor. When a black shadow within the locker stood up, D turned around, and at the very same instant Nan was freed from the paralyzing grip. Rubbing her eyes desperately, the girl tried to catch a glimpse of the battle taking place right in front of her. Perhaps she was lucky to at least see D's leap the instant her eyelids opened. A cry of astonishment spilled from her mouth.

The shadow was leaping as well. The two figures passed in midair, and the second the beautiful sound of their meeting blades reverberated, the strangest sensation took hold of Nan.

Black garb swishing out around him, D landed right in front of Nan. But D then leapt away from that spot, turning about-face in midair.

Nan thought her eyes were going to explode into flames of astonishment. The person opposite them—he was D, too, wasn't he? There were two of him?! Not only that, but the pose they both took now, with right hands holding longswords at the ready and left hands extended before their respective chests, were the same as their movements in midair—virtually identical!

Nan felt like there was a huge invisible mirror stretched between the two Vampire Hunters. Perhaps it was only natural that they both kicked off the ground at the same time. The movements of the two Ds were perfectly symmetrical—slashing down over their right shoulders for the left side of their opponent's neck, their blades then flashed to the side, spitting blue sparks as they met. Their weapons touching but not locking together, the two Ds once again switched positions and landed. While Nan was aware of the fact that the D who landed in front of her again was the *original*, the two of them looked so similar her mouth simply hung open. This eerie battle, where the true tussled with the false, would tolerate no interruption by a human voice.

But if both of them were D, just how would the real one defeat the false? The glittering sword reflected in an unseen mirror would doubtless cut both of them clear to bone.

Step by step, the first D advanced. His opponent followed suit. Though it may have been her imagination, Nan thought she caught a cruel smile on the other D's face. It was only a second later that the same face donned a perplexed expression. Without breaking his stance, D had turned his back to him. His foe didn't move. The thread linking the false to the true had suddenly been severed.

"Hey, what's wrong?" a voice spat mockingly. "Why don't you try getting some help from the other me?" the voice spoke to the other D—the one frozen behind the Hunter's back.

Nan got the impression that the words had spilled from the end of D's left hand, and no sooner had her eyes snapped wide with shock than the other D kicked off the ground without a sound. His blade ripped through the air, snarling like the breaking surf.

Making no attempt to parry that slash, the black darkness of D's coat spread its wings before the attacker. A blow that should've severed bone merely ripped the cloth on the Hunter's sleeve, and was no match for the blade that shot up from below and ran deep into the torso of the shaken and despairing attacker.

D dodged the body as it dropped in a bloody mist, and backed away. Though the corpse was the very image of him, it didn't seem to stir any deep emotion in the young man. As he put his sword away and turned to Nan, his face was completely devoid of sentiment.

"D, what in the world—" Nan finally managed to say, but the Hunter cut her short.

"Why did you come here?"

Cold was the only way to describe his question. Her eyes were trained on the shafts above her. All movement had stopped. "I thought I'd talk to you . . . about my dreams, since we never got to finish our conversation back in the bar." Nan's voice caught in her throat. Though she was a child of the Frontier, she'd never seen someone die up close like that before.

"The sun will be setting soon. You'd better go home."

D's curt dismissal finally drew a recognizable human emotion out of Nan's heart. Anger.

"You're awful. After I came all the way here—" she began to say, but no further words came from her mouth. Just what did she mean to this Hunter? Though she was fully aware it wasn't much, she certainly didn't want to be reminded of that fact.

"The night doesn't belong to mankind yet," D said quietly, as if the deadly encounter moments earlier had been merely a dream.

"That's not a problem in our village. I think . . . I can't say for sure, but it really should be safe. In the century since the last of our Nobility disappeared, no one's ever fallen victim at night."

"Maybe tonight someone will."

Nan was dumbstruck. Her eyes were hot and they stung, though this time not from sweat. "I'm going home," she said, trying to sound self-assured, even as she had little confidence it'd come out that way. Her voice quavered with anger. *Just turn and walk away and that'll do it*, she thought. She'd dreamt of him two nights more than the rest of the town. What was that supposed to mean? Didn't that count for anything with this young man?

Nan raised her face. Almost glaring, she said to D, "I have to finish telling you what I didn't get a chance to say back in the bar. You want to know why I'm concerned about Sybille? Because I used to be in the hospital room next to hers." And having said it all in a single breath, she turned herself around and walked away.

Going out into the corridor, Nan was on her way down the stairs when the tears spilled out. She tried to think about something else. Kane, a childhood friend who lived just a few houses from there, came to mind quickly enough. Though she could picture his face, no particular emotion was attached to his memory.

Outside was a land of darkness. At a loss for words, Nan came to a standstill and hugged her own shoulders. The autumn night had been lying in wait for her, armed with a terrible chill. It was a coldness that pierced her to the very bone, and she couldn't recall another like it. Without knowing why, Nan looked up to the heavens. Stars glittered in the night sky, each as sharp as the point of an awl. The wind whisked across a grove in a scene that hadn't changed at all since she was a child. It greeted her the same way now. *It'll be hard-cider season soon*, Nan thought hazily. But before she knew it, the chill was gone and she was left all alone.

III

Old Mrs. Sheldon's house was at the west end of the orchards. All of the evergreen grass bowed in unison with the breeze, changing the shape of the ground and hills every time they bent. The dilapidated old house with a weathervane on its red roof looked like the perfect place for a one-hundred-and-twenty-year-old crone to pass her lonely later years.

Mrs. Sheldon was sitting in a rocking chair on her front porch. Years must've passed since the last time anybody came to see her. Aside from the fact that her last callers had been schoolchildren, the old woman couldn't recall anything about that visit. From time to time the face of a gray-haired old man flitted through her mind, but she didn't understand why it made her feel strangely nostalgic. The fact that he was the man whose gravestone stood on the top of the little hill out back was something she'd long since forgotten. Thanks to a cyborg-conversion procedure she'd undergone more than a century earlier, all she needed now was to have her nutrient-enriched blood changed once every thirty years. Perhaps that was the reason people from town rarely called on her. That morning, as the old woman rocked back and forth for the two thousandth some-odd time, she saw someone for the first time in who-knew-how-many days.

Dismounting, D headed over to the old woman sitting in her antiquated but sturdy-looking rocking chair. "Mrs. Sheldon?" he asked.

"That's me. And you are?" the woman replied without a second's delay, watching D's face for a while before she smiled at him. "I've lost my touch. Back in the old days, I used to catch everyone off-guard when I shot back an answer real quick like that, whereas now they all take me for some sleepy old dotard who don't know which way is up no more."

"I came out here to ask you about something. They call me D."

"A name like that seems to say you come from somewhere else, and you'll be moving on soon. Of course, before you turn to leave, I reckon a lot of folks will be dying or crying. Step inside." Slowly getting up out of her seat, the old woman opened the door before her.

The interior was well-kept. Motes of dust dancing up in the morning light glittered like flecks of gold.

"Have a seat over there," the old woman said, indicating a chair as she headed for the kitchen. "I'll fix us some tea."

"Thank you."

The old woman disappeared, letting the door bang shut on its own, but soon enough she returned with a pair of steaming cups on a tray. "I got this from a merchant from the Capital fifty years ago. You know, I'd never use it for any of the folks from town. It's just for special visitors from far away."

"How do you know I've come far?" D asked, looking not at the cup her light brown and thoroughly creased hand had set in front of him, but at a face that seemed wrought entirely with wrinkles.

"You figure any man with the look you've got in your eye could stay put in just one village?" Pounding the small of her back a few times, the old woman settled into a chair. "You see, human beings pull around a whole heap of chains that the eye can't see. The other end of 'em is set in the earth, so folks can walk a mile or two, but they just can't go no further than that. Sometimes the chains are named 'home' or 'belongings,' and sometimes we call 'em 'sweetheart' or 'memories.' When we're young, we try to pull 'em out of the ground, but ten or twenty years go by and those chains just get thicker, and you've got more of 'em than ever. And when that happens, all you can do is set yourself down wherever seems proper. Once you do that, those chains start looking like solid gold to the human eye. What most people don't know is that it's just a thin layer of gold plating. See, the good Lord made it so humans can't see 'em for what they really are. You follow what I'm saying? What it comes down to is, people who aren't like that—whose eyes aren't clouded, and don't have a single chain on 'em —they must be made by someone other than God. Now, I wonder who that could be?" And with that she cast an all-knowing gaze directly at D and set her cup down on the table. "I'm sure you're in a hurry, so I thank you for indulging me in a cup of tea and listening to the ramblings of a foolish old woman. You'd probably cut anyone else's head off for saying what I did, so I reckon I have bragging rights there."

"Actually, I'd like to hear about the days when humans and Nobility coexisted," D said when he finally opened his mouth. "Anything at all. If you'd be so kind as to tell me about that time."

The old woman squinted a bit and folded her hands on top of the table. After sitting like that for several seconds without moving, she said, "There's too much to tell. So much that it'd be the same as me not telling you a blessed thing. But the lot of 'em went somewhere far away back when I was just a wee toddler. No one knows whatever became of 'em all. And after that, there was only one time they ever came back—and that was thirty years ago. If something's going on here now, I suppose that's the cause. Looks like when you come right down to it, Nobles can't change what they are."

"A girl was bitten," D said. "She sleeps even now, never aging. And as she sleeps, she makes other people dream about me."

The old woman picked up her cup. When she tipped it to her mouth, the steam seemed to billow from her lips. Pulling the cup the tiniest bit away, she said, "Thirty years ago, that girl was found lying in the woods just north of the village. There was a pair of bite marks on her neck. Truth be known, they were supposed to banish her on the spot, but they didn't. It's still anybody's guess which course of action would've been better. And she'd never met you before, is that right?"

D nodded.

Gazing steadily at the Hunter's face, the old woman continued, "As good as you look, *I suppose she'd want to see you even if she couldn't.* But, you know . . ." And then the old woman caught herself.

D didn't say a word.

"If it was me," she continued, "and I'd met you a million times, I still wouldn't want to dream about you because in the end, I'd wind up crying—no two ways about it. I doubt you can find a woman on the Frontier who's not used to shedding tears, but it doesn't get any easier—it still hurts just as much every time we do it."

And yet, Sybille dreamt of him. A man she'd never met.

"What kind of man was the Noble who bit Sybille?"

This time, D's question brought results.

"There was someone who actually spotted him. Sybille's grandmother. She passed away twenty years ago, but she used to tell people every single day how she'd seen him while she was searching for Sybille. Why, she made me listen to it so much I practically needed me a set of earplugs. Yes, he was a giant of a man dressed in black." And there the old woman stopped. Her eyes held a mysterious spark, and the spark became twin beams of light that could have bored a hole through D's face. "As for his features . . . he looked too good to be of this world—like you, you know."

D brought the cup to his mouth. His eyes seemed be gazing at Old Mrs. Sheldon, watching something else, and not focused on anything all at the same time.

"Why did he have to bite Sybille?" the old woman asked, the light in her eyes growing more intense, flickering with a touch of madness. "Why did he have to go and make her dream? And what kind of dreams did he give her, anyway?"

Of course, there were no answers so D answered with another question, because, after all, that was the whole reason he'd come. "Who was closest to the girl?"

"Let me see . . . Ai-Ling."

"Where is she?"

"Her home's a farmhouse a little over a mile southwest of here. I wager she'll be around at this hour."

D stood up, prepared to leave.

"Wait—" the old woman said, and the Hunter stopped. "Have another cup of tea, won't you? I don't want to let my first chance at conversation in a long time run off so easily. For all I know, it may be another ten years before I get a chance to chat with anyone again. The children don't even come out here to catch the sticky bugs anymore. This may be a peaceful village, but I'm lonely."

D reluctantly took his seat again.

"Not only are you handsome, but you listen to people, too. Someday I'm sure you'll settle down somewhere. Find yourself a good wife." And leaving him with those words, the old woman went into the kitchen.

"A peaceful village, isn't it?" D muttered.

"That it is," a hoarse voice responded from his left hand as it rested on his knee.

"Is it a good village?"

"That I can't tell."

"We're in the same boat then," D said.

"Just because it's peaceful doesn't mean I'd call it good. The same can be said for villages that aren't so peaceful. There's nothing good in this world. Not in Nobles, or in humans—or in you, for that matter."

D turned his face to look out the window. The plains changed from minute to minute; each and every verdant leaf was charged with the vitality of morning, declaring that there was still more of the blazing season of fall to come. In contrast to the white light that surrounded him, D alone was a wintry shadow.

Accompanied by a faint aroma, the old woman returned. "Here you go!" she said, setting down his cup. In the middle of the cup of thin, amber fluid floated a single blue petal. The petal was like a tiny blue sea.

D brought the drink to his mouth with his left hand. Needless to say, he kept his right hand free to be ready for any sudden attacks. Though his left hand stopped, it didn't seem like an interruption to his fluid movements.

"What is it?" the old woman asked, smiling happily.

"Drink some," D said.

"Huh?"

"Taste yours. It smells different."

"Oh, that? You know, I went and changed the tea leaves. This is homemade, grown in my very own garden out back. The last pot was some cheap stuff I got off a merchant from the Capital." Winking at her guest, she drew the steaming liquid through her wrinkled lips. "There. Are you satisfied there's no poison in it now, my suspicious Hunter? You've gone and spoiled the mood. It's okay; you don't have to drink it if you don't want to."

D brought the cup to his mouth. The old woman watched with pleasure as his Adam's apple bobbed up and down. Setting the cup down, D got to his feet. He was headed for the door, but halfway there he turned around and asked, "Did you dream about me, too?"

The old woman nodded.

"And what did you think?"

The brief silence that followed may have been her wrestling with concerns about what it would be polite to say. "I can't speak for the rest of 'em," Mrs. Sheldon finally ventured, "but I thought you were dangerous."

"Dangerous?"

"In the dream, you seemed to say you were a dangerous man as you walked along. Even though you didn't actually come right out and say it, I could definitely tell."

That was probably the best way to describe him.

"Thanks for the tea," D said simply, and with that he left her home.

"Godspeed to you," the old woman called from the porch. "We'll meet again soon. Next time, you'll have to listen to one of the songs I wrote. It's a good one, since I made it back when I was young."

Saying nothing, D mounted his horse, gave a single kick of his heels to its sides, and was off.

When the house was hidden behind the hill, a hoarse voice snapped, "I can't believe how stupid you can be sometimes. Drinking that tea of all things! It was probably poison."

"You mean to say you don't know what was in it?"

"Well, I could make out the tea well enough, but there was some other unknown substance in it."

"You'll have to do better than that," D said as if the matter didn't involve him at all. "A dangerous man, am I?" he muttered.

"That's for sure, as far as anybody's concerned. But remember what the old lady said—she said the whole village felt the same thing."

What they felt was that he was clearly a dangerous man. Dangerous for *them*, that is.

The voice continued, "That would mean the folks in the village called you here even though they think you're a threat to them. It's possible they called you here to kill you. If that's the case, what that farmer did would stand to reason . . . But I don't think that's it. Despite what the old lady said, I'm not so sure every last person in town felt the same way. It's pretty clear they weren't hostile. After all, this is a peaceful village."

"A peaceful village, is it?" As he rode, the words D muttered sailed off on the wind and the scenery streamed by on either side.

To any bystander, this conversation would've been unparalleled in its weirdness.

"You were gonna leave town . . ." the hoarse voice continued indifferently. "On your way out, you were attacked, but your attacker was killed with an arrow from your dreams. *He* must've wanted to keep you alive. And as a result, you wound up staying here. It may very well be the farmer who attacked you was part of *his* plan, you know."

Then suddenly, the hoarse voice was gone. Without a single world, D kept gazing straight ahead. The young man didn't seem to be concerned about the uncanny ring of this voice that seemed to come from nowhere, nor did he seem the least bit worried about the subject of its discourse. Perhaps the weirdness that existed beyond the mortal realm was something the inhuman never even noticed.

†

Back at the house, Old Mrs. Sheldon watched her departing guest until both he and his mount had vanished behind the hill. Then, in a manner that was totally unbecoming for her age, she seductively winked in their direction, before stepping off the porch and heading around to her back yard.

Mrs. Sheldon's yard was a fenced-off plot of over a thousand square feet, where colors beyond numbering competed in a floral arena. Stopping at a certain patch of pretty flowers with the same blue petals that were floating in the tea, the old woman said to herself, "Oh, he's a dangerous man all right, but I wouldn't mind getting into danger with him. In some ways, I want that tea to work, but in other ways I suppose I don't. Lordy me, it's been a long time since I felt like a mixed-up schoolgirl." And then, casually glancing down at the blue flowers at her feet, she said, "Well, this is certainly where that tea was picked . . . but I wonder how long it's been growing here? *I've never seen it before.*"

And just as the old woman bent over to pick a bit more of it, she heard the strident sound of something whistling through the air right by her ear.

The Sheriff

CHAPTER 3

I

After D galloped over a mile in under five minutes, a vast ranch suddenly appeared. Out on the rich pasture there was a herd of meat beasts, several of whom were munching the grass. Seven feet long and easily in excess of fifteen hundred pounds each, the barrel-shaped beasts were covered with armor-like plates that could deflect lasers. Their snouts were reminiscent of power shovels with a pair of curved buckets, which were actually their upper and lower jaws loaded with massive molars. Yet, despite their daunting appearance, nothing tastier had ever graced a dinner table. Though the aesthetic sensibilities of the Nobility had given shape to many ghastly creatures for the sole purpose of terrifying humanity, these beasts were perhaps the greatest exception to that rule in that they also provided food. What's more, so long as the beast wasn't fatally wounded, the flesh that'd been carved from it would begin growing back twelve hours later, while the creature itself felt no pain at all and offered no resistance. It was said that with a pair of these treasured beasts, a family of five would never go hungry. Unfortunately, these meat beasts were extremely limited in number, and they rarely produced offspring. Usually, if someone found one, they'd have a creature that could fetch them enough money to buy one of the Nobility's flying machines, and that's usually what they did rather than keep them for food. By the look of it, there were at least thirty of them on the ranch, leading D to the conclusion that not only was this region peaceful, it was rich as well.

As D headed straight for the main house, scarlet streaks of fire occasionally skirted the periphery of his field of vision. The streaks were flames disgorged by the scarlet moles that were supposed to guard the place, although their numbers were less than a fiftieth of what an ordinary ranch would have. With so few of them, you could never hope to see the hundreds of fiery pillars that usually erupted from the earth to greet intruders on the surface or in the air.

A sensor set forty feet away from the main house was tripped, and before D's horse had stopped, a woman appeared from the front door carrying an old-fashioned Tommy gun with a drum magazine. D halted.

As the woman stared at his face, a faint red glow rose in her cheeks. "Um . . . Can I help you?" she asked in a voice that had a touch of good-mannered timidity to it. Her black hair was tied back in a light brown scarf and her face was that of a woman long past her prime, hard around the mouth and razor sharp through the eyes in a way that let the bitter precipitate of her life bleed through. And yet, there was something refined about her, the clear line of her nose and her gracefully thin eyebrows suggesting a life far removed from that of her faded cotton shirt and long skirt. In addition to the Tommy gun, she had a well-weathered knapsack slung on her back.

"Are you Ai-Ling?" the Hunter inquired.

"Yes."

D advanced on his horse.

"You . . . Stop right there. I can't let you come barging onto our land."

"Sorry, but this is urgent," D said from up on his horse. Dismounting by Ai-Ling's side, the Hunter said, "I'd like to ask you a few things about the girl sleeping in the hospital—Sybille. My name is—"

"D," Ai-Ling muttered as she slowly lowered the barrel of her weapon. "I can tell you what I know. But right now, I've got to feed the beasts . . ."

"I'll wait."

An expression flitted across the middle-aged woman's face that straddled a line between resignation and delight. Shouldering the Tommy gun, she slowly headed toward the fence. D walked right alongside her.

"What did you come here for?" Ai-Ling asked. Perhaps she, too, sensed that D was dangerous.

D didn't answer. As Ai-Ling opened the gate and walked out to the middle of the pasture, D leaned back against the fence and watched her. It was clear he didn't have the slightest intention of helping.

Tucking the Tommy gun under her right arm, Ai-Ling stripped off the knapsack about forty feet from D. Quickly opening it, she knocked it on its side. Glistening crystals of synthesized feed for the meat beasts spilled out, and shrill cries arose from all sides as the ground began to rumble. The fifteen-hundred-pound mountains of black came running in unison. The thirty of them had a total weight of over twenty tons, which made the earth tremble and even shook the fence as they stampeded toward her. D alone was unaffected, with not so much as a single hair stirring. It was almost as if the vibrations of the fence the young man was leaning against were absorbed by his black coat before they could reach him.

Ai-Ling stepped away from the tremendous beasts as they greedily consumed the food they loved, but soon she was lost again in a mad scramble of black armor that seemed sure to trample her to death. And yet, when her slender figure stepped out from between the massive, thrashing forms, she suddenly delivered a kick to the rump of the closest beast.

"Bad boy, Ben!" Ai-Ling scolded the creature. "You've already eaten more than your share, haven't you? Be a good little beast and give Pluto some room. Don't give me any trouble now."

Although fierce, the meat beasts were also highly intelligent, and if handled properly, could be tamed. Doing so, however, meant risking life and limb day after day. It was said to take as much patience as finding a single grain in a mountain of sand, and yet, it looked like this woman with the cultured upbringing had managed to do just that. The beast she'd kicked ambled aside, but the one called Pluto seemed to miss the point entirely and just continued to hang back. "Get a move on, Pluto. You've finally got an opening, so get in there and chow down." Seeing that the beast still wasn't responding, Ai-Ling shouted, "You big dope!" and kicked it in the rump. It didn't move.

Ai-Ling took a step back and folded her arms. Eyes filling with determination, she grabbed the Tommy gun by the stock and held it like a bat.

"Now there's something," D muttered.

The woman had just taken the gun and smacked a creature taller than she was right in the middle of its ass. Beads of sweat flying from her, she delivered five or six blows before the idiotic beast finally nosed its way into the opening and started scooping up feed with its power-shovel jaws. Once she was sure of that, Ai-Ling went over to D again. Although she was probably mentally and physically exhausted from what she'd just done, her gait was incredibly steady.

"Sorry to keep you waiting, but I have to check the thermostats in the chickener coop, too." Her breathing ragged, the woman had D's face reflected in her beads of sweat. Her body shook. "Would you like to come with me? Ordinarily you could wait in the house, but I can't very well have a man in my home while my husband's out."

"Out here is fine with me." As D said it, he took a place by Ai-Ling's side and they walked off toward the building that stood to their left. "Don't seem too suited to farm life," he said after they'd walked a short distance.

It took a few seconds for Ai-Ling to realize he was talking about her. Shooting a look of surprise at D's face, she asked, "You concerned on my account?" Her expression was almost a tearful smile.

"Farm work is tough, even for a man," D remarked. "So, why did you give the meat beasts names?"

"The work's not really all that hard," Ai-Ling answered in a cheery tone. "You keep at the same thing for thirty years, and you'll get used to any kind of labor. And I gave them names because it makes it easier to work with them."

Upon reaching the building, Ai-Ling opened the steel door. A nauseating stench billowed out—the stink of wild animals and their excrement. Ai-Ling turned her face away and coughed. "I just have to check the thermostats, but we can talk while I'm walking around. Ask away."

Her voice traveled back from the darkness. The sunlight peeking in through the doorway provided a modicum of illumination for the building's interior, where there were rows of massive chickeners—giant chicks standing up to six and a half feet tall. The way they simply stood there motionless behind the high-voltage lines strung along either side of the pathway, scrutinizing the pair with glinting blue eyes but not displaying any of the rambunctious behavior of normal chicks, was as unsettling a sight as any.

These giant chicks were a crucial food source out on the Frontier. There were only a few special species that could produce chickeners, and they had extremely sensitive constitutions; a temperature deviation of a few degrees from their usual conditions could quite easily spell death for them. In addition, there was a multitude of problems involving their feed and their vicious disposition, so a family of five would usually face tremendous hardship in raising just one of them. What was taking place in this filthy, dimly lit hut was nothing short of a miracle.

Pale sparks shot out in the distance as a chickener touched one of the high-voltage lines. Oddly enough, the chick didn't let out a single cry of pain.

"As I recall, chickeners love human bones. Are you able to get them?"

Ai-Ling shook her head at D's question. "Not too easy to come by in our village. So I buy them off the dead carrier."

A wide variety of merchants came to Frontier villages from the Capital or other commercial districts. The fur trader, the repair man, the parts dealer, the fruit seller, the ice man, the dressmaker, the weapons broker, the magician, the traveling picture show—some stank of blood while others were cheery, some were stained with grease while still others were dressed in the finest of clothes, but each and every one of them was an indispensable part of the Frontier. The dead carrier was another such merchant.

Living as they did in such a brutal environment, people didn't always view the dead with reverence. Organs had their use in transplants, and human hair could be treated with a special animal fat to make communication lines that could carry a signal any distance. Even bones had an important role to play in fertilizer, thanks to their high calcium content. In addition, a guitar made from a carved pelvic bone and hollowed-out vertebrae, and strung with tough intestinal material by a veteran tuner, would make absolutely exquisite music. While the bodies of relatives were handled differently, those who died out on the road might receive a perfunctory memorial service, after which a coffin bearing only their meager possessions would be carried off to the communal cemetery while arrangements were made to bring the cadaver out to a "butcher" on the edge of town for dissection.

When they still didn't have enough corpses, dead carriers would sometimes supply bodies they'd preserved with their own flash-freezing equipment, while other times they would prowl around villages and towns like ghouls in search of fresh cadavers. Corpses were often sold as they were when demand called for it; otherwise, certain parts were marketed in their raw state, or were processed and then sold.

Ai-Ling checked the antiquated temperature equipment at each pen, which each held a trio of colossal, wily eyed chicks. When she got to the second pen's thermostat, she paused and turned around to face D. "You still haven't asked me anything. Afraid of distracting me? Even my husband isn't that considerate."

Saying nothing, D watched the chicks.

Smiling sadly, Ai-Ling reached for the machine. Suddenly, one of the chicks craned its neck, flames shot from the high-voltage line, and Ai-Ling pulled her hand back, a scream trailing out after her. The chick's sharp beak had gouged the flesh on the back of her hand. Instinctively, she pressed the wound with her other hand, but blood seeped out around it anyway. D's elegant white fingers touched the wrist of her topmost hand. Ai-Ling was speechless. She could only watch D's face raptly as he moved the hand she was using to keep pressure on the wound and looked down at her injury.

"It's nothing serious," the Hunter told her. "Put a compress of vajna leaves on it, and before the day is out—"

Suddenly, Ai-Ling jerked her hand away roughly. In the feeble darkness, it wasn't clear if D noticed how flushed her face was all the way to her ears. "I'm sorry," she mumbled softly. "It's just, it's been a long time since a man took my hand."

"Does that happen a lot with the chicks?" D asked as he watched the chick. Blue flames rose from its downy white chest—the work of the high-voltage lines. "And not a peep out of it—that's very polite of it."

"Every once in a while they get me," Ai-Ling said as she pressed a handkerchief to the wound. In a matter of seconds, vermilion laid claim to the white cloth. Seeming uneasy as she looked up at the rapacious bird, she continued. "But it sure caught me off-guard today. You know, I can usually tell whenever they're in that mood."

"We should go."

"Still got some to do yet," Ai-Ling said with a smile before moving toward another pen. Stopping in front of the equipment, she hesitated a bit before reaching out her hand. The upper body of the nearest chick shook a bit, and then it froze. D was reflected in its glassy eyes. It seemed as if the creature had suddenly developed an appreciation of beauty, but actually the remorseless eyes of the vicious bird were filled with a shade of horror that was beyond description. D's eyes were tinged a pale shade of red. Perhaps Ai-Ling also sensed something, because she looked up at the young Hunter with a pallid countenance, and then quickly went back to work. After that, the inspections were finished without further incident.

The sunlight was waiting to greet the two of them again. Once outside, Ai-Ling locked the door and tipped her head appreciatively to D. "Thanks for the help. Uh, try not to look at it so much. I mean, it's not a very pretty hand."

She wasn't talking about the hand she'd injured. The hand she covered it with had countless scars on the back, and the skin had hardened in a condition unique to toxic bites so that it was now like the scaly hide of a fire dragon. Perhaps D had noticed from the moment they'd met that she'd been trying to keep it hidden.

"What kind of girl was Sybille?" the Hunter asked, his voice cold and devoid of emotion.

Ai-Ling's expression grew stiff, remembering again why D was there. "Oh, she was a romantic," she replied flatly. "And she was so kind. What more could she possibly need? I'm sure she must be having some really nice dreams. If she's not, there can't be a God."

"What kind of dream would be a good dream?"

Thinking a bit, Ai-Ling turned her gaze to the depths of the blue sky. She had a faraway look in her eyes, like something important was up there. "The kind of story that traveling writers come up with for the young girls."

D remained silent.

Ai-Ling licked her faintly colored lips, and her eyes narrowed ever so slightly. "A dream," she began, "where people in love hold hands when they walk down the street. Where the library has all the books you ever wanted to read. A dream where no one threatens anyone else, and everyone thinks about other people and does things for them without ever being asked. Where new fashions arrive from the Capital every week. A dream where the pharmacist has all the medicine you need to soothe your child's fever. Where you can make ends meet without working like a dog. A dream where everyone goes down to the pond on a moonlit night to catch fireflies. And a dream . . ."

The rest of the final sentence was spoken by another voice.

". . . where humans and Nobility walk down the street side by side?"

Dazed, Ai-Ling stared at her mysterious visitor. "Are you some kind of sorcerer?" she asked.

"The Noble who bit Sybille chose her specifically."

Ai-Ling's eyes were glazed with perplexity. "What do you mean by that? Why was Sybille chosen?"

"An ancient mansion and blue light, white evening gowns and black formal wear, a cotillion—does that remind you of anything?"

Something sparkly pooled in Ai-Ling's eye. "And here I thought we'd just dreamt about you . . . but you had Sybille's dream, too, didn't you?" A tear rolled down her cheek. "That was what she wished for—to wear a white gown and dance the night away with a man in a tuxedo in the hall of some old mansion. The night wrapped in a blue light."

"She got her wish."

"The night in her dream never ends, does it?" Ai-Ling asked.

"I don't know."

"Do you think Sybille is happy?"

D had no response.

Ai-Ling pushed back the hair dangling before her brow. "Don't get me wrong, I'm satisfied with the life I have now. I really can't complain. We manage to get by, and I can feel how real the earth is beneath my feet. I may not have lovely dreams like Sybille does, though . . ."

"They may be lovely dreams, but that doesn't mean they're *good* dreams." D lightly touched his hand to the brim of his hat. That was his way of saying goodbye.

Ai-Ling stood completely still, wanting to say something else; she watched the black expanse of his back as he quietly walked away. The silhouette of her visitor made it quite clear it was all over. His outline was a steadfast refusal.

Not entirely convinced she was ready to say anything, yet realizing something important was on the tip of her tongue, Ai-Ling took a few steps forward. Before she reached him, D stopped and turned. It wasn't Ai-Ling that he faced, but rather the chickener coop. As her own dark eyes followed his gaze, the steel door burst outward and fell to the ground, pieces of its frame flinging everywhere. The frantic white creatures inside came into view and jostled out into the sunlight in a wild tangle of downy feathers.

II

The silence was shattered by a shrill cry every bit as horrifying as the roar of a gray bear before it attacks its prey. Seeing the blue light and purple smoke that rose from the white breast of each creature, Ai-Ling shuddered. "But that's just . . ." she stammered. "How on earth did they get by the high-voltage lines?"

"Go back to the main house. They're probably after me," a voice like bronze whispered in her ear, realizing just then that the Hunter was at her side.

"But—"

"Just go." His order was even gentler than his ordinary speech.

Without waiting to see that Ai-Ling made it back to the house, D turned the other way and sprinted into action. His coat fluttered out in the wind like a pair of huge black wings. Perhaps the reason he moved forward was because he'd sensed that the speed of Ai-Ling's retreat was far slower than that of the colossal birds as they charged toward her. Chicks or not, each of them was over six-and-a-half feet tall, and a blow from the beak or talons of one of these foul-tempered beasts was enough to punch a hole in titanium . . . to say nothing of what they could do to flesh.

When they had closed within ten feet of the Hunter, one of the death-dealers in downy white bounded up toward the heavens. Built to carry the creature's seven-hundred-pound frame, the chickener's legs had enough spring to leap over fifteen feet in the air, even from a complete standstill. With all of its talons spread as wide as they could go, the bird started to drop from the air right at the point where it would intercept D.

Perhaps the eyes of the bird caught the silvery path of D's weapon as it sliced off both the attacker's legs in midair. As D plowed straight into the flock of screeching chickeners, more black beaks than could be counted came down at his head. The human skull would be soft as a grape to them, but the parabolic arc of the vicious bird beaks was rewarded not with a taste of D, but with the glittering slashes of his sword. Bright blood scattered in the sunlight.

Less than two seconds later, over a dozen chicks lay on the ground. Fresh blood stained the green grass. Gory blade in one hand, D stood motionless. Though had he slashed away with his sword in the middle of a wild mist of blood, not a drop of it marked his clothes or his gorgeous face. The question was, why not?

Moments later, that small bloody part of the vermilion pasture started to rise without warning. But then it wasn't alone—the ground around it trembled and began to rise as well. Dirt and grass still sticking to them, these things rolled free of the ground and floated up into the air. They were bubbles, up to a foot and a half in diameter. Given their crimson color, the name "blood bubbles" suited them well. Like lava boiling from a caldera, like poisonous foam spawned by some crazed chemical reaction, these horrific offspring were born from the earth that'd drunk the blood of the vicious birds. Almost like sentient beings, the bubbles stopped at a height of six feet. One by one, their numbers grew. Perhaps that was all they were waiting for.

"What do you make of them?" D asked someone.

"Think maybe we should call them 'bloody foam eggs'?" someone replied. "I've never seen 'em before either. They're bubbles, so they've gotta burst sometime. When they do, shut down your senses. Just a

second," the voice added. "Nothing ventured, nothing gained. Want me to take a bite out of one?"

"That would be nice."

"Hey, don't be so damn casual about it. This concerns you, too." The indignation of its tone was further colored by swirls of weirdness that knew no depths. "Hey! Come and get us!" the voice shouted.

At some point, D had taken his left hand from his side and turned the palm toward one of his airborne foes. The wind roared. And with that, one of the mysterious blood bubbles quivered and was drawn toward D's hand. As its rounded contour touched the Hunter's palm, it stretched thinner, as if it was being drawn through a hole, and the other extreme of the bubble swelled grossly. The suction didn't end there. The swollen portion didn't pop, but appeared to be struggling even as its shape continued to change. In no time it shrank, displaying the sort of fear a drowning creature does, before it sank completely into the palm of D's hand.

"Wow! Pretty darned tasty," a voice said cheerily, but a second later, it became a cry of pain the likes of which the world rarely heard.

"Rather strong poison?" D inquired calmly.

"This stuff . . . it's pretty damn lethal . . . Don't think even I could take a second one . . . Better fall back."

And with that, there was movement. Not on the part of D, but by the blood bubbles. Perhaps the groans of their victim had filled them with confidence, or maybe they'd finally amassed the numbers necessary, but the bubbles split into two groups and zipped through the air in a beeline for D.

"Sheesh! Don't cut those things . . ." his left hand squealed.

D covered his nose and mouth with a scarf at the very same time the first rank of blood bubbles was bursting. A crimson fog stained the air, but there was no figure in black within it. Not making a sound, D ran through a world of red, where one blood bubble after another exploded. Up ahead of him, he saw Ai-Ling frozen in her tracks as other blood bubbles were flying straight for her.

"Hold your breath and hit the ground," D shouted, coughing a split second later. He'd been hit by the bloody mist from a bubble he'd shattered overhead. The bright blood seemed to pry his lips apart as it spewed from his mouth.

Though his own lifeblood streamed out behind him, D didn't falter in his pace. Grabbing the vulnerable Ai-Ling around the waist, he bolted for the fence. When the blood bubbles zipped toward the leaping figure, a flash of silver shot out for them. As if pushed away by the wind in his sword's wake, the blood bubbles receded. D slipped right through their midst. Sprinting a good forty feet, he turned to look behind him. There didn't seem to be any way to escape the swarm of bubbles fiendishly closing in on them. Just how much of their poisonous fog could he endure?

"It's okay now," D said, not seeming pained at all as he let Ai-Ling know it was safe to breathe again. "How about it?" he asked someone else.

"Do whatever you like. You're a regular slave driver."

On hearing that irritable reply, Ai-Ling started looking all around them with her flushed face.

Gently setting the woman on the ground, there was no telling what D was thinking as he dashed right for the blood bubbles that were closing in on them. Suddenly, the vermilion globes rose as one. Spacing themselves uniformly, the blood bubbles formed a circular canopy. Anything beneath that ceiling was sure to be attacked and trapped by their deadly mist, but D went right under the center of it. They were forty feet above him, a distance that, for all D's leaping ability and skill with a sword, would be too much of a gap.

D's left hand rose. If the blood bubbles had been equipped with eyes, they might've seen the human face that formed there. Eyes reminiscent of the tiniest bamboo leaves sparkled wickedly, and thin lips pursed. With a loud *whooosh* the air began to rush in one direction: toward the tiny lips. Caught in the extreme suction, every last blood bubble sank in a straight line toward the palm of D's hand. D's blade danced about and, with no way of escaping, the globes of blood burst wide open. Before the blood raining down from them could cover his body, D leapt back. Bubbles trying to rise to the sky once more were pulled along with the madly howling wind and then popped without ever being able to form a bloody and inescapable curtain around D.

Leaping back from where he'd dispatched the last of them, D drove his blade into the ground and fell to one knee, coughing horribly. A crimson stain spread across the blue scarf covering his mouth. His coughing stopped in a matter of seconds, and D got up. Taking the scarf away, he turned to Ai-Ling. Her deathly white face was struggling to form a smile. "You'll want to take a bath in the antidote later." And saying that, D took a few gold coins from an inner pocket on his coat and closed Ai-Ling's fingers around them. Payment for the chickeners he'd dispatched.

Ai-Ling was about to shake her head, then thought better of it and accepted the money. Out on the Frontier, even a single bucket could be a precious commodity. "What just happened?" she asked. "I've never heard of anything like that coming out of chickener blood." Her voice was tremulous—no doubt due to the fact that while hers was a hard life, up until now it'd also been a relatively uneventful one.

"Isn't your husband around?" D finally asked her.

"This morning, he headed off to town. He's got other work to do."

"Do you want to come with me? I can't tell you if staying here would be safer, but I can take you to your husband. After all, those blood bubbles went after you, too."

Ai-Ling bobbed her head with its fright-stiffened features up and down. After shutting the gate so the meat beasts wouldn't run off, the two of them got on D's cyborg horse and galloped away.

"Never seen fighting like that before . . . What in the world are you?" Ai-Ling asked, her arms wrapped tightly around D's waist.

"You said you dreamt about me, didn't you?"

"Yes, I did."

"And what did you think?"

Ai-Ling fell silent. Her hair, already tinged with gray, fluttered in the wind. "Do I have to tell you?" she finally asked.

"Not if you don't want to."

"It made me hate you so much that I could kill you."

One person said he was a dangerous man. Another said she despised him. Who could say that everyone in the village didn't fall into one of those two camps? Even in their dreams, D was something unsettling, something they found detestable.

"I don't know why that was," Ai-Ling continued. "I just found you truly hateful. Like you were going to destroy this life and everything we've worked so hard to build—but then, when I woke from the dream . . ." Her words trailed off there. It was some time before she resumed speaking. "I know I said I was happy before . . . but I envy Sybille. Never aging, just dreaming her dreams . . ."

"They're not necessarily pleasant dreams."

"That's what everyone says. But any dream that you never had to wake up from would have to be better than reality . . . even a nightmare. If she woke up, I wonder what she'd think of him . . ."

How did the first real emotion in the woman's weary tone sound to D? As he sat there on his horse, his face remained as cold and emotionless as ever.

They came to a road that ran back to the main street. As D was about to turn his mount toward the village, Ai-Ling said, "Go left—to the hospital. At this hour, my husband should still be there."

The horse galloped to the outskirts of the village, and in no time they were out in front of the white hospital building. Just as D was about to take off, Ai-Ling politely requested that he explain to her husband what had happened. Though this might be the Frontier, the battle that D waged at their ranch was like some conflict from the very depths of hell. No matter what she said, her husband probably wouldn't believe it. For once, indifference on the young man's part might cause a lot of trouble.

After some consideration, D got off his horse.

"This way," Ai-Ling said, walking ahead of the Hunter. After going down a familiar corridor to stand before a door he'd seen before, D realized what was going on. Ai-Ling knocked on the door, and when it opened from the inside, a man's face peeked out. The Hunter didn't even need to see him. The solemn face toughened by countless blizzards was that of Sheriff Krutz.

III

In a hospital room forever locked in feeble darkness, the three of them talked for several minutes. Of the three, it was actually Ai-Ling who explained what had transpired, with D merely offering a terse confirmation at the end that her account was accurate.

Giving no indication of being disturbed or even surprised, once the sheriff had finished listening, he said, "Earlier, you got into some trouble with Clements and got a hotel room burnt down. Now you've gone and killed the chickeners at my ranch, eh? What in blazes did you come to our town to do, anyway?"

"I don't know the answer to that either," D replied.

"Ai-Ling—go wait in the lobby," the sheriff ordered.

The woman wore an expression that suggested she had something she wanted to say, but a shade of something that resembled resignation came over her and she nodded.

When the door had closed again, the sheriff offered a chair to D. "This is fine," he said, leaning against the wall instead.

The sheriff threw a dispassionate gaze at D. "Would that be part of the iron code Hunters have about never leaving their back open?"

"Was she the love of your life?" D asked, not answering the lawman.

The sheriff's eyes shifted to the girl in the bed. "That was thirty years ago," he said.

"As far as your wife is concerned, she is even now. It must be painful, watching you go off to see your old girlfriend every morning."

"Drop the subject. What do you know, anyway?"

"I was led to this village by a dream the girl in that bed had. When I tried to leave, something got in my way and someone died. The key to solving these mysteries is held by your old girlfriend as she sleeps. The reason I was called here and the reason I can't leave seem to be one and the same. That's all I know."

"You mean to tell me you don't care about my personal life, then? Just dandy. Get out of town before you stir up any more trouble."

"That's fine with me, but there's something that just won't let me leave."

"Hogwash—I'll see you to the edge of the village myself. And don't you ever come back." Just as the sheriff stood up, D stepped away from the wall. And then someone knocked on the door. The sheriff went over and opened it. "Well, hello there, Dr. Allen," he said.

Men and women in white slipped in through the open doorway. The cart the nurses pulled in had several trays of surgical implements and a white device that made harsh mechanical sounds.

"Would you look at that . . ." the sheriff muttered in wonderment as the hospital director first smiled warmly at him, and then turned a sharp gaze at D. The figure in the black coat had already disappeared through the doorway. "Wait in the lobby," the sheriff called out after the Hunter before turning back to the director.

The director's heavily wrinkled fingers stroked the power generator as he said, "This just arrived from the Capital this morning. It's the latest development in brain surgery technology. I believe we just may have some success using this to transmit signals directly to her brain cells instructing them to wake up. It may seem like *ex post facto* approval, but we figured you'd be here at this time anyway. So, what do you say? Should we give it a try right away?"

The thoroughness of Dr. Allen's preparations, to say nothing of his strangely coercive manner, left the sheriff a bit confused. "You're talking about sending stimulus directly to her brain. Couldn't that be dangerous?"

"Even if I'm just putting medicine on a bug bite there's some danger, however small, involved."

"But we're talking about someone's life here," Sheriff Krutz said as he looked the elderly physician right in the eye. "If there's any possible danger, however small, I can't go along with this. Besides, if Sybille were to wake up, would she be able to stay the way she is now?"

"What do you mean by that?"

"Let's just suppose for a second that she might not sleep for all eternity, even if the wound on her throat remains. As long as Sybille has that wound, she'll remain a young girl . . . albeit a young girl in a dream. But when she wakes, isn't it possible her dreams and her flesh will return to reality?"

The hospital director heaved a heavy sigh. "Well—I suppose there's no way around that. But of the two, Sheriff, which scares you more?"

The sheriff's expression shifted. As if sunlight had suddenly shone down onto dark thoughts he'd been oblivious to, he let his eyes wander absentmindedly across the ceiling. "Which one?" the sheriff muttered.

"When the Noble's spell over her is broken, her physical body will lose its youth, and her dreams will be robbed of their youthfulness as well. But isn't that a fair enough trade for what she'll regain? Which scares you more, Sheriff?" The director's voice had the sharpness of a steely blade.

The silence began slicing into everyone present in the room; one of the nurses hugged her own shoulders.

"I don't know . . ." Sheriff Krutz groaned in a low voice.

In a room packed with ghastly expressions, Sybille's face alone was serene as a slow breath trickled from her.

†

As the figure in black returned from the far end of the hall, a faint voice called out his name. It was Nan. Her innocently smiling face blossomed like a flower in the gloomy lobby. Getting up off the sofa, she came toward him as if pushed along by a wind. "Thought you'd be here," she said. "I've been looking for you."

"How'd you know I'd be here?"

Furrowing her brow as if troubled, Nan touched her forefinger to the tip of her nose. "Intuition, perhaps? Yes, I'm sure of it."

"Ai-Ling was supposed to be here."

"She left a few minutes ago. I knew in an instant you must've brought her here."

"You have good instincts," D said, heading for the front door.

"Wait just a second, Mr. Impatient!" Nan called out as she scampered after him. "What are you gonna do next?"

"Leave the village."

"What?!" Nan gasped, her eyes going as wide as they possibly could. "But you haven't even gotten to the bottom of the mystery yet. And that other incident is still under investigation. Like I told you yesterday, the sheriff will go after you if you try to leave."

Turning his face back the tiniest bit in Nan's direction, D said, "That's right." His lips were molded in a rare wry smile. As they went out the front door, he turned to Nan and said, "The sheriff and Sybille were lovers, weren't they?"

Nan nodded. "If Sybille hadn't wound up like that, I guess they would've gotten married. They got along really great—and they were the best-looking couple in town."

"On the way up here, I heard that the three of them were apparently friends."

"You don't give a lot of thought to other people's feelings or relationships, do you?" Nan remarked sadly, but of course the comment garnered no reply. "What do you think it'd feel like having your husband go off every single day to visit your old best friend in the hospital? Especially when she's waiting there for him, looking just like she did way back when? I should think it hurts his wife just seeing herself in the mirror. And all of this . . . every last thing . . . is the Nobility's fault. If only he hadn't bitten Sybille . . ."

Savage emotions shot from the girl's innocent face, but D didn't divert his gaze.

Suddenly, Nan was looking at D through eyes damp with tears. Her pale hand pressed down on his black-clad shoulder. In a piteous tone hardly imaginable from such a naive young girl she said, "You're a Hunter, right? Then do something for her—help Sybille. If you can destroy the Noble, you should be able to save his victim."

"What do you mean?" D asked, keeping a grip on his reins. It was a question that would probably draw a frightening response. A gale carried the smell of fallen leaves through the sunlight around them. The distant mountains turned red and gold with the changing foliage; autumn was quietly strengthening its hold.

Nan didn't answer. Tears crept from under her closed eyelids, leaving trails on her pale cheeks as they rolled down. The hand pressing down on D's shoulder shook with her sobs. Even after he had pulled away, her hand remained extended for the longest time.

No word of parting was spoken, but soon enough hoofbeats could be heard growing ever fainter. Nan didn't turn around—for a long time she stayed there. She thought maybe someone would come for her. She was sure if someone would just speak to her and ask her what was wrong, she'd go back to being herself. A voice addressed her just then, but not the one she had in mind.

"What happened to the Hunter?" the sheriff asked.

Quickly wiping away her tears, she looked back at him and said, "He left just now."

"Well, I'll have to make sure," Sheriff Krutz said, going down to the end of the fence and getting on his horse.

"What's gonna happen to him?" Nan asked out of the blue.

"Not a thing. I'll see him to the edge of the village. After that, it'll be up to him to decide."

"I wonder if he'll be able to go."

Getting the distinct impression the Hunter had said nearly the same thing to him not so long ago, the sheriff forgot to goad his horse forward with a kick to the flanks. "He tell you anything?" he asked.

"Not at all," Nan replied, shaking her head. In all her life, she'd never shaken it so hard. Her hair swung out and around in arcs, and her glittering teardrops flew out on an identical course. "What'll happen to him?" she asked. "What'll happen to Sybille . . . or to you, Sheriff? And what'll happen to all of us?"

"Nothing's gonna happen," the sheriff said firmly. At one time, the villagers had been able to hear those words and sleep peacefully through dark nights rife with fluttering demons. When a trio of wanted men came down the main street, the sheriff told the frightened populace the very same thing before he coolly went off to deal with the matter.

The lawman drove his spurs into his mount's flanks. There was the sound of horse and rider thundering across the earth, and then Nan was once again left behind.

†

It took him less than five minutes to find D—there was only one road that connected back to town. About a third of the way from the hospital to that junction, D was out in the middle of the road. A sense of incongruity filled the sheriff's heart. D had stopped. *And he was facing the lawman.* Having halted his horse for a moment, the sheriff then closed the remaining distance with one burst of speed. At first, he thought this might've been some sort of setup, but he quickly thought better of the idea. He was convinced this Hunter would never resort to anything so crude. Scattering pebbles everywhere, the sheriff pulled up alongside the Hunter. The other man made no attempt to look at Krutz, but had his eyes trained straight ahead.

"I take it you weren't waiting around for me, now, were you?" said the sheriff.

"How did you come here?" D asked.

"What?"

"Rode straight from the hospital for about five minutes, didn't you?"

"Sure did," Sheriff Krutz replied, feeling somewhat bewildered. There was nothing unusual about their surroundings or the way the Hunter was acting. His voice had been ordinary when he asked the question, too. Only he was pointed in the opposite direction.

"Then this is where normalcy ends, I guess."

"What are you talking about? Didn't forget anything back in town, now, did you?" Although the last question had a pressure behind it meant to dissuade D from breaking their agreement, the Hunter didn't seem to notice in the least.

"I went straight," D said.

While Sheriff Krutz thought it was obvious the Hunter meant he'd come straight back from the main road, a heartbeat later another impossibility crossed the lawman's mind, making him squint suspiciously. *He can't mean to tell me he's been riding straight on since he left the hospital, could he?*

Before the sheriff could get the question out of his mouth, D had turned his mount around. The Hunter rode off without even asking the lawman to come along. It was only natural that the sheriff went right after him. Side by side, the two of them continued down the road.

"This is a peaceful village," Sheriff Krutz said. "Always has been—since long before I was born. It's not the sort of place for those with the scent of blood all over 'em."

"What did you want to be when you grew up?"

At that unexpected question, the sheriff turned toward D in spite of himself. By the look of him, he was a young man, no more than twenty. Being a man of the law, Krutz was accustomed to a certain level of formality, but for some reason this question didn't bother him. "This," the sheriff said, pointing to the badge on his chest.

"Did you ever tell Sybille that?"

"Why would you ask that?"

"You had the makings of a sheriff. That's probably what Sybille wanted for you. Your dream was her dream, too, wasn't it?"

"We never even talked about it. I was supposed to run the general store."

D didn't say anything.

"But forget about me. I want to know why you—" Realizing in the blink of an eye that he'd ridden ahead of D, Sheriff Krutz hastily pulled back on his reins.

"See if you can go on," D said.

"What?"

"Go straight ahead. I'm going to wait a minute."

About fifty feet ahead of them the road twisted to the right. Beyond that it was swallowed by the densely packed greenery of the woods. Throwing a sharp glance at the Hunter, the sheriff started off on his horse. Nothing happened. Slowly he turned into the woods. The sheriff couldn't believe his eyes. A black horse and rider suddenly stood before him. It was D, but even after Sheriff Krutz had ridden close enough to confirm the rider's gorgeous face, he still wasn't ready to accept it. To the Hunter still keeping his silence, he said, "Is this a sealed dimension?"

"Well, I've had some experience with those. This is something else."

"So, this is what you meant when you said something wouldn't let you leave the village?"

D gave no answer, but kept his eyes trained straight ahead. The sheriff turned around. Out of the woods, a low singing voice was growing louder.

> "Go take a peek if tomorrow's not along,
> Those old Nobles just might've been wrong,
> A world full of twisted creatures and such,
> Don't seem to bother anyone much . . ."

First, a pair of horses became visible. They were followed by a second pair, and then a third, before a wagon covered by reinforced vinyl finally appeared.

"Looks like people can still get through from the outside, though," the sheriff said in a low voice.

"You there—what are the two of you up to?" the middle-aged woman sitting in the driver's seat with the reins and an electronic whip in hand asked in a voice so big and bold it was clear she wasn't the least bit afraid. Come to mention it, her body was fairly huge, too. She was built like a keg of beer, unlike some other women who had waists thinner than this woman's upper arms. "Well, if it ain't the sheriff," she shouted. "How's life been treating you?"

D gave a quick look to the lawman.

"An acquaintance of mine," the sheriff commented morosely. "That's Maggie, a jack-of-all-trades. Comes by twice a month. Damn!" he added suddenly. "I'd better stop her, or she won't be able to get back out again!"

"It's no use," the Hunter said.

The covered wagon was far enough away that the driver couldn't hear what the two of them were talking about, but it stopped right in front of them soon enough. "Quite the looker you've got with you," Maggie said to the sheriff. "Seems like the rough-and-tumble sort, but I hope you weren't planning on running him out of town, were you? If you are, I'll thank you to hold up until we've been introduced." To the Hunter, she added, "Hello there, you sweet young thing. I'm Maggie the Almighty."

"They call me D."

"Well, I'll be!" The round eyes and mouth set in her big dinner-roll of a face all opened in unison. It took a few seconds before she could speak again. "You . . . you mean you're . . . Well, now, it's a pleasure to meet you. This is an honor."

"Any strange business on your way here, Maggie?" the sheriff inquired in a stern tone.

"Why, I haven't done a blessed thing! What'd I ever do to have you put a question to me like that? The nerve of some people! Say, handsome," she said to the young Hunter, "why don't you come into town with me? I'll even act as your guarantor. Though in your case, I'm sure there's no shortage of ladies who'd want to be with you, even if it meant getting bitten," she said rather impudently, quickly adding, "Oops," and clapping a plump hand over her mouth.

"Have we met before?"

With that question from D, Sheriff Krutz also trained a grave gaze on the hefty figure.

A bewildered Maggie replied, "Nope, never seen you before. Not even in my dreams." The last remark she said completely casually, but, with the way the sheriff's expression quickly hardened, she must've realized she'd said something wrong. Still, she hardly seemed unnerved. "Well, guess I'll be getting a move-on. I'll get my permission to set up shop later, thank you," Maggie said coolly, shooting a wink at D before she called to her team and gave a shake to the reins.

"What'll we do?" D asked Krutz as the lawman watched the departing wagon. "The other roads are probably just like this, in which case all we can do is head back." Without another word, D wheeled his mount around, and then suddenly behind him he heard the metallic click of handcuffs, so well known that even the smallest child on the Frontier would recognize the sound.

"I'm sorry, but we're gonna have to detain you until we can get this situation sorted out," Sheriff Krutz told him. "No matter how you look at it, you seem to be the cause of all this. If I don't do something, there's no telling what could go wrong next."

"And if I'm locked in your jail, nothing else will happen?"

"Not really. But as the law here, I can't very well leave you free, either." In the lawman's rough hand was a weapon that was exceedingly hard to come by, graceful and fierce and glittering in the sunlight—a sol gun. Amplifying the power of natural light, the gun could channel it into a fifty-million-degree beam that could go through three feet of titanium in a thousandth of a second. Unlike laser blasters or photon cannons, which were rendered useless if their ultra-compact nuclear power sources were destroyed, the sol gun only needed a piece of resilient photosensitive film to keep it running indefinitely. Thirty minutes of exposure on a sunny day or six hours on a rainy one was enough to keep the beam charged for over two hundred hours. Even D wouldn't fare very well if shot through the heart with that, never mind what would happen if it was fired at his head . . .

The sheriff quickly put some distance between D and himself. "See, I've heard that the Vampire Hunter D has a sword that's quicker than a laser beam," he explained. "Move along, now."

D showed no signs of resisting, and the two of them started back up the road that'd brought them there. Neither of them spoke at all. Soon, they could see the hospital once again.

"Aren't you going to swing by?" D asked out of the blue.

"What are you talking about?"

"I recognize the new equipment the doctors had. Are you sure you shouldn't be there?"

"I'm busy being the sheriff—or are you gonna give me your word that you won't take off?"

"If I did, would you believe me?" D asked.

"Nope."

The white building came up on their left, and fell behind them in no time.

"I suppose they just may wake her up after all . . ." the sheriff said, as if rationalizing. For words born of his iron confidence, they sounded strangely frail.

"So, if you plan on locking me up to prevent any trouble, I doubt that's going to do much good."

"Don't give me any more of your speculation. This happens to be part of my job. I'm not letting my personal life get mixed up with business here."

After remaining silent for a short while, D said, "You should let her keep on dreaming. No matter what those dreams may be." And then he quickly added, "Or is it too late?"

Realizing there was something more to the Hunter's words, Sheriff Krutz moved his horse to one side and turned his eyes to a little path that D's body previously blocked. It was as if the very balance between heaven and earth had been upset. "Sybille . . ." he said, calling out the name of the beautiful girl on the path in a voice that was thirty years older, but carried three decades of emotion. The golden hair that fluttered in the breeze was like a blessing from the goddess of fall. Clad in a white blouse and a blue skirt with stripes, she was an icon of youthfulness that had utterly absorbed the four seasons. "Sybille . . ." he called out once more, as if trying to gently cup his hands around some treasured possession.

†

How's that?" the old man in white asked, the silver needle he held still stuck deep into a blonde's head. A colored cord ran from the end of the needle, connecting it to a monitor on a nearby cart.

The woman watching the monitor, also dressed in white, looked up and said, "There's been a disruption in her brain waves. According to our data bank, we've got some leakage to the outside."

"Not good," the old man muttered as he pulled out the needle. "We can't have *this* leaking to the outside. Give me a reading on what needs to be modified."

"The seventh sector, point 989."

The needle moved to the new position and sank in.

"It's gone," the nurse announced as the elderly hospital director wiped the sweat from his brow with one hand.

"Well, at the very least, we've made the necessary arrangements to eliminate dangerous individuals. Transfer Sybille to the isolation ward."

A number of figures in white nodded in acknowledgment and dispersed in a flurry of activity.

The old man gently looked down at the placid expression of the girl who lay there sleeping. "I'm sorry, Sybille. I really don't want to interrupt your sleep. No matter what happens to me, you should just go on sleeping. We'll protect you."

There was no way the tragic tone would register in her ears. As Sybille Schmitz slept, her face was peaceful, as if all had been forgotten.

The Dream Assassin

CHAPTER 4

I

D went into the holding cell in the sheriff's office. Almost instantly, burdensome business took human form and started knocking on the office door. The first to come were those villagers who'd seen the sheriff bringing D in, the overwhelming majority of whom were women. When they asked what had happened, Sheriff Krutz told them they were interfering in official matters and sent them on their way. He also came up with a more personal reason—those who pressed for more substantial details were told the Hunter had picked a fight with him over the way he was caring for Grampy Samson's meat beast out at his ranch. Making it a work-related problem as close to his personal business as he could, he was able to set the villagers at ease—there was that much more distance between the case and themselves. Less than thirty minutes after D was taken into custody, even the mayor paid them a visit. Explaining the situation, the sheriff tried to get him to leave.

"That's not exactly what I'd call a very detailed explanation," the intractable mayor said.

To which the lawman replied, "The truth is, I'm questioning him as to why we all had that dream about him." And that did the trick.

†

D lay on his narrow cot, not moving a muscle.

"You're an odd one, you surely are," Sheriff Krutz said to him. Getting no reaction from the Hunter, but unable to keep his mouth closed, he continued. "This may sound funny, but I kinda get the feeling I've thrown royalty into my jail. Just take a look out the window. Every woman in town's watching this place. We might not be able to get the door open with all the baked goods they've been leaving outside for you."

"Why don't you go to the hospital instead of keeping a watch over me here?" D suggested, opening his mouth for the first time since he'd been put in the cell. "There's no way Sybille's appearance isn't connected to them treating her with that equipment. Or maybe—"

"Maybe?" The sheriff's tone suddenly dropped. "Maybe what?"

"You said the village was peaceful long before you were born, didn't you?"

"Yep."

"Ever had any big accidents or major problems?" the Hunter asked.

"Well, I can't say that we haven't. We are out on the Frontier, after all."

"How many times have you nearly been killed?"

The sheriff furrowed his brow at the rapid-fire questions. Ordinarily he was the one who did the interrogating. Though the tables were turned, he knew there was no way he could correct it. With some irritation the sheriff realized that the bizarre question had started a chain of ripples in some dark inner portion of him. "What would you ask a thing like that for?" he replied. "I'm sitting here talking with you, aren't I?"

"Whether you're alive now or not isn't particularly important," D remarked softly. "What I want to know is how you've managed to survive."

For a split second, the most virulent shade of hatred resided in the sheriff's eyes. Vigorously lowering the blinds over the window, he walked toward the cell. Tossing his coat down on the floor, he tugged his shirt off roughly. His hard pectorals looked sculpted from clay, and the few long scars that ran from his chest down to his tight abdominal muscles left a huge purple X on him. There were also scattered round scars that seemed to be from bullets, with four of them on the left side of his chest and three closer to the middle of his belly.

"I picked up part of this scar eight years ago, and the rest five years back. The color's strange because the swords had poisoned tips. Two of the holes in my gut are from steel arrows; everything else is from slugs." He turned his broad back toward D. Melted purple flesh covered him completely below the scapula. "All I'll say is . . . I got burnt. I don't mean to brag, but in twenty years I've only missed two days on the job."

The sheriff held his tongue and waited for a reply from D, then suddenly he heard a knock at the door. As he pushed his arms back through his shirt sleeves, he turned to the intercom and asked who was there.

"It's me—Bates."

It was the same deputy who'd questioned D the day before. The position of sheriff wasn't necessarily a full-time job on the Frontier, and the sheriff had—at his discretion—the ability to grant the title of deputy to anyone who requested it. Most of the time, Bates was just another villager. He'd been out patrolling the town, but now he was back.

"I hear you tossed him in the slammer," the deputy said as he bounded in energetically. "So, was there something fishy about him after all? That'd mean that Nan was—"

"This has nothing to do with the Tokoff incident," Sheriff Krutz said flatly. As Bates frowned in disappointment, he added, "I'm going out. You take over here. Keep a good eye on him. No matter what happens, don't you dare let him out. His blade's over there," he said, his eyes indicating the longsword propped against the side of his desk. Then, grabbing his hat off the hat rack, he left. Not once did he look at D.

Bates whistled enthusiastically. "Finally acting like his good old self."

"Is he the big hero in town?"

Still ebullient, Bates turned to the cells and said, "I suppose you could say so. Peace is good and all, but he was built to be zipping around taking care of business. Vampire Hunter or not, you'd be no match for him."

Locking the front door, Bates settled into his chair with nervous excitement and turned toward D. He was so eager to share the sheriff's glories he could barely contain himself. There'd been a showdown eight years earlier that he began to describe in utmost detail and with great respect.

It all started when a notorious group of roving criminals, the subject of warrants from the Capital, came to their village. Each of these villains had committed numerous murders, and each was heavily armed—packing both pistols and laser rifles. When a rider on a fast horse brought word from the neighboring village, Sheriff Krutz went out alone and waited for the three of them in the street. Until then, the three men hadn't met any resistance, but when they stopped in front of him, the sheriff told them to go right back the way they came.

"He said the same thing he always does: 'Don't bother stopping.' I was still a kid—had just turned twenty and was hiding behind a pillar—but it sent shivers down my spine. And what do you reckon happened next?

"Of course, the three of them started to get off their horses. 'Don't bother getting off,' the sheriff told them. It was three against one. Even with the disadvantage they had of drawing on horseback, the odds were still against the sheriff."

Bates continued, recounting that a heartbeat later, the battle began. The three of them reached for their holsters first, but Sheriff Krutz beat them on the draw. The blue flash from his sol gun reduced the face of the middle rider to flames. The sheriff rolled across the ground as roars and fiery streaks flew from the riders and tore through the spot where he'd been. Three times the blue beam flew off, and as soon as the last shot roasted the torso of the man to the left, one slug after another ripped into the sheriff's belly. An instant later, the face of the third man was reduced to its constituent atoms, and the battle was at an end.

"And if you think that's something," Bates added, "What happened next was even more incredible. He went to the doctor's without any help from anyone, had him put a bandage on the wound after the slug had been pulled out, and then went right back to work."

Bates's cheeks were red hot, and his eyes glittered. He was like a little boy boasting about his father.

Waiting a bit for the deputy's ardor to cool, D asked an odd question: "What do you think of the Nobility?"

"What do you mean?" Bates asked with a grimace. "What the hell are you—"

"Do you hate them?" D's tone was soft. The sound of it hadn't changed, but the intent behind it had.

Bates realized as much. "Not really . . . I don't like 'em or hate 'em. I can't say as I've ever heard my ma or pa speak ill of them, and back in the old days we used to get along with Nobles in these parts. I don't know how it is in other places, but they never caused us no harm."

"Sybille was bitten by one," the Hunter reminded him.

"Sure, but that was . . ."

When you thought about it, it was rather strange. Fear and hatred of the Nobility was handed down from parent to child, generation after generation. Yet this village seemed entirely cut off from that hatred—a fact that would have been startling to just about anyone, and probably considered miraculous by many. D never got to hear the deputy's reply because a ferociously spirited knock suddenly echoed throughout the office.

"Who is it?" Bates asked through the intercom.

"It's me. Open up." It sounded like Clements.

"What's your business here?"

"Well, it sure ain't with you. I need to see that Hunter you've got locked away."

"Hey, I'm busy now," Bates said into the microphone.

"Hell, so am I. Hey, I'll have you know I pay my taxes and all. That sure as blazes gives me the right to go into the sheriff's office."

Bates clucked his tongue. "Gimme a second," he replied, and then turning to D he added, "Looks like you've got trouble. But relax. I won't let any harm come to you."

D didn't move an inch.

When the door finally opened, Clements took his sweet time coming in, a pair of lackeys trailing behind him. While the man's brown double-breasted suit didn't merit particular attention, Bates's eyes were drawn to the weapon he had tucked under his arm. It was a three-foot-long cylinder about eight inches in diameter—a large-scale impact cannon.

"Were you thinking of taking out a Noble's tank or something with that?" Bates asked with his right hand resting on the old gunpowder-driven automatic handgun that was tucked in the holster at his waist.

"Aw, shit, no! We've just been out playing army. Me and my boys here, that is."

"Don't try anything, Clements. He's still a suspect in the—" Bates started to say, but then he remembered he didn't know exactly what charge the Hunter had been locked up for, so he just rolled his eyes instead.

"Hold it right there, Bates. Reach for the sky!" blustered one of the lackeys.

A muzzle so huge a child's head could fit inside it pointed in his direction. Bates brought his right hand away from the grip of his automatic. "C'mon, Clements. Don't be stupid. You do this, and the sheriff and me won't let it stand."

"Well, the rest of the village will sure as hell let it stand. You think they're all just gonna sit around doing nothing after some bastard they don't know from a hole in the wall killed one of their own?"

"In that incident, Tokoff made the first move. Nan saw it."

"You think that counts for shit?" Clements said, licking his lips. "That little bitch's at the age where she's got an itch only a man can scratch. All this guy'd have to do is nibble on her earlobe and she'd tell us whatever he wanted her to."

"What the hell's possessed you? Have you taken complete leave of your senses? You start swinging that cannon around in here and you're liable to take out the next three houses to-boot!"

That last remark had an unexpected effect. A thin film covered Clements's eyes, and for a few seconds he just stood there. Then he was suddenly back to his usual self, and he barked at his dumbfounded lackeys, "Well, what the hell are you waiting for? Take care of business!"

"Stop! You commit a murder in the sheriff's office, and they'll execute you, sure as shit," Bates yelled. He then tried, unsuccessfully, to get between the weapon's muzzle and the holding area, catching a severe blow to the cheek. The unpleasant sound of steel connecting with bone seemed to cling forever to the side of the impact cannon.

"Okay, now that there's no one to stop us, you can kiss your ass goodbye, pal!"

Still not having moved in the slightest, D said to the sneering Clements, "You had a dream about me, too, didn't you?"

"Kill him."

At Clements's rather softly spoken command, the two bewildered lackeys threw the switch on the impact cannon. The bars of the cell flew inward, and a shock wave that could have sent a charging five-ton beast snout-over-tail reduced D's bed to dust as it hammered a mortar-shaped depression into the floor.

D, unscathed, danced through the air.

With the slight sound of another discharge, a section of wall over six feet in diameter collapsed. The hem of the Hunter's coat fluttered out as a cloud of dust suddenly rose up and struck the outer surface of his garment. Had D's coat not absorbed half of the force of the blow, the shock wave that rebounded in the direction of the two lackeys would have killed them instantly. Instead, the pair sustained internal injuries as the force slammed them against the floor and bruised every inch of their bodies.

Having been struck both inside and outside by the shock wave, the set of steel bars that comprised D's holding cell began to break, shooting bolts everywhere and collapsing outward. With nowhere to escape, Clements let out a scream when he realized he was pinned under them. In no time at all, the air was crushed out of his lungs, his flesh and bones cracked and popped under the strain, and the agony was enough to cut his cries short.

"I'm going to take a little nap," D said, having just devastated three foes without lifting a finger.

"Okay," Bates said dazedly from his spot on the floor. He no longer had a clue as to who was the victim in the situation. He couldn't even remember the last words out of his mouth. Raising a bloodied hand to his brow, he repeated, "Okay. Pleasant dreams."

II

The sheriff arrived at the hospital, his heart grown as heavy as lead. As he got closer to the hospital, it became clear that gravity was tugging at it harder and harder.

"Sheriff—" the nurse at the front desk called out to get his attention, but his feet kept moving. "Sheriff, the director says he needs to talk to you."

"I'll get to him later," he replied tersely, advancing down the hall. His heart was growing heavier, and yet it was beating faster than before. Somehow he seemed to know that even after he reached her room it wasn't going to get any better.

A number of nurses and patients stepped out of his way, almost as if frightened. When he reached her room—in half the usual time—he grabbed hold of the doorknob and found, much to his surprise, that the door opened easily.

Not much had changed in the room—the bed and the curtains were still a part of that quiet, feeble darkness to which he had grown accustomed. Only Sybille was missing. His heart became a red-hot lump of steel.

"Sheriff!" someone called out down the hall.

From the sound of the approaching footsteps, he knew who it was. The voice was that of a male nurse named Basil, who was widely known as the hospital's bouncer. The lawman turned toward the door to find Basil standing there with a forced smile, two other men close behind him. The nurse at the front desk must've let Allen know he was there. That woman was a shrewd one.

"Sheriff, the director—"

Krutz lunged forward. He easily got a grip on Basil's throat and, giving one easy breath, the sheriff lifted all two hundred pounds of the strapping man off the floor with one hand.

"Sheriff?!" The powerful hands of the other two men grabbed hold of the lawman's arms and shoulders from both the fore and the rear.

"This is . . . Sybille's . . . room." Krutz forced out each and every word with the weight of three decades in his voice, and then, with every ounce of strength he could muster, he took a swing with his left hand. The two men, who were no strangers to violence, slammed back against the wall with a force that made it tremble, and then slowly slid onto the floor. On the way down, one of them managed to get his electromagnetic baton out, but the sheriff struck it out of his hand with a swift kick of the foot. The hand that gripped the weapon was crushed at the wrist—the steel baton shattered in a shower of blue sparks. Between the pain and the electromagnetic waves that bombarded him, the man lost consciousness.

"What the hell . . . are you doing . . . Sheriff?" Basil gasped, his hoarse words falling with his sweat.

"This is Sybille's room," the lawman repeated. "For thirty years, I've been coming up here to see her. You, me, this village—we all got older, but this right here never changed because Sybille was always here. Where'd you take her?"

"Don't . . . know . . . ask the director . . ."

"Where's Dr. Allen at?"

"I'm right here, Krutz. You'd best set Basil down. Another three seconds and he'll suffocate."

After the briefest hesitation, the sheriff released the man. "Don't try anything funny. I don't care how tough your boys may be, they're not in my league. That's why you need me." There was something about the last thing he'd said that lingered in his heart, but the sheriff soon put it out of his mind and asked about Sybille.

"She's been transferred to someplace safe."

"And what was so dangerous here?"

"Now, don't get all hot under the collar," Dr. Allen said. "There's no immediate danger, however, we have to be prepared in case something crops up suddenly. You should come with me, Sheriff."

The director turned then and stepped out of the room, motioning for the sheriff to follow. Out in the hall, a number of nurses and patients had formed a semicircle around the doorway. Just as the sheriff was about to turn around and leave the room, he lost consciousness and collapsed to the floor.

†

D walked through familiar woods in darkness devoid of sound. It was such a quiet night that it almost seemed possible to hear the thin fog whisper as it drifted about. Even in this dream world, D wasn't sure if the fact that his footsteps failed to make any sound as he stepped on the grass was his own intention or not. In any case, he supposed Sybille would be waiting for him at the mansion.

The iron gate stood in the moonlight as it always had.

D halted. This particular evening, he might be an unwelcome guest.

The man stood at the gate. Garbed in raiment like the very darkness, with his face covered from the nose down by a black scarf, he wasn't entirely unlike D. Two eyes set in skin redolent of bronze held D's reflected image. If the powerful emotion they were loaded with wasn't something special directed at D, then surely all he gazed upon must've been touched with fear.

"Don't intend to let me in?" D inquired softly. "There's no point fighting here. Any duel decided in a dream can't be called a duel at all."

His opponent stood there, looming like a wall of iron that had no answers for him.

"Like the mansion itself, you're just another one of the girl's creations. You led me here. You saved me. Now get out of my way."

"Go back," the man in black said, his scarf trembling slightly as he mouthed the words.

The two of them gazed at each other. Both of the man's black-gloved hands went into motion. Bringing together a bow and a single arrow before his chest, the man drew the steel bowstring back with tremendous power and determination. It was clear that no matter how fast D might move, they were too close for him to evade a shot.

"Go back," the man in black ordered him once again.

"Is there already another guest at the mansion? Or is another one on the way? If you use that bow, there'll be no taking it back."

The tension swelled. The moonlight froze, and even the fog stopped dead. In a world choked with a thirst for killing, the youthful Hunter was the only thing of beauty.

The steel flew.

D stopped it with his empty left hand, and as he caught it, that same hand blurred with activity. An instant later, D felt another presence off to his right.

Both D and the man in black kicked off the ground simultaneously and ran toward the presence. It came as no surprise that both of them sprinted forward in an attempt to discover the identity of whoever had invaded this dream. In the next instant, black lightning shot from the treetops at the two men as they sprinted toward it, side by side. The two figures quickly split to the left and the right of the lightning bold. Still holding the arrow that he caught with his bare hand when the man fired it at him, he hurled it again in the direction of the presence he detected. Apparently, that foe then hurled it back again. There was no blood on it. Did those who lived in this world of dreams even have flesh and blood in the first place? No, this was the dream of a young lady who slept ever on.

Suddenly, the man in black pulled out ahead of the Hunter. As he was a part of this world, it was only natural that he raced into the thicket with a speed D couldn't match. There were emanations of some awesome conflict from the area, and then the presence unexpectedly disappeared. Jumping in scant seconds later, D found a thin mist eddying sadly before his eyes. There was no sign of either the man in black or their unseen foe. Perhaps they'd awakened from the dream?

Noticing something on the ground, D bent over. What his black-gloved fingers touched was a scrap of cloth sticking out of the earth. It was clear from the jagged shredding at the edge of the cloth that it had taken incredible strength to tear it off—perhaps the man had torn it free in that brief second of battle. After trying unsuccessfully to pull the scrap from the ground with all his strength, D realized that it was going to be impossible. Perhaps in accordance with some physical law of this dream world, the cloth had become one with the black ground.

Drawing a slender dagger from his belt and cutting off the corner of the cloth, D left the thicket. Where had the two of them disappeared to? Were they engaged, even now, in supernatural battle without end in some other, unimagined world? There were any number of things that should've occupied the Hunter's thoughts, but he seemed aloof as he turned back toward the road. Perhaps the man in black had urged D to go back because he was expecting an intruder. Tonight it seemed, at the very least, that the man harbored no animosity toward the Hunter.

As always, the mansion towered majestically in the blue light.

Suddenly, D heard the most bizarre groaning—at first appearing to emanate from the highest heavens and then seeming to originate from the depths of the earth—a sound that stopped him dead in his tracks as soon as it reached him. Human groans. The groans of a woman.

Without a sound, D leapt back. The thin fog rising around his chest trembled—shook with regret. D surveyed his surroundings. There was no change. A band of white wove plaintively in and out of the grove—only the fog to the fore was clearly heading toward him, in defiance of the rules of this world. Surely he'd be able to elude it. However, if the fog's purpose was to cut off the area between D and the mansion, it would have to keep pushing him back indefinitely.

"Was this fog born after hearing the scream in this dream?" D muttered.

The fog kept closing in on him. D didn't move. His field of view became obscured by a world of pearly white. Was it coming? Even after the fog receded—trailing tails of white behind it—D continued to stand in the same spot for a short time longer.

Awash in blue light, the mansion showed no signs of being any different. Neither cautious nor hurried, D passed through the iron gate. Advancing a few steps, the Hunter heard the gate shut behind him.

"This is dangerous business," his left hand said in a hoarse voice. "There's something funny here. You can't be too careful."

Once inside the mansion, D caught sight of a figure in white at the center of the hall and halted. It was Sybille. Along with her white gown, she wore a sorrowful expression that she cast down at the floor. Even a sad dream was still a dream.

"My travels aren't particularly urgent, but it's getting to be a bit boring going to the same place every time I sleep. Today you're going to explain what you want with me."

At D's words, her slim face grew even more pensive and she hung her head still lower. Her shoulders were shaking. The trembling grew more intense. From beneath that downturned face, sobs trickled out. No, it wasn't sobbing—it was laughter. With D standing right there, the girl began roaring with laughter as if she were completely deranged. Slowly, the whole mansion warped.

"Wow! Looks to me like that fog earlier didn't belong here after all," the hoarse voice said with what sounded like admiration. "So, is this a dream within a dream, or has some other dream invaded the place? Whatever the case, it ain't good. Okay, now how do we get out of here?"

The voice seemed to suggest that the fog might be an illusion powerful enough to drive even the master of this dream mad.

"Can't we just leave the dream as a dream?" D muttered, seemingly oblivious to the mansion as it swayed like the whole place was underwater. His tone sounded somewhat weary. "It's horrifying, so it must be destroyed. It's beautiful, so it must be destroyed. It doesn't want to destroyed, so it must be destroyed. At this rate, what will humanity leave behind?"

These remarks likely weren't directed at the young lady before him. The girl's voice had already become something inhuman, and D noticed that fragments of it moved around her like a white cloud. Every time the girl opened her mouth, more sound poured out. This was truly a dream world, with clouds forming from her voice. Part of the cloud suddenly stretched out. A silvery flash sliced it in two.

Longsword in his right hand, D ran straight for the figure he now knew was a fake Sybille. Retreat was not in this young man's nature, yet clouds besieged him from all sides. As his longsword mowed through them, they wrapped around the steel like silk floss, one layer after another.

With the girl right before him, D made a swipe with his longsword. The blade should've taken her head off then and there, but it met stiff resistance and bounced off—the work of the clouds, no doubt.

Someone pushed the rebounding blade behind the Hunter's back. This person that even D hadn't detected was none other than Sybille. With one movement of her slim arm, she snapped D's sword in half. Taking the portion of the blade that remained in her hand, Sybille hurled it at D. The Hunter caught it with his left hand. The piece then stretched out between the fingers that gripped it, penetrating deep into D's chest.

Sybille grinned deviously, but her face stiffened, and surely at that very instant she was witnessing D's left hand slowly extracting the bizarre shard of his blade. Perhaps this young man wasn't subject to anyone's control, not even in their dreams.

Having extracted the shard that'd been poking all the way out of his back, D made a leap at this foe in the form of Sybille. In midair, his pose was disrupted. The floor he'd been standing on stretched like rubber, clinging to him and pulling him back.

Scattering clouds of white from her smile all the while, the fake Sybille turned from D and retreated toward the far reaches of the mansion.

Still in that awkward pose, D hurled his fragmented blade in her direction. Howling through the air, it went into the slim figure through the nape of her neck and jutted out through her windpipe, nailing the girl's body to the wall.

Feeling the pulsing of the floor beneath his boots like the beating of some vile heart with his every step, D walked toward the fake Sybille. Red bloodstains were quickly spreading across the back of her white dress. Almost like predefined shapes, the stains welled up from the very fabric of the gown like roses opening their petals. No, they actually *were* roses. And her gown wasn't the only thing that was blooming crimson buds. Red roses welled up on various parts of her body until each and every one of them blossomed in a riot of huge roses that covered every inch of her.

D didn't so much as raise an eyebrow at these weird proceedings, but surely his eyes caught the next eerie transformation to the girl's flesh. A number of black lines burst out of her body in different places, stretching out in all directions, sinking into the floor, walls, and ceiling. Yes, they sank in—everything in the mansion lost its shape, growing soft as watery paint and swallowing the vines that grew from the girl. But did D realize what it all meant? As he calmly looked over his shoulder, countless vines were sprouting back out of the walls and ceiling, intersecting and forming a fine lattice that, in the blink of a human eye, managed to completely contain the Hunter.

Tearing his boots free of the sticky floor, D went over to the closest lattice, put his left hand and both feet against the center of it, and then leaned his body against it. His brow crinkled ever so slightly. The lattice of thin vines had grown needle-like thorns that pierced his hands and feet.

"Oww . . . This is the real thing!"

Though the Hunter's left hand may have overstated the case, it was clear the pain from this was real. The blood running out of him was real, too—the dream's reality. In which case, a death in a dream might be a death in reality.

The walls began sliding closer, the ceiling lowered, and the floor slowly rose. As the walls reached the body of the fake Sybille still nailed to the wall, she melted away. In less than ten seconds, the three-dimensional jaws of death would make contact with D.

The dagger glittered in D's right hand. The blade was brought down with all the power he possessed, and sparks shot out as it bounced off the surface of the vines.

"Looks like we're cornered," the Hunter's left hand moaned almost nonchalantly.

"Why don't you try swallowing the ceiling or one of the walls?" D asked softly. Although he sounded as if he was talking about having a cup of tea, this was, of course, a grave matter that could mean the difference between life and death.

"You've gotta be joking. You think you can just drink a dream? If I did that, then everything would just turn to dreams."

"Okay, then," the Hunter replied.

"What'll you do?"

"What happens if you die in a dream?"

"I don't know," the left hand said. "And wouldn't you know it, there're no dead folks around to ask. Why don't you try asking the one who made all this in the first place? *You-know-who.*"

Giving no reply to that, D reached into his coat with his right hand. "Dying in a dream? That would be an interesting experiment—but we can't do that." As he spoke, his right hand was thrust toward the sky.

Something like a scrap of paper flew up into the air. It was D's dagger that then pierced the scrap. And then both items were driven right into part of the floor that was rising like muddy water, though the substance rang like something solid as he stabbed into it.

Suddenly, everything went black.

D opened his eyes and found himself in the middle of the lane that ran to Sybille's mansion. Waking from a dream within a dream, he'd returned to the first vision. Not saying a word, he looked down at his left hand. There wasn't so much as a scratch on the back or the palm. As for his longsword, it remained in its sheath.

"Hey! What did you do?" the Hunter's left hand asked in a surprised manner.

Bending over, D reached for something that glittered on the ground by his feet. This was the spot where he'd thrown his dagger, and what he'd picked up was that very same blade. To the tip of it was stuck a piece of brown cloth—the cloth that the assassin in the thicket had left behind. Because the twisted, melting mansion was some nightmare spawned by the assassin, a strike to the piece of cloth that linked it to Sybille's dream was all that was needed to deal a lethal blow to that dream within a dream. Nevertheless, waking from one dream into another was quite strange.

"What'll you do now?" the voice asked.

D began walking. In his dreams, just as in reality, the young man's steady pace was always the same.

III

As soon as he awoke, Sheriff Krutz opened his eyes and realized he was lying on a bed in an examination room in the hospital's internal medicine ward. When he tried to get up, something tugged strongly at his head. Bringing his hand up to it, he felt countless cords there. Some kind of pliable substance covered his scalp, and cords were stuck into it. It must've been the conduction paste they used when taking electroencephalograms.

Just as the lawman finished prying the whole mess off his head, the hospital director appeared in the doorway on the far side of the room. The speed with which the old man stepped aside belied his age. The gooey mass the sheriff had hurled slammed against the wall, cords and all. The only thing capable of marring his face any further at this point was retribution.

"I'd say our friendship has had it," the sheriff said as he got off the bed.

"Would you just wait a minute?" Dr. Allen said, raising one hand.

Though the sheriff had been about to uncork some choice vocabulary, the thing that kept his tongue in check was the depth of the pain the old doctor wore on his face.

"After having done this to you, it's only fair that I explain all the circumstances. The truth of the matter is, I don't want to tell you, and I believe you'll probably wish you'd never heard it, either. You see, I've come to a conclusion—a most unfortunate one."

"Where is Sybille?" Sheriff Krutz asked, as if brushing aside everything the hospital director had just said. He felt around his waist to make sure that his gun was still strapped to his belt.

"She's this way. Come with me."

"No more sneak attacks," the director said in a sarcastic tone.

"What did you do to me?" the sheriff finally inquired after a few minutes of walking in silence.

"We checked your brainwaves for abnormalities—although I doubt you'll believe that. Come with me and you'll find all your answers."

The two of them got into a wooden elevator and descended into the basement.

"Hey—we're in the emergency ward. Is Sybille's condition more serious now?" the sheriff asked, his voice echoing down the cold corridor. Before it had entirely faded, the two of them were greeted by a white door. Tough-looking male nurses stood to either side of it. The sight of one of them carrying an old-fashioned rocket launcher and the other cradling a photon-beam rifle made the sheriff's eyes glow with quiet determination. Whatever was going on with Sybille, it was extremely important.

"Was Basil okay?" the sheriff asked.

"Yep, he's resting now."

"Be sure to tell him I'm awful sorry about what I did."

One step through the doorway, and the sheriff froze in his tracks. The sound of the closing door was quietly embraced by the thin darkness. The bed that held the soundly sleeping girl, the curtains, the machine by her pillow, and even the feeble darkness of human design were all very much like her old room.

"I just stopped it a little while ago," the hospital director said, having noticed how the sheriff's gaze fell on the machine. "She was connected to your brain, and it was working beautifully, but things got fouled up when we were so very close."

"Don't you have any nurses in here?" the sheriff asked.

"They've finished up. From here on out, no one comes into this room except you and me. And if anyone else tries it . . . Well, I suppose a doctor committing murder does pose a bit of an ethical dilemma."

The sheriff eyed the elderly physician with something akin to anxiety. "And what reason would you have for going to that extreme to protect Sybille?"

The hospital director gestured to one of the chairs and seated himself in another. After he'd watched the sheriff seat himself in a chair with its back against the wall, Dr. Allen said, "I want to ask you the God's honest truth. *Are you sure you really don't know?*"

Feeling like he might be incinerated by the blazing spark in the other man's eyes, the sheriff replied, "I don't know. What are you talking about?"

The hospital director stared at him. The fierce light in his eyes had a hint of desolation to it that suited the perpetual twilight of the room. Suddenly, the active doctor looked like a tired old man covered with wrinkles and hung with heavy shadows, and Sheriff Krutz had trouble believing his eyes.

"Earlier, when I was bringing that Hunter back to town, I saw Sybille." As the lawman spoke, he paid special attention to the director's face to see what reaction it would register, but the old physician didn't react at all. Maybe he thought it was a joke, maybe other matters were occupying his mind, or just maybe—

Tracing back through his memories so he might describe Sybille better, the sheriff suddenly remembered something. Something he'd seen somewhere before. Her clothes . . . The white blouse and the skirt . . .

"The Sybille you saw was one I called forth."

The impact of the director's words jarred the sheriff back to his senses. The wind whistled in his ear. "What did you just say?"

"To be a bit more precise, I extracted Sybille's image from her dream. Using this device here."

"Then, does that mean you can use that thing to wake her up?"

The director said nothing.

"I guess that's what I should expect from a machine from the Capital. That's fantastic."

"No," Dr. Allen said as he looked down at the peacefully slumbering girl with a pained gaze, "this machine can't awaken Sybille. The only thing that can do that is the Noble who left his fang marks on her throat. And another thing—this isn't from the Capital."

"It's not? Well, who made it then?" Sheriff Krutz asked, suspiciously eyeing the complex arrangement of metal, crystals, and batteries.

"I did. And it took me just two hours."

The sheriff was at a loss for words.

"Two hours before I ran into you and the Hunter outside her room, I had just gone back to my office after finishing my rounds. I thought I'd stare out the window for a while, have myself a smoke, straighten up my desk—when I found *this* there."

The sheriff was still speechless.

"Well, not really *this*, but all its parts. They didn't even have plans with them. But I took one look at them and knew how to put it together. Now, don't you look at me that way," he said to the sheriff. "I'm not crazy. You should know better than anyone I'm not that kind of person. I always tell the truth."

"That's true, but—"

"Come on, Krutz," the hospital director said in a nostalgic tone. Very rarely did he call the sheriff by name, but what they were involved in now had made them compatriots, or, perhaps more accurately, co-conspirators. "It's been a long thirty years. When this happened to Sybille, I was just thirty-five, a doctor still wet behind the ears. I tried so hard to save her, like I was fighting for my very life . . ."

A ghastly spark resided in the director's eyes. It was as if something extremely precious had been taken from his soul, and that spark was a light shining out of the abyss left in its place.

"I can still recall how it was back then. You and Sybille walking home from school, holding hands. And Sybille making you garlands with flowers from the field out back. White and blue ones—maybe they were celaine blossoms? She put them around your neck, but you got all bashful and took them off like a big dope. On the other hand, that time Sybille fell into the river, you jumped in without a second thought—even though the current was wild enough to drag a man away in only knee-deep water. And when she went out grape picking with her friends and she was the only one who didn't come back, you were the one who went off with a beat-up old rifle in hand to search for her all over a demon-filled forest. Isn't that right?"

Sheriff Krutz nodded. His expression looked like he was staring at something right in front of him, but on the other side of an eternal gulf.

"Were Sybille's hands warm? Were her lips soft the first time you kissed them? Was that golden hair of hers as soft as silk? Well, was it?" Dr. Allen asked. "And when she pressed her feverish cheek against your chest, didn't she tell you it was like iron? And that she could hear the beating of your heart?"

"Probably."

The tone of the old man's voice suddenly dropped. "What if all of that was a lie?" he said.

For a brief while, the sheriff's expression showed he was still lost in remembrance. And then, slowly studying the face of the elderly physician, he said, "What?!"

"I'll tell you." Gently resting his hand on Sybille's forehead, the director muttered in a low voice, "I'll tell you something you're better off not hearing. Something you're better off not knowing."

†

When Sheriff Krutz got back to the station, D was lying down in the cell without bars.

"What happened here?" the sheriff asked, and Bates explained the situation. "As soon as Clements gets out of the hospital, lock him up," the lawman ordered. "We're gonna make an example of him. Give him two weeks. Now, get out there and patrol. I'm gonna ask our guest some questions."

"Yes sir." Wearing an expression that showed he didn't completely understand, Bates stepped out of the office.

The sheriff turned around to face D. There was an incredulous look in his eyes as he inspected the shattered wall.

"Did you solve the mystery about Sybille?" D asked softly.

"Nope. Think you know the answer?"

"How long are you going to keep me in here?"

"Until this is over."

"When will it be over?"

"I don't know," the sheriff replied wearily. Of course, D had no way of knowing the lawman wore the same tired air as the hospital director. "From what Bates tells me, you were sleeping. You dream about Sybille?"

"There was some interference," the Hunter replied.

"Interference?"

"It seems there are those who don't want me to respond to the girl's call."

"Are you saying a foe can get inside dreams?" the sheriff muttered as if in a daze. "In that case, could you even call it a dream? What do you think?"

"Maybe even dreams can dream." D quietly gazed at the sheriff. "I don't mind staying in here, but are you sure that's the best thing for the rest of you?"

"Just what's that supposed to mean?" Sheriff Krutz was gazing back at D. For the first time, a mood of impending violence hung between them.

Their eyes shifted in the same direction simultaneously. A plump female form burst energetically into the cell while her feverish knocking still echoed from the door. The face, now pale, was that of the jack-of-all-trades—Maggie.

"Sheriff, we've got serious trouble!" she bellowed, her tone perfectly matching the energy that carried her into the room.

"What is it?" the sheriff asked.

The woman pointed out the door. "Well, I hadn't been out there in a dog's age—to Old Mrs. Sheldon's, I mean."

D's eyes sparkled with sudden interest.

"But when I got there, you just wouldn't . . . When I got there, I found the old woman out back in her garden . . . with a black arrow through her throat . . ."

The Awakened

CHAPTER 5

I

It was thirty minutes later that a trio arrived at Old Mrs. Sheldon's house: Maggie the Almighty—who discovered the body—Sheriff Krutz, and D. The sheriff himself had requested that D accompany them. "Are you coming?" he'd asked, and D had stood up. That's all there was to it. For some reason, the sheriff had brought the Hunter's longsword with him. D didn't seem to care at all.

When the little house came into view beyond the ever-changing contours of the hill, the sheriff furrowed his brow and looked over at Maggie, who rode by his side. Smoke was rising from the chimney. Apparently she had noticed it, too. "That's odd. When I left, there wasn't anything coming out," she shouted.

Her words were soon obliterated by the thunder of hoofbeats as they quickened their pace toward the house. With riddles locked in their hearts, the three of them halted their mounts in front of the little house. The sheriff was the first one through the front door—where he froze on the spot. Peeking around from behind him, Maggie let out a scream of terror. "It can't be . . . When I saw her, I'm sure she was—"

"What's this you're so sure of?" Old Mrs. Sheldon asked, setting her steaming cup of coffee down on the living room table and glaring at her boorish intruders.

"We're not . . . It's just . . . We got word that someone had found you murdered, you see," the sheriff explained with a rare feebleness in his voice.

"I'm not sure I want to hear any more of that talk, Sheriff. Sure, a lonely old bird such as me likes to have company, but certainly not on account of that sort of rumor." The old woman closed the front collar of her coat as she stood up.

"But this can't be! I saw her lying in the garden out back, covered with blood," Maggie bellowed, her meaty jowls shaking. "Check into it, Sheriff. Check into it real good."

"Take a good look. The person you claimed was dead is standing right in front of us. If there's anything human that can survive getting shot through the neck, I'd sure like to see it." And saying that, the sheriff turned around and suddenly exclaimed, "Where's D?!"

It appeared that the Hunter had vanished from the doorway without anyone noticing.

Maggie and the sheriff circled around behind the house to the flower garden and found a tall figure in black swaying with the breeze.

"You stay where I can see you," the sheriff told him.

"There's not even a trace of the blood. That's impossible," Maggie said from behind them. Stepping in front of the two men, she extended her hand toward part of the riotous mix of blooms. Amazingly, her limb wasn't even trembling. It was this same courage that allowed her to work as a jack-of-all-trades visiting scattered villages across the Frontier. "She was lying right over there and the ground all around her was bright red with blood . . . There was a black arrow jutting out of her neck . . . What's this?!"

The sheriff squinted at her exclamation.

Maggie's hand then pointed to an area a little in front of the first spot she'd indicated. "Even the flowers have vanished!" she shouted.

"The flowers?"

"There were blue flowers in bloom. Right in here. Prettier than any I'd ever seen. And now, as you can see, they're just gone . . ."

As if in a daze, she turned to Sheriff Krutz, and as their eyes met, D asked the lawman, "When's the last time you were out here?"

"About five days back," the sheriff replied in a voice as thin as paper. "But I didn't actually see her then. I was just in the area—and I saw the smoke coming out of her chimney."

"Were there blue flowers in bloom then?"

Thinking a bit, the sheriff shook his head. "Nope."

"So, they bloomed and then disappeared, did they?" the Hunter mused.

"I think her eyes might've been playing tricks on her."

"Wait just one minute there—you think I dreamed all this?" the woman roared angrily, but she immediately fell silent at the result of her words.

The trio was enveloped by tension as tight as a nerve at the breaking point. D quietly looked at the sheriff. The stiffness that'd taken hold of Krutz's whisker-peppered cheeks was gone in an instant, and the placid atmosphere returned.

"What kind of flowers were they?" D asked Maggie.

Perhaps thinking him her ally, the traveling merchant stared at his profile as if hypnotized, then hastily made some gestures with her plump fingers. "They were about this big, and just the most beautiful shade of blue. Though I've never been there before, I have to wonder if it's the same color as the 'sea' that I've been hearing about since I was a kid."

The sea—a blue petal.

D turned right around. Faster than anyone else, he'd determined there was no use staying there any longer.

The sheriff apologized to the old woman for their sudden call, and then the three of them mounted up.

"You should show your face around here from time to time, Sheriff," the old woman called out, her words clinging to them as they rode away.

On the road leading back to town, D alone wheeled his horse around.

"And where are *you* going?"

"I can't leave the village."

"You're in custody," the sheriff said bitterly.

"Your wife told me all about the girl. Where's the shortcut to the dance?"

Giving it some consideration, Sheriff Krutz then pointed in the direction of the forest to the southwest. "Go about two miles," he said. "When you come out of the forest, there'll be a little path. Follow that for three-quarters of a mile."

"I'll come back when this is finished."

As D finished speaking and prepared to give a kick to his horse's flanks, a long, thin shape flew toward him. Catching the longsword in his left hand without even turning, D galloped off.

"Not the most social type, is he?" Maggie muttered as she smoothed her hair. "But that's how the lookers have to be. I don't care how cold he was to me; I suppose I'd still try to move heaven and earth for him . . . even knowing he'd leave me for sure."

"You can tell how it is?" the sheriff said as he watched the dwindling figure.

"Hell, anyone can tell. He's not trying to do it, but he makes the people around him unhappy. At my age, and with me leaving the village behind real soon, it's not a big problem . . ." She looked at Sheriff Krutz with a sort of pity in her eyes, then turned the same gaze toward the old woman's home. "But I figure it's gotta be pretty hard on the rest of you folks . . . Gotta wonder if it wouldn't have been better if you'd never let him in."

†

By the time D arrived at the vacant lot, the sunlight was already fading and the sky was graced with a languid blue tone. Tethering his horse to a tree trunk, D trod across the yellowed grass. The scene around him was a familiar one. The lot was fairly large—some might even call it vast. At present, it held no mansion steeped in blue—just a grassy field stroked by the wind. Not speaking a word, D stood in the center of the lot where, in the dream, the great hall would have been. Here, the girl the sleep-bringer loved had imagined dance parties every night, and here in this overgrown lot she'd danced with furtive steps. And her partner had been—

"Can she come out of the dream?" D asked, as if putting the question to the wind.

"I don't know," the unsociable reply came, riding on the wind.

"Shall we give it a try, then?"

"Sure, why not?" the voice said.

D moved a little to the right. The tall grass hid him completely where the garden would have been. If he went still further to the right, he'd come to the gate, and beyond that, to the road that led to the mansion.

Catching strange sounds on the wind, D quietly turned around and saw two figures approaching from the path at the opposite end of the lot. The slender one was a little quicker. Squinting, he saw that it was Nan. The young man behind her was about the same age, though his face was quite boyish. The two of them probably lived close by.

"Aw, don't get so mad about it," the young man said, trying to keep his tone down, although the wind carried it clearly enough.

"I'm not mad at all. Go home," Nan said tearfully. This wasn't a quarrel between siblings, but between lovers.

"I didn't mean to say that, it just came out. You don't have to get so hot about it," the boy said. "C'mon. Let's go back. The sun'll be going down soon."

"There's nothing to worry about. I've been coming here for a long time. You can go home alone."

"Stop being such a ninny," the boy said, anger tingeing his words. Then he reached around from behind Nan and grabbed her by the wrist. Nan shook her arm free of his grip and quickened her pace.

The boy stopped following her. Cheeks flushed with indignation, he shouted, "Do whatever the hell you please, then. No matter what happens, your precious Hunter's not coming for you!" And then he turned his back on her.

Nan stopped in her tracks. Once the young man had vanished down the road, she turned around. She looked worried. She looked sorry, as well. Standing on tiptoe, she was about to go after him, but she soon abandoned that idea and settled back down on the ground. With the back of her right hand, she rubbed both her eyes. If silent tears could be called crying, then that's just what she was doing.

Waiting for her to finish dabbing at her eyes, D came out of the grass. When he was about fifteen or twenty feet away, Nan casually turned in his direction, and then finally she noticed him. Her eyes opened wide and her cheeks flushed instantly. "Oh, no!" she gasped. "How long have you been here?"

"I just arrived."

Nan seemed relieved. No one liked to be seen crying by other people. "But you saw us, didn't you?" she asked bashfully. Voice dipping lower, she said, "And I suppose you . . ." She wanted to ask if he'd overheard the boy mentioning a certain Hunter, too, but caught herself and never finished.

"You shouldn't fight like that."

"Stop it. You sound just like one of my teachers at school. It really doesn't suit you. And it wasn't even anything worth fighting about."

D said nothing.

"When I said I'd dreamt about you a few times, he said that was really strange because he'd only had the one dream. That irritated me, so I went ahead and told him I'd gone to see you and talk about it. And that's where the argument started . . ."

What would D make of this little dispute that centered on him?

"One of your childhood friends?" the Hunter asked.

Nan nodded. "The boy next door. His name's Kane."

After answering, Nan noticed that D had turned his back to her, and she went off after him. The same boy was coming back down the road. D was ready to move away.

"Don't. Stay here," Nan said, clinging to his arm. Perhaps she was just being obstinate.

Kane froze in his tracks and stayed that way for a while. It was hard to tell whether he was angry or amazed. "Asshole!" he shouted.

Nan hollered back, "Too bad. Looks like I already have a date!"

"The night creatures can eat you for all I care. Hop in a grave with the Nobility, why don't you?" And with those typical Frontier curses, the young man ran off.

"He's worried about you," D said, his voice calm. For some reason, the young man's voice got like that when he looked at a youthful, lively figure.

"What, that little bastard?" Nan sulked. She tried to act like an adult, but that unbelievable bit of childishness made her expression run the full gamut.

"Why did you come out here?"

"No reason. It's close by, and I've been playing here since I was little."

"Apparently Sybille used to come here a lot, too," said D.

"How do you know that?"

"Do you want to go to dance parties, too?"

"You don't talk about yourself at all, do you?" Nan said angrily. The Hunter was the cause of her quarrel earlier. She felt like since he knew it, the very least he could do was be a little kinder when he talked with her. But he was far too distant for her to ever say such a thing to him. After all, he was from another world. So, why did she have to dream about him three times? All of a sudden, Nan felt a sense of hatred toward someone, but she didn't know who—a fact that only further churned the emotions inside of her.

"You said you were in the bed next to hers, didn't you?"

"The *room* next to hers," Nan corrected him. "I spent two years in the hospital with foam worms eating through my chest. You know what happens when you get a case of those buggers?"

"I hear it hurts."

"Yeah," Nan said, holding her left hand over the soft swell of her bosom.

The worms were a favorite food of spear-carrying sprites, but the girl didn't realize they were part of the air that filled her lungs until the damage was done. If even one of the thousandth-of-a-millimeter-long creatures was allowed into the body, the toxins it contained could turn the victim's every breath into flames. Yet they actually hardened the lining of the lungs, so their host went through an agonizing hell before their body was completely burnt. When treatment came too late, the flaming breath could spread throughout the entire body, eventually serving up a corpse that had a glossy sheen on the outside, but was charred and crumbling on the inside.

A case of the foam worms was only treatable if caught during the first four weeks in the body—Nan had barely made it in time. Strapped down to her bed, she was pushed to the brink of madness by the pain, begging more than once for them to kill her. What saved her was the encouragement she got from her parents and Kane, and the wisdom the hospital director showed in the decision to move her bed.

Dr. Allen had used these words when he introduced the quietly slumbering girl in the next room to the agonized Nan: "You're going to get well someday. I know it hurts, but that's just proof that your condition is improving. If you just bear with it another year or two, you'll be able to race around under the blue sky again, free as you please. You'll be able to kiss boys, too, I suppose. But that girl won't. Chances are she'll never awaken again as long as she lives. All the things you're going to go on to experience ended for Sybille thirty years ago. And now she just sleeps, never aging. Is that any kind of life?"

"So, I just suffered through it," Nan said, gazing at D with sparkling eyes. "Knowing I'd get well someday—that someday, I could get out of bed, run across the ground, pick apples in the fall, go skating in winter, and swim in the lake in summer. And listen to Kane play his guitar again. That's what I thought about."

Having said all of this in a single breath, Nan suddenly looked down bashfully and played with her hair. The dusky light painted her profile a rosy hue as D remained silent and gazed at the eighteen-year-old girl. "What you said earlier . . . " Nan ventured in a tiny voice, still looking at the ground.

"Yes?"

"About the dance party—I heard about it from the sheriff. He said it was Sybille's dream—that he was sure every night she was throwing a dance party."

"Do you envy her?" D asked.

"Sure I do."

"This is a peaceful village."

"I still envy her. A lot more, recently." Nan stopped herself then. Frightened by D's eyes as he watched her, she froze. What was going to happen? The thrill that accompanied her shudders made her very pores open.

What actually happened was unexpectedly simple.

"How recently?" the Hunter asked her.

She didn't answer right away, but when she did speak, her voice was husky. "Since you . . . since you appeared in my dreams."

II

Did you get them?" Dr. Allen asked.

In lieu of a reply, Sheriff Krutz removed a thick wad of papers from the chest pocket of his coat and held them out. "Which one?" he said, teasing Dr. Allen by casually moving the mass of papers away from the older man as he reached for them with his blotchy finger-tips. Suddenly, there was a sharp crack. The sheriff's eyes shifted from the papers he'd just smacked into the palm of his otherhand and looked up at the hospital director. Krutz's eyes were ablaze, kindled by grief and an intense hatred.

The director took his gaze impassively. His iron will ruthlessly deflected the sheriff's arrows of fiery sentiment. An incredibly powerful sense of duty was supporting him. "You know what happened to Clements?" the director asked.

They were in Dr. Allen's private office. While flames fed by petroleum and a light that was a complex arrangement of lenses kept the dark at bay, the two of them were like darkness in human form.

The sheriff gave no reply.

Folding his hands on the table, Dr. Allen said, "He's in serious condition—broken ribs punctured both his lungs. Even after he heals, he's never going to be very spry again. Makes you wonder if he wouldn't have been better off dead. If nothing else, he was a fair bit more adventuresome than you."

"You think he knew what's going on here?" the sheriff asked in a hoarse voice.

"He doesn't seem to be aware of the situation. But from here on out, there'll be a lot more like him. We won't be able to say this is a peaceful village anymore."

The sheriff once again smacked the bundle of papers into the palm of his hand.

With the pile of papers now tossed down before the director's stormy eyes, Allen picked them up and began reading them. He pored over the pages with a prudent gaze, as if he were studying a patient's charts. "Alexis Piper: at least seven counts of murder, uses an electric whip . . . Belle Coldite: seventeen counts, trained in demon kempo . . . Maddox Ho: twelve counts of murder, uses a knife . . . I don't think any of them could stand up to the Hunter," Dr. Allen mused. "Hmm . . . The Bio Brothers . . ."

Eyes shining brightly, the director went on scanning through the rest of the papers. While he was doing so, the sheriff seated himself in a chair by the wall and gazed out at the darkness massing beyond the windows, never moving a muscle.

An hour later, the hospital director came to a decision, saying, "These guys are it."

"Can you get them?" the sheriff asked.

"I'll manage something. It may take some time, but time isn't a problem."

"You mean because he can't leave?"

"Precisely."

"Killing that Hunter's not gonna be easy," Sheriff Krutz stated. "Not even in *this world*."

"I realize that. That's precisely why Sybille called him here. But now that he's in here, there has to be some way he can be killed. Just as we can die, so can he."

"Well, I saw him a little while ago, and there wasn't a scratch on him."

"That's just because our preparations were inadequate," said Dr. Allen. "But I've continued to make improvements to the machine. This world and everything in it is on our side."

"For all the good it'll do us." The sheriff's words were accompanied by a metallic squeak—the sound of a trigger being pulled tight.

The hospital director gazed disdainfully at the muzzle of the missile gun that Krutz leveled at him. "Traded up for something to use against a Hunter who can chop down a laser beam, did you? You'd certainly be better off using that against him, but you really can't do that, either. You'd still have to worry about him coming back to life. Have you thought about blasting someone else with that thing?" His tone was inflammatory.

"You talking about Sybille?" Sheriff Krutz said, spitting the words.

"At the very least, it would settle matters here. Though I don't know exactly how everything would wind up," the director said, leaning back in his chair. "I was born in this village. It was a good village. Ever since I was a little boy, I thought there couldn't possibly be a more wonderful world anywhere. Every child eventually gets the urge to leave their birthplace, but the thought never even occurred to me. It was my sincerest wish to live my whole life here—to grow old and die in this village."

"Me too."

"But," the elderly physician began, his eyes colored as never before by weariness and despair, "I never would've guessed the whole thing was a sham . . ."

"Don't start that!" the sheriff moaned. The finger he had around the trigger was white from the strain.

"I believe I showed you proof of that not long ago. This world and everything in it is just Sybille's—"

Dr. Allen may have actually caught himself at the very end. The instant the ultra-compact missile flew from the twenty-millimeter-wide barrel it reached maximum velocity, slamming into the elderly physician's chest at a speed of fifteen hundred miles per hour before exploding. The detonation was the work of an impact fuse. A half ounce of explosive gel blew open the hospital director's chest and his left shoulder, killing him instantaneously.

"The Bio Brothers?" the sheriff muttered as he caught the foul stench of burning flesh and fat. Getting to his feet, he looked down at Dr. Allen with a touch of sadness in his eyes. "I was born here in the village, too, and swore to the people that I'd be their sheriff. And I can't be a party to murder, no matter what the reason."

Holstering the weapon at his waist, the sheriff grabbed the list of criminals and walked out of the room. There was no sign of anyone in the hall. Normally, he'd pass a few nurses at this hour. Come to mention it, there wasn't the smell that was unique to this time, either—the aroma of supper.

Sheriff Krutz went down into the basement. In front of the room where Sybille slept he came to a halt briefly. He tried to think about what he was doing, but couldn't get his thoughts to come together. He went in.

The machine, the feeble darkness, and Sybille were all sleeping.

There ought to be a few nurses around, the sheriff thought. It was like an empty hospital. He stared at Sybille's face, propped up on the pillow like a pale moonflower. Her serene breathing served to lessen, at least a bit, the burden of the darkness crushing down on his heart.

"Is it true, Sybille?" he called out to her. "Are all our memories just made-up stories? Was all that stuff about you and me just a dream? Is me being here now a dream? Hell, are the things I'm thinking now not even my own will? Is it all really just some dream you're having? Or something the *other* you dreams?!"

The sheriff slowly brushed his hand against the missile gun on his hip. He hesitated when his fingertips met the grip, but, after repeating this gesture a number of times, he finally grabbed the grip firmly and drew the weapon, pointing the barrel at Sybille. All part of a single action. That the barrel of the weapon shook was completely natural.

And then, a pale hand gently came to rest on the sheriff's.

"Ai-Ling?!" Open wide with amazement, Sheriff Krutz's eyes reflected the quietly smiling image of his wife. "But how . . . ? When did you get here?"

"Please, stop already," Ai-Ling said. She sounded so sad.

For a second, the sheriff got the impression that for the longest time he hadn't seen his wife wearing any other expression but sadness.

"It's already begun," Ai-Ling said. "No matter what you do, it won't help anything. The Sybille we have here isn't the real Sybille, you know."

"No. She *is*. I know she is."

"No, you don't. You don't know anything at all. Not even about yourself. Probably not even who you love."

"But I . . . You're the one I . . ."

"That's a lie," Ai-Ling said with a thin smile as she shook her head. "You're just trying to love me. But even that's just because *Sybille makes you do it*. The same goes for me hating you. Don't you see? I'm very happy now. Of course, that's due to Sybille's control, too . . ."

"No," Sheriff Krutz said, shaking his head. The sweat that had seeped from him, while he was unaware of it, now did a sparkling dance through the air. "That's not true. I'm me. I love you with all my heart. And you hate me with every inch of your body."

Ai-Ling was speechless. Something began to glisten in her eyes as they watched her husband.

The sheriff was pierced by a near-indescribable fear. That fear spoke to him.

What exactly are you?

I'm the sheriff. My name is Krutz Bogen. Age: forty-eight. Weight: one hundred and fifty-seven pounds. Height: six feet three inches. My favorite food is . . .

What are you? Why are you here? How did you come to exist?

I was born. I came from my mother's womb.

Where is your mother? What do you mean by "mother"?

The woman who gave birth to me. Her grave's in the cemetery on the outskirts of the village.

"Krutz! Darling!" his wife called to him. "Give up already. Let's just accept our fate. That's the best thing we can do."

"You've gotta be kidding me," the sheriff moaned. His hair was standing on end. But this phenomenon was more the result of anger than fear. "I don't care what my fate may be—if it's something someone else would assign me, then I'll be damned if I'm gonna submit to it. I'm me. I'll live by my own thoughts."

"Yes, that's it. It's all about living," Ai-Ling whispered gently. "Even if we are just part of some other Sybille's dream, we still have a right to live. This whole world does. Please, you've got to help me with this."

Sheriff Krutz shut his eyes. His wife's request overflowed with the sincerest passion . . . but even that wasn't her own doing. He recalled what the hospital director had revealed to him just before he'd gone back to the jail to visit D.

This village, this world, even we ourselves are a dream—a dream Sybille has. All of this will vanish like a popped bubble if she awakens even once—that's what we all are. And that includes the Sybille who sleeps in our world, too.

When Krutz still refused to believe, Dr. Allen manipulated the machine connected to Sybille's head to give substance to her image so the lawman might see. The image was a copy of the girl as she made herself appear in her dreams, a copy that disappeared less than two seconds later, but even after that the sheriff was a tangle of doubts, standing still as a statue. And now–

"It's a lie," he groaned.

"Please, help me with this," Ai-Ling begged him. "So we can continue to exist . . ."

"And do what? What's the point? Suppose we *are* just the dream of the other Sybille . . ."

The words of the hospital director came back to him: *Since we are dreams, in order to continue to exist, we must see to it Sybille continues to dream. That Hunter came to disturb everything.*

How do you know that? Krutz had asked.

Because . . .

"Sybille!" the sheriff screamed. The frantic cry gave him the determination to stick to what he believed. His thumb cocked the hammer of the missile gun.

"Don't!" Ai-Ling cried.

"What are you afraid of? The director said this Sybille is just part of a dream created by the other Sybille. Just like us."

"We'll disappear, too."

"If Sybille wants to wake up, then that's fine," said the sheriff.

"How can you do this?"

"You said all our emotions are just something someone else gave us, right? In that case, maybe I really don't love Sybille at all," Sheriff Krutz said. "If this Sybille is just part of the dream, sleeping and dreaming within this dream . . . then, if I kill her, the other Sybille might wake up . . ."

"Darling!"

Taking her cry as his cue, the sheriff pulled the trigger. Bright red flames enveloped the bed. The sheriff stared at the missile gun like an idiot. Sybille was sleeping peacefully. Not a trace remained of the flames now.

If we're lucky, perhaps this world has broken off from Sybille's dreams and now has a will of its own, the words of Dr. Allen came back into his

mind once more. *The world doesn't want to be destroyed. That's why it put me to work.*

Sheriff Krutz lowered his weapon. The frosty beauty of the Hunter drifted to the forefront of his mind and a strange peacefulness came over him. D alone, he knew, was a separate entity. The missile gun sank slowly.

"Darling . . ."

Not answering his wife's call, the sheriff calmly walked toward the door.

"Where are you going?"

"I'm gonna leave the village."

"How?" Ai-Ling asked.

"I don't know. But I'll go around and around a thousand times if need be. Maybe I'll die in the process."

Ai-Ling said nothing.

The white door pinched the form of the sheriff from view.

"My darling . . ." Ai-Ling fell to her knees, sobbing. Up 'til this very day, she'd lived with the knowledge that her husband's heart would never let go of Sybille. She'd always believed the passing years would eventually sweep away the anger and sadness she felt watching her husband go off to see the girl. Thirty years had passed before she finally realized she was used to it. But a resolution was coming–now.

"It's an awful dream, isn't it?" the voice of the hospital director echoed over her shoulder.

"But, my husband . . ."

"Can't be helped. Wouldn't you agree?"

Ai-Ling closed her eyes and nodded. A tear left her cheek, falling to strike her knee.

III

When darkness ruled the world, people went in-time. Ten thousand years of memories of the creatures in black were locked into the populace's DNA, and the nocturnal cries of the beasts only served to multiply their fears. Even now, night didn't belong to humanity—with the exception of this one small village. Normally, lamps glowed between the trees here, the long shadows of lovers flickered on paths, and the mirthful voices never ceased. But tonight, all that had changed. There were no human forms out on the moonlit streets. The door to every house was barred; people were huddled around their fireplaces, unable to move, as if that was the only place they'd have substance. Each and every villager was straining his or her ears to catch the movements of a single man.

Moonlight falling on every inch of him, D slept in part of the vacant lot. Propped up against the trunk of the same demon's scruff oak tree that his horse was tethered to, his torso looked ablaze in the light. A few minutes earlier he'd shut his eyes and immediately fallen asleep. He was once again heading to the blue mansion to ask its mistress why she'd called him there. Suddenly, a gust of wind blew against his body and D's eyes opened. The echo of iron-shod hooves came down the road, and before long a horse and rider appeared in the lot. They were heading straight toward D, who made no attempt to get up.

"Thought you'd be here," the sheriff said. "Did you meet with her in your dream? With the real Sybille, I mean."

Lightly raising the brim of his traveler's hat, D stared at the sheriff's honest face. "Finally found out, did you?" he asked.

"Yep," Sheriff Krutz said with a nod. "When did you know?"

"When I called on Old Mrs. Sheldon's place with you. I remembered that I'd had a cup of tea there with a blue petal floating in it. After that, it was just a matter of adding things up."

"I don't know exactly how, but Dr. Allen intends to get the Bio Brothers. Ever heard of them?" the sheriff asked, smiling wryly. After all, he couldn't tell if the information in this world would match that of D's own.

D didn't say anything. The sheriff believed his silence wasn't due to his being uninformed, but rather because he knew who he was going up against and it didn't matter to him in the least. How torturous had the times he'd lived through been? Thinking of this, Sheriff Krutz felt the heavy, dark sediment that had collected in his heart suddenly disappear; he smiled without even knowing it. "That's all I had to say. Looks like I went and woke you up, though. Did you see Sybille?"

Meeting the lawman's searching gaze, D shook his head. "No."

"Haven't slept yet, then?"

"I didn't dream."

The sheriff didn't quite know what to say, but then D answered his question for him.

"Probably due to the machine the hospital director was using."

"In that case, the dream you had would be the same one the Sybille in *this* world is having, wouldn't it?" Sheriff Krutz asked.

"Probably."

"Wonder if it's the same one the *real* Sybille has."

D nodded. "The blue light and the white gown really suit her."

Staring at D for a while, the sheriff then thanked him. "Dr. Allen and Sybille are in the basement of the hospital. That's all I really came to say. Good luck to you."

"Where are you going?"

"Out of the village," the sheriff said. "Don't know where I'll go once I'm out, but I've gotta give it a shot. If Sybille wakes from her dream in the meantime, that's fine by me, too."

"Good luck."

"Same to you."

Sheriff Krutz wheeled his horse around, and D watched him until he'd vanished down the road. Apparently, the only way the Hunter would be able to ask Sybille why she'd called him here was to go to the hospital.

"Well, are we off then?" his left hand asked.

"There's no other option."

"Why don't you try talking to the girl? You know, persuade her to go on sleeping. No matter what you try, nothing you do will counter the effect of his bite. The girl the sleep-bringer loved will never wake again. You ought to tell the doctor and sheriff of this fact and set their minds at ease."

D pulled a dagger from his coat and slowly began digging up the ground. "Maybe the girl won't ask me to wake her up," he said.

The voice in his left hand seemed bewildered by his statement. After a short time, it said in a vaguely buoyant tone, "You sure do say some crazy stuff for a pretty boy. So, what'll you do if that happens, eh?" The voice stopped suddenly, making a sound like something was stuck in its throat. D pressed his left hand against the mound of black soil he'd dug up. And with that, a sound that anyone would recognize as chewing began, and the mound of dirt dwindled swiftly.

What was happening went without saying. Powered by the four elements of the universe—earth, wind, fire, and water—the counte-nanced carbuncle was taking his sustenance. And yet, it seemed to be eating out of frustration. D simply kept his eyes pointed straight ahead at nothing and didn't move a muscle. In no time, the exag-gerated sounds of mastication faded; a rude smacking of lips ensued, followed by a belch that shook the darkness.

"They've taken measures against you, haven't they? If we can't do what we like in this world, we might not even be able to ask the girl what she wants," the now mean-spirited voice informed him. "That guy from the hospital's been meddling with the brain of this world's Sybille. If the dream you have is the same one she's dreaming, you probably won't be able to see her again." And then, as if suggesting something the Hunter hadn't thought of, he added, "But wouldn't that wrap everything up all neat and tidy? The dream just wants to stay a dream, after all. I mean, even for the girl, I don't think this world is all that bad, as dreams go."

"You're not the one who has to dream it . . . and neither am I." D got up without making a sound. Bright in the moonlight, his profile was cold and beautiful enough to astonish any dreamer.

†

Even as Krutz came up on the last curve, he didn't sense anything out of the ordinary. *Is it gonna send me around in a circle again?* The lawman paused and wondered. *If it does, that's just fine by me.* Sheriff Krutz rode on, regardless. The scene around him was unchanged. He finished making the turn, and could then make out the dome-shaped watch post on the outskirts of the village. It looked like he was going to be able to get out.

The watch post was manned twenty-four hours a day by three shifts of young men from the village. He took a peek inside, but there was no one around. If there'd been anyone in there, he'd have felt them or heard their breathing, but there was nothing like that–only the cold atmosphere on what had been an unattended post from the very beginning pierced the sheriff. Perhaps this was a dream, too?

Getting off his horse, he went into the watch post and pushed the control button. There was the low whine of a winch as the four bars that comprised the roadblock were hoisted out of the way. The sheriff mounted his horse again and took a hold of the reins when all of the sudden a low whinny entered his ear and raced through his whole body. There were two sounds–the sounds of a horse and another animal.

Forty-five to fifty yards ahead of him, the road was intersected by a broad strip of white. Sheriff Krutz concentrated his gaze on the right side–off to the south. If he couldn't see that far in the darkness, he never would've been cut out to be sheriff. Although it wasn't a particularly common occurrence, rescuing those careless enough to travel by night was part of what he was paid to do.

The moon was bright. And yet, the two approaching silhouettes seemed to have an undulating darkness trailing along behind them. One of them was a man in a coat on horseback. The other one was doubled over the back of some black quadruped shape, which at first appeared to be just a hump on its back. The sheriff's memory informed him of who they were. Giving a light kick to his mount's flanks, he rode out to the road.

The strange silhouettes continued to draw closer, not seeming the least bit unnerved.

"Hold it," the sheriff called out to them from twenty feet away.

The two men halted as if on cue. Their stop had been so well synchronized, it almost seemed like they were telepathically linked.

"You're the Bio Brothers, aren't you?" the lawman asked.

There was no reply.

"I'm the sheriff in this village. Krutz is the name. You keep riding on straight to the north."

As soon as he'd finished speaking, there was some reaction from the others. The man on the horse said nothing, but smiled. The quadruped shadow bared its fangs. Either side of the muzzle it extended had a gleam of emerald—its eyes.

From his seat on the back of a cruelly snarling black panther, the shadowy figure said, "He told us to be on our way down the main road, big brother." The tone was mocking. Scorn was a common camouflage for anger. "He's telling us to keep out of his village." Below the source of that voice, there was a wet sound, like flesh ripping. The little man who looked like he'd been lying on his belly had risen. The flesh of his abdomen continued to rip free from the black panther's back.

"We're here because we were sent for," the man on the horse said. He was a figure of imposing proportions, every bit as tall and broad-shouldered as the sheriff. His tone was as dark and heavy as the earth. "You ought to know that. You'd know *one of our jobs*, at least."

"Yeah, *one of them*," the man on the panther's back said. The little man was dressed in black from top to bottom. It was impossible to tell whether or not his lower body was actually fused to the panther's back.

"Really, now. How many more are there?" Sheriff Krutz asked, lifting the bottom of his jacket and brushing the grip of his missile gun with his right hand. He was well aware of the ruthless ways of the Bio Brothers. Two of the most dangerous killers on the Frontier, the pair were known to tear those that faced them limb from limb, while the panther filled its belly with their victims' innards before they finished ripping them to shreds. *Could he take them?* He tried to imagine it, but wasn't so sure if he could. The two of them would be bad enough, but he sensed something else waiting behind him.

"Just one," the man on the horse replied. "Getting rid of you."

The sheriff kicked his horse's flanks. At the same time, the two men across from him also began to advance. Sheriff Krutz figured the battle would be decided in an instant. The distance between the two factions was definitely diminishing, and the darkness between them made sounds as it began to coalesce. A lust for blood blew at the sheriff's face like a gale-force wind. The panther sprang at him from the left, like pouncing darkness. In midair, its claws grew a foot long.

The very instant the sheriff vanished from the beast's field of view, the little man on its back leapt into the air. "What the hell?!" the little man cried out in astonishment. Although he'd followed the sheriff's leap and was launching an attack on the lawman, the knife that gleamed in the little man's right hand had been deflected by the barrel of the missile gun. To make matters worse, the gun Krutz was holding also smacked him in the forehead, knocking him backward.

Even in midair, the sheriff kept an eye on his foes on the ground. He turned the missile gun that'd smashed open the brow of the little man—who was apparently the younger brother—in the direction of the big man on the horse and opened fire.

"Hyah!" the man cried, and a second later, he was galloping across the earth.

Equipped with a laser-targeting unit, the missile limned a gentle curve.

Touching down again, the sheriff fired a second shot at the black panther that'd bounded off the back of his horse in another direction.

The panther didn't dodge it. In fact, the flames from the missile imbedded in its forehead vanished unexpectedly. Was it a misfire? Or was that the world's way of trying to save itself?

Time for a third shot. The sheriff's fingers worked reflexively, and even when he found the pale flames of a projectile sinking deep into his chest, his digits didn't stop. When the unholy conflagration finally died out, a shadowy figure stood up in the spot where, until then, the sheriff had existed. It was the man on the horse–the older brother. The missile had been aimed at him, however, the target that'd apparently run away had appeared again from the completely opposite direction.

"Wasn't as easy as I thought it'd be," the younger brother spat from the panther's back, one hand pressed to his forehead. He then licked at the blood dripping from his fingers with his hideously long tongue.

"Excuses about being out of practice aren't gonna cut it," the older brother said reproachfully.

"You're right."

"Our next opponent is a heavyweight."

The younger brother stopped moving. As he did, the black panther bared its fangs and let out a menacing snarl. The moon alone remained bright as the two shadowy figures headed into the village.

†

It's getting rougher on her," Dr. Allen muttered as he watched the blue line on the display panel. "Sybille's putting up quite a fight, too, as I thought she might. Of course, that's not surprising, as this world was hers to begin with."

"Will it be all right?" Ai-Ling asked. "That machine of yours will only work on our Sybille, I take it. What'll happen if the other Sybille intervenes?"

"I don't know," the hospital director said. "I don't even want to consider it. All we can do is pray it doesn't come to that. That is, if we even have the right to pray."

"I should hope we at least have the right to live," Old Mrs. Sheldon said, sitting in her favorite rocking chair over by the window. "Not that I mind, as it'll be time for me to call it a night soon. Of course, I can't even get a decent night's rest with the thought of this world of ours bringing me back from the dead whenever it pleases. What in blazes is gonna happen next? Who gets to decide our fate? *This world?* The other Sybille you folks have been talking about?"

She turned her face toward the floor in contemplation, as Ai-Ling said in a brooding tone, "D. What if we explained what's going on to the Hunter and tried to get him to help us? We could ask him to ignore Sybille's request."

"I'm thinking that'd be a big waste of time," Old Mrs. Sheldon replied, shaking her head. "Sybille went to all the trouble of calling him here. Whether he wants to or not, he's gonna wake Sybille up."

"I have to agree with that," the director said as he adjusted the energizing crystals.

"Wake her up . . ." Ai-Ling muttered. "Wake up someone who received the kiss of the Nobility . . . I wonder if he could?"

"What other point would he have in being here?" said Dr. Allen.

Ai-Ling was about to open her mouth to speak when the old woman's harsh tone stopped her.

"Leave your thoughts as just that. I certainly don't wanna hear them."

Silence descended on them until the intercom set in the wall started to buzz softly. Getting to his feet, Dr. Allen pushed the talk button and asked, "What is it?"

The nurse's voice wasn't very loud, but the other two heard her well enough.

"So, they're here, are they?" the director muttered, confirming that he'd gotten the message before he released the talk button again.

"What'll you do? Are you going to leave Sybille's dream erased?"

Dr. Allen shook his head at Ai-Ling's question. His gesture carried something more with it, but the woman didn't want to interpret it as despair.

"Is there anything else we can do?" the old woman asked as she rocked.

"We won't know until we try," the director said, reaching for his machine.

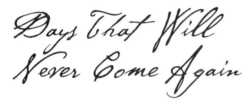

Days That Will Never Come Again

CHAPTER 6

I

When D entered the hospital, he was greeted by the stark emptiness of the hallways and the white lighting that made it look as still as the bottom of a lake.

"Welcome," someone said from behind him.

Turning, the Hunter found a nurse standing there.

"Director Allen is waiting for you. Allow me to show you the way." Giving a slight bow, she walked ahead. D followed after her. "You know, I had a dream about you, too," the nurse said.

D didn't respond. The nurse probably hated him as well. D was the enemy of all who wanted to continue living in this world. Even here in a world where they'd once been fond of the Nobility, there was no place for him.

The two of them got in the elevator. In no time, they arrived at the bottom floor. A hallway devoid of life seemed to continue on without end under the harsh white lights. The nurse's footsteps were the only sound that rang through the stagnant air. Just as the sound of them stopped, the scene around D grew distorted. It was full of light . . . natural light. What kind of power did one need to turn a subterranean passageway at night into a field in the daylight?

The world was covered with a green so lush it seemed to saturate his eyes. A young man and young lady raced across the plains, apparently headed toward the forest. The sunlight and green grass bestowed their blessings on the couple. The magnanimous will of nature seemed to bid all the joyful things in the world to serve the youthful lovers. The young lady turned. It was Sybille. The boy turned as well. Strong traces of the sheriff's face were visible. Laughter could be heard. Anyone would love to have such a dream.

D was standing in the forest. A bittersweet odor invaded his nose, and the trees were awash with crimson. It was late autumn. Ripe apples rolled by his feet. Chasing after them, Sybille dashed right at D, passing through his body like a ghost. The sweet product of life drooped from the branches of every tree, sparkling red in the light borne on the wind. Farmers with baskets on their backs smiled as they watched Sybille, and then walked away. Tonight, there'd surely be fat slices of apple pie on the dinner table.

Once again, the scene changed. The distant ringing of a bell shook the falling snowflakes; figures in black overcoats, grouped in twos and threes, lined up and filed into the mere skeleton of a building. It appeared to be the frame for a community hall. Inside were Sheriff Krutz and Sybille. Dr. Allen was there, too, and off to the side stood Ai-Ling and Old Mrs. Sheldon. Snow struck their faces and dyed their overcoats white. The pale lace patterns it left weren't quick to melt. All present exhaled white plumes as they listened with gleaming eyes to speeches by the mayor and the principal, then prayed for the future of their village.

Gradually the village grew larger. Old folks died, children grew up, clouds rolled by, old houses were rebuilt. Damage due to malfunctioning weather controllers was close to nonexistent here; very few people perished from accidents. On evenings in the spring, little girls changed into white dresses, children ran with fireworks in hand and left a rainbow of sparks in their wake like some fantasy. Everyone hastened down the main street to the site of the dance party being held at the vacant lot. Oddly enough, Sybille didn't dance even once, but sat enviously watching the men and women cavorting with their partners in the moonlight. The young sheriff danced with Ai-Ling, but as they danced he looked at Sybille. Ai-Ling sadly pressed her cheek to the lawman's chest. The village was peaceful.

D was in the cemetery. White gravestones in orderly rows paid respect to those now gone. There were also a number of moss-covered marble tombs among them, and as twilight drew near, the children visited and called out the names of those interred there. When a bit more time had passed and the last remnants of the day vanished, deep blue shadows rose from under the gravestones. And then the shadows joined hands with the children to form a big circle and recounted with pleasure tales of the Nobles' world, showing the villagers graceful dances quite unlike their own and teaching them how to make apple pies. From time to time, one of them would be pained with thirst, so one of the villagers would cut their wrist without any reluctance at all, catching the crimson fluid in an empty milk bottle and delivering it while it was still fresh. Here, consideration and coexistence and sympathy ruled the scene. An ideal had become reality. It was a dream, however, a dream where the dreamer mustn't awaken.

A faint voice reached D's ears. This particular voice always sounded so sad. *Why have you come?* it asked. But not with words. Just with a question. *Why have you come here? This is a peaceful village. Isn't this what you always had in mind?*

D didn't reply. He stood like a beautiful and intricately worked statue.

Eyes beyond numbering stared at him: the sheriff, the hospital director, Old Mrs. Sheldon, the hotel manager, countless other men, women, and children, and those with pale skin and ivory fangs. And Sybille, too.

Remain here, the pale ones said. *Live here in peace. No one will shun you here. This is the world he made.*

"That's right," D said, responding at last. "It was made by drinking the blood of a girl. What about her?"

That can't be helped. This is a beautiful village. And that was her dream.

"Perhaps it was *his* dream. The girl called me here. She hasn't told me what my job entails yet."

And do you intend to take it?

"I don't know."

You are a Vampire Hunter. Don't concern yourself with this.

A mysterious spark resided in D's eyes. "You're right, I am," he said.

Perhaps some deeper emotion lay behind those words. The intent gazes of the villagers that were trained on him accusingly suddenly froze . . . then glittered brighter than ever.

A heartbeat later, his surroundings were masked by pitch darkness. All that was left was D–and one other person, the hospital nurse.

"Would you lead the way?" D said to her softly.

The nurse turned around. She had Sybille's face. "Leave, D. Just leave the village," she said. "Everything will be fine then."

"Which Sybille are you?"

"I am myself. Please. If you do anything, I'll cease to exist in this world. Don't say anything or do anything. Just leave."

D began to walk slowly.

"D." Sybille's expression changed.

D walked away again.

†

Dammit, he's here. Your brain manipulations don't seem to be doing the trick, and things are starting to get hairy," Old Mrs. Sheldon said.

"What'll we do?" asked Ai-Ling.

"We'll just leave it all to this world," Dr. Allen replied.

"But this all originally sprang from Sybille's dreams. Can it break free of her?"

"I don't know," the director said. "After all, Sybille is putting up an awful lot of resistance."

The crystal shards that made up part of the machine gave off pale purple beams of light.

†

As D calmly walked away, the nurse swung at his back with her right hand. A knife she'd produced from somewhere glittered there. Before her blade had moved more than a few inches, a flash of silver slashed through her svelte torso. The nurse faded away, too. Even D couldn't tell whether she was a product of this world or a phantasm conjured up by someone manipulating Sybille's brain.

Once more the hallway stretched on forever. D halted. A number of doors were lined up on a wall that shouldn't have had any. He opened the closest one.

The image of Sybille floated in the darkness. "Leave our village," she said.

D closed the door without saying a word. He then opened the next door. His surroundings were masked by a thick white fog that clung to his skin. "Watch yourself now," his left hand said. "I can't quite analyze the components of this stuff. There are dream enzymes mixed in it."

D looked over his shoulder. The hallway was fading into the mist, too. Direction was ceasing to exist. D advanced toward where the door had been.

There was a slight creaking sound. Quickly enough, he remembered that familiar sound as Old Mrs. Sheldon rocking back and forth in her favorite chair. As she came into view, he saw she had a gray blanket on her lap, a tray with a teapot and steaming cups balancing on top of it. D noticed that the steam they gave off took the color of the sky as it rose in the air. This was all probably an illusion, too.

D's left hand was a blur of action. A needle of unfinished wood seemed to sprout from the left side of the old woman's chest. It'd been thrown by D. With the tiniest sound, she collapsed in her rocking chair. The old woman's body then disappeared.

"Seems whoever it is isn't as powerful as the dreamer," the Hunter's extended left hand said. "Still, you can't let your guard down. If we get taken out, it might mean more than us just vanishing. Here it comes!"

By "it," the voice meant the bluish smoke spreading through the air that was heading for them. No sooner had D held his breath than the smoke dropped, like it had real weight, and crushed around his upper body.

A flash of silver shot out. Two silvery slashes formed a cross that quartered the blue smoke, but it quickly fused together again and rushed through the air in pursuit of D as he leapt away. Trying to leap again, D found his feet stuck to the ground. Old Mrs. Sheldon lay on the floor, and she had a grip on the Hunter's ankles. D's upper body turned blue. He could feel the smoke seeping in through his skin.

The wind howled as the blue smoke became a single stream that was sucked into D's left hand. In less than a second, the world of white had returned. His left hand coughed. On the surface of his palm, a human face swiftly formed. "Shit . . ." it gasped. "Damn smoke . . . Probably shouldn't have swallowed that."

"It works by osmosis," D said, not seeming the least bit upset.

"I'm analyzing it now, so keep your pants on. Gonna have to try breaking the dream down to the elementary particle level." Just then, the voice gagged, and the tiny mouth disgorged blue smoke. It almost looked like he was blowing out a long drag from a cigarette.

Mingling with the white fog, the smoke soon vanished.

"I've got it! This stuff is–?!"

Suddenly, the cries of D's left hand were interrupted by a bizarre chill enveloping the Hunter's frame. With a sickeningly loud tearing sound, furry tentacles burst out all over his body. A monster within him–created, perhaps, by the combination of the smoke and the blue petal tea the old woman had given him before—was being born. Wriggling tentacles ruptured D's chest, stomach, and face. The back of his head flew off and something that looked like a cross between a spider and a scorpion peered out.

D's left hand grabbed the creature by the neck. It was like a vision of hell. With just one hand, D yanked out the creature that'd formed in his body. Flesh ripped and bones snapped. As the creature plopped to the ground, D's longsword split its brain in two. D stood there impassively.

"Well, I must say, I'm downright amazed at your power today," someone said with admiration. "If you weren't fully aware this world is no more than a dream, I fancy you'd be in a body bag right about now."

D turned around completely. There was no trace of the old woman, but D perceived her presence, despite the fact that she couldn't be seen.

Not at all ruffled, D began to walk. Even as he made his way through the fog, he maintained his impressive good looks. After taking a few steps, he halted. Ai-Ling stood before him.

"D," she said.

He couldn't tell if she'd shouted it or whispered it. Nevertheless, D continued walking once more.

"Wait! I'm the same Ai-Ling you met before!" Hers was a sorrowful cry. Surely it was painful that she even had to say this. Living with a husband who'd fallen for her best friend, stoically defending her home and family even though she knew her husband still loved the other girl—what had become of this woman's true nature? Was this just a role she played?

"Step aside," D said softly. "I have to go see Sybille."

"Stay here in the village, or forget about seeing her and just leave."

"Tell Sybille to let me," the Hunter replied.

"If you'll stay here in our village . . . in our world . . . I'll always—"

D kept walking. Ai-Ling didn't move. Putting his hand to her shoulder, D pushed her out of the way. It was a gentle nudge that wasn't like the young man. There was a door behind him.

"D . . ." Ai-Ling mumbled behind him. "Kill me . . ."

D grabbed hold of the doorknob. Behind him, the air stirred violently, and he went into action.

Ai-Ling had a knife in her right hand and had tried to stick the Hunter with it, but D grabbed her wrist with his left hand.

"I'm begging you, D," she said. "Please, just kill me . . . I can't die on my own, you see. This world just brings me back to life. But if you were to cut me down . . ."

D—the bringer of death—made a motion with his black-gloved hand and Ai-Ling fell to the floor. By the time low sobs spilled from her, the young man in black had disappeared through the door. He hadn't so much as glanced at the hysterical woman.

He was in the feeble darkness of the hospital room. Next to the bed sat a device, and next to that stood the hospital director.

"Here at last," Dr. Allen said happily. He wasn't talking about the Hunter.

D turned around.

Two figures appeared on the far side of the room—a huge man sitting on a horse and a little man lying on the back of a black panther. Though the room was small, there was more than enough space between them and the Hunter.

"D, I take it? We've heard talk about you," the man on the horse said. The ring of fear in his voice was probably due to his believing the talk they'd heard. "I'm Harold B., the senior Bio Brother. That there's my kid brother."

"Duncan B. is the name." The eyes of the little man and the panther brimmed with unearthly hostility as they looked up at D.

"We meet at last. We don't mind if we get destroyed," Harold said from over by the window. "Of course, if you take us down here, it looks like we'll be brought right back to life anyway. I don't suppose you're gonna turn around after all this and say you'll just settle down all peaceful-like in the village, now will you?" Harold brought his left hand to the breast pocket of his coat, pulled out something shiny, and tossed it at D's feet. It was a silver star.

In a heartbeat, the entire room froze. The director, the brothers, and even the black panther all saw something there so terrifying that it made their hair stand on end. D's eyes gave off a blood light. The instant it faded, the panther leapt without making a sound.

Bisecting the animal with the silvery flash that shot up from below, D held his longsword at the ready again. Just now, the panther's body had offered no more resistance than cutting through thin air. Instantly, the black panther was over by the wall again, its eyes wildly ablaze with a lust for killing. A moment later, the two halves of its bisected torso were connected again. Both the man on the horse and the one on the panther smirked. When the front half of the panther thudded to the floor, however, Harold's eyes filled with the first real look of fear.

"You . . . You *sonuvabitch* . . ." moaned the little man who'd tied his own life, or at least his upper body, to that of his beloved beast.

Not even bothering to look at the little man, D leveled his longsword at the man on the horse. "One on one won't be easy for you," the Hunter said in a low voice.

Harold gave a little nod. "Yep, we must've been out of our minds, I suppose, to throw down with Vampire Hunter D, of all people."

"Hold on, there. It still ain't over yet . . ." Duncan groaned from the floor. Copious amounts of dark red blood gushing from his wound, he dragged himself toward D. The sword the little man held in his right hand was proof enough he hadn't given up the fight yet.

D advanced smoothly. Not toward Harold, but rather toward Duncan. Though his foe could do no more than crawl, the Hunter's cruel blade came down at an angle, decapitating not only Duncan, but his black panther as well. Without a moment's delay, D leapt into the air and thrust his gore-stained blade right through Harold's chest. As the huge man dropped helplessly, the Hunter lopped off his head. The geysers of blood didn't erupt from the wounds until a second after D landed again.

Intensely silent, D turned to the hospital director.

"So, that finishes it, then?" said Dr. Allen. "You are one fearsome character, to be sure. Exactly what we'd expect from the one chosen to save our princess from her eternal slumber."

"I can't wake her up," D told him flatly. "All I want to know is what I'm supposed to do. Give *this* Sybille back her dream."

"If I refuse, will you cut me down?"

The Hunter didn't reply.

The hospital director soon nodded. His hair was standing on end. "This may be a dream, but still," Dr. Allen said, "I'm afraid to die."

The Hunter watched as the man reached for the machine with both hands. A second later a burning hot blade ran into D's back and out through his chest. Turning, he met Harold's face, which was plastered with a hideous grin.

"Too bad, eh?" Harold said with a wink. "And, you know, I ain't the only one still kicking. My kid brother's fit as you please, too."

The panther head on the floor bared its fangs, and the two halves of its torso balanced uneasily on two legs each. Of course, part of Duncan remained on top of all three pieces.

"The two of us are the product of some science from thousands of years ago—what they called biotechnology," the older brother explained. "See, we were made to be different, right down at the cellular level, namely, like this."

As he said that, Harold thrust his chest forward. It was literally as if he'd shed his skin. A semi-translucent Harold broke free of his body, floating a few feet in front of the spot where his physical body stood. And then, almost simultaneously, this new form took the color and texture of his original body. Then, his original body suddenly lost its color and substance, becoming like the reflection of a statue in a pool before disappearing without a sound.

Pulling these false images from his actual body, he could produce copies of himself. Perhaps even D hadn't imagined his opponent could form doppelgangers like this. Harold B. used these false images to confuse his foes while his real body crept around behind them and brought down a lethal blow with his weapon.

His younger brother, on the other hand, had vastly accelerated cellular activity. As a result of this, his limbs could continue to function even after they were severed from his body, and he could fuse with other living creatures to make them do his bidding. Who could hope to be a match for these brothers?

"End of the road, Hunter," the older brother said. Perhaps knowing something of D's nature, Harold didn't pull out the blade he'd run through the Hunter, but rather drew another one and lashed out with that. A heartbeat later, the arm wielding the new blade fell to the floor, severed at the shoulder. Realizing D had accomplished this with his sword without turning, and with a blade still stuck through his heart, Harold sputtered, "You *sonuvabitch* . . . You're no plain old dhampir . . . are you?!" With one hand clamped down on his shoulder while fresh blood gushed from the wound, Harold shook all over with pain and rage.

The only reason he managed to avoid the full damage of the flash of silver that zipped through the air was because D was fighting with a knife still stuck through his heart. It was a frightening display of stamina, the way the Hunter stood with only the slightest wobbliness before quickly shifting to the most exquisite combat stance. Harold and his indestructible brother Duncan, who still lay on the floor, backed away with a tinge of amazement in their eyes.

With his right hand leveling his blade at the two brothers, D reached around to his back with his left. Grabbing the knife by the handle, he jerked it free. And yet, the blade protruding from his chest seemed to go in precisely the opposite direction, pushing out further! For a heartbeat, D's expression seemed tinged with pain.

Three objects flew toward him. The black panther's head, its forequarters, and the hindquarters from which they'd been sliced. While the two halves of the torso each had a pair of legs, how the head had launched itself into the air was a mystery. Baring fangs that grew long and curved like those of a sabertooth tiger, the head made a huge turn in midair, bringing its jaws down toward the top of D's head.

A flash of silver light ripped through the beast from its fang-filled upper jaw to the base of its snout, and D sailed through the air without a sound. His coat fluttered out to deflect both halves of the torso.

A split second before the Hunter landed, the world around him spun a hundred and eighty degrees. The floor was above him, the ceiling below—and yet, D was still on his way back toward the floor. An odd sensation struck D, completely upsetting his sense of equilibrium. Although gravity was pulling him down toward the ground, his senses were telling him exactly the opposite.

"Kill him!" Harold shouted from horseback.

The fangs and claws closed down on D from above—although to the Hunter, it felt like they were coming from below. The teeth jutted from the severed upper jaw. There really weren't words to convey how bizarre it actually looked.

In an incredible display of skill, D parried the attacks—and fell to his knees. Fresh blood dripped from his chest, staining the floor.

"Your death in this world will mean death in reality," Dr. Allen said from somewhere unseen.

And it was at that very moment that D's form warped.

"No!" Dr. Allen screamed, but he wasn't alone. Harold B. cried the very same thing. The knife that'd left his hand had gone through D's body and stuck in the wall.

"He vanished . . ." Harold muttered in disbelief. A flash of silver had gone right past the end of his nose, knocking a crystal shard from the machine next to the bed.

"Damnation!" Dr. Allen shouted.

Harold's vicious gaze shifted to the bed with intense speed. Even after seeing the sorrowful visage of the beauty lying there, the beastly light didn't fade from his eyes. "What happened?" he asked. "Was it because that machine of yours started acting up?"

"No," the director said, shaking his head. "It's not the machine's fault. Control of this world is shifting, you see. But it's essentially the same as if the device had been destroyed."

"What are you gonna do?" Sounding very much like a curse, Duncan's question drifted up from the floor. He looked over the head of his panther, which had its snout sliced off, with eyes as red as blood and glaring at the hospital director. "If you just let him be, he's gonna see Sybille. And if that happens . . ."

"We're finished," Old Mrs. Sheldon said from the doorway. "If I were you, I'd be trying to come up with another way to stop that real fast. But it don't matter all that much to me."

The old woman sounded easygoing, apathetic even, but her words made Dr. Allen knit his brow. "There's still a way," he said. "Just you wait. Dream or not, a whole world is no easy thing to destroy."

II

D was back in the vacant lot—the same lot as always. The grass glistened in the moonlight and swayed in the breeze, just as it had when he left.

"Just so you know, that wasn't my doing," said the voice that spilled from D's left hand.

Ignoring the remark, D said, "Shall we take a little nap?" He must've known it was Sybille that'd transported him here from the hospital. The machine keeping her dreams in check was destroyed by Harold's dagger, which D threw just before he vanished. A vermilion stain spread across his chest.

"I suppose we should," his left hand said. "Two forces are competing for this world. Both are pretty tough. As a result, the opposition's just gonna keep escalating. But enough about that—I guess we should find you a bed, eh? If you've gotta go to sleep, at least after what just happened you're nice and tired for it."

D turned around. His cyborg horse was tethered to a tree not far away—his mount had been transported, too. "Watch the place while I'm gone," he said. And with that, he walked over to the nearby grove.

"Very interesting," his left hand said. "Plan on sleeping here, do you? You've got nerve, I'll give you that. They'll find you here in a second." The voice sounded almost excited about the proposition, as if the idea of D getting killed was so entertaining he could barely contain himself. For D, it would be the same no matter where he slept. The whole world was his enemy. But knowing this, he still chose to go back to sleep in the vacant lot, the very first place his foes would think of looking for him—indeed, he was no ordinary young man.

As he lay down, a slight sigh spilled from his thin lips. Most likely it was just his chest wound having its say. Of course, no one else would ever know for sure. D's sorrow, his joy, and his pain belonged to him alone.

Taking the longsword off his back and setting it down in the bushes to his left, D shut his eyes. Immediately, he was enveloped in blue light. He was in the hall of the mansion and a sad but sweet melody twined around him, and then flowed away. Why had Sybille chosen music so light but so sad?

A number of shadowy forms flowed in around D. The next thing he knew, the figures in the hall had begun to sway. The graceful steps of dreamers. Voices humming with laughter. Weaving his way through men and women who were like phantoms, D came to the center of the hall. All movement stopped. The dancers remained with hands together, chatting guests still held champagne glasses, all of them frozen for eternity in those poses. All except one—Sybille.

Saying nothing, D stared at the pale girl who stood there quietly. "It's about time you finally told me what it is you need," he said. "What do you want from me?"

"Please, kill me."

What had she said?

Could the words of this pale young lady, the one with these beautiful dreams, have said this? *Please, kill me.*

D's face was reflected in the black of Sybille's pupils. He was cold and beautiful . . . and completely removed from the deeper emotions.

"Why don't you just go on dancing like this?" the Hunter asked. "This night will never end. This is what you wanted. *He* knew that when he bit you."

D turned his eyes to one of the nearby dancers. The man's face was the color of darkness, but the fangs in his mouth were conspicuous. And his partner was an ordinary woman. It was a dance party for humans and Nobility—hand in hand in a world swimming with kindness and blue light. But what could all this mean if the Noble responsible for this had known about it, too? Perhaps the one who bit Sybille and made this wish of hers come true had wanted the very same thing. In the end, however, it had come down to this—

"Please, kill me," Sybille repeated. Her words were sincere—no anger, no pain, no weariness in them. That was what she desired from the very bottom of her heart.

"If you die," he said, "it will all fade away. As will this world. And everyone you've made. And everything they've dreamed." The Hunter's words were heavy with conviction. Could the young lady truly wish for death if it meant throwing everything away?

"Kill me—" she said.

D turned around to leave.

The hem of her white gown flapping wildly, Sybille dashed out in front of him. "Please, don't go. Don't leave until you've killed me. That's the whole reason I brought you here."

Not even bothering to shake free of her hands, D left the hall.

"Kill me," Sybille pleaded, tears glistening in her eyes.

D stopped on the veranda. On the brick path that led to the iron gate there stood a figure in black, an arrow already notched in his bow. "So, if I won't kill her, then they'll kill me?" D muttered. Was that how badly she wanted to die even though she had the perfect dream?

"I'm begging you."

Giving the girl no reply, D went down the stone stairs. The bow shook slightly. D's left hand raced out for the steel arrow howling through the air. Realizing that the little mouth in his palm had stopped his missile, the figure in black was thoroughly shaken.

Using the moment as an opening, D made a mad dash. As the shadowy figure kicked off the ground, a deadly thrust stretched toward his torso. The blade went into his chest through his black garments. Leaving only the jolt of that contact behind, the man leapt back to the iron fence.

D threw his sword, his beloved blade—a truly frightening move. It pierced the man's heart, went right through him, and didn't stop until it struck one of the iron bars of the gate.

D looked around. There was no sign of his foe in front of the iron gate. Then D saw him behind it, holding the left side of his chest as it dripped bright blood, slowly retreating into the depths of the forest.

Removing his sword from the fence, D pushed against the gate. With a slavering sound, his left hand spat out the arrow, and the missile fell against the bricks. A chain had been wound around the gate repeatedly. Raising his right hand, D swung it back down without particular difficulty. White sparks flew, and the chains dropped off like a lifeless serpent.

"Please, don't go," Sybille said, her voice mingling with the creak of the iron gate. "If you won't kill me, I'll—"

"—kill me?" D said.

Kill to destroy. Kill to not be destroyed.

"That's a human for you," the voice in his left hand muttered.

At that moment, pale blue sparks shot from the iron gate. D furrowed his brow as purplish smoke and faint groans rose from his left hand as it wrapped around the fence.

"Don't go. I beg of you!"

D pushed the gate open. All at once, the wind buffeted him. The moonlight scattered, and the forest wailed. Shredded leaves whirled around D like a cyclone. Fine lines of vermilion raced across his pallid cheeks. The foliage had become razor-sharp fragments of steel that slashed his skin.

Like great black wings, the hem of his coat spread, whistling as it dropped again. Every bit of airborne foliage was batted away, and they imbedded themselves in the ground.

"Stop your idle threats," said the Hunter. "If you want to be killed, you'd better try to kill me, too."

"But . . . If I did that . . ." Sybille said, her voice borne on the wind.

D's left hand chuckled with delight. "That was an awful thing to say. But at least you're showing your true colors . . ."

The left hand then gave a muffled cry of pain as D squeezed the melted flesh into a tight fist and walked away.

"Where do you think you're going?" the woman called out. "Unless you wake up, you can't get out of here. There's nowhere for you to go." Her voice seemed to follow him forever.

No place to go. For D, that made this place no different than anywhere else.

Thunder rumbled in the distant sky.

†

Nan entered the vacant lot. It was a pale, moonlit night. Her eyes were incredibly sharp, and she just couldn't get to sleep. Her quarrel with Kane was part of it, but at the same time, she was also aware that it wasn't the main reason. As she lay in bed, she couldn't close her eyes without seeing that Hunter's face. It rose in her heart just like the pale moon.

She'd gone outside to cool her head a bit. As the wind pushed her around her yard, she'd gotten an urge to go for a walk, and the next thing she knew, she was on the path that led to the vacant lot. She didn't have the faintest idea why she was going there.

On entering the lot, she immediately spotted D leaning back against a tall tree at the edge of the grove with his eyes shut. Jealousy filled her as she surmised that he was probably visiting Sybille's mansion. Muffling her footsteps, she walked over to his side.

As the girl gently reached out to touch D's shoulder, his eyes opened. Unfathomable in their hue, his eyes gazed at the paralyzed and dumbstruck Nan. "I'm glad you woke me up," he said. "Well done."

"Sure," Nan replied, her eyes wide. She had no way of knowing D had been stuck in a dead end in the dream world.

"What brings you here?"

"You—you're covered in blood . . ." the girl stammered.

"The wound has healed."

"But it looks awful," she said. "Come to my house. I'll clean it up for you."

"Just leave it be," D said, lightly shutting his eyes. Then he quickly asked, "Did you make up with that boy you were arguing with earlier?"

"Why, that's—" Nan began, about to tell him it was none of his business, but in the end she merely shook her head. The gorgeous young man, arrogant and cold-blooded, had suddenly looked so isolated and weary to her. Though she couldn't tell what his hat, boots, and coat were made of, there wasn't a loose thread or a mark on them. But the body they sheltered had no place to call home, and the reality of that hit her painfully hard. Surely this young man hadn't known even one night's peace. Tears filled Nan's eyes as she closed them, trying to chalk her own reaction up to adolescent sentimentality. Wiping away her tears, she opened her eyes again. D was looking up at her, and she began to blush.

"What's wrong?" asked D.

"Nothing. Please, don't say anything to scare me."

"Are you still afraid of me?"

Nan had no reply.

"You're the only one who dreamt of me three times. Do you have any idea why?"

"None whatsoever." As D's gaze left her, Nan damned her luck. "Um—aren't you even gonna ask me what I'm doing out here?" Though she'd broached the matter timidly enough, D didn't answer her. Nan could've cursed herself for asking such a stupid question.

"I couldn't get to sleep, so I decided to go for a walk. It's not like I went out looking for you or anything. Don't get the wrong idea."

While she realized she was just going to end up hurting herself, she couldn't help speaking. She'd probably hate herself in the worst way for it later.

"It's a lovely night," D said suddenly. "Quite appropriate for a peaceful village. Do you wish it could always be this way?"

Not fully understanding what he was getting at, Nan nodded anyway. She just felt like she had to. "This is where I was born," she said. "There's no place else quite as nice."

"Ever thought about leaving?"

Nan shook off the moonlight. "You mean to go to some distant village?" she asked. "Sure, I'd like to go, but I don't know what I'd find there. That scares me."

"How about your boyfriend?"

"You mean Kane? Give him another year and I'm sure he'll zip out of the village like an eagle freed from a snare. All the boys are like that. They're not the least bit afraid of the unknown. Or maybe they go *because* they're afraid."

Out on the Frontier, there weren't all that many young people who left their home villages. For villages that relied solely on local industries to support themselves, young people were an irreplaceable labor force—more precious than anything. Because the young men and women themselves understood this, the vast majority of them were destined to reach maturity, grow old, and go to their eternal reward all in that same village. Still, there were some young people who set out seeking the world beyond their village, while the ones that remained at home kept their love of unexplored territory burning deep in their hearts, with all the fire of a youth's feverish imaginings.

"How about Sybille?" D asked. His voice stirred the moonlight.

A strange turmoil engulfed Nan. Her lips trembling, she said the name of the dreamer. Why did D ask her such a thing when she'd never known her as anything but a slumbering princess?

"I don't know . . ." Nan replied, not surprisingly. "But . . ."

D watched the girl quietly.

"But I think a girl like her would just stay here and pass her whole life in the village, even if she wanted to go somewhere else. And if her own children wanted to leave, it would bother her, but she'd keep her peace and watch them go. After all, what she wanted more than anything was a peaceful village."

"Compared to other places, this village has a lot more young people who leave. Do you folks ever hear from them?"

"Yeah, sure," Nan said, nodding firmly. It was almost guaranteed that the young birds who left the nest would send money and letters back to their families. On very rare occasions, when the parents wished to see their children living in distant lands, back they came, as if they knew of their family's desires.

D listened, not saying a word. Somehow, Nan got the feeling he might be bidding this world farewell, but she quickly discounted that notion. He wasn't the kind of person who'd have anything to do with sentiment.

"I kinda get the feeling I know why she called you here," Nan said. Even she was startled by how smoothly the words came out. "Mind if I tell you?"

"Go ahead."

"Because you don't have any connection to this village or our world. I don't know why that'd be important, I just think it's the reason she chose you. Because you're someone who won't be moved by the joy or grief Sybille feels while she sleeps, or by the hopes and despairs of our world. You come, you go. That's the kind of person you are."

Once she finished speaking, she had the feeling it hadn't been a nice thing to say, but D didn't seem to mind in the least; he just kept staring straight ahead. As she gazed at his perfect profile, Nan felt a fire she'd never really known before welling up in her heart. While she was fully aware he wasn't the kind of person who got involved with others, that made her feel all the more like she wanted him to be someone special. And she wanted him to feel the same way about her. She'd seen D more than anyone else in the village had, after all. This thought rose from the deepest reaches of Nan's psyche, easily weaving its way through the safeguards of rationality before it moved the girl's hand. Another thought, a different thought.

The girl's fingers touched D's shoulder. Somewhere inside her, an image of Kane may have remained, but it swiftly vanished. "D," Nan said to him, "this is probably the last time I'll ever see you."

She had no proof of that, but it just felt so incredibly true. Nan quietly brought her cheek to rest on a powerful shoulder that spoke volumes about how solid he was. It was the only thing she could do, even though she'd seen his face in her dreams three nights more than the rest of the villagers.

D didn't say a thing. At least Kane would've hugged her to his chest and stroked her hair.

"D," Nan said, not expecting anything, but still wanting something nonetheless. Once more she called his name, but it was then that she was pushed away, and the Hunter rose with such speed he whipped up a black wind.

"Stand back," was all he said. Ringing cruelly as the crack of a whip, the words drifted off into the forest as Nan and D both turned their gaze in the same direction.

"Papa—" the girl cried out reflexively when she saw what was clearly her father at the entrance to the vacant lot. And it wasn't just him. "Mama, and Kane, too?!"

Perhaps the three figures had heard her voice, because they looked at each other and hastened closer.

"Nan, what in blazes are you doing in a place like this?" her father shouted, but the girl averted her face from his admonishment.

"We looked in on your bed and found you gone. And Kane was so worried, he came along, too," Nan's mother said, driving the girl's spirits still lower.

"I suppose you're gonna tell us you didn't lure her out here, eh?" Kane spat, his fiery words prompting all to turn in his direction.

D was in front of the boy. The Hunter stood a head taller than him. Though the other man was like a massive wall before him, Nan's boyfriend focused every bit of defiance he could muster on the Hunter.

"Kane, he had nothing to do with it," Nan protested. "I came up here on my own, I'll have you know. I couldn't get to sleep."

"Now, you listen to me," the boy said, thrusting a trembling finger at D. "Me and Nan are gonna get married one of these days. I don't take kindly to some lousy wanderer coming in and dirtying her up."

"Kane, quit it. I don't recall promising you any such thing."

"Hush, Nan," her mother said in an attempt to stop her. "At any rate, if nothing's happened, then we're fine. C'mon, let's go home."

"And I'll thank you not to come nosing around these parts again," the girl's father said as he glared at D.

"I just can't walk away," Kane said, shaking his head. "Someone takes my girl out in the middle of the night, and you think I'm gonna just let that go? Duel me!"

Nan felt like she'd been paralyzed. "What did you say?!" she shouted. "Stop it, Kane!" But it was the next words she heard that made her hair stand on end.

"Fine. Let's do it," D replied.

Dumbfounded, Nan turned to her father. Stern as ever, his expression plastered a look of ghastly terror to his daughter's face. "Papa?!" she exclaimed.

"It's no use. Come with me," Nan's mother said, grabbing hold of the girl's shoulders and dragging her back. Even her mother was going along with this . . .

She watched as her father said, "Here," and handed Kane an ax. Just as he took it, Kane backed away a few steps, and Nan's father stepped back, too. D stood still. Completely forgetting to put up any kind of struggle against her mother, Nan was rooted to the spot. What was happening was so hard to believe that she thought it must be a nightmare. At that moment, there was a weirdly colored explosion of light inside her head. *This is a nightmare. A dream . . . I'm–*

A weird cry brought the girl's eyes around in D's direction. Kane had brought his ax down. It whined through the air. Though it didn't look like he'd done anything at all, D had smoothly moved over to the grass. The air was crushed with a heavy *whoosh!* The very instant a horizontal flash seemed to be swallowed by the Hunter's black torso, a streak of silver shot up from below, causing Kane's hand and the ax it gripped to vanish. Nan held her breath. D watched silently as Kane collapsed backward with a cry like a beast. Behind the Hunter, another figure was drawing closer.

"Papa?!" the girl exclaimed, but her cry wasn't as fast as the sword that pierced her father's chest as he was about to pounce. Slumping across D's back, the girl's father let the machete he'd hidden fall from his hand, and a cry of pain spilled from his mouth. By the time he hit the ground, he was already dead.

"Papa! How could you do such a thing?!"

Flicking the gore from his blade with a single shake, D headed for his horse without saying a word. "I don't want to kill, but I can't die just yet, either," he finally said. And then his words were all that remained in the night air.

As Nan stood there frozen in her mother's arms, her brain incapable of forming even a single thought, she heard the sound of dwindling hoofbeats ringing in her ear.

III

So, what are you gonna do?" D's left hand asked with laughter in its voice as the Hunter galloped for the edge of the village. "Some want you to wake her up, and some don't—and both sides are pretty damn serious about it. Hell, both sides are trying to settle the battle themselves. To be destroyed, or not be destroyed? You're the man of destiny for them. What kind of star were you born under?"

"I'm leaving the village," D said as they tore through the blue darkness ahead of them.

"It's no use. This is a dream world. You can't leave unless the dreamer lets you."

"Take in the wind," the Hunter said. His words were as hard as the slap of a gale.

Almost immediately, his left hand went out by his side as if to challenge the winds buffeting him, and his palm inhaled with an incredible whistling sound.

"We'll make it out at this rate," the Hunter said, but it wasn't clear if the remark was directed at his left hand or himself. D's feet struck his mount's flanks, and the creature galloped on madly.

D turned to the right suddenly and caught sight of a black shape racing right with him along the fence. It was the black panther.

The instant D saw Duncan sitting there on the beast, a flash flew from the Hunter's right hand and his reins sailed through the air.

The rough wooden needles sank into Duncan with fierce accuracy. But a heartbeat later, the panther's charging body split into three parts, all of which leapt straight for D. As they came down at him, the fangs and claws grew like silver serpents. All of them were deflected with a beautiful ring, and, as they hung in the air helpless and unprepared for another engagement, the Hunter's weapon once again flashed out. This time, the three pieces were bisected by a horizontal slash, but by the time the bloody mist shot out, D had already galloped ahead another forty feet. Behind him, the forelegs and hind legs gave chase—though they were now reduced to mere chunks of flesh. The distance grew swiftly between him and the remnants.

Ahead of him, a stand of high trees was visible. D was at the edge of the village. Perhaps he had a chance of escaping after all.

His left hand reached out before him. A human face formed on its palm—and the lips on that face pursed. The wind howled. Before, it had inhaled, but now it exhaled.

It wasn't clear exactly what kind of infernal manipulations his palm might've done to the air in the interim, but the scenery ahead of it began to quiver like mist. Like a thin sheet of paper shredding in the face of a hurricane, the fence and the forest beyond grew hazy. Behind them, another scene came into view—though there was no way to gauge the distance to it. A vague, phantasmal grove of trees and a dawn sky—that had to be the real world out there.

His horse picked up speed. Just before the fence, its four hooves left the ground in a mighty leap. Headlong, it rushed at a scene that was like a double exposure in some gorgeous, mesmerizing film. But the beast floundered in midair.

Leaving his horse as it dropped like a stone, D sailed through the air, then came back to earth. His sword raced out, deflecting a knife flying at him.

"Just as I expected. When I go after you head on, I ain't much of a threat."

D threw his gaze in the direction of the voice, having determined that the knife had come from the huge form on horseback lurking behind the trees. It was none other than one of the infamous Bio Brothers—Harold B.

"And that's exactly why I'm gonna take you on from every which way—Look!" With these words, Harold's body bent backward, and a false image pulled free from him.

A wooden needle shot out, passing in vain through the original body before imbedding itself in a tree behind it.

The false image grinned at the Hunter. Another transparent image flew to the fore. But the one that'd created it didn't fade, and the newer image also went on to create another false image, as did the one it made, and the one after that—and in the space of a few seconds, the area around D was filled by countless images of Harold. That wouldn't have been a problem if it was clear which one of them was real, but there was no sign of the true Harold. Even D, with his incredibly acute senses, found all the false images to be exactly like the real thing.

"This time, we'll be using these," dozens of mounted Harold images declared in unison, showing the weapons they had in their right hands: rough wooden stakes. "I hear these things work just dandy on dhampirs, too. And just so you know, we're all real. If there're a hundred of us, we'll drive a hundred stakes into you. Except we're gonna do it a little differently. Like this!"

Streaks of white light flew from the right hands of a few of them. As the whirling stakes rained down on him from horseback, D became a black wind and dashed into action.

Perhaps the images of Harold in the foremost ring knew what they were doing as they called out to attack in low voices, each with a stake in one hand. The question remained: what would happen when the lone beautiful figure collided with the countless black ones?

If Harold's plan had a single miscalculation, it was from experience rather than the lack of it—and from conjectures he'd made about D's speed and strength with a sword based on their previous battle. None of the wooden stakes the false images brought down met anything but air. Every time the black shape moved between them like a mystic bird with the hem of his coat flashing out around him, countless Harold images were cut in half, merging with the air as they vanished.

Less than twenty seconds later, D stood motionless and alone on the clear, moonlit ground. "What are you going to do? If you retreat now, then there was no point calling you at all," the Hunter said in a low voice.

There was no answer for him, only a cold wind blowing by.

D's gaze dropped to the corpse of his horse lying there on the ground. A knife was sunk deep into its neck. "Can we make it out without any acceleration?" he asked.

"Not on your life," his left hand replied. "At times like this, what you need is for someone to just plunk you down a brand new horse right here and now. You know, as far as dreams go, this one ain't very accommodating."

Saying nothing, D shook the gore from his blade and returned it to the sheath on his back.

It was a second later that he did an about-face. Stopping an unseen attack with a metallic *clang!* and a shower of sparks, the Hunter's blade slashed into a certain spot in the sky with overwhelming power. The unmistakable sound of flesh being rent resounded, groans of someone in their death throes rang out—and with these sounds, the badly battered form of Harold B. came into focus right in front of D.

"Don't be thinking . . . you're safe now . . . This . . . ain't your world . . ."

As Harold finally finished getting the words out, blood spilled from his mouth and he fell flat on his face. The only reason he'd been able to wound D earlier was because the Hunter had been distracted by the hospital director and his machine.

"That was a lot easier than expected. So, what do we do now?"

Not even bothering to glance at Harold, D replied to his left hand's question, "Nothing we can do but wait, even though the very shadows are our enemies here."

"Yeah, that's all well and good, but you can't just stand around in one spot either. Well, are you gonna get walking or what?"

Even before his hand finished speaking, D had already started walking toward the fence. It was only a little over six feet high, but it was three layers thick. Lightly kicking off the ground, D landed easily on the other side of the fence. But he didn't start walking right away.

There was no road on the other side of the fence. There wasn't even a forest. The edge of the grove was off in the distance now, and before him the ground was cleared of trees, but well covered with gravestones—round ones and square ones, large and small. It was a cemetery. If this was to be the final battle, then this truly would be a fitting place for it. This place that Nobles and humans had once shared as friends was now desolate and decaying, and a stifling miasma shrouded the area, despite the fact that it was now night.

D advanced a step. He was in the center of the cemetery. Off to his left was a particularly large crypt made of marble. The domed roof was equipped with a parabolic antenna for an information satellite service and a laser detection system. It was also thoroughly covered with dust. A dark line ran right down the middle of the polished doors. As they swung open without a sound, D watched silently. What else could be coming out of the home of a Noble but one of the Nobility? Undoubtedly, this was a final assassin the world was sending after D. Even after the form of Sheriff Krutz pushed its way out of the darkness, D's expression never changed. The scrap of cloth left by the assassin that'd targeted him earlier in the dream was a piece off the hem of the sheriff's coat. He'd been under their control for a while.

The sheriff held a stake-firing gun. Below his vacant eyes, his lips rose and a pair of fangs peeked from his mouth. Apparently, the world had given Sheriff Krutz exactly what he needed to fight D on equal terms.

"Looks like we've finally come down to it," the sheriff muttered grimly as he stepped down to the ground from the crypt. "I'm not in control of myself anymore."

Ten feet lay between the two of them. D would be a heartbeat too late to do anything about the stake gun.

"I can't miss you with this gun, and I won't," the sheriff continued softly. "Even now, I'm not entirely sure whether I should be defending this world or not, but I can't help it. When you see Sybille in the hereafter, give her my apologies."

"And if she's one of the Nobility, just how is she supposed to die?" D asked. His gaze and his tone were those of a Vampire Hunter. "Sybille will continue sleeping, and your wife will keep waiting for you to come back to her. It would seem the world you're trying to protect isn't all fun and games."

Sheriff Krutz pulled the trigger. The pressurized gas cylinder inside the firing mechanism gave the one-pound stake a speed of twenty-three hundred feet per second, but it was struck down before D's chest by a silvery flash of light. As the saying went, D's sword could cut down a laser beam.

A flash of white flew from D's left hand. The pale needle vanished in the darkness, and the sheriff's body leapt to an unbelievable height. With a *fwissssh!*, a couple of silver missiles launched from the tip of the sheriff's extended hand, spitting tiny flames from their tails as they flew at D down on the ground.

Gathering up the hem of his coat, D pulled it to his chest and then flung it wide. His timing was exceptional—the coat changed the direction of the missiles without striking their fuses, and the three harbingers of death, unable to assume a new course, turned the ground into a fiery patch of hell.

In midair, the two shadows passed. As the figures came back to earth a few yards apart, one of them wobbled badly and fell against the gravestone beside him. "If they change me again . . . will it change *this me*, D?"

"I don't know," the Hunter replied.

"Either way . . . I don't want to get up again . . . Godspeed to you." Braced against the gravestone, Krutz quickly grew weaker in his movements. As the sheriff slid down the stone, a softly mumbled word could be heard.

"That was a name, wasn't it?" D's left hand muttered. For once, his tone was incredibly serious. "So, what did he say? Ai-Ling, or Sybille?"

D didn't answer. The flames painted his face with ghastly shadows and colors.

Even if there were others still who didn't want the girl to awaken and planned to continue to act on their beliefs, it was safe to say that here the curtain had fallen on at least one of their attacks on D. But what awaited him next?

D was about to walk away when suddenly a presence stirred around him. Every single gravestone began to shake. D stopped.

Whump! One of the gravestones fell over. The sound was heard time and again. Even when the first figure got up out if its grave, the sound of the falling monuments didn't stop.

"D," Dr. Allen called out.

"D," Mrs. Sheldon called out.

"D," Ai-Ling called out.

The hotel manager politely asked him to stop.

Clements told him not to do it.

Bates groaned at him not to let her wake up.

Tokoff was there, too.

All the villagers were there. Everyone was pleading with him. They told him not to let her awaken. With pale hands outstretched, the herd closed in on D.

The young man had never been one to show mercy to his foes. With a potent aura emanating from every inch of him, D readied himself to attack. The wave of humanity surrounded him like a tsunami, but, at the very instant they were about to break, something split the air.

Some didn't make a sound, others keeled over screaming, but all of them had the ends of black iron arrows poking out of their chests or throats. In their final moments of life, those who didn't die instantly continued toward D with vindictiveness fixed on their previously vacant and pallid faces. The steel arrows raining down dropped them one after another until finally the last of them fell. As D stood in a world strewn with corpses and choked with the stench of blood, he suddenly noticed a man and a woman standing at the edge of the cemetery. The archer in black, and Sybille in white.

The dream of the Sybille within the dream had finally become reality in this world. And it was probably only in a dream that a lone archer could drop hundreds of villagers.

"We won't kill you," Sybille said, boundless hatred and grief hanging in her voice. "Because you're going to kill me." Her pale finger pointed at D.

The man drew back on his bow. A steel arrow sliced through the wind.

D saw that single arrow become multiple shafts in midair. The hem of his coat flew up to counter the attack. Deflected arrows sank into the ground, but still others pierced D's shoulders and abdomen.

"How was that?" Sybille asked with a smile as D dropped to his knees in pain. "Still not in the mood to kill me? And here I thought the one called D was supposed to deal death to all who challenged him. I beg of you—kill me."

Arrows jutted out all over D's body, but his expression was no different from usual.

Tears glistened in Sybille's eyes at the Hunter's stern refusal.

The archer in black notched another arrow. Before he had finished, D raised his chest. "Don't," was all the Hunter said.

If the next shot went through his heart, the wound would be fatal.

The bow released with a *twang!*

At the same instant, a silvery gleam shot from D's hand. He'd thrown his longsword. Faster than the arrows, it pierced the heart of the man in black, and he fell to the ground with a force that knocked the scarf away from his mouth.

As Sybille stood there stunned, unable even to speak, D staggered toward her. "Do you still want to die now?" he asked.

"Yes," the girl replied joyfully, neither nervous nor distraught.

"You were one possibility," D said softly. The bright blood dripped from countless points on his body and stained the earth. "A certain man chose you to entrust with his hopes. Here in your village—in your world—humans and Nobles lived together in mutual understanding. This was through your power."

"And it was a wonderful thing, but it truly pained me . . . Always sleeping . . . Forever dreaming, and nothing else. Never knowing joy or sorrow or pain . . ."

D looked at the corpse in black by her side. The scarf had flown out of the way, and he could see the face clearly. It was Sheriff Krutz. Choosing the man she loved more than any other as her protector was probably a natural move on the part of her heart.

The saddest of melodies came to D's ears. The ground became a highly polished floor. He could tell without even looking that the figures swirling around him were dancing a waltz. The ball was in full swing now.

"D . . ."

As Sybille called out his name, a certain emotion seemed to echo in it. In her pale hand, a knife glittered coldly.

Sybille advanced. Their bodies overlapped into a single form. As if pierced by pure delight, Sybille shut her eyes and shook with ecstasy. Her tears gleamed with blue—and then all movement stopped.

After D pulled his blade from the sheriff's chest, he ran it through Sybille.

The girl's knife was still tight in her right hand. The real question was whether D knew she'd never intended to stab him.

The weight of her body against him suddenly vanished. He turned around. The dancers stood like phantoms, then vanished just the same. And Sybille's face . . . was that of Nan. The girl who'd slept forever in this world must've transferred her consciousness to Nan so that she might live a life. Both D and Sheriff Krutz had probably known. After all, when the vision of Sybille had appeared before them for the first time, she was wearing the same clothes as the girl.

Staggering, dragging one leg behind him, D went around behind the girl. He looked at the face of her partner. It was Sheriff Krutz. And it was D. It was both, and it was neither. The man she'd danced with for three decades under the blue light of the moon, and the man summoned to wake the slumbering princess.

D's eyes dropped to the sheriff/archer's face. Pulling all the arrows from his own flesh and throwing them to the floor, the Hunter headed for the door. Even as he pulled the arrows out and walked away, his expression remained immutable—just as it was when he stabbed Sybille.

Nan was in her room, lying on her bed, when she realized the awakening had come.

Old Mrs. Sheldon was out on her porch in her rocking chair.

Ai-Ling was staring up at the night sky.

Dr. Allen was watching over Sybille as she faded from existence.

All was still. It was a truly quiet night.

†

D opened his eyes. The rays of dawn were bleaching the world. He was in the middle of the forest. Considering the position of the sun and the time he'd gone to sleep, no more than two hours could've passed. D still remembered every detail of the strange dream. This was the same vacant lot where the mansion had been located.

And then he noticed something. His position had changed. The tree he'd been resting against towered from a spot some forty feet to his left. His cyborg horse was over there, too.

"A hell of a dream that was," a mocking voice said, although it sounded somewhat weary, too.

The reason for this new location was immediately evident. A lone corpse lay at his feet. Hidden in the high grass, it showed every sign of having been there for many long years. It must have been there at least—

"Thirty years," the voice said. "There's a stab mark on the chest. Well, now we know."

The real Sybille had been banished from the village and discarded in this forest. Thirty years—perhaps it was only natural that as she lay there all that time, lashed by rain, shivering in the wind, dreaming of a perfect community of humans and Nobles, her heart had taken measures to find peace for her, as well.

D headed for his horse. He'd been summoned to a village, and had to be there by the end of the day. Loading his gear up behind his saddle, D was about to mount up when a spirited voice called out to him.

"Say, you there—isn't there supposed to be a village around here?" As the woman on the wagon gazed raptly at D, she added, "I don't know—maybe it was just my imagination. But I had this dream about it last night, and it all seemed so real. Hey! What are you looking at?!" she asked the young man.

"Nothing," D replied, giving a slight shake of his head.

"Then I'll thank you kindly to spare me the funny looks. I may not seem like much, but everyone in these parts knows Maggie the Almighty. But, you know what?" the woman began, knitting her brow, "now that I think about it . . . Haven't we met somewhere before?"

"No. Never."

"No, I guess not. If I'd seen a looker like you before, I sure as heck wouldn't forget it. And yet . . ." the woman started to say, looking astonished as she gazed at the young man on horseback. A rosy glow quickly suffused her face.

In the end, she never actually knew that she was responsible for the smile etched on the lips of the young man in black as he rode off into the distance, but for a long time after that, her feelings of good fortune took the form of the young man who visited her dreams each night.

Do vampires dream? And if so, what manner of dreams do they have? This *Vampire Hunter D* novel was the product of just such speculation. If vampires dream, then theirs would be the dreams of the undead. But if *their* dreams were to be superimposed on those of the living, what shape would these new dreams take? Nobles who dance in the daylight? Humans who stride silently through a world of darkness? Whatever the case, it would certainly be something beyond human or Noble imagining. I'll have to wait for the reaction from you, my readers, before I'll know whether this volume conveyed that effectively or not.

Japan, the land of my birth, has developed a culture quite different from that of the English-speaking world. And after living nearly sixty years in such a place, I suppose that even when I use something like the European vampire theme in my work, it differs fundamentally from what might be created in your world. Perhaps that's what makes the *Vampire Hunter D* series so enjoyable.

In the postscript to the previous volume I touched on England's Hammer Films and their production *Horror of Dracula*. As I watched that movie in a theater in my hometown, I trembled in my seat and came under the thrall of the vampire as surely as one who'd felt its bite. In Japan, there are no legends of humanoid creatures that drink human blood. This is because blood here isn't surrounded by the same air of sanctity. Therefore, vampires—as creatures that intermingle elements of life and death and ultimately achieve immortality through blood—were horribly attractive. Add to that the fact that their immortal existence carried an eternal curse, and you could essentially say they were made just for me. To wit, it wasn't my blood but rather my very soul that was consumed by the film *Horror of Dracula*.

At the tender age of eleven, however, it wasn't Christopher Lee's Count Dracula I wanted to be, but rather Dr. Van Helsing, as portrayed by Peter Cushing. As a child, I didn't wish to be a fiend, you see. And I can't really blame myself for wanting to switch to the vampire-slaying side back then. After all, I was simply too terrified of Dracula to think of becoming like him. The reason I chose to make D a Hunter who destroys vampires even though he's related to them probably had something to do with that trauma in my youth.

Unlike the various ghosts and spirits in Japan that can appear virtually anywhere and follow whomever they choose, and also quite different from the Count Dracula of legend who lived in the same land as the rest of the people, talked about the same things, was carried around in his coffin by a horse-drawn carriage, and had to slip into other people's houses through doors or windows, the Dracula that Christopher Lee embodied seemed entirely too real to me as an eleven year old. The idea of him certainly remained with me. As a child, fearing a visit from the Count, I fashioned a cross from a pair of chopsticks and slept with it by my pillow.

Horror of Dracula was a huge hit in Japan, and it was adapted into comics, plays, and movies. I was surprised by a comic that used the story just as it was, but shifted the setting to Edo-era Japan. Although Dracula in this tale is a vampire who's come over from a foreign country, the Dr. Van Helsing character is a young Japanese warrior schooled in Western matters, Harker is a friend from his school days, Mina and Arthur Holmwood are his parents—and his father is a samurai, of course. As you may know, Christianity was prohibited here during the Edo era, so the crosses normally used against Dracula are Japanese talismans instead, the wooden stakes are replaced with Japanese swords, and Dracula is turned to dust by the talismans and the rays of the sun. Now, doesn't that comic—*Ma no Hyakumonsen*—sound like something you'd like to see?

Hideyuki Kikuchi
March 17, 2006,
while watching *The Revenge of Frankenstein*

VAMPIRE HUNTER D

VAMPIRE HUNTER D

VOLUME 6

PILGRIMAGE OF THE SACRED AND THE PROFANE

Written by

HIDEYUKI KIKUCHI

Illustrations by

YOSHITAKA AMANO

English translation by

KEVIN LEAHY

Dark Horse Books

Milwaukie

VAMPIRE HUNTER D

Prologue

S ome called this town the journey's end, others its beginning. Mighty gales blew across the sea of golden sand that stretched from its southern edge. When those mighty winds hit the great gates of steel, pebbles as big as the tip of a child's finger struck them high and low, making the most plaintive sound. It was like a heartrending song sung by someone on the far side of those sands to keep a traveler there.

When the winds were particularly strong, fine sand drifted down on the streets in a drizzle, amplifying the dry creaking of things like the wooden sidewalks and window frames at the saloon. And on very rare occasions, little bugs were mixed in with the sand. Armed with jaws that were tougher than titanium alloy and stronger than a vice, the bugs could chew their way through doors of wood and plastic as if they were paper. Luckily, the petals of faint pink that always came on the heels of the insect invasion killed the bugs on contact—an event that imbued the whole encounter with a kind of elegance. As the order and timing of the arrival of these two forces never varied, the homes in town had to weather the ravages of the tiny killers for only three short minutes.

And yet, on those rare nights when there were great numbers of the bugs, the town was enveloped by a harsh but beautiful hum, like someone strumming on their collective heartstrings. The sound of the bugs' jaws did no harm to humans, and before long the scene would be touched with the flavor of a dream, and then vanish as surely as any dream would on awakening. Some considered it a song of farewell or even a funeral dirge, and people in town grew laconic as the fires in their hearths were reflected in their eyes.

No one knew where the pale pink petals came from. While more than a few had headed off into the desert that was burning-hot even by night, not a single traveler had ever returned. Perhaps they'd reached their destinations, or perhaps their bodies had been buried by the sands, but no word ever came from them. There were some people in town who'd happened to meet such travelers, however, they'd only occasionally be able to raise some fragmented memory of a vaguely remembered face, and then turn their gaze to the gritty winds that ran along the edge of town.

This particular day, the song of the bugs was much sharper than usual and the faint pink rain seemed a bit late, so the townspeople looked out at the streets in the afterglow of sunset with a certain foreboding. The funeral dirge faded, as the time had come for those performing it to die.

And that's when it happened. That's when the young man came to town.

The Hidden

I

The sound of the bugs grew more intense, and the men encamped around the tables and seated at the bar turned their fierce gazes toward the door. Grains of sand became a length of silk that blew in and then almost instantly broke apart to trace wind-wrought swirls on the floor. The door was shut again.

Eyes swimming with indecision caught the new arrival. Was this someone they could take in, or should the newcomer be kept out?

It took a little while before the floorboards began to creak. Time needed to decide which direction to creak off in. Done.

The piano stopped; the pianist had frozen. The coquettish chatter of the women petered out. The men's noisy discussions ceased. Behind the bar, the bartender had gone stiff with a bottle of booze in one hand and a glass in the other. There was curiosity and fear about just what was going to happen next.

A table to the left of the door and a bit toward the back was the newcomer's destination. Two figures were settled around it—one in black, the other in blue. Wearing an ebony silk hat and a mourning coat with a hem that looked like it reached his ankles, one evoked a mortician. The deep-blue, brimless cap and the shirt of the same color that covered the powerful frame of the other were undoubtedly crafted from the hide of the blue jackal, considered by many to be the most vicious beast on the Frontier. Both men were slumped in their chairs with their heads hung low as if they were sleeping.

The source of the creaking footsteps surely noticed something very unusual about the situation—all the other tables around the pair were devoid of customers. It was as if they were being avoided. As if they were despised. As if they frightened people. Another odd thing—it wasn't a whiskey bottle and glasses that sat on the table before them. Black liquid pooled in the bottom of their brass coffee cups, which still had swirls of white steam lovingly hovering over their rims.

Even after the creaking stopped, the two men didn't lift their heads, but every other sound in the place died when the footsteps ended. Several seconds of silence settled. Then a taut voice shattered the stillness.

"We don't take kindly to folks with no manners, kid!" the figure in blue said.

And immediately after that—

"Your mistake, Clay," the other one remarked, his very voice so steeped in black that it made everyone else in the small watering hole tremble.

"Well, I'll be," the first man said, his blue cap rising unexpectedly to reveal his eyes; set in his steely face, they were even bluer than his attire. Though he'd called the person he heard walking over a kid, he was only about twenty years old himself. His face looked mean enough to kill a timid man with one glare, but he suddenly smiled innocently and said, "They say you can disguise your face, but you can't do a thing about how old your steps sound."

"Too bad, sonny," the newcomer said. The voiced spilled from lips like dried-out clay, as cracked and creased as the rest of his face. More than the countenance so wrinkled that age could no longer be determined, more than the silver hair tied back with a vermilion ribbon, it was the slight swell in the gold-fringed vest and blouse that gave away the sex of the speaker. "I happen to hate being ignored," she continued. "I don't care if you're the biggest thing to ever happen to the Outer Frontier; I still think you ought to show your elders the proper respect. Don't you agree?"

The rest of the customers remained as still as statues. Even so, an excited buzz filled the room. Suddenly, someone said, "That old lady's looking to start a fight with Bingo and Clay Bullow!"

"What do you want?" Clay asked. His tone was incredibly light.

"Well, tomorrow, I'm heading across the desert to the Inner Frontier. And I want the two of you to come with me."

Clay's mouth dropped open. Without taking his eyes off the crone, he said, "Hey, bro—some old hag I don't even know says she wants us to keep her company on a trip through the desert."

"There'd be a heap of pay in it for you," the crone told him. "I'd like you to watch out for me and another person, you see. With you two along, I figure we'd get there in less than a week. . . and alive, to boot."

"Bro—"

"You don't know her, you say?" another voice said. Calling to mind rough-hewn rock, his tone didn't exactly match his spindly, spider-like limbs. "Little brother, you'd best jiggle that memory of yours a bit more. We might not have met her, but we know her name. You'll have to pardon me," he told the old woman, "but I'm asleep at the moment. Wish I could greet you properly, Granny Viper, People Finder."

The silent saloon was rocked. She was Granny Viper: the chances that the Inner Frontier's greatest locator of those who'd been hidden would run into the Outer Frontier's greatest fighters had to be about ten-million-to-one. They were really in luck.

"I couldn't care less about greetings. So, how about it? What's your answer?" the old woman chirped like a bird.

"We're waiting for someone," the face beneath the silk hat replied.

"Whoever it is, I'm sure they'll be dead before they get here." The crone's mouth twisted into an evil hole. Her maw was a black pit—without a single tooth in it. "And if they do make it here, they're gonna have a little run-in with you, I suppose. Either way, it's the same thing, am I right?"

354 | HIDEYUKI KIKUCHI

"Without a doubt," Clay said, throwing his head back with a huge laugh. "But this time, we've got a real job cut out for ourselves. Depending on how things go, we might end up—" Staring at the back of the hand that'd appeared before him without warning, Clay caught himself. "I know, bro—I've said too much already."

Bingo's right hand slowly retracted.

"Sure you're not interested?" the crone asked in a menacing tone.

The man in the silk hat didn't answer.

"Sorry, but I just *have* to have you two along," Granny insisted.

The wall of men and women around the trio receded anxiously, and all eyes focused on the hands of the old woman and the two brothers. In light of what was about to happen, it was a completely natural thing to do. Their gazes were filled with consternation—even an old woman like Granny Viper had to have some sort of "weapon" if she lived out on the Frontier. Her lower back looked like it'd snap in two if someone even touched it, and just below it she wore a survival belt with a number of pouches on it. Still she had no bowie knife or machete—the most basic of equipment. But what everyone's eyes were drawn to was a large jar that looked like it was ceramic. It had an opening that seemed wide enough to easily accommodate the fist of a giant man, but it was stoppered with a polymer fiber lid. And although it looked like it would be fairly heavy even if it were empty, the old woman walked and stood as if unconcerned with its weight. One of the taller spectators had been up on the tips of his toes for a while trying to get a good look at it, but the lid was the same gray color as the jar, and its contents were completely hidden from view.

Similarly, the weapons of the two men were every bit as eccentric as hers. What hung at the right hip of the younger brother, Clay, couldn't have been any more inappropriate for him—a golden harp strung with silver strings. As for the older brother, Bingo, what he carried was more surprising than anything. He was completely unarmed.

"Granny Viper, People Finder" and "The Fighting Bullow Brothers." Getting a sense that an otherworldly conflict never meant for human eyes was about to be joined here between some of the Frontier's most renowned talents—and the weird weapons they possessed—the saloon patrons were all seized by the silence of the grave. The crone's right hand slowly dropped to her jar. At the same time, Clay's hand reached for the harp on his hip. Bingo didn't budge an inch. And just as the three deadly threads were about to silently twist together . . .

The black bowler hat flew up in the air. The wrinkled face of the crone looked back over her shoulder. The gaze of the youth in blue was there just a second later, at the door. Closed since the crone entered, the door now had the eyes of all three of these rough customers trained on it. There was no one there—at least, not in front of it—so what were the three of them looking at?

At just that moment the door knob turned. Hinges squealing as they bit down on sand, the door became an expanding domain of darkness on the wall. Perhaps the figure it revealed had been born of the very night itself. The saloon patrons backed away, and the hue of the black garments that covered all but his pale and perfect countenance made it seem that he blew in like a fog of fine sand. As if the countless eyes on him meant nothing, the young man shut the door behind him and headed over to the bar. What they were dealing with now was something even more unusual than the Bullow Brothers or Granny Viper, People Finder. With every step forward the figure in black took, grains of sand dropped from his long coat. To the women in the bar, even these seemed to sparkle darkly. As soon as the young man stopped at the bar, the people heard him say in a voice like steel, "There's supposed to be someone here by the name of Thornton."

Swallowing hard, the bartender nodded. Though he was big enough to serve as the bouncer too, the man's colossal frame grew stiff. It sounded like he was barely squeezing the words out as he said, "You're Mr. D . . . aren't you?"

No reply was needed. Though the bartender had only heard about one characteristic of the Hunter, he knew this was unquestionably the man who stood before him.

"He's out back right now," the bartender said, raising his right hand to point the way. "But he's having himself a little *entertainment* at the moment." It was common knowledge that in many cases, Frontier town saloons also doubled as whorehouses.

D walked off in the direction the man had indicated. He'd gone about a dozen steps when someone said to him, "It's a pleasure to meet you."

It was Bingo.

"Bingo Bullow is the name. That's my younger brother, Clay. You might've heard of us. I was thinking we might get to know the greatest Vampire Hunter on the Frontier."

Bingo looked at the back of the figure who'd halted his step. Like his body, the elder Bullow's face was extremely thin, and his chin was covered by a wild growth of beard. Seemingly hewn from rock, his expression shifted just a bit then.

As if he'd merely stopped there on a whim, D started walking again.

"Well, shut my mouth!" Granny Viper exclaimed in an outrageously loud voice, indifferent to all the other spectators. "This *is* a surprise. I didn't know there was a man alive who'd turn his back on Bingo Bullow when he offers an invite. I like your style! Indeed, I do!"

"Hold it, you!" Clay shouted as if trying to destroy the old woman's words. He jumped to his feet. His cruel young face grew red as hot blood rushed to his head. As he reached for his elegant weapon with his right hand, another, thinner hand—that of his brother—pressed against his stomach stopping him.

"Knock it off," Bingo told him.

The older brother's word must've been law, because the younger Bullow didn't utter a single complaint after that, and the anger that radiated from his powerful form rapidly dispersed.

"I'll be waking up soon," the elder Bullow informed him. "We'll have to wait until the next time I'm asleep to pay our respects."

Out of the countless eyes there, only those of the crone sparkled.

The door to the back room opened and then closed again, swallowing the darkness given human form in the process.

The cramped room was filled with a lascivious aroma. Long, thin streams of smoke rose from an opening in the metallic urn that sat on the round table. It was an aphrodisiac unique to the Frontier sectors, and all who smelled the scent—young or old, male or female—were transformed into lust-crazed beasts. On the other side of the table sat an ostentatious bed that'd been slathered with the gaudiest color of paint imaginable, and on that bed something terribly alluring wriggled: a knot of naked women, all of them dripping with sweat. It was probably the influence of the aphrodisiac that kept them from so much as turning to look at the intruder as he entered.

Perhaps wondering what was going on outside the intertwined flesh, a raven-haired head popped out of the middle of that pale pile of femininity even as feverish panting continued to fill the air. From the man's face, it was impossible to tell whether he was young or middle-aged. He must've been the only one who'd responded to D's knock. Roughly pushing his way free of the women clinging to him, he finally stopped what he was doing, and stared directly at D.

"Well, I'll be . . . Just goes to show you can't believe everything you hear, I guess. Your looks are so good, my hair's practically standing on end." And then, as he hastily began shoving the women out of the way, he hissed, "C'mon, move it!"

Although his squat form looked to be less than five feet tall, he had a considerable amount of fat on him—evidence of days spent in pursuit of culinary delights. He didn't bother to cover himself as he slipped on his underpants. Once the man was wrapped in a robe, he actually looked quite dignified. Digging a thick pair of glasses out of his coat pocket, he put them on. He almost looked like he could pass for a scholar from the Capital.

"This isn't exactly the most appropriate place to receive a guest who's traveled so far, but, you see, I wasn't expecting to see you so soon." Glancing then at the electric clock on the wall, he added, "Actually, you're right on time. But back at the hotel, I heard that a cloud of moving miasma had shown up on the road, and that no one would be able to get through for a couple of days . . . Guess I should've remembered I was dealing with the Vampire Hunter D."

In what was surely a rare occurrence for the young Hunter, he received a somewhat sheepish smile from the other man, but when the man in black failed to move even a single muscle in his face, Thornton shrugged his shoulders and said, "Well, I suppose I should tell you about the job, then."

The reason he averted his gaze at this point wasn't so much to change the tone of the conversation, but rather because he'd reached the point where he could no longer stand looking at D head-on. Regardless of gender, those who gazed at the young man's gorgeous visage for too long began to hallucinate that they were being drawn into the depths of his eyes. Actually, the women that Thornton had shoved out of the way had been ready to voice their dissatisfaction when D suddenly entered their field of view and left them frozen with their mouths agape.

"Okay, get your asses out of here! I'll pay you twice what you had coming," the little man—Thornton—said, but even as he shoved them out, the women kept their dumbstruck gazes trained on D until the very end.

"Care for a drink?" Thornton asked the Hunter as he picked up the bottle of liquor sitting on the table, but then he shrugged his shoulders. "Oh, that's right—you dhampirs like to say, 'I never drink wine,' don't you? Sorry. I may be a lawyer, but I'm still just a plain old human. Pardon me while I have one."

Filling his glass to the very brim with the amber liquid, Thornton pressed it to his lips. Time and again, his Adam's apple bobbed up and down before he exhaled roughly and set his empty glass back on the table.

As he nervously brought his hand up to wipe his lips, Thornton began by saying, "I wrote to you for one purpose and one purpose alone. I want you to cross the desert. To go all the way to the town of Barnabas, across this 'Desert of No Return' where so many have never been seen again."

"For what purpose?" D asked, opening his mouth at last. "In your letter, you said you could furnish me with information about someone I have a great interest in."

"That's correct," Thornton said, nodding his agreement. "And the reason I can do so is because the request to send you out into the desert comes from that very person."

II

Now that it was late at night, the sound of the bugs had only increased in its plaintive rhapsody. A few minutes later, blossoms covered the town and the sounds died out, began anew, and then vanished again . . . as if the night would never end, and the song of parting would never cease.

It was at that moment that a wrinkled hand knocked on the door to a room in a hotel on the edge of town. There was no answer. Without waiting very long, the hand pushed against the door. It opened easily. The interior was claimed by the same shade of darkness as the world outside. The reason Granny Viper turned to the right side without hesitation wasn't because she'd memorized the location of the bed, but because she could see as well in the dark as she could at midday.

"Pardon the intrusion," the old woman called out in a hoarse voice, and although she received no reply to her greeting, she could see the tall figure that lay on the bed clearly enough. "Ordinarily, I'd call you careless, but for the Vampire Hunter D, having the door locked or unlocked probably makes no difference. Anyone who came in here with evil in mind wouldn't live to tell about it." Her tone was buoyant, and she meant her words as a compliment. As always, there was no reply, so the hunched-over figure said, "Sure, I'd heard of you before, but I never could've imagined you'd be so incredible. Obviously, you're awful good-looking, too, but what I couldn't believe was that someone actually ignored the Bullow Brothers. That's when I thought to myself:

That settles it. At first, I was aiming to ask the two of them to help, but forget that now. Who needs a couple of punks fresh outta short pants, anyway? I've decided to go with you instead."

Here the old woman paused and waited for the Hunter to respond, but there was no reply. Perhaps he was just a shadow that had taken human form? She strained her ears and still she couldn't hear him draw a single breath, nor could she catch the beating of his heart. The crone realized that if her night vision wasn't so keen, she'd never have noticed his presence.

Any ordinary person would've lost hope at this exercise in futility, or grown indignant at his cold-heartedness. But the old woman went on talking. "When I first came in," she said, "I didn't feel the urge to kill from you, and I don't now, either. I've been to other Hunters' rooms, but it's unbelievable. They're always on edge, never knowing when somebody's gonna try and get the drop on them, and you can feel the violence just hanging around in the air outside their rooms. No matter how big they are, *you're* above them all. If someone came in here, they'd take you for a stone until the second you struck them dead. On the other hand, if you wanted to, you could stop a foe cold through a stone wall with just a harsh look in their direction. But I suppose I'd be surprised if you had a mind to do that even once in your life. And that's why I've pinned all my hopes on you."

In a manner of speaking, all the old woman's efforts were rewarded.

"What do you want with me?" asked the shadow of all shadows.

"I already told you, didn't I? I want you to come with me. You know, across the desert to the town of Barnabas. There'd be a nice piece of change in it for you. Enough for all the booze and broads you'd ever want. I just know you couldn't say no to a sweet deal like this."

"No." His concise reply had an intensity that completely severed the discussion.

"Well, why the hell not?"

"Leave."

"Stop mucking around," Granny said to him. "I just told you how set I am on having you. Maybe you think you're too good to listen to some old bag, eh? Well, I'll show you. You might not think so, but I'm pretty well known across the Frontier. And while they may not be quite as dangerous as you, I know a lot of people—folks that'll come running just as soon as I give the word. No matter how tough you are, up against a hundred of them—"

The crone's voice died there. As if pushed by something, her stooped figure leapt back. Perhaps unable to weather the other-worldly air that staggered the imagination, she flew out of the room with terrific speed. Light flowed in from the corridor.

"Stop it," Granny shouted. Her words had the ring of an entreaty. "What, do you plan on killing me? I'm more than a hundred years old, you know! What'll you do if you give me a heart attack or something?"

Yet the unearthly air continued to creep toward her.

"Just stop it, or this kid—this girl—will die, too!" she shouted, slipping around the door and reappearing in the rectangular space pushing another figure. Someone with eyes that could pierce the darkness would see the shoulder-length black hair and the soft lines beneath the simple flesh-tone dress, and might even determine that the girl was about seventeen or eighteen years old. Without saying a single word, she just squatted there, hugging her own shoulders. The Hunter's ghastly aura was merciless.

"Please, stop," the crone cried out from behind the door. "The girl's name is Tae—she was one of *the hidden*. What's more, it was the Nobility that hid her!"

The girl's rigid body collapsed unexpectedly. Bracing one hand against the floor, she heaved a few short, sharp gasps. Rather attractive in its own way, her face was as expressionless as stone now, as if it terrified her to draw even the smallest of breaths. The girl seemed to have the world crushing in on her from all sides.

Granny's face peeked around from behind the door as her expression turned deadly serious. She came out slowly, moving with a weighty and plaintive gait. Circling around behind Tae, she put her hands on the girl's pale shoulders. Turning to the darkened depths of the room, she asked, "Do you know what my trade is?" Quickly realizing she wasn't likely to get a reply, she said, "I'm a people finder. I've been nicknamed Viper, like the snake, but I'm not one of them dala-a-dozen orphan trackers they've got hanging around here. I specialize in children who've been taken—I find *the hidden*. You know," she said to the Hunter, "I can't very well stand out here talking about it. Let me come back in for a second. C'mon, stand up," she told the Tae as she forced her to her feet, went back into the room, and closed the door. What's more, she then pulled out a chair, told Tae, "Have a seat," and settled herself in another chair, in a display that took presumptuousness to laudable heights. And yet, the reason she didn't complain about D's rudeness as he continued to just lie there was because his ghastly aura still permeated her flesh. "This girl—" she began to explain before she was interrupted.

The darkness was split by the voice of its master. "You mentioned the Nobility, didn't you?"

"Why, yes, I do believe I did," the old woman said, fighting back her delight. "She's a genuine, bona fide victim of hiding by the Nobility. I nearly killed myself getting her out of Castle Gradinia."

For all the supernatural phenomena that occurred out on the Frontier, the notion of *the hidden* had an especially chilling connotation. Unlike profit-motivated kidnappings, these could suddenly happen right out in public or under conditions where it should've been impossible to just vanish. The victims could be young or old, male or female, but in the case of young ladies it was almost certain to conjure images of a dreaded fate that would make anyone quake with terror . . . even as it robbed them of their tears. There were several possible causes for these disappearances, and they were sometimes attributed to unknown creatures or to the dimensional rips that appeared at irregular intervals. But in cases where members of the Nobility were suggested as the culprits, the terror sprang not from the disappearance itself, but from the anticipated result. What kind of fate might befall a young lady in such a situation? If they were merely prey to satisfy their captor's taste for blood, they might be saved. Luckier still were those who were given positions as maid-servants on the whim of the Nobility, though this was less common. A fair number of girls were rescued under those circumstances, but there could be more to it than that . . .

"A hell of a time I had there," Granny said, twisting her lips. "I was thinking I'd taken out all their defensive systems, but there was still one left. Damned thing put me to sleep until night. Well, I'd already made up my mind about what I was gonna do, so I drove a stake through the bastard's heart just as he was getting out of his coffin. Still, he was thrashing around like nobody's business, and I had to keep that accursed stake stuck in him for a good three hours before he simmered down. After that, I searched the place, and happened to find this girl. Not to worry, though, I've checked her out, and as far as I can tell, there's nothing wrong with her. I had her hypnotized so deeply it would've driven her mad to go any further. And, naturally, she can walk around in daylight."

"How did you find her?" D asked, his query free of inflection.

Tae shivered with fear.

The crone shrugged her shoulders and said, "There really wasn't much to it. Once I went down into the basement, I found a prison where they kept humans. She was locked in there. I asked her a few things, and by the sound of it, they had her slaving away as a maid of sorts. You can guess the rest. She was still right in the head, so she remembered which village she hails from. The sheriff in Gradinia even had a request from her parents to look for her. And that's how I ended up transporting her. That's what I do, you know." Granny nodded in a way that made it clear she was quite proud of what she did, too.

"And the Noble—what was his name?"

The old woman didn't answer that question. Although the Hunter's tone and the direction he faced hadn't changed, the crone understood that this query was directed at Tae.

Tae's body trembled, but her face remained aimed at the floor. She didn't say a word. It was almost as if she was erecting shields of incredible density all around herself.

The old woman, however, grew agitated and barked, "What are you doing? Hurry up and answer the man! This could mean the difference between us getting to the town of Barnabas safely or not!"

Tae said nothing.

"Oh, you stupid little twit!" Granny shouted, raising her right hand violently while keeping her back as straight as an arrow. Apparently, her hunching had been part of an act to get his sympathy, but there was no need for her to follow through with the blow.

"Leave," D said, making it clear that their visit had concluded.

"Wait just one second. I'm not done speaking my piece yet," the crone cried out in a pitiful tone. There wasn't an iota of the bluster she'd shown the Bullow Brothers left in her voice. The sudden and complete reversal was a nice change, though. "Like I just explained, we're in a situation where we've gotta get across the desert . . . and we've got a time limit, too. If we don't make it in four days, counting tomorrow, we're out of luck. See, the girl's family is in the town of Barnabas, but on the morning of the fifth day, they'll be moving on to somewhere else. Given the size of the desert, it's gonna be a close call. If we were to go around it, it'd take us more than a week, which is why we definitely need us some heavy-duty backup. Now, I don't know just what brings you to town, but if you haven't taken care of whatever it is, I'd like you to put it off for a while and come along with us. I don't care whether you wanna do it or not; I've already settled on you. Hell, even the girl said she likes you. Didn't you, sweetie?" the crone said, seeking some corroboration, but the girl remained as stiff as a board. "See what I mean? She likes you so much that she's at a loss for words. Of course, that's only natural, you being so handsome and all." Chuckling, she added, "This may sound strange, but if I was a tad younger myself, I don't think I could keep away from you, stud."

Of course, D didn't move a muscle.

Seeing that this was having no effect, Granny changed tactics. Her tone suddenly became tearful. Sobs echoed through the darkness. "Have you no pity for this poor child?" she asked, her entreaty coming in a nasal tone. "She was only ten when she was taken, and she spent eight years locked up in a Noble's castle. Even I don't know what happened to her during all that time—and I'm not about to ask. Can you blame me? Somehow, though, the girl survived. That's right—she kept herself alive for eight long years, a girl all alone in a world we can scarcely imagine. Doesn't she have the right to live the rest of her life in happiness now? When I found out her family was still alive and well, it brought tears to my eyes, I tell you. Her life's just about to begin. Now, wouldn't you wanna do everything in your power to help her out?" Winded from her speech, Granny caught her breath. Tears glistened in her eyes. It was all terribly impressive.

D's answer was brief: "Leave." The word had a forceful ring to it.

The crone was about to say something, but decided against it. "Okay, I get the message," she spat back in a rancorous tone that would've raised the eyebrows of all who heard it. "I'm gonna call it a night, but there's no way we're giving up on this. We need you. I don't care what I've gotta stoop to; I'm gonna get you to come along with us. C'mon, Tae."

As she indignantly turned to the door, the old woman cursed in a low voice. Her back suddenly hunched over again. Taking the girl with downcast eyes by the hand, Granny dragged her out into the hall and disappeared.

The door closed with a force that shook the room. The reverberations were absorbed then by the air and building materials, and mere seconds later, when silence once again ruled the darkness, the chirping began. It was the small and distant sound of the bugs pecking at the dark of night, scratching at the hearts of all who listened. It was the sort of sound that made those who heard it want to lie down deep in the earth. To those who were leaving town, the songs seemed to bid them adieu. Who knows how many listeners likened the melody the bugs continued to play to a funeral dirge. The sound continued just a little while longer, and soon, outside the room's tiny window, the light pink petals began to rain down. Yet even then, the figure lying on the bed did nothing, as if melodies of parting and funeral laments held no relevance for him.

III

The next day, the world belonged to the winds. Every time they whistled forlornly, a thin coat of what looked like gold dust was thrown onto the streets.

It was still early morning when the angry voices surrounded the hotel. The number of people around the building and packed into its lobby looked like it encompassed the entire population of the small town. They demanded that the hotel manager chase off the Vampire Hunter that was staying there immediately, and although he was reluctant at first, he consented after hearing all the circumstances. And while he understood the reasons, his heart must've been heavy at the thought of dealing with the greatest Hunter on earth, because his steps were sluggish as he headed to the stairs from the front desk.

All of the townspeople behind the manager were armed. Although there was usually comfort in numbers, the reason their faces were as pale as paper was because they, like all residents of the Frontier, were well-informed about the general capabilities of Hunters. The fingers wrapped around their stake-firing guns and long spears were stiff, cold, and clammy.

It was probably the manager's good fortune that he didn't have to knock on the door in the end. The door creaked open before his trembling hand, and the room's occupant appeared. As that handsome countenance silently watched them, the townspeople forgot their murderous rage and were left dazed. But it was the manager who noticed D was prepared to set off on a trip. Bringing his hand to his heart in relief, he asked, "Will you be leaving, sir?"

"I can't rest here any longer." D's eyes gazed quietly at the men filling the hallway. The lust for violence that'd churned there had already disappeared, and they were gripped now by a sort of lethargy—just from a single glance from the Hunter. As D walked ahead, the mass of people broke to either side, as if pushed back by some unseen agent. The only thing showing in the eyes of the men pressed against the wall was fear. D went down the stairs. The lobby was a crucible of furious humanity. Like the sea in days of old, they parted right down the middle, opening a straight path between the Vampire Hunter and the door.

"Your bill has been paid," the manager called from behind him.

D went outside. In the street, there was a furry of wind and people—and eyes steeped in hatred and fear. Just as he took hold of the reins to his cyborg horse in the shack next to the hotel, a cheerful voice called out to him.

"Scaring the hell out of a group that size is quite a feat," Clay Bullow said, donning a carefree smile, but D didn't even look at him as he got up in the saddle. "Hold up. We're leaving, too. Why don't you come with us?" Clay suggested, seeming just a bit flustered. The hot-headedness of the previous night had burned away like a fog. He was also on horseback, with the reins in his hands. "My brother's waiting at the edge of town. You know, I'm not talking about us all being friends or nothing. We wanna settle up with you."

As D casually rode off, Clay gave a kick to his mount's flanks and headed after him. Flicking the reins, he pulled up on D's left side.

"Now, this is a surprise! Guess I should've expected no less," he said, eyes going wide. His exclamation was entirely sincere. "You draw your sword over your right shoulder. If you leave me on your left, you can't try to cut me without turning your horse and everything this way. Have you got so much confidence that you don't care about something like that, or are you just plain stupid? Just so you know, this is my good side."

By that, Clay must've meant the hand he'd use to fight. His harp was on his right hip. His hand glided toward the strings.

"Care to try me?" the Hunter asked.

Clay's hand froze in midair. All it had taken was that one question from D. The Hunter was rocking back and forth on his horse.

The people saw Clay's mount halt, and the other rider rode away at a leisurely pace.

D turned the corner. The great gates that separated the town from the desert were hazy through the clouds of sand. They lay straight ahead of him. D advanced without saying a word.

Massive forms challenged the sky to either side of the gate—enormous trees that were the deepest shade of blue. Looking like thousands of giant serpents twisted together, the trunk of each had countless cracks running through it. There were no smaller branches or twigs. Naturally, there were no leaves, either. The two colossal trees had died ages ago. Beside the huge tree on the right, a figure in a silk hat sat on a horse, and next to the tree on the left rested a wagon with a cylindrical cover. Covered on three sides by a canopy of reinforced plastic, the driver's seat was occupied by Granny Viper and Tae. All of them were waiting for D—but the Hunter rode by without glancing at either party.

"My younger brother was supposed to go collect you," Bingo said. Perhaps he was still "sleeping," as his face was turned to the ground under his black bowler hat. As he spoke in his sleep, his voice seemed unbounded. "But I guess the Hunter D was a little too much baggage for him to handle after all," the elder Bullow continued. "Someday, we'd like some of your time to settle things nice and leisurely. We're headed down the same road you are. What do you say to going with us?"

Granny Viper cackled like a bird of prey, blowing aside the dusty clouds. "You think our young friend here travels with anyone else? Looks like the Fighting Bullow Brothers have gone soft in the head! He's always on his own. He was born alone, lives alone, and he'll die alone. One look at him should be enough to tell you as much."

The crone turned an enraptured gaze on the pale profile riding past her. "But this time," she said to the Hunter, "I need you to make

an exception. Now, I don't know what you're up to, but if you're going across the desert, then Barnabas is the only place you could be headed . . . which happens to be where we're headed, too. Even if you don't want to come with us, we still have the right to follow along after you." Glaring in Bingo's direction, she added, "Sheesh. I don't know what you boys are trying to prove, but we could do without you. I'm giving you fair warning," she said to Bingo in a tone that could cow even a giant of a man. "If you make a move against D, I'll take it as a move against us. Try anything funny, and you'll find yourselves with more than one foe on your hands."

And then the crone pulled back on her reins. An electrical current passed through the metallic rings looped around the necks of the four cyborg horses in her team, triggering the release of adrenaline. A hot and heavy wind smacked the horses in the nose as they hit the street. Beyond the great gates that opened to either side, D's shape was dwindling in the distance. The wagon was close behind him, and Bingo's horse was about a minute behind the wagon. Another five minutes later, Clay passed through the gate as well. As soon as he'd gone, a sad sound began to ring out all over town. If the wind was a song that bid them farewell, then the cries of the bugs were a funeral dirge. And before long, even that died out.

The crone's covered wagon soon pulled up on D's right-hand side. Golden terrain stretched on forever, and the sky was a leaden hue. The thick canopy of clouds that shrouded the desert was almost never pierced by the rays of the sun; in the last fifty years or so, the sun had only been seen once. Somewhere out on the line that divided heaven from earth, a few ribbon-like beams of light had once burst through the sea of clouds in a sight that was said to be beautiful beyond compare. Some even said there was a town out where it'd shone. But after that, the light was never seen again.

"Oh my, looks like those two really are coming along," Granny said after adjusting her canopy and peering into the omni-directional safety mirror. Made of more than a dozen lenses bent into special angles and wired in place, the mirror not only provided clear views of all four sides of the wagon, but of the sky above it and earth below as well. The figures that appeared in the lens that covered the back, of course, were the Bullow Brothers. "Why do you reckon they're following you?" the crone asked as she wiped the sweat from her brow. Though sunlight didn't penetrate the clouds, the heat had no trouble getting through. In fact, the inescapable swelter was a special characteristic of this desert. "They say a fighter's blood starts pumping faster when he finds someone tougher than him. Well," she laughed, "it sure as hell ain't anything as neat as all that. You know why you were thrown out of that hotel?"

D didn't answer her. Most likely, it was all the same to him. He'd probably have just left his lodging at checkout time. No matter what the townspeople tried, it wouldn't have mattered, because in truth, they wouldn't have been able to do anything to him.

The old woman looked to the heavens in disgust. "Unbelievable! The mob back in town was ready to kill you. You must've known as much. And yet you mean to tell me you don't even wanna know *why?*"

Waiting a while for an answer, the old woman finally shrugged her shoulders.

"Watch out for those two, you hear me? The reason everyone in town was after you is because the daughter of some farmer out on the edge of town had her blood drained last night. They've probably got her in isolation by now, but when they found her in that state this morning, they just jumped to the conclusion you were to blame. After all, you are the world-famous Vampire Hunter D. And you're a 100 percent genuine dhampir."

As Granny said this, she took her left hand off the reins, got the canteen that sat by her feet, and brought it to her mouth. The temperature continued to climb rapidly—a sure sign that the world humans inhabited was now far away.

"Now, I can tell with just one look at you that you're not that kind of weak-willed, half-baked Noble, but the world don't work that way. Everyone got all steamed-up and figured it was entirely your fault, which is why they formed that big ol' mob. Hell, they don't even know for sure if she was even bitten or not. Truth is . . . any quack in town could've easily made a wound that'd look like that. Give the girl a shot of anesthetic, and she'd have the same symptoms as if one of the Nobility fed on her, and she wouldn't be able to eat for four or five days, either. It was them," the crone said, tossing her jaw in the direction of the Bullow brothers. "They did it. To get you thrown out."

Seeing a slight movement of D's lips, the old woman had to smother a smile of delight.

"Why would they want me thrown out of town?" the Hunter asked, though from his tone it was completely uncertain whether or not he was actually interested. It was like the voice of the wind, or a stone. Given the nature of the young man, the wind seemed more likely.

"I wouldn't have the slightest notion about that," the crone said, smirking all the while. "You should ask them. After all, they're following along after you. But it's my hope that you'll hold off on any fighting till our journey's safely over. I don't wanna lose my precious escort, you see."

Not seeming upset that he'd been appointed her guardian at some point, D said, "Soon."

The word startled the old woman. "What, you mean something's coming? Been across this desert before, have you?"

"I read the notes written by someone who crossed it a long time ago," D replied, his eyes staring straight ahead.

There was no breeze, just endless crests of gray and gold. The temperature had passed a hundred and five. The crone was drenched with sweat.

"If the contents are to be believed, the man who kept that notebook made it halfway across," D continued.

"And that's where he met his death, eh? What killed him?"

"When I found him, his arm was poking out from some rocks, with his notebook still clutched in his hand even though he was just a skeleton."

The old woman shrugged. "At any rate, it probably won't do us much good, right? I mean, you must've gone as far as he did."

"When I found him, he was out in the middle of the Mishgault stone stacks."

Granny's eyes bulged. "That's more than three thousand miles from here. You don't say . . . So, that's how it goes, eh? The seas of sand play interesting games, don't they? What should we do, then?"

"Think for yourself."

"Now I'll—" the old woman said, about to fly into a rage, but a semitransparent globe drifted before her. The front canopy was in the woman's way, so she touched its curved plastic surface and it quickly retracted to the rear.

The thing was about a foot-and-a-half in diameter. It was perfectly round, too. Within it, a multicolored mass that seemed to be a liquid was gently rippling.

"A critter of some sort," Granny remarked. "I've never seen anything like it before. Tae, get inside."

Once she'd sent the girl into the depths of the covered wagon, the crone took the nearby blunderbuss and laid it across her lap. With a muzzle that flared like the end of a trumpet, the weapon would launch a two-ounce ball of lead with just a light squeeze of its trigger. Pulling out the round it already contained, the old woman took a scattershot shell from the tin ammo box that sat by the weapon and loaded that instead. Her selection was based merely on a gut feeling, but it was a good choice. From somewhere up ahead of them, more globes than they could count began to surround the wagon and the rider.

"Looks like the Bullow Brothers are gonna wet themselves," the old woman laughed as she eyed one of the lenses in her mirror. "What the hell are those critters, anyway?"

"I don't know," D said simply.

"What do you mean?! Didn't you just say they'd be attacking us *soon*?"

"There was nothing about them in the notebook."

The crone's eyes went wide. "Then this is something new, is it?"

The question was barely off the old woman's tongue when their surroundings were filled with light. Not only had the globes taken on strange colors, but they'd begun pulsing with life.

"God, these things are disgusting. I'm gonna make a break for it!" Granny shouted, forgetting all about the man she'd asked to guard them as she worked the reins for all she was worth. The cyborg horses in her team kicked up the ground in unison. The intense charge pushed the globes out of the way, leaving them spinning wildly in the vehicle's wake. Racing on for a good four hundred feet, the crone then stopped her wagon. As her eyes came to rest on D by their side, she was all smiles.

"Stuck right with us, didn't you?" Granny said to him. "Forget what you said—I just knew you'd be worried about the two of us. Good thing for us. That's just what I like to see in a strong man."

The old woman was about to lavish even more praise on the Hunter when suddenly she stopped. D had taken one hand and slowly pointed to their rear. "Take a shot at them," he said in a low voice. Perhaps he'd only kept up with her to see what effect it would have.

Though her face made no secret of her apprehension, Granny must've shared his interest, because she raised her blunderbuss. "Oh my," she said. "Those two boys are coming, too. Hold on a minute."

"Now," the Hunter told her.

"What?" said the old woman, her eyes widening. She then found out why D had instructed her to shoot—the globes they'd knocked out of the way were now rising without a sound to disappear in the high heavens. They were moving so quickly that hitting them would be no easy task, even with scattershot. The globes that surrounded the galloping Bullow Brothers also broke off immediately and headed for the sky.

"You are one scary character," Granny muttered, not exaggerating her opinion of him in the slightest. And as she spoke, she brought the blunderbuss to her shoulder and leaned out from the driver's seat. She didn't have time to take careful aim. A blast of flames and a ridiculously loud roar issued from the preposterously large muzzle of the weapon, rocking the world. Globes shattered above the two brothers, sending out spray. There wasn't enough time to get off a second shot.

D and the old woman waited silently for the pair of riders approaching in a cloud of dust.

Clay was the first to speak, shouting, "What the hell were those things? We're not even three miles out of town yet!"

Head still drooping, Bingo swayed back and forth on his horse. He was fast asleep, but the fact that he'd raced this far without being thrown made it clear it was no ordinary slumber. Bingo Bullow, after all, was a man who conversed in his sleep.

As Clay gazed up at the unsettling leaden sky, Granny Viper caught his eye. The old woman was bent over in the midst of concealing her blunderbuss.

"Hey! You lousy hag!" Clay shouted at her. As he kept watch over D out of the corner of his eye, he added, "That was a damn fool thing to do. Just look what you did to my hat!" Pulling his cap off, he put one of his fingers into it. His fingertip poked out of a hole near the top—a piece of shot had gone right through it. If he'd been wearing the cap all the way down on his head, it probably would've hit him right in the forehead.

And what did Granny do when met by a look of hatred that would've left a child in tears? She grinned from ear to ear. The smile she wore seemed so amiable, not even the sweetest, kindest woman in the world could've hoped to match it.

"What a piece of luck, eh?" the crone said with sincerity. She then told the astonished Clay, "I wasn't the one who decided to take the shot, though. Our handsome friend here made the call. And I was sure he was likely to cut me down if I didn't do like he said."

That was true enough.

"Is that right?" Clay asked D. In stark contrast to the tone he'd used up until now, his words were soft. He seemed ready to have it out with the Hunter.

And D's reply . . . was no reply at all. "Looks like you didn't get any of their contents on you," the Hunter said, filling his field of view with the two brothers.

Clay gave a knowing nod. "So, that's how it goes, is it? That's your game, then? Well, that's too damn bad. If it was that easy to get the stuff on us, we'd be ashamed to call ourselves the Bullow Brothers."

"The next time they show up, you might not be able to avoid it. Besides, I doubt it would've been life threatening, even if you got some on you."

"And how the hell do you know that?" Clay cried out.

"A hunch," D replied.

"Don't give me any of that shit!"

"Give it a rest," Bingo muttered in a tone as flat and gray as the sky over them. "The Hunter D had a hunch about it. We would've been fine even if we got wet!"

"Spare me. I don't need to hear it from you too, bro."

In a soothing voice, Granny spoke to the frenzied Clay. "Settle down, there. No harm came to you, so everything's okay, isn't it? We'll have no fighting amongst ourselves in this party."

Silence descended. It wasn't a quiet interval for introspection, but rather one brought on by sheer astonishment.

"Who the hell ever said we're in your party?!" Clay shouted, more blood rising to his face.

"Why, you did, the second you left town. We've got the same destination, and we've been traveling less than five hundred yards apart. What's more, it seems our Mr. D has a head full of info on half the nasty critters waiting for us out in the desert."

Holding his tongue for a minute, Clay turned to his older brother and asked, "You think that's true, bro?" His tone was like that of a gullible spectator putting a question to a bogus clairvoyant.

"I don't know," Bingo replied, his head swaying from side to side. "But under the circumstances, traveling together could make things a lot easier later on. And you know what they say: it's the company you keep that really makes the trip."

Eyes that Gleam in the Dark

CHAPTER 2

I

Night soon fell without further incident. After tethering the horses to hooks on the back of the wagon, the whole group settled down for the evening behind a sand dune. A certain air of dignity prevailed over the world. Though darkness had covered everything, the heavens hadn't lost their dull gray clouds, which continued to hang over the heads of the little group. As the temperature fell rapidly, no one said a thing. White breath alone spilled from their lips.

"A hell of a desert this is," Clay groused as he warmed himself by the electronic heater he'd set down in a firmer spot in the sand. "Hot as a bastard by day and cold as a bitch at night. I don't mind it cooling off some, but the damn temperature's dropped more than sixty degrees!"

"There's a good side to it, though," Granny interjected as she held her hands out over Clay's heater.

"Hey, don't be sidling up to my stove like we're best buddies or something. That lousy wagon of yours has a heating system in it, don't it?" the younger Bullow said harshly.

Not the least bit fazed, Granny replied, "That's pretty tight-fisted talk for someone who calls himself a man. Well, with a temperament like that, I'm not surprised you start blubbering at the first little chill.

Sure it's cold, but see how the grains of sand get heavier in the lower temperatures so it's not blowing around like it does all day? Of course, it helps there's no wind, either."

"Damn straight," Bingo concurred in a deep voice from a spot some eight or ten feet from Clay. Now the younger Bullow couldn't possibly argue with Granny. But what kind of man could his older brother be? He wasn't by the heater. Why, he wasn't even lying down. He was still astride his cyborg horse, sitting in the kind of hard saddle that ordinarily left a rider numb below the waist after three or more hours of riding.

Granny muttered, "Strange tastes your brother's got." And it came as little surprise that she sounded a bit unnerved.

"Not really. You wanna talk about strange, there's your guy!" Clay said, tossing his jaw in the direction of Granny's wagon.

Leaving his cyborg horse beside the vehicle, D had lain back against a nearby sand dune with his sword in his left hand and his eyes shut.

"If that guy don't look like the loneliest thing ever. And it ain't because he's turned his back on the world. With him, everybody's happy to see him coming, but no one's sorry to see him go. And anybody who catches sight of him is bound to step aside on account of that intense scent he's got about him."

"Yes, the scent," the crone said with a nod as she followed Clay's gaze. "The smell of blood. The scent of solitude. But you still don't get it, do you?"

"Get what?" Clay asked, eyes opening wide.

"She's right," the slender black shadow on horseback said.

"Not you too, bro! You're siding with an old hag over your own brother?"

Before Clay had finished airing his complaint, D sat up without making a sound. Grains of sand spilled like waves down the slope he'd been leaning against. Eyes still closed as he stood up straight, he then froze in place like a bronze sculpture.

"What is it?" Clay asked, squinting his eyes.

Granny's face grew tense, too. There was no trace of movement around them—just the night frozen solid. That's all that was out there.

D's silhouette shifted. With a movement just as brusque as the one that'd put him on his feet in the first place, he seated himself again in the same spot.

Clay and the crone looked at each other.

"What is it?" Clay said again.

The old woman went over to D. "Did something happen?" she asked.

D didn't raise his eyes. "It rained sand," he said.

"Sand?"

"In this desert," the Hunter continued, "what we know about the world doesn't count for much, it seems."

"Did you sense something?"

"It's going to get more dangerous. Try not to make things any worse."

"Is that a fact? Well, we'll be counting on you, in that case," the crone remarked, pursuing the matter no further. If she left things to the Hunter, she couldn't possibly go wrong. Her feelings on the subject were more a matter of rationality than trust—she didn't want to be burdened with too much information when she could have D shouldering it all. Cold air suddenly snaked into her nostrils, and Granny sneezed loudly.

"Hey," Clay called out to D. "You seem to know an awful lot about this desert. So, why don't you tell us what's lying ahead? We're in this together, and we're all headed the same way. Why not share the wealth, eh?" His tone was somewhat belligerent.

D didn't move a muscle.

"Hey, don't play games with me. You plan on keeping everything to yourself?" Clay blustered, not giving up. In a desert crossing such as this, any information about the vicious creatures it contained could literally mean the difference between life and death. He was deadly serious.

"Wait just a second, you two," Granny interrupted. "We've barely finished our first day out here, right? We have a falling out this early in the game, then there's no point in traveling together in the first place. Think about it, D. There's some sense to what he's saying. We don't want to go plodding off across the sands without the slightest clue now. Tell him some of what you know."

"Not some of it. *All* of it." There was composure to the warrior's tone. He was ready to fight if need be. His right hand drifted toward the harp at his waist.

"Come now, D," Granny prodded.

Clay's index finger was poised by his harp. He pulled back on one of the strings, and then he stopped. He saw D open his eyes. Cold water rushed down from the nape of his neck to the base of his spine—the Hunter's glare was that powerful.

"If I tell you, you'll have to go first," D said in the kind of voice that crept along the ground.

"Fine by me," Clay replied with a magnanimous bow. It was no bluff. He seemed to have considerable confidence in himself. "I wouldn't be a weasel and ask you to go first anyhow. I'll plow dead ahead wherever we gotta go. So, just put your mind at ease and tell me all about it."

"The moving forest," said D. Clay noticed that the cloud of white that spilled from the Hunter's lips with his breath was far fainter than that of the rest of them. "If the notes I have are correct, it was about a dozen miles southwest of here. But it *is* a moving forest, after all."

"Meaning there's no telling where it's gone? That's a hoot!"

"The person who left those notes only saw it in motion from a long way off, but didn't go any closer. Whether or not he was lucky in that respect, I can't say."

"I see," said Clay.

"And another thing—there are people."

"What?!" Granny cried, her eyes bugging out. She'd thought whatever else slipped from D's lips couldn't possibly surprise her, but she was wrong. "People out in this desert? Stop pulling my leg."

"That's what it said in the notes," D continued softly. "About thirty in all. Apparently, they attacked on cyborg horses about a hundred and twenty miles south of here. Killed almost a dozen of thetraveler's companions and made off with their goods and the corpses."

"What would they take corpses for?" Clay asked.

Giving him no reply, D simply said, "There's more. It seems they were shot and stabbed but did not die."

Silence descended.

Bingo's torso rose from his mount. "Immortal, are they?" he said in a low sleepy voice.

"That's all I know," D said. His eyes were closed.

Clay shrugged his shoulders. "That's no big freaking deal, is it, bro?" he said to the figure on horseback. He sounded thoroughly relieved. Perhaps a desert plagued by beasts and immortal bandits was nothing to them. "That right there scares me a lot more," Clay said, tossing his jaw in the wagon's direction. There was no one but Tae inside, but everyone was well aware of what *the hidden* represented.

It was at just that moment that the wagon's door opened. Clay grimaced awkwardly and rubbed his scruffy beard. Tae's head hung low; it seemed to be something of a habit with the girl. Perhaps averting her gaze had kept the weight of her fate from crushing her.

"Get back inside. It's cold out here," Granny shouted. The rebuff had a touch of animosity to it. While it was her job to find children who'd been "hidden," she was entitled to feel however she liked about her charges.

"Aw, why don't you just leave her be?" Clay said as he glared at the crone's wrinkled face from the corner of his eye. "It's a hell of a lot more comfortable here than blasting the heat in there. Besides, a person's got a right to do whatever they damn well please. She don't have to take orders from anyone. And I'd be tickled pink to have a cutie like her out here instead of all these ugly mugs I'm traveling with."

Knowing as he did Granny Viper's name, Clay also surely had a good idea of the girl's circumstances, but his tone held neither fear nor loathing. No doubt he'd be brimming with confidence until the very moment he died.

Tae quickly ducked back inside.

Giving an appreciative whistle, Clay said, "Now, ain't she a beauty. What's her name, anyway?"

Granny met the man's cheery inquiry with a stern visage. "Let's be perfectly clear on something," she said, her voice rolling across the ground like a toxic cloud. "That girl is my merchandise. Try anything funny and you'll find yourself in hell trying to get some action from a she-devil."

"Well, that'd have to beat looking at your ugly kisser," Clay sneered back. "Your merchandise may be pricey, but that don't mean it's good. We all know what happens to most *hidden* who go back home, so you'd best pray that she ain't one of them."

"You needn't worry about it," Granny replied snidely. "My job just entails getting them home. What happens after that doesn't concern me. On the other hand, until I get 'em there, I'll look out for them even if it costs me my life. And I'm not letting anyone pull anything funny with her."

"Interesting," Clay said, licking his chops. "Well, just let me give you fair warning then. Before this little trip of ours is done, I'm gonna leave my mark on your precious goods."

"Oh, is that right?" Granny shot back, her eyes growing wider by the second.

"Knock it off, Clay," a sober voice said, shattering the tension. It belonged to Bingo. "Well," he continued, "it looks like the best thing to do is pull out of here as soon as possible."

Both Clay and Granny turned in the direction that the skinny figure indicated with a toss of his chin. White sand was dropping all around a form of unearthly beauty. Returning his weapon and sheath to his back, D stared out at one point in the darkness.

"What is it now?" Clay asked with seeming relish.

"Can you make something out?" Bingo inquired sleepily.

"Butterflies," D replied, walking over to his horse without making a sound.

"Hey, Hunter! You just gonna turn tail and run then?" Clay sneered, as if he'd been waiting for the chance to say these exact words.

"So, we've got no choice but to plow right through them?" Bingo added.

Not replying to Bingo's query, D merely said, "I don't think this is a job for me." He was looking right at the old woman.

"So you know what I have up my sleeve, then?" Granny said, her eyes going wide. "If my moves have become public knowledge, I may have to learn a whole new bag of tricks."

Just as D mounted his horse, Granny seated herself in the wagon. With an expression that said he didn't have a clue what was going on, Clay put his feet into the stirrups. Though all of them strained their eyes, they didn't see anything—the darkness drank up every sound, leaving everything in a state of utter silence. D's mount took a few steps away from them.

"Hold up a minute. Won't we be tackling this together?" Granny called out to D.

"I don't remember asking you to follow along after me."

"When you said this wasn't a job for you, was that supposed to mean you're leaving the rest of us to our own devices then? You're not a real compassionate man now, are you?" Granny railed at the Hunter, but D had ridden his horse beyond the reach of her abuse.

Perhaps nothing save the hyper-keen senses of a dhampir could've detected the paper-thin presence that was closing in on them from the depths of the darkness. At long last, the wind moved around them. The flowing air came from the beating of countless wings, yet was still strangely light. The mass consisted of butterflies beyond number—a swarm of thousands, or even tens of thousands. But where did they live, and what did they seek?

They rushed at D, enveloping the tall figure in black with the color of darkness. His blade flashed out. Without so much as the sound of a slash through the air, all of the bisected butterflies started to drop to the ground as D galloped through them. As the mount and rider advanced in a dusty cloud, the wave of black drifted away as if frightened of the Hunter, but an instant later it became a broad band that began following after him. It was only natural that the rest of the swarm set upon the wagon and the other two riders.

"Damnation! What in blazes is this?" Granny screamed from the driver's seat.

"These little buggers sure have some nerve!" Clay shouted as he plucked off a few that were covering his face. The black butterflies relentlessly besieged his livid countenance; Bingo had already been reduced to an ebony sculpture.

Suddenly the world of darkness felt a protest of orange light. Caught in three thousand degrees of flame, the butterflies themselves added fuel to the fire.

Pulling a tank filled with fire-dragon oil and a leather pressure-pump up onto the driver's seat, Granny waved the reinforced plastic nozzle around as she cackled, "Well, how do you like them apples?! Have another taste of one of the Capital's very own flamethrowers. I've still got plenty of this fuel to go around."

And in keeping with the crone's haughty talk, tongues of flame licked out in all directions as helpless butterflies fell like blazing scraps of paper. Not quite so conspicuous due to Granny Viper's furious battle, Clay and Bingo nonetheless were engaging the butterflies about forty feet away. The odd thing was, the butterflies really weren't doing anything. There was no sign of them injecting some solvent to melt the travelers' flesh or clogging their windpipes to suffocate them; they merely kept going after them.

"Damn! No matter how many we fight off, they just keep coming. At this rate, there'll be no end to it, bro."

There was no answer to Clay's remark—Bingo's entire body was draped in black cloth. While the younger Bullow struggled to pull the insects off his own face, his older brother sat on his horse without moving a muscle. As a result, it looked like he'd grown twice as fat.

"Damn you little pests!" Clay shouted through the airborne butterflies that eclipsed the darkness. And then a beautiful note rang out that sounded like someone strumming a guitar. But what happened when that sound melded with the darkness, and then became a wave that rippled out?

The swarm of butterflies that appeared to float on into eternity all disappeared within a ten-foot radius. Another note resounded: every time the mellifluous sound rang out, the maddening black swarm of insects that rushed in to replace their fallen comrades disappeared. And in the center of the gap that'd opened so suddenly was Clay. His right hand was on the harp he wore on his hip. He kept one eye on his older brother.

"Bingo's fine," the younger Bullow told himself. "The old bag's giving them a hell of a fight, too. Now where the hell's that Hunter gone off to?"

While Granny was indeed on top of the situation, Clay's older brother was blanketed, mount and all, with black butterflies. What was fine about that?

At that very moment, the swarm of butterflies smoothly drifted away. Because the creatures did no harm but merely trailed along after them, Granny and Clay found them all the more disturbing, and their expressions stiffened accordingly.

Gasps of surprise slipped from two pairs of lips at the same time.

The butterflies had begun to glow. So like the darkness in hue, first the contours of their wings and then their entire forms had suddenly begun to take on a silvery light.

"What the hell . . ." Clay muttered as the silver butterflies formed several thick bands before him that then intertwined and began to leisurely eddy about.

This wasn't merely some pattern formed by the capricious flight of the creatures. It was clearly a configuration purposely orchestrated by some higher intelligence. Straight lines and curves, polyhedrons and circles all existed in the same place and time, twisting together and pulling apart again. Yet for all that activity, the swirling figures remained focused on a single point in space.

While they weren't sure how long they'd watched, Granny and Clay felt like they were being pulled into the center of that vortex, and the two of them frantically shut their eyes. A few seconds passed.

"Looks like it's over," said a cold voice that sounded equidistant from the pair as it set their eardrums trembling. Opening their eyes in unison, they found a man on horseback stopped about fifteen feet from them. It was D.

"I just knew you'd be back," Granny exclaimed with joy, still holding a nozzle that dripped liquefied fat.

"Looks like he came back once he found out the butterflies were harmless," Clay muttered scornfully.

"I just came to tell you something," D said dispassionately from the back of his horse.

"Oh? And what would that be?"

"A tornado has sprung up nearly a mile ahead of us. Not a very large one, but enough to pick all of us up. It'll be here in about five minutes."

Of course, Granny and Clay must've wanted to know how the young Hunter had eluded the swarm of butterflies, and whether or not he'd watched their dizzying display until the end, but the threat of natural disaster took precedence over all else. As she stowed the flamethrower again, Granny asked the young man apprehensively, "You'll be going with us, won't you?"

Needless to say, his reply was the same as always: "You're free to follow me if you like."

II

While a pale ash colored the east, light began to rain down at the same rate the darkness dissipated. It was dawn.

The group had moved about three miles west from their first encampment and was sheltered behind a sand dune. When the wagon door opened quietly, a pale and reserved-looking face peered out. Roaring snores crept from the vehicle's interior—the whole group had gone to bed about three hours earlier. Tae looked around sleepily at her surroundings, but they weren't particularly terrifying. Behind a dune to her right lay a lumpy blanket where the toes of a pair of boots jutted from the end. Apparently, that was Clay. There was no sign of his older brother, and his horse wasn't with Clay's, either. There was no telling where a man like that could've gone. Sweeping another seventy degrees, Tae's eyes then halted. A figure in black was reflected in her widened pupils.

D was on the crest of a dune, staring off to the west. His form was reminiscent of the most exquisite sculpture, and as he focused solely on the direction they were headed, he had an air of intensity about him that suited the situation perfectly.

Tae climbed down from the wagon and headed for the dune. For a girl who seemed to have lost her own will and who was manipulated like a doll by the old woman, this was an unbelievably purposeful course of action. Climbing the dune, she was a few yards from the Hunter when she came to a halt. It was the words that came over the back of his black coat that stopped her.

"What brings you out here?" he asked.

Tae didn't answer.

"There's no telling what'll come at us next out in this desert. Go back to the wagon." His voice was soft, but it allowed no debate.

Tae closed her eyes. Her head still hung low, and her thin, bloodless lips trembled with fright. "I . . . I thought I might . . . answer your question . . ."

Back at the cheap hotel, D had asked the girl the name of the Noble who'd abducted her. Now it was a different question he put to her. "Do you want to tell me?" he asked.

Tae looked up at D with an expression that betrayed her surprise.

"Why have you decided to talk about it? If you don't want to, don't force yourself to do it."

The girl didn't know what to say.

"Did Granny put you up to this?"

Tae looked down again. It took a few seconds before she could speak again. "If you didn't feel like helping . . . she said none of us would make it across the desert alive . . . that's why . . ."

"Your parents are in Barnabas, aren't they?"

Several more seconds of silence followed.

"It seems both of them are dead," the girl replied. "But my big brother got married and took over the house."

"In that case, you needn't burden yourself unduly for the rest of the trip. I can't take you there, but you're free to follow me."

Tae looked at D strangely. The black expanse of his back spoke volumes on loneliness and complete isolation. Somehow, she got the impression that the young man had nothing more to say to her. Tae backed away a few steps; she was too afraid to just turn around. Right as she was about to go, the girl hesitantly said, "I don't remember anything at all. Just . . ."

Just what?

"In the darkness, there were always these two red eyes, blazing like rubies . . . watching me . . ."

The Hunter hadn't turned toward her, and the girl then turned her back to him, too.

Not long after the sloping dune had hidden the tracks she left in the sand, another voice—a hoarse one—could be heard where D seemed to be alone. "Well, it looks like *he* got a taste of her after all," it said with a chuckle. "In which case she'll never know happiness no matter how she might try, eh? So, what do you suppose he did to her?"

There was no reply. D just kept his eyes trained straight ahead at the cold world of sand that seemed shrouded in gray light.

The voice laughed with amusement. "She may be behaving herself right now, but he isn't crazy enough to snatch a human girl just so she can be his maidservant. Sooner or later, that girl's bound to show her true colors. Our foes aren't on the outside, but rather—"

"There are some girls that nothing happens to," D finally replied.

"Sure, but that's maybe one in ten thousand," the voice shot back ruthlessly. "And just think about the miserable end this world has in store for all the rest of those girls—and I don't just mean the ones *he* took."

If that comment had been directed at anyone but D, they would've grown pale as they tried desperately to strike the answer from their brain, or perhaps they would've frozen on the spot from the overwhelming horror of it.

For *the hidden*, the tragedy really began when they were found and brought back to the world of humanity. There were girls who might suddenly sprout fangs and tear into someone's throat the very day they were reunited with their parents. There were boys who might live uneventfully for months, or even years, before going mad without any warning whatsoever. There were actually records of a case a dozen years or so earlier where such children abandoned their parents again to live someplace in the mountains, but even there the madness in their blood set them to killing each other, until in the end they were all dead. You could say both the beginning and the end of *the hidden*'s tragic tale was penned when the children disappeared.

"You know how it is," D's left hand continued. "In the end, nothing good can come of that girl going back to her family. At first, her parents will weep for joy. They'll probably want her to live with them, even if it means hiding her from the neighbors or moving to another region. But after a while, they'll get to wondering if maybe her eyes don't have a strange glint to them. Not that you can blame them. To eyes that have peered into the darkness of the other side, this world is a hollow reflection. And could anything shy of the sights of hell ever move those kids again? No, not till the end of time. And there's the first act of the tragedy. The very parents who would've died to have their kid back now can't even look at them. They lock the kid in their room. And then one day the two of them pack up a wagon and take off out of the blue, leaving just their kid in the house."

The voice broke off there; D was squeezing his left hand into a fist. He did so with such force it wouldn't have been surprising to hear the bones cracking.

But from his fist, a tortured voice said, "I suppose you could say the kids that get left behind are the lucky ones, though. Some parents are more . . . *thorough*. The same parents who spent their last dalas searching for their kids one day start whittling down a piece of wood and putting a point on the end of it . . ."

Something red had slowly begun to seep from between D's fingers.

"Oof . . . No one can really say . . . who it's harder for . . . the parents or the kids . . . But I can tell you this . . . If that girl there never goes home . . . no one . . . gets . . . hurt . . ."

At that moment, D quietly turned around. Seemingly following Tae's tracks, he went down the dune. After mounting his cyborg horse, he wheeled around in the direction of Clay and the wagon.

"There's a tornado approaching," the Hunter declared. "We're moving out."

After just enough time to contemplate his words, the blanket rose and the door to the wagon opened. Both the old woman and the warrior had been awake for some time. They certainly weren't average travelers.

"What, again?" Clay complained.

"Seriously?" Granny Viper asked, just to be sure. "I mean, it's not like that sort of thing springs up all the time. So, I take it this is a different one from last night, right?"

"No, it's the same one," D said flatly.

"Meaning all of *what*, exactly?" Clay asked, his lascivious expression twisting into a sneer. "Are you trying to tell us ol' Mr. Twister's out looking for us or something?"

Ignoring him, D started riding to the east.

"Son of a bitch," Clay growled, hatred in his eyes, as he hustled after the Hunter and toward his own horse.

Granny made haste, too.

No sooner had the wagon taken off than Clay did something rather strange. Looking all around, he cupped one hand by his mouth and shouted as loudly as he could, "Bro, I'm going on ahead. You catch up with me later, okay?"

Though Bingo didn't seem to be anywhere within range of Clay's cries, it seemed like his younger brother might have been able to see him. Saying nothing more and not seeming at all anxious, the warrior lashed his horse into action. As he galloped toward the wagon that was already twenty or thirty yards ahead of him, he looked over his shoulder.

"God, that's unbelievable," Clay said, the words spilling from him like a trickle of disbelief.

Distance-wise, it must've still been a couple of miles away—a line that looked like a twisted metal wire tied the heavens to the earth. It was bizarre the way that either end was blurred, seemingly dissolving into the sky at one extreme and the ground at the other. As far as Clay could see, it just kept growing thicker and thicker.

Riding full-tilt, the younger Bullow pulled even with the wagon. Granny Viper also wore a look of desperation as she gripped the reins. She recognized the tornado for what it was now.

The door opened, and Tae's face appeared.

"Don't come out here," Clay barked, but it was the old woman's expression, instead, that stiffened at the remark. Tae remained as devoid of emotion as ever.

Clay rode up on D's right-hand side. For a split second the desire to take a shot at the Hunter from behind surfaced in his brain, but it quickly faded again. "What the hell's the story with this tornado?!" he shouted. "It's following us! A while back, I joked it was looking for us, but this is just—"

"It's a strange desert, isn't it?" D said in a rare response.

"Damned if I ever heard of a tornado chasing travelers all night long. But we managed to give it the slip once already. We'll just do it again, right?"

Giving no reply, D flicked his gaze to the rear.

Imitating him, Clay looked back as well . . . and groaned despite himself.

The tornado looked like it was three feet thick now instead of a thin wire. The distance was dwindling; it wasn't a mile away now, or even five hundred yards.

Shouting something, Clay kicked his horse's flanks. As he shot away from D, he heard the Hunter behind him say, "The wagon's going to be sucked in." His voice was cold, like a machine's. Clay quivered, as if an electrical current had just shot through his powerful back.

"Do something, D!" Granny cried, her voice trailing after the Hunter.

Grains of sand buffeted all of their faces.

"This seriously ain't good," Clay muttered as he pulled back on the reins. Letting D pass him, he pulled up next to the wagon. "Granny, send the girl over here," he shouted. His eyes were glittering.

"Don't make me laugh! Why, I'd no sooner trust a goddamn rapist like you than—"

"I'm a lot faster than your wagon. We might just be able to get away."

"Give it a rest. Before I'd ever give her to you, I'd let the whirlwind have her."

"If that's the way you want it."

Clay flew into the air. His huge form seemed to become feather-light, and he landed right next to the old woman. He then bulled his way to the door.

"Stop it. If you don't, I'll—"

Powerful winds tore away the rest of Granny's cry. Not only did it tug at her words, but her body as well—the instant the edge of the fiercely writhing, sand-lifting pillar of black touched the wagon, both the vehicle and its three passengers were thrown high into the sky.

III

As Tae's consciousness pulled away from the darkness, the conviction that she had returned to reality hit her. She was lying down. Beneath her, it was soft. Sand, no doubt. And it was hot. The sand was scorching. Slowly, Tae moved her limbs. She wasn't in great pain. The dull throbbing she felt here and there was from being tossed around inside the wagon when it was picked up by the tornado. Propping herself up with both arms, she looked all around. A sense of incongruity dug into her spine.

The endless expanse of sand was gone; right before her towered a fairly high mound of stone. It looked about a hundred and fifty feet high. Come to mention it, she was surrounded on all sides by rocks large and small. As it occurred to her that it wouldn't be that strange to find such a rock formation in the desert, Tae picked herself up off the ground. Sweat spread across the back of her neck. She had no idea what time it was.

"Well, little lady, looks like you made it okay," someone called from the rock behind her, prompting her to turn in a daze. When she did, her eyes caught the massive form of a man in a brimless blue cap. Feeling the malicious lust in his eyes as he watched her, Tae backed away a few steps.

"Don't go being so cold with me, now," Clay said, a broad smile creeping across his face as he approached her. The beads of sweat covering his face glistened. "I just came to a minute ago myself. This is a hell of a place to find ourselves. Could be me and you are the only two who survived, you know. In which case, it'd be better for both of us if we could play nice, now wouldn't it?"

"Keep away from me."

"Well, now. You got a lot more to say than I thought, don't you? I didn't really get to hear what you were jawing about with the Vampire Hunter. But I'd sure like to hear me some of that sexy voice of yours."

Before Clay had finished speaking, he pulled the girl's tiny body close to his own massive form. Given almost no time to resist, Tae was pushed back against the sand.

"Stop it!" Tae screamed as fingers hard as rock sank into her breasts through her blouse. When she tried to push the warrior off, her hands were caught by the wrist and twisted up over "her head. Clay's lips came closer. The girl desperately turned her face away. His lips touched her cheek. Suddenly all the strength drained from the girl, and Clay knit his brow. Regardless, he sought her lips again. She was as unresponsive as a wax effigy.

"What the hell?! You giving in already? That's no fun at all. C'mon. Scream or cry or something!"

Though the younger Bullow believed his words had carried sufficient threat, Tae's expression hadn't changed at all. This wasn't just some trick to rob him of his carnal urges.

Unable to stand it any longer, Clay shouted, "Hey!" and shook the girl by the shoulders. Taking her chin in hand, he turned her face back. The instant their eyes met, a moan slipped from him. What occupied Tae's eyes was something humans were never meant to see. Sadness and hatred, suffering and fear—all of those emotions commingled in her eyes, but more than anything they were shrouded with a distant coldness beyond imagining.

"You felt that all those years . . ." Clay muttered absentmindedly.

"I remember . . . a little . . ." the eighteen-year-old girl said in a tone that could freeze even a hardened fighting man. "A little of what happened to me there . . . You're exactly the same . . . All of you . . . Humans and *them* . . ."

"You mean you were . . ." Clay muttered, and then a harsh sound rang out. With a cry like a wild animal he pulled back, and then sprang forward. A howl through the wind followed after him: a mighty lash from a leathery whip.

"Prepare to take your medicine. I'll flay the hide off your hands and face!" Granny shouted from beside a massive boulder five or ten feet to the right of where Clay had first appeared. The whip whistled; it hardly seemed possible that an old woman was manipulating the whip as it dealt Clay a blow that stung to the bone.

Eyes still shielded by both hands, he hurled a single insult: "You fucking hag!" Once again, Clay leapt back, and a beautiful sound rang through the air. A split second later, half of the whip that was snaking after the man's massive form disappeared like a puff of smoke. At a loss for words, Granny stiffened with tension.

"I'm gonna punch your ticket, you old bag!" Clay shouted, his right hand creeping across his harp. A prismatic cloud suddenly spread before his eyes.

It was sand. The very instant that she saw Clay was drawing on his own skill, Granny quickly discarded her whip and pulled the sand from the jar at her waist. However, the strange color of the sand and the way she used it made it clear that this was no simple trick to blind her opponent.

The sand that fell between the crone's feet and the tips of Clay's boots began to take human form—an image of Clay himself appeared on the ground.

Something gleamed in the old woman's right hand. The moment the short knife she kept hidden on her stabbed into the sand painting on the ground, Clay clutched his right ear with one hand. Redness seeped out between the palm of his hand and his cheek, but he didn't make a sound.

"What do you want carved up next? An eye, or maybe your nose?"

Buffeted with the kind of threats that made grown men and fire dragons alike freeze in their tracks, Clay smirked as if the situation was so amusing that he just couldn't help himself. "Granny Viper, People Finder—I guess the name ain't just for show after all," he said. "Now things are starting to get good. This is just the way I like it!"

"I was about to say the same thing myself," Granny said, licking her lips. The situation was rapidly escalating to a dangerous boiling point where more blood could be spilt and lives could be lost.

And then someone said, "Hold it right there."

Both of them froze at that pitch-black voice. Two pairs of eyes zipped halfway up the rocky mound, where the hem of a black long coat billowed out in the scant breeze. It wasn't clear whether it was Granny or Clay who mumbled D's name.

"Put your personal differences aside until we figure out what's going on with the desert. Where's the girl?" the Hunter asked.

Clay and Granny finally noticed that Tae was no longer there. An almost pitiful look of distress rose on the old woman's haughty countenance.

Tae came around the rocks and wiped her lips. Bewilderment and despair were rising from the pit of her stomach, spreading through her whole body. She didn't know what she was going to do next, or even what she should do. She started walking. She didn't want to sit there crying, though she wasn't really sure why she shouldn't. She wasn't sure where she was going; all she knew was that wanted to get away from everyone.

As countless phantoms flickered in her consciousness, one vivid image came to the fore, and then faded: crimson eyes glowing in the darkness . . . coming closer.

Where will I go? What will I do?

Those eyes were peering into her patiently. As she tried to squeeze out a scream, her throat convulsed, barely choking it off. From behind the crimson glow, a pale visage vaguely drifted into view. It was a face that was incredibly beautiful, manly, and above all, sad. An emotion that felt like crystal-clear water filled the girl's heart.

Compared to that, she thought, *compared to the fate that fashioned those eyes and that face, my pain is nothing.*

The red points of light faded.

Tae noticed she'd come to a standstill. *I should go back*, she thought. Though she had no idea what awaited her, she decided to forge ahead anyway. Then suddenly Tae turned right back around as she heard something stir behind her. She looked over her shoulder. A good two seconds passed before she could push a scream past her lips.

The first one to race over to the girl was Clay. The instant he came around the rocks, he saw Tae running toward him. Steadying the girl who'd just thrown herself at his chest, he then concentrated his gaze on the person before him. It was a man clad in a tattered shirt and trousers. Covered with a bushy overgrowth of hair and beard, his face looked emaciated, although his physique was relatively well-defined. The man stood there dazed for a few seconds and then fell to his knees on the spot.

"What in blazes do we have here?" Granny said from behind Clay.

"I don't know. By the look of him, he seems like a traveler lost in the desert. But how the hell could he get by living in this hole in the rocks? Could be dangerous."

Grabbing Tae by the arm and pulling her away, Granny told the warrior, "You'll have to help me while I bring her away someplace safe. If you're a real man, you'll take care of matters here." And then she beat a hasty retreat.

"Who the hell are you?" Clay asked, his fingers still poised on his harp. Murderous intent billowed from every inch of his body—it would've been enough to make the average person collapse on the spot. He was head-and-shoulders above the warriors and Hunters found everywhere else.

Scared perhaps by the younger Bullow's demeanor, the man shook his head repeatedly and raised both hands defenselessly. "How . . . how did all of you get here?" he asked. It almost sounded like his windpipe was clogged with sand.

Odd as it was, it prompted Clay to reply, "We got scooped up by a mean old tornado and went for a little flight."

Clay watched with surprise as the other man's shoulders slumped part-way through his reply. His hands came down to hide his face. "It got you, too? I just knew it. We'll all be stuck here for the rest of our lives . . ."

"What's that?!" Clay bellowed. "Just what do you mean by that? And who the hell are you, anyway?!"

When Clay took a step toward the other man, his eyes were drawn to several riders coming around the base of the mountain. Perhaps noticing them too, the man who'd been crouched there suddenly leapt back up, gave a frightened cry, and raced over to Clay. Just as the ragged man was about to collide with him, Clay dodged easily to the right and stuck his foot out. Falling forward with great impetus, the man threw a cloud of dust high into the air. But he quickly got back up again. He might have clutched at Clay's legs, but the warrior effortlessly backed away to keep the contact from happening.

"Please, help me," the man groaned. "I ran away from them. Up until yesterday, I was one of them. There was no use trying to escape . . . no one's getting out of this damn desert!" the man cried with the most appalling look of hopelessness hammered into his worn face.

But Clay did him one better as he glared back at the stranger with an almost demonic expression. "Don't make me laugh, you little coward. Unless you want me to turn you over to them, you'd best promise to answer me straight about everything I wanna know. If you do, I'll chase 'em off for you. If not, I'll personally see to it that they butcher you on the spot."

"Okay," the man said, nodding without complaint. Although his face didn't look like that of a weak-willed person, the man exhibited considerable fear.

"Just so long as we're clear on that. Wait behind me, then. Oh, and one more thing: you gotta promise me you'll keep your mitts off the girl."

"Whatever you say."

"Good. Get back there. You can relax now." As he listened to the man scurrying behind him for cover, Clay stood there waiting for the approaching dust cloud.

Though the man said that these were his compatriots, there must've been a grave mistake. Astride cyborg horses that looked brand new, the group of men wore shirts so neat and starched they looked freshly laundered. There were four of them.

"Hey there!" Clay called out, raising his left hand in greeting. The gazes that met him were like stone. His smile never fading a bit, the warrior continued, "We went and got ourselves carried off by a tornado. We're in a spot of trouble, seeing as we don't know where we're at now. So, this is great. You guys sure are a sight for sore eyes. Just whereabouts would this happen to be?"

"We came for the man," said the middle-aged man who stood at the fore—a powerfully built character, who seemed to be their leader. His voice was impenetrable. It was devoid of every emotion a human—or any creature, for that matter—normally possessed. Actually, the voice would've sounded more natural coming from a rock. "You're coming with us, too."

Clay bared his teeth in a pearly smile. "That's fine by me. I had me a good upbringing, and I ain't too tough. See, I hate to go anywhere alone. But this other guy says he don't wanna go back, so I don't reckon there's any way to satisfy everybody here."

The men didn't even exchange glances with one another.

"Is that a fact?" the leader said. "In that case . . ."

Seeing the middle-aged man's hand go for the firearm in his belt, Clay swung his right hand up from below. The broadsword he'd hidden up his sleeve became a flash of white that pierced the man's throat. The man's hand was on his gun; Clay saw the muzzle of it turn toward his chest. It disgorged flame. The breechblock moved back, and a sleek empty cartridge flew from the weapon.

Taking a hit from an explosive round that could've easily blown a human head apart on impact, Clay just smiled. The inner lining of his shirt came from the bark of the armor oak, which was harder than rock. His right hand flowed across the strings of his harp releasing a tremendous sound.

The man at the fore of the group became an ash-gray statue, and an instant later the same fate befell his horse. They both fell to the ground in a dusty cloud. There would be no further attacks; the three others behind the leader had turned to dust, too. Perhaps the only reason one rider and mount at the very back still retained their original shape in this sandy form was because they were at the very end of the audibility range for the sound.

"Maybe they don't die, but they seem to turn to dust just fine," Clay said as he raised his right hand and hacked off one of the motionless horse's legs. Not bothering to watch the new pile of sand the collapsing figures created, Clay looked up. He had no idea where they'd been hiding, but another horse and rider now galloped away about fifty yards from him. "Son of a bitch!" he moaned, cursing his own carelessness.

Taking his harp in hand, he turned it toward the rider fleeing over a rise. The device generated ultrasonic waves that destroyed the molecular structure of any material, and as if to compensate for the cruelty of those sound waves, the vibrating strings also created splendid melodies.

However, Clay didn't have a chance to unleash another deadly attack with his fingers. The one surviving attacker suddenly saw a figure standing in the road before him. His horse didn't stop. The moment it looked like the beast's iron-shod hooves were going to trample him, the shadowy figure leapt up. Even after D landed, with his long coat spread out around him, the horse and rider kept right on running. But when the longsword clicked smoothly back into the sheath on D's back, the rider's head finally left his shoulders and rolled across the road.

"Glad you could pitch in at the end there," Clay said as sarcastically as possible to D, who walked toward him without even glancing at the results his own skill had wrought. "Where the hell did you run off to after you found out the girl was missing? Weren't trying to get a preview of my skills, were you? No, you wouldn't do any petty shit like that. Went to check out the neighborhood, right? You're a cold customer. Didn't you give any thought to what'd happen if I found the girl? And you left me to handle all of them, too. If I got killed, the old bag and girl would've both been goners, you know."

"You didn't get killed," was all D said.

Clay had no reply, and that was the end of it. But three pairs of frightened eyes greeted the approaching beauty in black.

The Living Desert

CHAPTER 3

I

The man said his name was Lance and that he was part of a farm group improving crops in the northern Frontier. The group had developed a new strain that would bear fruit even in cold areas without water; they'd selected this desert to stage their experiments some five years earlier. Traveling in a caravan of five trailers bearing a hundred thousand seedlings, the farmers fell victim to a sandstorm and were attacked by a pack of bandits. Regardless of whether they offered any resistance or not, all were slain. Lance himself had been hit, but for some reason the bandits pulled out the gun they'd shoved in his mouth and brought him back to their hideout. The reason Lance went along with all of this was because, in the heat of battle, he'd seen that no matter how many times the bullets and blades of his compatriots had found their mark, the bandits had been utterly unfazed—and he valued his own life. As soon as they arrived back at the bandits' lair, however, Lance realized he'd been drawn into a world beyond imagining.

"You see, the first thing they did was tell me their age. The leader said he was going to turn two hundred that year. And the other bandits did the same, saying they were a hundred, or a hundred and fifty, or whatever the hell they felt like. I laughed at them—at least I had enough backbone left for that. It's what they showed me next that tore the very soul out of me."

"And what was that?" Granny asked eagerly.

"Their stomachs. One by one they took off their shirts. And then . . ."

Lance pressed both hands over his face. They were in a cave they'd found in a rocky mound. The air was sultry, but it was better than being outside. Luckily, they also found Granny's wagon intact, so for the time being they were set as far as food and weapons went.

"What did you see?" Granny asked, growing pale as she did so.

"They were mummies, you see." Under the fresh new shirt of every last one of them, the stomach-wrenching remains of desiccated flesh clung to their bones. "Yet they were perfectly normal from the neck up—as you saw earlier. They turned their ordinary faces at me and grinned. I tell you, I thought I was done for then and there."

The mandate Lance got from them was strange and cruel; he was to work alongside these living corpses as they carried out their mission of slaughtering any travelers who ventured into the desert. How could Lance refuse them?

"In the past five years, we've attacked four parties," Lance said. "I killed folks, too. Men, women—people I didn't know at all. If I didn't do it, they would have killed me. One of them was a girl about your age, too, Miss. Now, I won't tell you I was out of my mind when I did it. I puked my guts up every time I did someone in. But that didn't mean I was happy with the way things were going, either. When I heard you'd been brought here, I decided I'd get away for sure this time no matter what happened to me."

"You said we were brought here. What do you mean by that?" Clay asked as his eyes moved to the cave's entrance.

D was leaning against the rock wall. At that distance, it was difficult to tell whether or not the Hunter could overhear the group's conversation. As he'd helped cut down Lance's pursuers, one would think he'd be quite interested in this discussion, but he didn't ask a single question or even move from where he stood. Ordinary expectations couldn't begin to apply to the Hunter.

"So, who the hell controls the tornado? You've been living out here for five years. You gotta at least know that much. And those freaking mummies gotta be working for the same person, right?"

"No doubt," Lance replied, nodding feebly. "But I can't even begin to guess who—or what—might be behind all this. All those years I watched them carefully, hoping to get some clue as to who it was, but I don't even know if it was someone human or not. Something tells me they don't work for any mortal."

The reason Lance believed this was because of the way he'd been kept alive. His sustenance had consisted of one meal a day of some unknown leaves and berries that were left piled unceremoniously in front of his quarters. Though he tried, he was never able to see who placed the meal there. Lance's meals usually were brought to him while he slept. If he stayed awake to keep watch, nothing would come. After a few weeks, a strange sensation came over Lance. No matter where he was, he had the feeling he was being watched constantly. Even out in the barren desert without another creature around, the feeling remained with him. Of course, escape was impossible. When they weren't attacking travelers, the mummies lay in their cave. Any getaway plans Lance might've come up with were always foiled by sandstorms—or something even stranger.

"And what the hell was *that*?" Clay asked.

Lance merely shook his head at the question. "I don't know. Well, I'd heard about it, but I'd never seen it before. It was water that just stretched on forever. I guess it must've been that 'sea' thing folks talk about."

Clay and Granny exchanged glances.

The Nobility's transportation system was still operational in the Capital, but the further away from the city one went, the worse traveling conditions got. Aside from a few exceptions, people had only the most primitive means of transportation to rely on almost everywhere on the Frontier. Not only did most people live their entire lives without ever seeing the sea, but many died without ever setting foot outside their own village.

Lance's words were sufficient enough to amaze both Clay and Granny.

"There's no sea in the desert," the old woman groaned. "It might've been a spell, or something set up by the Nobility, I guess. What do you think?" Her query was aimed at D.

Lying down in a hollow about ten feet from the rest of the group, Tae turned her eyes toward the Vampire Hunter for the first time.

"The tornado is under someone's control," D said, his eyes still trained on the vista before him. "Whoever controls it brought all of us here. There can only be one reason for that—to have us do the same thing it made him do, I suppose."

"What, you mean plundering?" Clay blurted out without the slightest reserve. "But nobody's loony enough to try crossing this desert anymore. No one other than this old bag, my brother, and me, that is. Anyway, we haven't been attacked by the freaking mummies. What's that supposed to mean?"

"That the desert has some purpose other than killing us, and so it lets us live," D replied plainly. "The man said he was being watched. Now, it's our turn for the same."

"Wait just a minute there!" Granny interrupted. "Just now, you said something about what the desert wants. What's the story? You mean to tell me everything that's attacked us so far is following orders from the *desert?*"

"It shouldn't come as a surprise. I told you about the moving forest. And I suppose you know about the living mountain in the northwestern sectors of the Frontier."

"Sure," Granny said, shivering at the thought of fifty billion tons of rock moving along the horizon. "But that's just a simple mineral-based life form that can't do anything aside from move. Of course, it only occurs maybe once in a decade, but then again, thousands of people get crushed when it does."

"It wouldn't be that unusual for a more complex creature to exist," D said, though it hardly sounded like a rebuttal. "Because the metabolism of mineral-based life forms is greatly restricted by their weight, they really can't hope to develop any further. But the same might not be true for the desert."

"You keep talking about this desert, but I just don't get it. You mean to say—"

"It could be a living creature with a developed nervous system and circuits for thought. But even I can't say exactly what either of those would be like."

"Okay, let me see if I've got this right. You're saying that the tornado was some kind of 'hand' that brings what the desert needs here? That it had 'eyes' that watched this guy? Just where are the nose and mouth then? Oh, I suppose you're gonna tell me those were the globes and butterflies we ran into at the start?"

D didn't respond.

"See, I've got another theory," Clay said, brushing off the dirt as he stood up. He'd been kneeling there listening to what Granny said. "For the time being, let's just forget why this character might've been brought here. But the reason other travelers were robbed and killed is pretty obvious. It's because whoever's pulling the strings is greedy, of course! And so far as I know, there ain't nobody with that kind of greed—nobody but humans."

"You know, you just might have a point there," the old woman said matter-of-factly.

But it was Lance himself that refuted the younger Bullow. "If you turn south from here," the man said, "there's a huge depression in the ground. Everything we stole is sitting in it, rotting or rusting."

Granny and Clay exchanged glances.

"You mean to say someone just chucked it all?" the warrior asked incredulously.

"I really can't say, as I never actually saw it being thrown away. But every last thing we took went off to the dump after about a week."

"So, what did they do with the goods while they had them then?"

Lance just shrugged at the old woman's query.

"At any rate, the first thing we gotta do is get the hell out of this hole in the wall," Clay said, looking around at his companions. "Hey, old lady—get in your wagon. We're getting out of here."

"It's no use," Lance said in a weary tone. "Hell, I tried a hundred times myself. But sometimes there'd be sandstorms, other times it was mirages of the sea. Oh, yeah—there were times I'd walk out and nothing at all would happen and I'd think to myself I was in the clear. And then there'd be this big damn mountain towering right in front of me."

"Well, this time it's gonna work just fine," Clay spat back. In his eyes, Lance must've been nothing more than a coward. "I hate to break it to you, but if we don't get out of here, you ain't either. According to what 'pretty boy' says, it seems we were brought here to take your place. Meaning, whoever controls this here desert don't have any further use for you."

A look of incomparable horror shot across Lance's face.

"Those creeps didn't come here to take you back earlier—I bet they came to kill you. Hell, we can leave you here and let them finish you off, if you like." Watching with relish as Lance's shoulders drooped, Clay then turned to D and said, "You're coming, too, right?"

"It's no use."

Realizing that the Hunter's frosty response was exactly the same as Lance's, Clay got a gleam of light in his eyes—a vicious spark. "What do you mean it's no use?"

"Is your wagon still in one piece, Granny?" D asked.

"Yeah, she'll move somehow or other. Horses are fine, too. But I don't think either could go through that again."

"If we get picked up by another tornado, her wagon will be ruined. Then we'll be out of luck."

"Well, what do you suggest we do, then?" Clay asked, suddenly kicking at the ground. A few small stones vanished into the dark reaches of the cave. "Are we just gonna sit here with our thumbs up our asses? You planning on staying here for the rest our lives, eating nuts and berries like this chump?"

"Do whatever you like," D said, pulling away from the rock wall. It was probably his way of saying he'd handle things his own way. Silently, he moved to the cavern's entrance.

"Is something coming?" Granny asked, squinting her eyes.

"Horses. Ten or so, with riders. His compatriots, no doubt."

"Came to shut him up, did they?" Granny replied, putting her right hand on her jar. "Hell, if there's only a dozen or so, I can take care of 'em one-handed," Granny quipped, but her words met only the empty space where D had been.

"D," Tae mumbled softly.

II

D stepped out into the light, although it was really only light in comparison to the cave. The sky, as always, was shrouded in clouds. At the entrance to the cave, the Hunter looked up at the sky. It was dim—so dim that it merely served to make D's gorgeous countenance seem all the more radiant. He stood quietly, without moving. It was as if he was looking at something beyond the lead-gray sky. But what? Glistening green plains or bright tropical lands would surely mean nothing more to this young man than an arrangement of air and land and colors. What of life, then? Or death? Or fate? Darker than dark and colder than cold, his crystal-clear eyes reflected nothing save the dusty cloud that had twisted around the rocky crag.

There were ten riders. They were the living dead, and a fair bit cleaner than Lance. Surely they'd come here because their earlier colleagues had failed to return. They didn't look at the faces of the four men that Clay and D had dispatched. It appeared the false life the desert had given them once couldn't be theirs a second time.

The living dead formed a semi-circle in front of D. A man with a mustache took a half-step forward. For all intents and purposes, he appeared human. "You're all going to be staying," he said in an almost mechanical voice. A gunpowder pistol hung at his waist. The rounds it could hurl from its six tiny chambers would go right through a tree trunk. "If you give us the man, you have our guarantee you'll be allowed to live here. You'd be wise to take us up on that," the man said flatly, and then he waited.

There was no reply. He was dealing with D, after all.

"Then I guess we can't avoid this, can we?" the man with the mustache said, raising his right hand.

The air was filled with the sounds of gears meshing. All the men on horseback had cocked their guns.

"You, in particular, interest us greatly," he told the Hunter. "If at all possible, we'd like to avoid a confrontation."

Wind buffeted the man's cheeks. And then laughter did the same. Not from D—that young man didn't even know how to laugh. The voice came from the Hunter's left hand, which he'd lowered naturally.

A dangerous silence came over the world.

The mustached man's hand went for the grip of his gun. That was the signal. The row of men pulled their triggers. Or rather, they tried to. But a cloud of yellow sand spread before them like a wall.

Weapons roared. There was the sound of the combustible gas in one tiny metal cylinder after another propelling wads of lead from the weapons' barrels. Orange sparks flashed somewhere in the sandy cloud, and between them streaked a silvery gleam. What happened within that cloud of sand was anyone's guess.

The billowing curtain of sand suddenly dropped to the ground. And with it fell the horsemen. Only D remained standing.

All of the other men had their heads split open and had turned to ash, but D didn't even look at them as he walked over to the only one of them who appeared to have fallen to the ground unscathed— the man with the mustache. The blade the Hunter thrust smoothly under the man's nose was not only free of blood, but of the faintest speck of dust as well.

"The dead should stay that way," D said softly. "How do we get out of this place?"

"I don't know," the man replied, shaking his head. He was pale. His lack of color seemed to spring not so much from fear as from

pain. With utter loathing, he added, "And I hope you all wind up like me. Used for the rest of your life by this desert—whatever the hell it really is—and brought back again when you're dead . . . That'd be just perfect," the bandit laughed.

There was a smooth *clink*! D had just sheathed his longsword. At the same time, the man's torso slipped off to the left. Sliced from the right armpit to the left hip, his body turned to dust and vanished before the two pieces could fully separate.

"This is a fine mess you've made," D's left hand chortled. "I don't think that Lance character knows the way out, either." Surely not even the mummies could've imagined the curtain of sand that'd issued from that very same mouth.

"And do you know?"

"More or less. But I haven't been fed enough to know an exact direction when one might not even exist."

D turned right around. Four people stood at the entrance to the cave. Even Clay couldn't hide the surprise that colored his ferocious countenance.

"Ten of them . . . and in less than two seconds. You're a goddamn monster . . ." the younger Bullow fairly groaned. "I wanna kill you more than ever now. With my own two hands."

"I'll thank you to hold off on that until we're across this desert," Granny said in a strident tone. Turning to Lance, she said, "Well, that takes care of the mob that was after you. Now, relax and see if you can't remember something better to tell us, okay? I'll be damned if I'm gonna hang around here playing bandit."

Putting his hand to the brim of his hat, D looked over his shoulder. "Escape is possible," he said.

"What?" more than one person exclaimed as they opened their eyes wide with amazement.

"But as long as we're out in the desert," he continued, "it'll probably keep chasing us. Before we leave, we'd better settle this."

"And just how are we supposed to settle it?"

"We wait."

And saying that, D went into the depths of the caves. The Hunter was hopelessly indifferent.

Clay and Granny looked at each other.

"I'm gonna take a peek outside," Clay announced. "If I gotta stew in this hole all day, I'll go nuts. If any strange characters start trouble, you'll have to deal with it."

Before Granny could stop him, the man in the blue cap had vanished in the sunlight.

"Dear me, if that man don't have ants in his pants," the old woman griped to herself. "Looks like we're left with just the cool and composed one to rely on now. You really are our guardian angel, you know."

Their guardian angel was deep in the recesses of a hole in the rocks, shrouded in shadows.

"So, what are you folks, anyway?" Lance said meekly. He rubbed his jaw incessantly, which seemed to be something of a habit with him. "I didn't think you were ordinary travelers, but it's like you're all freaks or something. Where are you headed, and what'll you do there?"

"We're pretty much just like you, you know. Relax. We'll get you out of here safe and sound, sure as shooting."

"I sure hope so . . . but I don't even know where the stuff they gave me to eat and drink came from. At this rate, I'll waste away to nothing out here."

"But you were willing to take that chance when you ran away, weren't you? I don't wanna hear such nonsense from a grown man. If you hadn't run into us, you'd have just grit your teeth and forged on, am I right?"

Lance shut his mouth.

"Well, if you're hungry, there's food over in my wagon. Come with me and I'll get you something to eat."

The old woman stood up, and Lance left with her. Only Tae and D remained. D was behind a rock with his eyes closed. About fifteen feet lay between the Hunter and the girl.

"Mrs. Viper just . . ." Tae began to say softly, her face still pointed toward the floor. Her tone was so weak it wouldn't have been at all surprising if it didn't even reach D. "She just left me here. I suppose she thought I'd be safe with you around . . . even though you're the scariest of them all . . ."

There was no reply. Even if Tae's voice was audible, it only would've sounded like incoherent mumbling.

"I never dreamed I'd be able to go home . . . I really thought I'd have to spend the rest of my life in that Noble's castle."

"You remember the Noble's name, don't you?"

When the darkness emitted these words, Tae trembled. It was quite some time before she managed to nod and reply, "Marquis Venessiger . . ."

"Just him?"

"Huh?" Tae cried out softly, turning in D's direction. She could see only darkness.

"Castle Gradinia had a special purpose. Was that the only Noble you met there?"

Tae was silent. Seconds passed. And then, as if unable to bear the silence any longer, she said, "There was another . . . He was taller than the marquis, and more regal . . . I never saw his face, though . . ."

"But his eyes were red. Blazing like rubies."

"Exactly," Tae said, nodding in amazement. But it didn't take long at all for her expression to become completely vacant. She was in the dark. And through that darkness so deep she could even feel the weight of it: two red things were coming closer. A pair of eyes.

"What kind of eyes were they?" D asked, not inquiring at all what sort of man it was.

"Bright red and piercing . . . Eyes that seemed to drink me up, body and soul . . . All they had to do was take one look at me . . . and then I couldn't even think at all . . . Come to think of it . . ." Tae said in a strangely relaxed tone. "Come to think of it," she repeated, "they were kind of like yours. I wonder why that is? Oh, I know now . . . Because they seemed so terribly sad . . ."

"Did he do anything to you?" D asked, changing his tack unexpectedly.

Tae was horribly shaken. "Not a thing . . . Nothing happened to me . . . I really just met him. Why would you ask me something like that? You're a Hunter, aren't you? Don't ask me anything you don't need to know."

"The one with the red eyes is a ruler." The darkness didn't move in the slightest, but smoldered behind the rocks. "The sun is setting on the Nobility's influence over our world, and yet the gusts from their black wings still bear mystery into so many lives. Yours may be one of them. What did he do?"

"Stop it!" Tae cried, covering her face as she got up. "Nothing happened to me at all. If anything did, I don't remember it—so please don't ask me such horrible questions." Her tone sounded cold enough to freeze a stone.

A tear glittered as it trickled down her cheek. Scattering those sparkling droplets to the wind, Tae raced from the cavern.

A few minutes later, Granny Viper showed up in the cave. "D—you in here?" she called out.

"Over here."

"You said something to the girl, didn't you? She came running back to the wagon, bawling her eyes out, you know," the old woman said in an uninflected tone.

"And that bothers you?"

"A little, I guess. After all, she's valuable merchandise."

"You've been traveling with her a while. Have you noticed anything about her?"

"Like what?" Granny asked, a fine thread of tension stitching through her flesh.

"Any physical irregularities? Swings in her mental state?"

"Sure, there's some of that to a degree," Granny replied, her tone already relaxed again. "But then, she's a girl at an impressionable age who's spent quite some time living with the Nobility, and now she's on a long, long journey home. If there wasn't anything weird about her, that in itself would be pretty weird. Look, I'm gonna be on my toes to see to it that nothing strange happens to her until I can hand her over to her family. And I'll thank you to keep any funny remarks to yourself. You should be thinking of some way to get us out of this godforsaken land as soon as possible."

"The girl has to be brought home," said a voice from the darkness. "Her family's still around, I gather."

"Yeah. Her parents passed on not long after she was taken, but her brother and his wife have a farm."

"*Alone* she might've been okay, but the *two of them* are in for a hard life."

"Just what's that supposed to mean?" Granny snapped, a heavy shade of dismay rising in her face.

Hearing a knock, Tae looked up. The forearms her face had been buried in were damp to the elbows. Quickly pawing at the corners of her eyes with the backs of her hands, Tae said, "Come in."

Expecting to see Granny Viper, the girl was actually a bit surprised by who opened her bedroom door. It was Lance. Scratching his head uneasily, he said, "Sorry to bother you. It's just that I heard crying . . ."

"It's nothing."

"Well, if you're okay, then. I was just worried, is all. Well, see you."

"Don't go," Tae cried out reflexively.

Lance didn't know what to say. As he stopped there in spite of himself, his eyes caught Tae crumpling on the bed. "Hey!"

"Don't mind me. Just let me be."

"But you just—" Lance began hesitantly. "I can't just stand idly by when a girl's crying. At times like this you shouldn't be alone. If you had someone to talk to, it'd be—"

"I'm fine, so get out."

Like a razor through the conversation, her tone was so intense Lance finally grasped the situation. "I get it. I'm sorry."

As he slowly turned his back, Tae called out to him huskily, "Wait—" It sounded like her nose was stuffed. "I'm sorry. But I'd just like to be alone. Please."

"Okay. But keep your chin up," Lance said, having nothing but a trite expression for this situation.

"Sure," Tae replied in the brightest tone she could manage.

Donning a smile that suited his bony face, Lance took his leave.

As the door closed, all the strength drained from Tae's body. Her hands rested naturally on her abdomen. A heartrending sigh spilled from her. That sorrowful breath carried the girl's curse on the universe. Her dainty shoulders trembled. Sobbing split her lips. There was little else she could do.

Tae watched as a number of sparkling beads shattered in her lap. Even after those beads had become stains, her eyes didn't move. They had a dangerous hue to them.

Standing, she pulled a leather bag out from under her bed. Her pale hand was swallowed by it, and then came back out with something long and thin and shiny. She tugged on one end with her other hand and it came apart in two pieces—a short knife and a sheath. When her eyes were reflected in the tempered steel, a spark of urgency resided in them.

Slowly the blade rose. At its tip sat Tae's throat. A light push made it dimple the flesh. As the blade moved forward the tiniest bit, its edge was stained red with blood.

Her trembling ceased. A decision had been reached. With the same speed that she raised it, she pulled the knife away again. Tae heaved a heavy sigh.

Just as she finished sheathing the knife, the door flew open without warning. It was Granny Viper. The first thing she saw wasn't Tae's face, but rather what the girl had in her hand. As she wrested the weapon from the girl with incredible force, Granny was probably disappointed by the complete lack of resistance. "Why you—"

"I'm fine. You don't have to worry about me," Tae said in a voice so faint it was barely audible.

An instant later a harsh slap landed on the girl's cheek. Exposed by the way the shock of the blow turned her head, the other cheek resounded with another smack. A wrinkled hand seized the girl by the collar and shook her.

"Listen—and listen good," Granny said, hammering the words into the face of the young girl gazing back at her absentmindedly. "You're valuable merchandise to me. It'd be a hell of a thing if you went off and damaged yourself now. I've got a duty to deliver you to your home without a mark on you. *I'm* responsible for you. And I've always met my responsibilities. Now, I'm not about to let you blemish my tidy reputation, either. You hear me? The next time you pull something like this, I'll forget all about bringing you home and I'll kill you myself. You remember that!"

Tae waited until the old woman had finished her threats. "Please, just kill me," the girl then mumbled.

It took Granny a few seconds to realize what she'd just heard. "What did you say?"

"I never even wanted to go home in the first place. So, if there's anything you don't like about me, go ahead and kill me here and now." Though her tone was hollow, a resolute will lay behind it.

"So, you don't wanna go home then?" Granny said, sounding somewhat obtuse. She wasn't badly flustered. In fact, the look she gave Tae was almost gentle.

Tae was silent. A great weight had suddenly been lifted from her chest.

"Swear to me you won't try any more of this foolishness," Granny bade her in a low voice.

The girl's pale visage was still aimed at the floor. For the longest time, the two of them simply stood there.

Clucking her tongue, the old woman said, "You're an obstinate one. But let me make it perfectly clear I'm pretty obstinate myself about you not doing anything else stupid. I don't care if you try hanging yourself or drinking poison—I'll bring you back to life and deliver you home. I'm not about to let a slip of a girl like you soil the name of Granny Viper. The Nobility did something to you, didn't they?"

Tae's face shot up. "Don't ask me about that," she said.

"Good enough," the old woman said with a nod. "It seems just asking you was effective. Well, I suppose if you've come around that much, you're not likely to do away with yourself so easily. Until we can get across this desert, just keep remembering all the bad things that happened to you."

"As far as memories go—I don't really have any."

"Is that a fact? Then you just have to think about what lies ahead. A person can live without memories if need be."

Tae's eyes shot up to the old woman's face. "Is that what you do, Mrs. Viper?"

"Spare me," Granny Viper said with an exaggerated frown. "I've got hopes and dreams, too, you know. I'm out to make a load of money quick, then open myself a fabric store."

"A fabric store?" Tae said with amazement.

"Yep. It may not look like it now, but I have really fine taste in clothes. See, before I got into this line of work, I had a place in the Capital. I always made children's clothing, and eventually I even made a business out of it."

"A fabric store," Tae muttered once more.

"Traveling together all this time, I've noticed you like kids, don't you?" Granny said in a gentle tone. "And since we're on the subject of fabric, you may as well know there's a sewing machine in the storage compartment under your bed. You can use it if you like."

"Can I really?"

"You can't wear that miserable puss forever. I just said I'd let you borrow my precious sewing machine, and I've never let anyone touch it before. Have to get you to cheer up, anyway. You sure look happy as a pig in slop, but are you sure you know how to use a sewing machine now?"

"When I was back home, I used one a little bit."

"Then give it a shot. But I'm not about to let you use it for free. After all, it wears down on the parts. I was thinking if you had the know-how, I'd have you make me a children's outfit." Indicating the far end of the wagon with her left hand, Granny said, "The material's in there. But if you make a mess of it, your family will have to reimburse me when I turn you over. Okay?"

Not waiting for a response, Granny turned her back. Once she'd reached the door, she looked back.

"I understand the Vampire Hunter might've said some callous things, but don't let it get to you. He might wear a sour puss all the time, but he's not the kind to bully folks. However, he does have to say some hard things to stay true to himself. It's a hard life, being so tough on yourself like that. And I hear it's a lot worse in his case. If you could get inside his skin, it'd be so sad in there it'd kill the likes of you or me."

Tae didn't know what to say.

"Oh, I saw our new arrival coming out of here earlier," the old woman continued. "What was he up to in here?"

"Not a thing. He just came in to cheer me up, is all."

"Hmm, must be nice being a pretty young thing. But I'll have to have a word with him. I can't have you getting all infested with bugs and such."

Granny stepped out of the wagon. A figure in black stood right there.

"Heard us, did you?" the old woman asked.

Not answering, D just put his hand to his traveler's hat and tugged the brim down a bit.

"Here I was, thinking you're cold as ice, and then you go and do something all considerate like coming out from the shade under the wagon for me. You really are worried about the girl, aren't you?"

"Something strange is happening to the desert," D said tersely.

Granny's expression changed. "What?" she asked in equally terse fashion.

"I don't know. Though something's clearly not right, I can't be certain just what it is."

"You saying we should move out, then?"

D didn't answer her, and Granny soon fell silent, too. They'd come to a conclusion about that earlier. For the time being, they could merely wait. D's eyes shifted ever so slightly to the east.

"What is it?" Granny asked, unable to see anything there.

"I hear a sewing machine."

"Looks like she's finally turned around," Granny said with a wry smile. "Now all we have to do is get out of this desert and get away from you."

"From me?"

"I'm sure you're not so thickheaded as to miss what I'm driving at. You're a dangerous man, not just for that girl, but for all women. Hasn't anyone ever told you that? If they haven't, it's because one look at you scrambles their brains."

The old woman stared at D's face, waiting for some reaction. Even out in the sunlight, he looked as beautiful as a crystal that'd formed somewhere in the darkness and then been worked by the chisel of the Almighty. A weird sensation surged up from Granny's lower half, making her shake. The praise of the present world meant nothing to this young man. Only those dead and removed from the material world could pay him his due.

"'There's no place like home,'" D said dispassionately. "At least, that's the maxim of travelers on the Frontier. But is that really the case?"

"I don't necessarily know how relaxing it'll be, but if you've got one, it's generally best you go back to it. You're talking about the girl, aren't you? You trying to suggest I shouldn't bring her home?"

"Are there any hidden who've settled back at home after you delivered them?" the Hunter asked.

"I wouldn't know," Granny said, turning away disdainfully. "I'm only responsible for 'em until I get 'em home. But once they're there, it's somebody else's problem, you see. I'm not really in a position to provide maintenance and upkeep, you know."

"I met one once," D said. His darkness-hued words melted in the sunlight.

Granny gazed vacantly at his beautiful countenance. Unrestrained curiosity and excitement colored her eyes. She couldn't conceive of this young man ever turning his thoughts to the past.

"It was in a village in a southwestern sector of the Frontier. Apparently, he'd been run out of town by the whole community. This boy of about eight was freezing to death by the banks of the river. Not long after I heard the particulars, he died."

"He must've done something or other, right?"

"Don't you see?" said the Hunter.

"No, I don't."

"He didn't do anything at all."

"Is that so? Then, why would they do that?" Granny asked, seeming a bit peeved.

"The boy had been with the Nobility for three months. That was all. A doctor had even verified there was nothing out of the ordinary. He could walk in the daylight, too. And in six months with him, his parents hadn't noticed any strange symptoms."

Granny was at a loss for words.

"However, a certain woman had her suspicions about him, and she went to the mayor and the leader of the Vigilance Committee and complained to them that she'd been bitten. Though they could tell at a glance that the wound had been faked, the two men chose to interpret it differently."

"They wanted to get rid of a nuisance, eh?"

"Within the hour, the whole village was beating down the boy's door. His father was killed trying to stop them, and the house was put to the torch."

"How awful," Granny said, shrugging her shoulders coldly. Tilting her head to one side, she added, "But I'm a bit surprised a lad at death's door could hold out long enough to tell you such an involved tale."

"The explanation came from his mother, who was right by his side."

"So, he had his mum there at the very end to look after him, did he? Well, that's something, isn't it?"

"She was the same woman who'd tipped off the mayor."

White sunlight held the two of them in its embrace. The world was unspeakably peaceful.

Granny awkwardly made her way over to the wagon. "Well, then. We don't have the faintest clue what's bound to happen, but I warrant the safe thing to do is have everything ready for departure. You said there was something strange out there, but do you think it'll be headed this way soon?"

"I don't know," D said, coming out of the shadows.

Granny casually remarked, "I hear it hurts you dhampirs quite a bit to be out in the sunlight. If someone wanted to kill you, daytime would really be the only time to do it. I guess you really can't fight your blood—" the crone said, stopping and clamping one hand over her own mouth mid-sentence.

Her mouth may have been covered, but her feelings showed in her eyes. They were laughing. Laughing maliciously.

Not seeming the least bit bothered, D walked out onto the sea of sand.

"Er, pardon me," Lance said, coming out from behind the rocks to the Hunter's left. Apparently, he'd been keeping out of the sun there ever since Tae had chased him off. D didn't stop walking, so Lance jogged after him. "Your name's D, isn't it?" he asked. "Back in my village, folks used to say that out on the Frontier there was this one incredible Vampire Hunter who was unbelievably handsome. That'd be you, wouldn't it? In which case, the girl and the old woman are connected to your business, right? I mean, I don't know the first thing about this. One of them's unbelievably gloomy, and the other's real testy. Say, speaking of the girl—she wouldn't happen to be one of *the hidden*, would she?"

"What if she is?" D asked as he walked.

"Hey, it doesn't matter to me. But shouldn't you be comforting her or something? She's had it bad enough up till now, and no matter where she goes, folks will give her a hard time if they find out what happened to her. The least you could do is be nice to her until she gets where she's going."

D stopped in his tracks and looked at Lance. "And why are you telling me this?" he asked.

Lance diverted his gaze. His cheeks wore a thin flush—even men blushed when they were subjected to D's gaze. Coughing, he replied, "Well, because you're the only one for the job. Girls her age always fall for the good-looking guys. I guarantee you that. And given that, you're far and away the top out of the three men here. Why don't you spend some time with her? I saw her crying earlier. A girl like her doesn't deserve to suffer like that."

D watched the man without saying a word. Soon he turned to face the desert. It was an endless sea of sand. "Don't leave this spot," he told Lance in a low voice.

Leaving the other man behind as he nodded his agreement, the Hunter advanced about twenty paces, and then stopped. As his face slowly scanned to his right and to his left, there wasn't a trace of tension on it.

"Well, there's something wrong here, and then again there isn't," said a hoarse voice that slipped from the vicinity of his left hand. "But something's sure to happen all right. Better be damn careful."

At that instant, darkness hid the sky. D's coat had fluttered out around him. As he whipped around, his eyes found nothing. There was naught but waves of sand dunes slumbering out in the white sunlight. Lance wasn't there, nor was the old woman and her wagon. Even the rocky mound was gone.

"Oh, boy," D's left hand moaned. "Just perfect. We've been hit with another psi attack."

Psi Attack

CHAPTER 4

I

How strong is the attack?" D asked, not sounding at all distressed. "As if you couldn't tell already. Well, I'd say it's about five thousand rigels on the Noble scale. Enough to drive the entire population of a city mad in a millisecond."

"The desert doesn't pull any punches."

"You said it," the laughter-tinged voice concurred. Both he and the Hunter had far more nerve than any human.

The sound of the wind died out.

D looked down at his feet; waves were lapping at them. His entire field of view was filled by an expanse of deep blue sea. Crests broke here and there, turning the rays of the sun into droplets of light. It looked as though the trip across it would span thousands of miles.

"And the purpose of all this—well, I guess it's to gauge your abilities. What are you gonna do?"

Giving no reply to the voice's query, D stood there. His legs then went into motion. The waves pulled away. Before the sea could help it, the Hunter was waist-deep in the water. The waves were sensors, and their very movements most likely served to relay the results of this test.

"Very interesting," the voice chortled. "So, the desert is a sea, then? Seems it's trying to surprise you, but we'll see who gets a surprise."

Even before the voice had finished speaking, the veracity of its claim became evident. A "feeling" that certainly seemed like astonishment raced across the surface of the sea around D. Silence shrouded the world.

"Looks like it doesn't know quite what to make of you," the voice said, seemingly beside itself with joy. "It's times like these it pays to stick around with you. So, what move will it make?"

D supplied the answer. He was gazing at one spot in the sea. A white wake was drawing closer at a considerable speed.

"Here it comes. There's a shark in the water."

Whether or not D knew what the voice was pointing out, he remained stock-still.

The range was about fifty yards. Forty yards . . . Thirty . . . Twenty . . .

The wake faded into nothingness. Whatever had been knifing through the surface must've gone back underwater.

"Gotta stay on your toes. Your opponent's only an illusion," the voice told D. "You'll have to beat it with just your psyche. Carving it up won't do you any good."

Suddenly, the surface of the water bubbled up. The dark blue form of a fish broke the surface as it leapt into the air. It was a streamlined behemoth, nearly twelve feet long and weighing a good five hundred pounds. The front end had a gigantic mouth open wide and a red gullet. The teeth were like white spearheads.

A flash of silver tore through the entire body. D ducked ever so slightly, and the colossal fish split in two over his head, dropping into the water with an incredible plume of spray. Watery beads reflecting the white sunlight quickly turned to purple with the fresh blood spilling from the beast.

However, D's eyes were drawn to the two bloody trails running behind the creature. The trails had drawn closer together almost instantly, converging to form a single wake that began leisurely circling D.

"Looks like the other side's no slouch, either," the voice said, its tone tense. "If your mental powers beat it, we should've gone back where we were the second you sliced into that thing. But since it didn't play out that way, this could be trouble. You can kill this thing over and over, and it'll just keep coming."

D's reply was placid. "Still, it has to die eventually. Even if it's just an illusion."

"Kill a dream?" the voice snickered. "I suppose *you* probably could, at that. Here it comes!"

The wake died out; D felt the wall of water pushing against his lower body. Apparently his foe intended to attack from underwater. Deadly as D's blade might be, its speed and power would be halved when underwater. In that respect, the phantasmal sea would be real enough.

D sank below the surface. Shifting his sword to his left hip, the Hunter was poised like those who drew and struck from the waist. The movements of the water relayed the speed and distance of his foe—and for a second, a flash of crimson zipped right by D. In stark contrast to the blue sky, the streak didn't fade for the longest time. The Hunter's submerged foe writhed in agony.

A second later, the world went black.

His long, gorgeous shadow stretched across the white sands.

"Wow," the voice said in a hushed tone. "Good work. But who in the world did that . . . ?"

D turned to face the person he sensed coming up behind him.

"You okay?" Granny asked, still breathing heavily as she held the blunderbuss ready. "You were acting kind of funny, and the sand sort of welled up out there and was making a beeline for you, so I put a round into it. What the hell was that thing anyway?"

"A shark."

"Huh?" the old woman said, her eyes wide in disbelief.

D turned back to the rocky mound as if nothing had happened at all.

Lance was still standing where the Hunter had left him. "What in the world—" he muttered like a mental defective, wiping the sweat from his brow. "You were standing there stock-still the whole time, so I figured you were up to something, and then all of a sudden you pulled out your sword and *Whap*! Of course, I couldn't exactly catch you drawing your blade, though. What on earth did you lay into?"

"A shark."

"What?!" Lance exclaimed, mouth dropping open.

"You mean to say you didn't see it?"

"Nope."

D turned his back to the man.

"What'll we do next?" Granny asked apprehensively.

"We wait." And with that alone as his reply, D returned to the cave.

Evening came. But something was missing: Clay. He'd gone out, but had never returned.

"What do you suppose happened to him?" Granny said with seeming concern, but she was actually more worried about losing some of their muscle than about Clay's safety as such. D didn't seem to care much at all. "You think maybe the desert finished him off? Well? Do you?" the old woman asked. "I don't believe this! If you're not the coldest customer ever. We're all in this together now. The least you could do is show a little concern, you know."

"You took it upon yourselves to follow me," D said. He'd merged with the darkness in the depths of the cave. The lamp Granny had in her hand was the only source of light, and it threw an orange veil over her surroundings.

"True enough," the crone replied, "but you could come up with a little nicer way of putting it, I'm sure. If push comes to shove, you plan on taking off and leaving us behind?"

"It's up to you whether you come or not. I'll let you know when I'm leaving. That's it."

"Curse you," Granny shouted, stomping her feet in anger. "I'm not out here alone, you know. You mean to tell me you're not worried about Tae?"

"How is she?"

"See! I just knew you were!" Granny exclaimed, breaking into a grin at her own cleverness. "I don't care how cold you might look; you've got redder human blood running in your veins than any of us. And it's warm, too. My guess is it's a lot warmer than most folks'. Relax. The girl's been fixed on mastering that sewing machine since noontime. She learned how to use one before, and she's sure got a knack for it. I warrant she'll have an outfit finished pretty soon."

"What's she making?" D inquired.

"Actually—" Granny said, hemming and hawing a bit, "— she's not about to show anyone."

"If our foe is coming for us, it'll be tonight. If nothing's happened by dawn, we'll move out. You're all set, aren't you?"

"Good to go anytime!"

As Granny replied, someone moved around outside the cave.

"Hey there!" a voice called out.

Jumping nearly three feet in the air, Granny brought her hand to the jar on her hip. As for D, he must've sensed the new arrival, because he didn't move an inch. It was Clay.

"Sure took your sweet time coming back, didn't you?" Granny said sharply, with a trenchant look that matched her voice. She may have already noticed that something wasn't right.

"There's something I want to show you all. Come with me," Clay said in a tone that was as stiff as a board. It was clear at a glance he was under some sort of spell.

"It's come, sure enough. It's come to get us," the old woman groaned. "What'll we do, D?"

The darkness to the rear took on human form, and Clay turned around and slowly headed back the way he'd come. D followed after him. He didn't even glance at Granny.

Outside was a land of darkness.

"Just a second. What about the other two?" the old woman asked Clay.

"They've already been taken away."

Granny's eyes bulged in their sockets. The fact that their foe could abduct the two of them without her noticing, let alone D, was simply mind-boggling. Teeth grinding together fiercely, she reached for her jar with her right hand.

"Later," D told her.

"Why wait?! If we grab him now, it'll be easy enough to get him to spill where the other two are. It goes against my grain to just waltz into whatever the enemy's got set up for me."

"He's not what we're up against; whoever's controlling him is. Break the spell over him now, and we'll be left with a man who doesn't know anything."

Granny let the strength drain from her form. The Hunter's assessment of the situation was sound. Her hand came away from the jar.

The three set off into the desert; there was nothing but sand. The moon was out. With every step they took, the ground made a strangely plaintive sound. Clay continued on without hesitation—surely whoever controlled him was also taking care of his sense of direction.

The rocky mound had long since been swallowed by darkness. They'd walked for perhaps thirty minutes and then Clay halted.

They were out in the middle of the desert—nothing but the shadows of the three of them stretched across the silvery sands. Suddenly, there was a voice in D and Granny's heads. Neither the sex nor age of the speaker was clear. They couldn't even tell whether or not it was an organic being.

I have never encountered beings—humans—like you before. It would appear there are all manner of things beyond my world.

"What have you done with the others?" Granny shouted as she looked all around. "One of 'em I could care less about, but the girl's valuable property of mine. If you've done anything to her, it won't end well for you."

I'm currently inspecting the one to which you refer. Quite an interesting human specimen.

"Hmph! If you're so interested in humans, you had all the time in the world to study Lance. Oh, I get it. First time you've ever seen a girl, right?"

No.

"Well, it doesn't matter either way. Where's the girl now? You're gonna give her right back to me. And then you're gonna let us go on our way without any more trouble. After you tell us how to get where we're headed, of course."

The voice fell silent. Back out of the darkness came a feeling that someone was mocking them. But that ended in a heartbeat. A voice deeper than the darkness made sure of that.

"Are you the desert itself?" D asked, still gazing straight ahead. Unlike Granny, he wasn't wound tight. However, the one he addressed knew that if the need arose, every inch of the Hunter would be transformed into a spring of coiled steel.

Yes, the voice replied a bit tardily.

"How long have you been sentient?"

I don't know. But if someone could tell me, I would very much like to know.

"What do you plan on doing with us? Get information from us, or keep us like pets for the rest of our lives like you did with the man?"

I wouldn't do that to you. Or rather, I couldn't. Even if I tried to, you wouldn't let me. You're so dangerous, the other humans can't begin to compare to you.

"Then what will you do?"

I put the very same question to you.

"Leave."

Once again, both sides were enveloped by silence. The sandy plain had nothing to say, but listened intently.

Very well, the voice said without emotion. *I'm aware it would be extremely dangerous to fight you. I will do nothing, and neither will you.*

"I'm going to leave now."

Do as you like. I'll seek the information I desire from the rest of them.

"Hold on there just a minute," Granny said, throwing a stern gaze at the young man in black. "Don't tell me you plan on pulling out and leaving all of us here."

"I don't have any plans one way or the other. The rest of you just followed after me."

"Okay. Then we'll follow along after you now, too. You wouldn't have a problem with that, would you? And if we run into trouble, help us out."

Suddenly Granny's body grew rigid.

I still have business with the rest of you.

The crone's head rung with same voice D heard.

I'll dispose of the man for his treachery, but I should like to investigate you and the other two at greater length. Come to me.

"Help me, D!" the old woman shrieked. The sand was up around her ankles. She was sinking. "D!" Granny cried.

Go in peace, the voice told D. *I would do nothing that might snuff their lives. These are the precious samples that will allow me to learn about human beings.*

Let me ask you something, D said without using his voice. *What will you do once you've learned about humans?*

Say no more, and be gone. You should consider yourself fortunate to be allowed to leave in one piece.

One more thing—what were those globes and butterflies for?

They were tools to ascertain your whereabouts. When the globes proved ineffective, I sent the butterflies. On seeing those patterns, the brain gives off special radio waves.

"Help, D!" Granny shrieked from down by his feet. "Forget about me, but save the girl—save Tae!"

A gag spilled from her throat, and the old woman's head sank into the sand. Clay disappeared right after her. A funnel-shaped depression remained for a moment, but sand soon tumbled in from all sides to fill it again.

Not even reaching out for them with his hand, D simply stared at the sandy surface, but then quickly started to walk back to the rocky mound. After a few steps, he halted. Slowly turning, he headed back the way he'd just come.

You are a fool, the voice scoffed, the hostility naked in its tone. *Reconsider what you're doing. A battle between us is in neither of our best interests.*

Naturally, there was no reply.

Standing in the spot where Granny had disappeared, D raised his left hand.

An intense turbulence spread from somewhere unseen.

Stop it, the voice said.

At the very same time, both heaven and earth howled. The snarling winds turned hard as steel and slammed against D, carrying him away. Caught in a massive gust, he flew far across the desert. The wind was blowing at speeds of well over a hundred miles an hour.

D's left hand hadn't come down. Fingers spread wide, his palm was suddenly filled by someone's face: a face with sarcastic eyes, an aquiline nose, and a tiny mouth. As soon as that mouth opened, it instantly swallowed the howling winds.

His foe had lost the strength to speak, while D stood there without making a sound.

"Good stuff," a hoarse voice said. "This wind is pretty damn tasty!"

Sailing back down to earth as swiftly as the gale had carried him off, D turned his left hand to the ground, toward the spot that had swallowed the old woman. If Granny Viper had been there to see the tiny lips pucker, even she would've been shocked—even more so when a powerful new gale rushed from those same lips.

The sand shot away. In no time at all, a hole six feet in diameter had been dug in the ground.

Stop it! the voice exclaimed, the words exploding in D's head. *Stop it! Stop it! Stop it!*

A heartbeat later, the figure in black was swallowed by the earth.

II

For several seconds, he was aware of traveling down through the sand. Just as the sand's resistance ended, D's speed increased, and the Hunter landed on his feet on a firm base. It was a stone floor. Incredible mass surrounded him on all sides. He was in a large subterranean cavern—a natural one.

So, you've come, have you? Fool.

Oblivious to the condescending remark, D surveyed his surroundings dispassionately, and then soon angled off into the darkness to his right. Was it that absurdly easy for the young man to tell where his abducted compatriots were? He was surrounded by true darkness, yet he walked impassively through it. The blackness was so thick that it seemed not even light itself could ever penetrate it. It took about fifty seconds for his eyes to find human forms there: four figures lay on the stone floor. As he walked toward them, the air before him stirred.

Something buzzed through the air. Giving a scream, it fell at D's feet in its death throes. At first glance, the winged creature was built like an evil sprite. Though it no doubt made flight easier, its body was disturbingly thin. The fangs jutting from its mouth—and the claws stretching from its fingertips—hadn't escaped D's notice, either.

One thing after another ripped through the air. If there'd been the slightest bit of light, the deadly little oddities zipping at D from all directions would've been apparent, as would D's consummate fighting skill. There was no telling when he'd drawn his longsword, but the elegant blade danced in his hand, sending each and every one of his attackers crashing to the ground.

Not bothering to sheathe his sword, D walked forward. Suddenly, there was nothing there for his foot to rest on. The ground had opened wide. In a fraction of a second, D kicked off the ground with his other leg. As he was leaping, he lost his balance, and the earth continued to crack open. D began to descend instead. Unable to correct his form, he couldn't get much distance from his leap. Into the abyss his body dropped.

The Hunter's left hand reached out, only narrowly catching hold of the lip of the ever-widening gap. D sprang up at once. Just as his two feet touched back down on the floor, the crevice stopped growing. D turned around. His darkness-piercing eyes found the ground still lay there, innocent in every regard. It'd all been a psychological attack. If he'd fallen into that nonexistent pit, his own belief in it might've kept him falling for all eternity.

D went over to the other four and knelt by Tae's side. His left hand hovered over her lips—her breathing was normal. The same hand moved to her brow. He must've employed a trick of some sort, because Tae's eyes then opened.

"You okay?" D asked succinctly.

Tae latched onto his arm with both hands. "D—is that you?" she asked.

"Yes."

"I can't see anything at all. Where are we?"

"Underground," the Hunter replied. "Can you walk?"

"Yeah."

Still clinging to D's arm, Tae got to her feet as fast as the Hunter rose again.

"Wait here," D told her. "I'll go wake the others."

"No. I don't want you to leave me alone in the pitch black," Tae said, refusing to relinquish her hold on him.

"Okay, grab onto my coat then," the Hunter told her. Still, the girl wouldn't move. Reaching up with his right hand to where Tae clung to him near the shoulder, D caught hold of her wrists. Speechless, the girl trembled slightly. Once both her hands had been pushed down by D's waist, Tae took a tight grip of his coat. Whether or not D noticed how flushed her face was in the darkness was anyone's guess.

The Hunter's left hand pressed against the foreheads of the other three, waking each of them in turn. Unlike Tae, all three of them immediately grasped their situation.

It was Granny who asked, "Is there a way out of here?"

"I don't know," D replied with his habitual bluntness. "We're underground, but it could be we're not really."

"What?!" Clay said, eyes bulging, although no one but D could actually tell that. "What's that supposed to mean? Oh, I see—this is some kind of mind game, eh? Very fucking impressive."

"Real or not, how are we supposed to get back to the surface?" Granny asked.

"That's obvious," said Clay. "We settle the hash of whoever's running all this. Hey, Lance . . . you there?"

"Yeah."

"You sure you don't have some idea where we can find him?"

"Not a clue."

"Sheesh, you're worthless," Clay spat. "Well, never mind. He's gotta be hiding around here somewhere, and I'll ferret him out soon enough. Hey, Hunter—move everyone back behind me. I'm gonna pluck me a tune."

Harp in hand, Clay stood up.

"I'll be using my focused sonic waves of destruction. Might make you a little nauseous, gang, but just suck it up."

His coarse fingers touched the fearsome musical instrument.

It was at that moment that light sprang up in the darkness. All around the other four, countless globes of light had winked on. At long last the four of them could see each other's faces.

"Not those . . ." Lance groaned.

"Recognize these things, do you?" Granny asked.

"Yeah. Those are the same things that showed up the night they first brought me back. They're guards. One touch and you're paralyzed."

"Really? Then they gotta be like the hands and feet of whoever controls them," Clay said, licking his chops.

Seeming to sense something in the warrior's tone, Tae clung tightly to the Hunter's black coat.

"This'll be fun. I'm gonna give this thing a good long lesson in what you get for trying to use good ol' humans as guinea pigs. Have some of this!"

A note of unearthly beauty shot off, with death as its passenger. The globes of light directly in front of Clay shattered without a sound.

"Serves you right," the warrior sneered when he sensed obvious pain from nowhere in particular.

"Get 'im!" Granny shouted encouragingly.

"You got it!" Clay replied, spinning around. But a scream from Tae froze him solid.

"Why, what is it?" Granny asked, seeming terribly upset as she turned around. A second later, the old woman's eyes opened wide.

The same cry of "Monster!" flew from both Granny and Lance's mouths.

Still clinging to D, Tae screamed again when she looked up at him.

"Close your eyes!" said a steely voice that knifed through the maddening darkness. Low though it was, it had the power to make all of them comply. "It's just a psi attack that makes each of us look like a monster to the others. Don't open your eyes again until I tell you to."

Eyes shut tight, Clay turned in D's direction. A shout split his lips, a battle cry of "Goddamn freak!" In unison with his cry his right hand danced, wringing the sweet sounds of death from the instrument at his waist.

Zipping over Tae's head after D shoved her out of the way, the ultrasonic waves disappeared into the darkness. Somewhere out there, something collapsed.

"D, I still see it, even with my eyes shut!" Granny Viper shouted, her face pale.

"Look down," D told them, and then he leapt.

Darkness melted into darkness. Only D's perfect pale countenance revealed his location. Sailing over Clay's head as he made ready to recklessly launch another note from his harp, the Hunter landed right behind the warrior. Screaming, Clay spun around. He wore a crazed look. D's sword limned an arc as it came off his back.

In both narrowly evading the blade and leaping a good distance away, the younger Bullow truly deserved to be counted among the most renowned warriors of the Frontier. However, just as Clay came back to earth, a dull thud echoed from the back of his head. Before the warrior could launch any more ultrasonic waves at whatever he thought his pitch-black retinas reflected, he unceremoniously collapsed to the floor.

"Got 'im!" Granny was heard to exclaim.

D's eyes discerned the old woman standing there, still facing down but with an old-fashioned firearm in one hand. Tae and Lance were lying on the ground—that was the best possible solution.

"Is this a psi attack?" Granny asked.

"That's right."

"What should we do?"

"Stop it," D replied tersely.

"Good," Granny replied, sounding like she must've had the biggest grin imaginable plastered on her face. She was eager to counter-attack. "What do you suppose it'll throw at us next?" As she spoke, she unconsciously looked around her. "Hey, everything seems normal now . . . which basically means I can't see anything at all again," she said.

In response, D told her, "Here comes the next one."

"What?!" As Granny frantically spun around again, two figures emerging from the depths of the darkness entered her field of view. Dimmer than the very blackness, one was faintly recognizable even in this murk. The one on the right wore a wide-brimmed hat, and the hem of his coat fluttered in a dark breeze. Spying the much smaller figure with wild, disheveled hair, Granny muttered, "It's me—and D."

Perhaps D had already realized the truth. He took the sword he had in hand and put it back in its sheath. It clinked home with a beautiful sound.

"Are they illusions?" Granny asked, poised for battle.

That's very perceptive of you, the voice said. *But they are no mere phantasms. As you shall see.*

Was the purr of a blade through the air faster? Or was Granny swifter as she leapt out of the way? Still poised for action as if nothing had happened, the old woman now had two blackish streaks dripping down her deeply wrinkled face. Real blood.

That blood should be flowing through your veins. Even in a world of dreams, death may come. Here, reality itself is little more than a dream. If you believe you've been cut and think you'll bleed, then bleed you truly shall, just as you see. The two of them were created using all the data I currently have on you, but I believe you'll find their strength and constitution are perfectly matched against your own in virtually every regard. Meaning neither you nor they could ever win or lose to the other in all eternity. I look forward to seeing what sort of fight it will be.

The false D leapt. Coming from above with his full body weight and all his speed added to that of his blade, he brought a blow down at the top of D's head. The painful sound of metal-on-metal gave way to blue sparks that shot through the air.

Keeping his freshly drawn blade at the same height as when it'd parried his foe's deadly attack, D made a horizontal slash with the longsword. It met with nothing. His foe was D, too.

The two figures glared at each other across a gap of less than ten feet. Who would make the next move?

Knowing all the tricks his foe possessed, the false D readied his sword nonetheless. Seeing that a prolonged battle would be to his disadvantage, he intended to gamble everything on one lethal blow. The air whistled with a slash from above one shoulder to just below the other. He was close enough for that attack to actually work.

D took a step forward. As he did so, he simultaneously brought out his sword. The instant the false D's blow had bitten into his shoulder, the tip of D's blade could be seen slipping into his opponent's chest.

"Not bad," D said. Just as he'd taken a step forward to throw off the balance of the false D's attack, so his foe had managed to avoid a thrust through the heart by the merest fraction of an inch—an exquisite move executed in a hundredth of a second. Apparently, what the voice had told him was no lie. The two of them were deadlocked. Whoever made the next move would die.

They leapt in unison. Streaks of light crossed in midair. The sound of blades knifing through the wind only followed later.

As D landed, a black line split his forehead—the work of a blow from his foe's blade as they flew past each other. His foe smirked at him. No one save D could see the torrent of fresh blood spilling down his opponent's clothes from the horizontal slash across the false D's chest. Such was the difference between fighting with a shoulder wound versus a hole in the chest.

His opponent dashed into action.

D's field of view wavered—one of the streams of blood running from his forehead had changed direction and run into his right eye. The blade meant to meet his foe was off ever so slightly, shaving the flesh from his opponent's cheek while the flashing steel of the false D pierced the real D's heart. As D dropped to his knees without uttering a word, the callous blade was driven in much, much deeper from above.

That finishes him, then, the voice said wearily.

But who would've thought the voice would gasp just then, or that the false D's eyes would go wide with astonishment? His foe watched as a hand gloved in black grabbed his blade from below.

D raised his face. His eyes gave off a reddish light.

You couldn't be . . .

Strength surged into D's lower body. Perhaps the Noble blood that coursed through the young man's veins gave him unnatural power, for even after being pierced through the heart, he was very slowly rising to his feet.

His opponent struggled to pull the blade free or force it in deeper. It didn't move an inch. The balance of power had been broken.

A low moan spilled from D's lips. Something else accompanied it—a pair of fangs. Did his foe see how the tracks of the rolling drops of blood from his forehead vanished at his lips?

When his opponent tried to leap away, it was a second too late, and D's blade came straight down to split the other man's head. Whipping around in a flash, the same sword then pierced his opponent's heart. His foe crumbled to the ground.

Expressionless though he was, D somehow seemed satisfied with the way the false D's countenance had never betrayed any terror even at the bitter end, when his head turned to dust.

The pressure of the darkness was suddenly gone. D was gazing down at his feet and the shadow he cast there. It fell across silver sand.

Having slain the phantasm his foe had conjured, he'd thwarted the psychological attack. There was no sword through his chest, no blood coursing from his brow, but he was still holding his longsword. The psi attack had been ingenious; it had managed to rouse D's demonic nature. But had even *that* part been real?

"That was a hell of a scary character to deal with. I mean, whoever made him, of course," a low, decrepit voice commented from somewhere around D. "With all the power it invested in that, I'd wager it took a terrible hit just now. If you plan on getting out of here, now would be the perfect time for it."

Not replying, D looked around at their surroundings. Three figures were stretched out on the sand. A diminutive fourth stood ready for battle: Granny Viper. She was probably still squaring off against an opponent. Apparently, the psychological assault had affected her much more than it had D.

D returned his longsword to the sheath on his back. At the pleasant metallic song of it sliding into its sheath, Granny shuddered a bit. Dazedly, she surveyed her surroundings. Noticing D first, she blinked her eyes. "What on earth did you—? Why, I was fighting right here and . . . Oh, I get it—you broke the psi attack, didn't you?"

She quickly turned and looked for Tae, a show of her sincere devotion to the job. Racing over to the girl with a cry that bordered on a scream, the very first thing she did was check for a pulse. Having enough foresight to take the possibility of internal injuries into consideration, she was careful not to move the girl too much.

Seeing the crone's shoulders come down in manifest relief, D then turned his eyes to the heavens. The moon was visible in the clear sky. D began walking back toward the rocky mound. "You can handle the rest," he told Granny. "We leave in twenty minutes."

III

Three hours later, the horizon donned a tinge of blue. In lieu of a rising sun, the air filled with rising winds. The hard-flung grains of sand beat against the wagon's canopy mercilessly, making a sound like the peal of a bell. Granny spat a grit-laden wad of saliva from the driver's seat. Both D and Clay had scarves to shield their nose and mouth, and they rode on either side of the wagon. The vehicle was renowned for its ability to reach speeds of seventy-five miles per hour on level ground, but now it barely managed a tenth of that.

Granny was anxious—the damage D had dealt their enemy wouldn't be enough to destroy it. Once its wounds had healed, it was sure to make its next move against them. If it threw out another tornado, they'd be right back where they started from; in fact, some result even more miserable definitely lay ahead for them. You could say the first order of business was to get as far away as they could before their foe had a chance to recover. In her heart of hearts, the crone prayed the enemy's power didn't extend across the entire desert.

But the real question was, just where were they racing now? Though they knew the direction they were headed, their present location was a mystery.

D was riding ahead of the wagon and off to the right, and as Granny gazed at his back, she had a strange look in her eye. According to the Vampire Hunter, the town they were bound for lay more than a hundred miles south by southwest of there. She'd asked him just how he knew for sure, but he hadn't answered her. Ordinarily, she'd have accused him of pulling her leg and raised a big stink. Even Granny herself wasn't sure yet why she'd let the matter rest so easily. She knew he was a dhampir. There was no need to be surprised when a man with the blood of the Nobility in his veins displayed such an incredible ability. However, she got the impression there was more to this young man than this fact alone.

Granny was quite familiar with ordinary dhampirs. While it was true that they were several ranks above humans, they still had their limits. If you tried hard enough and were willing to die in the process, you could even kill one. But that reasoning didn't seem to apply in the least to the gorgeous young man before her. Could he be killed? The very thought of it had never occurred to her. Like darkness given form, the young man could send any opponent at all into the depths of the abyss, if he so wished. From her own intuition, Granny realized the Hunter's knowledge was surely instinctive as well.

Finding something disturbing about the black back of the man they were supposed to be relying on, Granny finally decided to speak to him. "Tell me something, D. Just what do we have to do to stop this desert once and for all?"

As she expected, she got no reply. But she did hear another voice from off to her left.

"Sheesh, how the hell would he know? How could anybody possibly know anything that crazy?" Perhaps feeling somewhat humiliated after learning from the old woman that he'd been used like a puppet on a string, Clay sounded more vindictive than ever.

Granny just smiled sweetly at him and cooed, "Now, don't go saying that. After all, he had a little part in saving you, you know."

"Hmph. I'll square things up with him sooner or later." Clay then turned and looked at the wagon. "All that aside, you sure it's a good idea having them two riding in there together? That sodbuster might look all well-behaved, but down deep he could just be some hot-handed operator for all we know."

"We don't really have a choice. Unlike you, the two of them are ordinary folks. See, they still haven't shaken off all the aftereffects of the psi attack. But just let me warn you—"

"I know already! If I go touching your precious goods, you ain't responsible for what happens next, right? Shit, if you're that worried about it, why don't you put a chain around her neck and keep a hold on one end of it? I ain't promising you a damn thing. To tell the truth, I've always wondered what it'd be like to put it to one of *the hidden*. Oops..." Clay said, smirking as he pulled away. No doubt he'd felt the urge to kill radiating from every inch of the old woman.

Turning forward again with a disapproving cluck of her tongue, Granny then stiffened with tension. D had come to a halt. "What's wrong?" the old woman asked with fear in her voice, though that was just a part of a plot she'd set in motion to get his pity.

"It's a sandstorm. A little more than a mile ahead of us."

"Not a twister?"

"No, a sandstorm."

The old woman squinted her eyes. "Well, I can't see anything."

"If we keep going straight, we'll run right into it," said D. "This calls for a detour."

"But, wouldn't that put us behind schedule? I mean, that'd be a problem for you too, right?"

"If we're lucky, it's just a normal sandstorm."

"Stop feeding us this load of crap," Clay snapped. "I don't see a damn thing either."

"I can see it."

That one softly spoken phrase was enough to silence even the irrepressible Clay.

"Or would you rather try and risk it?" the Hunter ventured.

"Great idea!" the old woman exclaimed, slapping her knee noisily. "That's just what we'll have to do. I mean, what's a sandstorm or two? Let a little thing like that stop you, and you could hardly call yourself a man the rest of your days."

"You gotta be shitting me. I'm completely against this," Clay groused.

"Oh my! I thought you were one of the greatest warriors on the Frontier, but I guess you ain't all you're cracked up to be."

Granny's retort brought immediate results. Blood rushed into Clay's face. "Don't make me laugh," he snarled. "I ain't saying I'm afraid. I just gotta find my brother, is all."

"Oh, you poor thing, you. Say, D—how far is it from here to the place we got scooped up?"

"About seventy miles, I'd say."

"Now, I don't care how chock full of fraternal love you are when you gallop off, you won't be able to cover that kind of distance. You'll just have to leave your brother's fate to the heavens. If luck is on your side, who knows—you could run into him again somewhere outside the desert in two or three years. And if it's against you, he'll bake in the sun and die like a dog."

At that point, a bizarre reaction came over Clay. A smile that really had no business on a wild beast of a man like him—a smile some might even call spooky—spread across his whole face. "My brother Bingo baking in the sun? Did you say something about dying? That's just too funny. I'd sure as hell like to see that with my own two eyes," he spoke in a voice like a corpse, with a grin that was almost unimaginable from someone with such a ruthless, fearless image. Even Granny's expression grew stiff.

Just then, the back door of the wagon suddenly started to open, leaving the crone at a loss for words.

Scrambling down the built-in set of steps, the pale figure kicked up the sand as she ran down the right side of the wagon.

"Tae!" Granny shouted, standing like a vengeful demon. "Get her for me, D!"

In response to her cry, the Hunter wheeled his cyborg horse around. It was a heartbeat later that the horse tumbled forward, just as he was about to gallop off. From its back a figure in black flew like a mystic bird. Landing in a spot some fifteen feet away, D plunged the sword he'd already drawn deep into sand at his feet.

"What's going on?" Clay asked as he looked all around.

"It looks like it's come back around," D told the younger Bullow. While he was speaking, the figure of Tae dwindled between the dunes with a speed never anticipated from such dainty little legs.

"Wait up, Miss Tae!" Lance cried, clutching his head as he tumbled from the back of the wagon.

"What on earth happened?"

Stopped short by the question Granny had barked, he replied in an almost tearful tone, "I don't know. We were talking, and then all of a sudden she whacked me over the head with a wrench."

"You stay right there. I'll do something about this," the old woman said. Still standing in the same spot, she reached for her jar with her right hand. D, however, didn't move, and Tae just kept getting farther away—she was already more than a hundred yards from the wagon.

Granny's hand came out of the jar balled in a fist. From behind her, Clay saw that countless multicolored particles had begun to trickle smoothly from between her clenched fingers, but the flow quickly ended. And just what had become of those particles that fell on the floor of the front seat by Granny's feet and down onto the desert sands? Driven by what might be called a warrior's instinctive curiosity, the younger Bullow was just about to spur his mount forward when Granny bent low. For a split second, it seemed like a flash of blue light shot by her feet.

Tae was just about to disappear behind a dune. Seeing the way the girl collapsed completely made Lance's eyes bulge out of their sockets.

"D—how're things over there?" Granny cried out.

"Better for the moment."

Apparently it was no exaggeration, as the Hunter's cyborg horse had gotten back up and was shaking off the grains of sand.

"In that case, go! The girl's out cold."

The figure in black dashed off, coat fanning around him.

"What did you do, old lady? What the hell is that sand, anyway?"

Granny turned and smiled at Clay's query. "That's a trade secret," she replied.

"Don't give me any of that crap!"

"It is, just as sure as your little tricks are."

By that, she clearly meant the way he did battle. The gazes of the two—ferocious and cruel—collided in midair in a shower of unseen sparks.

D scooped up Tae. The reason she'd collapsed so suddenly surely had something to do with the crone's mysterious skill, although D didn't know exactly what that was. Judging from the way Tae's hair stood on end, she must've been hit with some sort of electric shock. However, D had seen with his own eyes that nothing had passed between the old woman and the girl. How, then, had it happened?

A light tap on her cheek, and Tae quickly opened her eyes. "D?" she said.

"Don't move. What happened?"

"I don't know," Tae replied, her eyes tinged with terror. "I was talking with Mr. Lance, when I just got this feeling that I had to get out of there. This voice was telling me to go outside—"

It was clear then that the desert had indeed returned to the way it had been.

D reached out with one hand to pull the girl up, and behind him a flume of sand shot up unexpectedly. Not simply sand, this had a humanoid shape. Tae's eyes were wide open now, and they caught the silvery flash of light that shot through the air. The outline of the figure that'd pushed just its upper body from the ground suddenly crumbled, and a heartbeat later it was again a golden pile of sand melting back into the desert. Tae gave a scream.

To either side of them the sand rose in one place after another, taking human form everywhere it did. The forms almost looked like the miasma rising from a solidified swamp. Pole-thin arms reached for D's neck.

The silver flash that shot up diagonally took the limbs off at the elbow. When all of their arms had fallen to ground, the shapes flopped backward in what seemed like pain and slowly sank back into the earth.

"There're still more of them," Tae said, her eyes reflecting the countless round heads springing from the sea of sand around them. Would they be able to get back to the wagon? A hundred yards seemed completely hopeless.

A powerful arm wrapped around the girl's waist. As Tae gazed at the gorgeous visage of her sturdy guardian, his name came to her lips. Her anxiety burned away like a fog.

"Here we go," said the Vampire Hunter.

"Okay," Tae replied. She was no longer afraid.

A cloud of dusty creatures was closing in on them. Their heads lacked eyes or noses or mouths. Their bodies were like short, fat rocks with a couple of logs stuck in them, but completely smooth. These unsettling interpretations of the human form were more than six feet tall and born of the sand.

A black figure raced like the wind between those sandy shapes. Any hand or body that threatened to block his path was promptly severed, with some of the would-be assailants turning to dust on the ground and others doing so in midair.

Having already covered more than twenty yards at full speed, D artlessly slammed his blade into the right shoulder of yet another foe that stood in his way. True to the strange feel of what it was cutting, the blade hacked halfway through the creature's chest before stopping. As the Hunter pulled his blade free, his foe pounced, turning back into sand over D's head.

Ignoring the sand men that were springing up all around them, D quietly inspected his longsword. Black grains clung to the blade—iron dust—causing his weapon to lose its edge. If it stuck to steel it had a powerful magnetic charge, and that had to be what helped the sand men keep their humanoid shape. But understanding the reason did nothing to help the irrefutable fact that D's offensive might had dropped considerably.

Sand creatures were packed all around them. Tae clung to D's waist while D gazed at his blade without saying a word. It was a cold, clear gaze that seemed to suggest that this young man would greet life and death, joy and sorrow, all with the very same look.

The wind snarled loudly.

As an eerie shudder climbed her spine, Tae saw the sand men stop . . . and then back away immediately. When the girl looked up at D again, she learned the reason: his eyes were giving off a red glow.

D dashed forward, carried by the wind. He landed right into the heart of the sand men. With the coolness of an artist raining destruction on a group of standing sculptures, the Hunter swung his longsword in wide arcs. His blade was already thick and black with the iron particles that clung to it. As if to demonstrate the power of his Noble blood, he left a few of the sandy monstrosities split from head to crotch, while others were sliced clean through the torso. Without exception, they all returned to their original material. As the wind blew the dust from the crumbling bodies into D's face, his crimson eyes gleamed beautifully and with ineffable mystery.

Someone was shouting in the distance. D leapt into the air and over the edge of a nearby sand dune. Off to his left, the upper body of another sand man stretched from the ground.

Tae was about to scream when right before her very eyes D's left hand snapped closed on the featureless face of a sand man. Dust spilled from between the Hunter's fingers, and the creature's head broke apart like a clod of dirt.

But the sight that greeted them next was like some sort of miracle. The countless sand men crumbled to pieces in a matter of seconds and mixed with the dusty clouds, as if some titanic hand had wiped them all out of existence.

The Dark Forest

CHAPTER 5

I

As the Hunter and the girl returned to the wagon, they were met by Granny's wrath-filled visage. Despite having defeated the sand men by some means even D didn't understand, she didn't seem confident in herself. There would be more trouble related to Tae, it seemed.

"The water's shot," Granny said, pinning Tae with a reproachful gaze as she did so. "Before she ran off on us, the girl left the spigot on the tank open. We've shut it again, but given the number of us, what we have won't last half the day. If we spread it thin as possible, we'd still only get three days."

"If there were only half as many of us, it'd last six days," Clay interjected with amusement from high in the saddle. "Care to see who's gonna get to drink that water?"

The space between all of them was strung with invisible threads of tension.

"You've got a point there," Granny said, looking as she did at Lance from the corner of her eye. "I suppose we can't let those that aren't pulling their own weight drink our water."

Lance lowered his eyes. He was well aware of where he stood.

"How long would it last between four people?"

At that abrupt question, Granny stared at the young man in black with astonishment. "Well," she replied, "barely a day and a half, I suppose."

"Make it two."

"I suppose we can manage that. But traveling by day should be a lot more painful for you than it is for us."

"The night makes up for it. He can have my share."

The old woman turned and exchanged glances with Clay. "Now, this is a surprise. I didn't know you were one to worry about anyone else. And here I thought you had liquid darkness flowing through you instead of blood. That's very kind of you, but me and Tae will take it instead."

But Granny was in for yet another surprise.

Sulkily, Clay said, "I don't want any either."

Not only did Granny have her mouth agape, but Lance did as well.

Gazing steadily at D, Clay said, "If he ain't drinking, there's no way I'm gonna keep wetting my whistle. If anybody could accuse me of taking the easy way out, I'd never live it down."

"Oh, dear me, if that's not enough to bring a tear to my eye," Granny said, bowing her head as if deeply touched. "I've lived a good long time, but I've never heard anything as fine as all that. Yes, indeed—you men can be mighty impressive. Good enough. I'll give both your shares to Tae."

It was just like the crone to make no mention of what would become of her own share of the water. But just then a third shock was delivered to Granny.

"That won't be necessary," the girl declared.

"How's that?" asked Granny.

Everyone turned to the girl, who met them with a distant look in her eyes. She was staring off in the same direction she'd headed during her escape. The fact of the matter was that Tae had someone to guide her.

"What do you make of this?" the old woman said to D.

"Apparently there was no need to bring her back," the Vampire Hunter muttered in a low voice from the back of his horse. A weary shadow hung on his gorgeous countenance. The sunlight and scorching heat of the desert were foes of the highest order for those who descended from the Nobility. Even for the greatest of dhampirs, the physical exhaustion was far more intense than it was for human beings.

Tae leapt down from the driver's seat. Granny reached out for her with one hand, but D stopped the old woman.

"The desert's definitely calling out to the girl," the Hunter said. "Given how it wrecked our water supply, it could be calling us, too."

"What do you suppose it's up to?"

"We'll just have to go see."

"Isn't that dangerous?" asked the old woman.

"There'll be danger no matter where we go."

"Okay. I can't very well let my merchandise run off. I'll follow along right behind. Right behind *you*, that is. Otherwise, you're liable to say none of this is any of your concern and keep right on going."

"Would I?" D muttered, tugging on his reins.

Tae was already walking away. The footprints she left in the sand were pathetically small. As if guided by those tiny tracks, the rest of the party advanced. The moment the girl disappeared behind a massive sand dune, D turned and looked back.

"Worried about the sandstorm?" Granny asked.

Needless to say, she got no reply.

Clay passed his vigilant gaze from left to right. While he was on his guard for sand men, it should've come as little surprise that a mischievous grin lingered on his lips. Even matters of life and death were little more than a game to this warrior.

The group continued for more than three hours. The sun had risen even higher, burning deep black shadows of the party into the sand.

"Say, mister," Lance called out to D from the driver's seat of the wagon, where he'd taken Granny's place. Having cowed him with threats about his share of the water, the crone was now stretched out beside him with the canopy shading her face—her concern for Tae keeping her from going inside. At first, Granny had been quite worried about the girl as she headed off so purposefully, but after seeing the steadiness of Tae's steps, the old woman complied with D's instructions not to interfere. She refrained from calling out to the girl as she walked away, however, anxiety about protecting her merchandise kept her countenance stiff.

"What is it?"

On hearing D's reply, Granny was more surprised than anyone. Having this Hunter actually reply when someone called out to him was like seeing the whole world turned upside down.

"How about you switch with me and come take the driver's seat?" Lance suggested. "It'd be a lot easier on you. There's shade from the sun and everything."

"Don't worry about it," D replied.

"Yeah, but—"

"I'm used to it. Have you ever ridden a horse before?" the Hunter asked.

"A little. I could handle one if it was just walking along like that."

"Your job is to make the wild places green."

"I've lost my faith in doing that," Lance confessed.

"Why?"

Granny had been silently listening to the pair's conversation, but her eyes bugged out then. Anyone who knew D would've had exactly the same reaction. The very thought of D—the great Vampire Hunter D—wanting to know anything about anyone else boggled the mind.

"All you folks have these incredible abilities," Lance replied. "By comparison, I'm just a plain old farmer. I can't do anything but reclaim soil and plant things. And then, when I found myself out here in the middle of the desert, I couldn't even save myself without help from all of you. I'm pathetic. You know, I'm twenty-five now. Do you suppose there's still time for me to become a Hunter?"

D's head didn't turn, but his eyes slid to the side. "What do *you* think?" he said.

Finding himself at the end of D's question, Clay clucked his tongue. "Sheesh. If it was that easy for every sodbuster and his brother to become one, we'd be up to our asses in Hunters. Guys like you should be Vegetable Hunters or Piglet Hunters," he told Lance.

"That might not be bad," the man replied.

"Bah," Clay said, spitting in disgust. "You're completely hopeless. You could die out here and I bet there ain't a single soul who'd miss you."

"You're right. My mother and father were both carried off by a flood."

Sitting there beside Lance, Granny donned an expression that seemed to say, "Heaven help us."

"What sort of things did you plan on planting?" asked D.

"Anything. If it'll grow with fresh air and water and sunshine, then anything at all."

"Well, that's what you should do."

"Damn straight. That sort of shit suits you," Clay said spitefully.

"It's a job we can't do," D remarked, putting a sullen look on the younger Bullow's face. "I can swing a sword, but I don't know how to plant seeds. I can kill Nobles, but I can't raise a single vegetable. There wouldn't be a problem if all the Hunters were gone, but people can't live without food."

"Maybe in theory that's true . . ." Lance conceded. "But a Hunter gets some appreciation when he takes care of something, right? No matter how much of the earth we've made green, no one has ever thanked us for it. Yeah, I sure wish I could use a sword a bit more like a dhampir."

His envious remark was rocked from the air by an explosion of laughter.

"What's so funny?!" asked Lance.

Holding her belly, Granny said, "How could you *not* laugh at that? You're the only person I ever met who wanted to be a dhampir. I get it now. Seems farmers don't know a whole lot about the world. You'd best stick to planting seeds for the rest of your days."

"What's so funny about dhampirs? That's a pretty good thing to be, isn't it?"

"Take a good look at our young friend here," Granny said, staring at D with a fierce look in her eye. Her gaze seemed to harbor what could be taken for hate, which surprised Clay as well as Lance. "Absolutely perfect from head to toe," she continued. "What more could you ask for? Any woman—any man, for that matter—can take just one look at him and get lightheaded. But he treads a path that's painful as hell."

Lance didn't know what to say.

"Tell me," the old woman said, "have you ever fished off a riverbank? Fun, isn't it? I'm sure you've picked flowers and seen sunlight sparkling in the breeze, too. Everyone does those things, but he can't. Sunlight burns his flesh like a blowtorch. If he fell into running water, he couldn't even move his limbs properly. Touch a rose, and he'd scream and wither away. A gentle breeze? If it blew against him, it'd rip the skin and muscle from his bones. Did you say something about people appreciating dhampirs?" Granny asked. "Let me give you some facts about just what sort of rigmarole goes on when one of them comes to work for a village. For starters, while the dhampir is there, no women or children are allowed to leave their houses at all. In cases where it's really bad, they're all locked up in one spot and don't come out again until business is taken care of. Any hand or foot that comes into contact with the dhampir gets scrubbed and disinfected until the skin comes right off it, and in the case of livestock, the animals are put down on the spot. That much they could stand. But the whole time they're in a given village, not a single person will ever look them in the face . . . and that's hard to do."

The words came like flames from the crone, but D listened without comment. Stunned by this bombshell, Lance and Clay both gazed at the woman's wrinkled face in disbelief.

As if she'd just noticed them, Granny snapped back to her usual self. "Goodness me," she said, pressing her hand to her mouth as if she'd just told a joke. "That was terribly rude of me. Let's just pretend

I didn't say any of that. Okay, everyone? Is that all right, D? Don't make such a stern face," she told the Hunter. "Oh, I'm sorry," she added, "That's the way you always look, isn't it? Well, at any rate, tell me you don't hold it against me."

The Hunter said nothing.

"Oh, come now. You can't take the hysteric outburst of an old lady that seriously. Please. Just say this one thing for me. Tell me you don't hold it against me."

"It didn't bother me," said D.

"Don't tell me it didn't bother you; say you don't hold it against me. As a special favor to an old woman."

"I don't hold it against you."

"Thank you kindly," the old woman exclaimed, breaking into a grin as she raised one hand in thanks.

Wearing a look that absolutely defied description, Lance gazed at D.

"I guess dhampirs got it pretty hard, too," said Clay, who sounded unusually introspective.

Ahead of them, a few low mountains of sand appeared. They were perhaps twenty feet high or more, but the inclines were gentle. Tae began climbing them with a regular gait. Granny switched her wagon into low gear.

Tae and D were the first to reach the summit; next came Granny's wagon. Then Clay galloped up last. All halted there. There was no wind to welcome them.

"I see," Granny said, sounding deeply impressed. "I suppose that'd make anyone want to give up farming."

About two hundred yards off, the desert underwent a remarkable transformation. No trace remained of the boundless sea of sand. Lush green filled everyone's field of view, and it stretched off without end to either side. The scent of cool ozone tickled the nostrils of all. The towering trees seemed to reach heights of easily four hundred feet. The desert had chosen to greet the party with a massive forest.

II

Though they all recalled what this had to be, it was Granny that said its name. "So, this is the moving forest—it has to be a trap, right?"

"More than likely," the Hunter replied. "But at least we should be able to find water here."

"It's a damn good trick. Never seen an oasis like this before," Clay said, his eyes sparkling with admiration. But this was no mere oasis. It was a vast forest the likes of which couldn't be found even in the heavily wooded regions of the north. The vista was more than just magical . . . it was close to miraculous.

"What do we do, eh?" the crone asked.

"Unless we want to roast here, we have no choice but to go on. We have a guide," D said, turning his gaze to Tae, who'd stopped a few yards ahead of him.

"You have to do something for her," Granny said. "If you don't wake her up fast, she'll wind up serving the desert for the rest of her life."

"There's nothing we can do for her at the moment. We'll have to take the desert itself out of action. For the time being, our hands are tied."

"Hmph!" the old woman snorted. "Here you are, a dhampir, and you're completely useless."

"At any rate, let's go," Clay said, raking the fingers of one hand through his hair. Grains of sand rained noisily to the ground. "This trip's just about bored the hell out of me. I need me a bit of stimulation, I think."

No one had any objections, and there was little else they could do. Tae began walking again. With nothing to stop them, the party followed along after her into the vast forest. As they entered the shade, cool air swept over every inch of them. They suddenly stopped sweating. Granny shivered.

Tae continued between the boles and their endless verdant riot, her steps free from trepidation. It was obvious she was under someone else's control. The only sound the party heard was that of grass and dirt under hooves—absent were the songs of the birds and the chirping of the insects. Apparently, nothing lived in this forest save the trees.

"Hey, sodbuster," Clay called out. "This is a hell of a place we find ourselves. You happen to know what kind of trees these are?"

"Pretty much."

"Well, I feel so much better then," the warrior said, his explosion of laughter coursing out between the trees and then disappearing. But Clay soon clammed up.

"This is a psi attack, right?" Granny asked.

"No," D replied, never taking his eyes off Tae. "This is the real thing. But it's definitely under the desert's control."

"What in the blue blazes does it want with us anyway?" Granny said irritably, and then she quickly looked up.

Lance, who'd been straining his ears, had clapped his hands together. "That sounds like . . . water!" he exclaimed.

"Seems this confounded desert might be good for something after all," said the old woman.

"Only because it has to keep us alive," D remarked.

"With that kind of thinking, you're not cut out for anything but Hunting."

D looked up. The colossal branches overlapped above them, forming a dense canopy. The reason it remained bright despite the fact that sunlight couldn't get through was because bioluminescent fungi clung to the bark of the trees.

"There's something out there," Clay muttered.

"You're right," Granny said. "I can feel it. There are a lot of them, too. I just can't tell where they're coming from."

"I'm sure we'll know soon enough," Clay said, putting his right hand on his harp.

After they'd gone on for five minutes, the sound of water was even more obvious to their ears. Another ten minutes passed, and suddenly a waterfall and pool appeared before them. The silvery ribbon of water dropped straight down from a height of thirty or forty feet.

"This is nice! I'm gonna have me a swim."

But just as Clay made that carefree remark, Tae thudded to her knees ahead of them. Strength draining from her body, she collapsed on her side.

Leaping down from her vehicle, Granny raced over to the girl.

"Is she okay?" Lance asked as he jumped to the ground, too.

D and Clay alone gazed at the dark blue waters that reflected the greenery.

"Doesn't seem to be anything here," Clay said after a while.

Without a word, D rode his horse over to the edge of the lagoon. He didn't so much as glance at Tae or the other two with her. His left index finger went to his mouth. When it quickly came away again, a bright red bead welled from the tip of it. Turning his finger toward the ground, he pressed his thumb against it right next to the bloody bead. A drop of scarlet fell between the waves lapping at the shore, and then vanished in the blink of an eye. Watching the placid surface for a while, D then said, "Looks like you can swim here."

Choosing a flat spot near the water, the group set up camp. By the time Lance finished taking care of the water tank, it was evening. But that only applied to the world outside the forest—D and his companions were still surrounded by the glow of the luminescent fungi.

"That looks like the end of our water woes," Granny said with a satisfied nod when she returned to the driver's seat from an inspection of the tank.

Sitting by the campfire gobbling down the contents of a can of food, Clay remarked, "Sure, but the long and short of it is, we ain't getting out of here till we put this desert down once and for all. We gotta do something fast. Where's the thing's heart, anyway?"

"If we knew that, we wouldn't be busting our humps," Granny replied in a bitter tone as she glanced out of the corner of her eye at D, who reclined against a rock some ten or so feet away.

"What'd you do with Tae?" Clay asked as he looked all around.

"She's in the wagon with Lance."

"Again? You're playing with fire there."

"You needn't trouble yourself about it. I'm sure he won't let his guard down this time."

"I'll take the next shift from him," said the warrior.

"Let the wolf watch the sheep? Don't make me laugh."

"A wolf, am I? That guy's a hundred times more dangerous than me," Clay shot back, his eyes creeping over to D in the shade of a rock.

"That one's had a different upbringing from you. Got a better character, too."

"He's a dhampir. He's bound to get thirsty for blood sooner or later."

"If he does, I suppose I'll just have to chalk it up to bad luck," Granny replied.

"Have it your way then," the warrior said. Clay then hit the outer wall of the wagon with his ridiculously large fist. "Hey! Come out here a minute. I gotta have a word with you."

Both Lance and Tae stuck their heads out.

"My business is with the man of the wagon," Clay said. "I thought we could take a little stroll and chew the fat."

"What, with me?" Lance asked, his eyes wide.

"You got a problem with that?"

"No."

"Then leave the dhampir to watch the women and come with me."

"Don't you hurt him," Tae cried. "He was only looking after me."

"Relax, missy. I might not look it, but in warrior circles, I'm known as something of a gentleman," Clay said with a smirk as he tossed his jaw in Lance's direction.

"D! Granny! Stop him!"

"Let 'em be," Granny said with a wink. "When men get to quarreling, this is the only way to put an end to it. Now you stop for a minute and think about what it means if a couple of boys are ready to throw down over you. And once you're done doing that, get back to your sewing."

"D," Tae called out, her last hope bound to his name. But then she realized that her expectation wouldn't be met. There was no sign of the gorgeous youth in black anywhere.

"He's probably off checking out the area," remarked the old woman.

Now down on the ground, Tae could be heard to say, "I . . . I'll go look for him!"

"Now, just hold on!" Granny cried at the slender back of the girl dashing off toward the rocks. The crone reached for the jar on her hip, but stopped in mid-motion. "Ah, to blazes with it!" she said to herself. "She's at that age, after all." And then she turned to the two men with great dissatisfaction and said, "Unless the two of you are trying to see who can be the world's biggest idiot, you'll knock this off right now."

Going to the side of the rock, Tae looked toward the forest. Between the green leaves, a figure in black could be seen in the distance.

"Wait!" she cried out, and just as she did, the black shape melted into the forest. Before she could even think about turning back, her body was moving forward. As she ran, she called out, "D!"

Stopping where D had disappeared, she looked all around. Twenty or thirty feet off to her left there was a section of open ground, and D stood in the center of the nearly circular clearing.

"D!" the girl cried out. She was about to dash over to him when a low command sharp as a blade stopped her.

"Hide."

Frantically, the girl ducked behind a tree. D had become a statue. Though she strained her eyes, Tae could see nothing around them; perhaps only D knew what it was. At just that moment, something black bobbed up over D's head. Looking at it from a logical standpoint, the object dropping from above with incredible speed had probably slowed its descent at the end to lessen the shock of impact, but to Tae it seemed to just pop up instead. The slight glint the girl saw was like a blow to her heart.

"D!"

The flash of silver that flew up from the ground forced the girl's cry back down her throat. Cut in half around its middle, the dark figure thudded to the ground at D's feet. It was a stark-naked human. However, the hands that grasped something metallic and the legs were abnormally long, reminiscent of a spider. As similar forms dropped from above one after another, Tae gasped.

D's longsword flashed out, and those it touched fell to the ground dead. A trio of figures that'd landed out of reach of the blade took to the air. They had incredible leaping power, but that was all they had a chance to show. Without time to use the weapons they had in their hands, they were split in half by the arc of the longsword. D moved lightly. A bloody mist billowed toward him, skimming by his body before it hit the ground.

At some point, enough spider people had descended that their milling shapes blotted out the darkness. If they came at D en masse, even he wouldn't be able to stop all of them at the same time. Perhaps realizing as much, the figures creeping across the ground crouched as one. Before they could advance, they stopped suddenly. A horrifying aura had paralyzed them all—an aura which emanated from D.

"Heading back?" Tae heard the Hunter ask in the same steely tone as always.

The spiders scurried into action. They seemed relieved. For some reason, Tae felt relieved, too.

The bodies of the spider people floated up into the air. Although Tae's eyes couldn't detect what supported them, they rubbed their hands and feet together as they vanished into the treetops. No doubt the reason they seemed to be moving in slow motion compared to their earlier descent was because D's aura had seeped into their marrow.

Suddenly, Tae realized that the two of them were alone.

Turning to her, D asked, "Why did you come here?"

At a loss for words, Tae then remembered what her original motivation had been. "Er . . . Mr. Clay and Mr. Lance are about to . . ."

Her voice petered out. She'd just realized D didn't have a whit of interest in that. What became of his fellow travelers was no concern of his. "How can you be so cold . . .?" she said, the words creeping from her mouth unbidden. She had to wonder what her face looked like as she stared at D. She'd tried to regain some composure, but one after another the emotions seeping from her heart became words. "You don't care at all what happens to anyone else, do you? You're nothing but darkness and ice to the very core. No matter what anyone else thinks of you, you can just ignore them like some little puff of wind. I've heard that dhampirs have human blood mixed in with the Noble, but that's a lie. You've got nothing but the cold, dark blood of the Nobility flowing in your veins!" she shouted.

As Tae shouted at him, she shook. It felt like the blood was coursing through her body in reverse, and that it was going to freeze—from fear. No matter who or what they might be, anyone who crossed this youth would be cut down. Tae realized for the first time what this Vampire Hunter *really* was. However, another emotion had welled up with her fright, and it was on this that Tae's consciousness became fixed. The feeling became a sob, and Tae spun around. If nothing else, she wanted to at least keep him from seeing her cry. Leaning back against a nearby bole, Tae sobbed.

"What happened in Castle Gradinia?" the Hunter asked.

The girl heard his voice, but didn't sense him drawing any closer. "Don't come near me," she said. "Just go back. Leave me alone."

"This is dangerous territory. Those things I just fought haven't given up yet. Cry as much as you need to, then I'll take you back with me."

"Stupid Hunter," Tae cried as she turned around. A powerful wall of black blocked her way. "Stupid, stupid, stupid!" Repeating the word over and over all the while, Tae pounded him with her fists. It felt like she was hitting solid rock. "I thought you might be okay. I was so happy, because a man like you could be a dhampir."

"Which of the Nobles fathered the child you carry?"

Tae stopped what she was doing. She thought her blood would freeze, and that even her heart might stop. The girl tried to shut her eyes, but her eyelids wouldn't budge at all. Words alone came to her with usual ease as she said, "What are you talking about?"

"You're pregnant. Which of the Nobles is the father?"

Tae couldn't feel anything anymore. "I don't know," she replied.

"Is it *his*?"

That was all he had to say for Tae to understand. Out of the darkness, eyes that were fiery red points of light drew closer.

"Is it *his*?" D asked once more.

"I couldn't help it, you know," Tae said. The girl thought she sounded like an old lady. "What could I do? Either of them could've killed me with just one finger. I had no choice but to do as they told me."

"When did you realize it?"

"Back when I was still in the castle. Do you know what month it'll be born? Ordinarily, it's supposed to take ten months and ten days for a baby."

"Yes, ordinarily. In the case of this child, it'll be about six months after you noticed the first indications."

As if to distance herself from something unseen, Tae took a step backwards. "What do you mean, 'in the case of this child'?"

"If it's *his* child, your baby will be no ordinary dhampir."

"What are you trying to say?"

"Let's go back."

"No. Tell me. What'll my baby be like? It couldn't be," Tae mumbled. "It couldn't be . . ." The second time she said it, she tried to invest the words with nothing but horror. But something had welled up inside her. Although she wasn't even aware of it, Tae was now hopelessly in its power, under the sway of a sad yet mysterious delight. "Just like you . . ." she continued.

Something cold touched her cheek. Before Tae realized it was D's left hand, her consciousness had become one with the darkness.

"An awful tale it is, but interesting still," D's left hand muttered as it caught the collapsing girl. "I wonder what road the girl will take? Anyway, those characters you faced just now have been keeping tabs on you ever since you were down by the water. That's why you drew them out here, isn't it?"

"That was a test, I imagine. For me."

"Testing your abilities? What for?" asked the voice.

"Don't you know?"

"Nope," the voice said, its reply vested with laughter. Malicious laughter. "Come now. You know just as well as I do. This desert has a real nostalgic feel to it."

D put Tae over his left shoulder.

"Just when and how did things get so crazy?" the voice continued. "I remember something a woman we met once said. She wanted to know why something so good had to end so badly."

"Do you think this is something good?" the Hunter asked.

"I don't know."

D started to walk back. And the voice wasn't heard again.

III

By the time D came back with Tae over his shoulder, the fight between Clay and Lance had ended. Lance lay stretched out by the edge of the lagoon, spread-eagle. His face was swollen to nearly twice its normal size, and his nose was a bit crooked.

Detecting the Hunter as she washed out a cooling cloth, Granny raced over to him.

"She's fine. I just put her to sleep. She'll come around in about ten minutes," the Hunter said. A light flip of his black shoulder put Tae's body into the air, and an agitated Granny caught her. Taking a quick glance at Lance, D remarked, "He won, didn't he?"

"I'm surprised you could tell," Granny said with a grin. "That fool Clay is laid out in the bushes over yonder. The farmer gave it to him pretty good. But Clay's not all bad, either. He fought bare-handed to the very end."

"Get everyone into the wagon. I'll stand watch," D said, his eyes on the flow of the waterfall all the while.

"You mean those two yahoos, too?"

"You can have them sleep outside if you like," D told the old woman.

"I'll do just that. Good luck with the guard duty."

As Granny carried Tae in both arms and walked unsteadily toward the wagon, Lance got up. His face was a mess. "Is she okay?" he asked.

"You needn't concern yourself with her, you useless thug. The nerve of you, going off like you're something special and getting your good-for-nothing face beat purple in a fistfight. And just so you know, I won't hear of you asking me for the day off tomorrow," Granny snarled.

Even after the old woman had vanished into the wagon with Tae, her ill-tempered remarks still hung in the air.

"It seems you beat him," the Hunter commented.

Raising his head, Lance looked at D with a strange expression on his face. He couldn't believe the young man would bother to say that to him. "Back in the old days, I was a little hellion," he said. "Besides, you can't beat a farmer barehanded. Hunters and warriors came to my village a lot, and they taught me some fighting moves, too."

"Sounds like he bit off more than he could chew," D said as he turned toward the bushes Granny had mentioned. The head of a shadowy figure was listlessly rising from them. "Was this about the girl?" D asked Lance.

"Yeah."

"You really went at it, didn't you?"

"I didn't have a choice. I couldn't just stand there and let him beat the hell out of me."

"Well, that may be a bit of welcome news," said D.

"For who?"

"There're not a lot of men who'd get their face blown up to twice its normal size for someone else. I bet the girl's never met anyone like that before. I'll tell her what happened."

"Don't bother. That's not what I had in mind," Lance said, sighing.

An arm sheathed in black was offered to the young farmer, making his eyes go wide. Grabbing it by the wrist, Lance pulled himself upright.

"So there you are, you lousy sodbuster!" Clay roared, his massive body being carried closer by an uncertain gait. When his face came into the light, it was nearly twice as swollen as Lance's. "What do you say to a rematch? I ain't taking no for an answer."

"Maybe later," Lance said, smiling for some reason.

"Shut your hole!" Clay bellowed, and he was about to grab hold of the smaller man when an arm in black restrained him. "What do you think you're doing?! Let go of me!" he shouted at the Hunter.

"Let him go, D," Lance said as he rubbed the back of his neck to loosen it up. "I thought I'd settled this once and for all, but if he hasn't given up yet, there's not much else I can do. Okay," he told Clay, "now swear to me again that if I win, you'll stay the hell away from the girl."

"No problem, and Vampire Hunter D is my witness."

The figure in black stepped away from them.

Shouting something, Clay took a swing at Lance. The warrior was stumbling over his own feet.

After ducking the blow, once Lance heard it whistle through the air above him, he rammed himself headfirst into Clay's stomach.

Ouf! With a howl more akin to an explosion, the warrior's massive form flew into the air with ease, and Clay landed on his back in the same spot by the water where Lance had been lying. The ground rumbled.

Leaping into the air, Lance slammed his elbow down on his opponent's solar plexus with the full weight of his body. Something resembling water sprayed from Clay's mouth; his body shuddered, and the battle was over.

"There won't be any more rematches."

Lance nodded at D's remark. Clay didn't move a muscle.

Getting to his feet, Lance looked down at his vanquished foe. In a matter of seconds, the same grin he'd worn moments earlier covered his face again. For although Clay's fierce countenance was contorted with pain, it was also etched with an undeniable smile.

Two hours passed.

Even the activities of the fungi might've been governed by biorhythms, for a deep blue filled the darkness and enveloped the party by the water's edge.

D set his saddle down by the campfire and rested his head on it as he reclined there. The men with the badly swollen faces lay covered by blankets a few yards away. Had the moon been out that night, it was so silent that they would've heard its beams raining down.

D mentioned the incident with the spider people to no one. His eyes were shut. The Hunter might have considered himself to be the only one they were after, or perhaps he was confident that if they attacked him there he could carve his way through them. Whatever the case, as his gorgeous form lay at rest, there was no hint of tension about him.

The wagon's door opened without a sound and Granny peered out from the driver's seat. She was about to say something to D down on the ground below when a rusty voice beat her to the punch.

"Get some sleep." Most likely, the Hunter had caught some otherwise imperceptible creak from the door.

"Well, I can't," Granny said, wearily muttering encouragement to herself as she hobbled down from the wagon and headed over to D rather nonchalantly. The jar on her hip swayed back and forth. Though she gave the impression of being fiercer and more determined than the average old lady, seeing the way she walked just then with her wrinkled cheeks and bleary eyes was like catching a glimpse of some gorgeous dancing girl's true face laid bare when the makeup comes off back in her dressing room. Surely there were nights when the crone felt an acute longing to open that fabric store.

Circling around behind D's back, she took a seat. "Have some?" she asked, thrusting a jug of liquor at his refined countenance. It was the cheap sort of fruit spirits that could be found in great quantities at the general store in any post town.

"No."

Curt as D's reply was, it was odd that it didn't seem at all intended to offend the listener.

"Oh, that's right. I must've mistaken you for someone else," Granny said. Pulling out the cork, she took a swig. Three times her throat bobbed, and after pulling the jug away, the crone wiped her lips with the back of her hand. A long sigh escaped her. "About some of the things that were said to you today—don't take it personally. And I don't just mean what I said. From what I hear, Tae had some pretty harsh things to say too, right? Well, I'd like to make up for that. Kindly accept my apologies."

"Don't worry about it."

"Honestly?" Granny said, breaking into a broad grin like a little kid. "Ah, I'm glad to hear you say that. I didn't think you were a petty man or anything, but it's still a relief. We've got a long ways to go yet. And we really are counting on you."

"You should get some sleep."

"Stop trying to get rid of me," the old woman replied. Wrapping both hands around her knees, Granny watched the endless ripples on the water's surface. "You know, don't you?" she said after some time passed. "You know about the girl—that she's pregnant. And that it's probably a Noble's baby. If someone doesn't fix it, she'll be having that kid sooner or later."

Saying nothing, D continued to lie there with his eyes closed. As to what sort of thoughts passed through his mind, no one could say. "What'll you do?" D then asked, muttering the question.

"What's this? You're actually interested in someone else's fate? I'll take her home, of course. That's my job, after all."

"In that case, you didn't need to bring it up at all."

"Well, there are times I just feel like doing or saying something funny. I bet you get the urge sometimes to just lie out in the sun and get a tan."

"She's not going to be very welcome, even back at her own home," D said, returning to the topic of Tae. "Especially not if she's going to have a Noble's baby. And she won't be able to hide that. It doesn't matter how strong anyone says she is; strength probably won't be enough to resolve this problem."

"You trying to tell me not to take her back?" Granny said in a tone charged with defiance. "Because that's the one thing I simply can't do. I've said it before, and I'll say it again—this is my job. No matter what happens later, everyone's overjoyed at first, and there's coin in it for me. What comes next—well, forget it. I'd just be repeating myself. You've already heard my spiel on the matter, and hearing it again ain't gonna make it any more interesting."

"How's her sewing?"

"She seems to have a real knack for it. She was rattling away at it earlier, too. Not that I have a clue what she's making," the old woman said. "So, what do you suppose will happen with her kid? It'll be a dhampir, won't it?"

"If it's a Noble's child."

"I was wondering if maybe you couldn't look after it . . . you being a fellow dhampir and all. You could teach it all it needs to know from the very start. I mean, you're Vampire Hunter D, after all. It's not like you couldn't afford to feed a girl and her baby. I'm sure you of all people could find some way of making a living besides being a Hunter, couldn't you?"

"Is that what you think?" D asked.

"Yes, indeed."

"Then why am I still a Hunter?"

Granny nodded gravely, as if she'd been waiting for him to say that. "Because you're too awkward. Your pride won't allow you to mix with normal people and live the slow life. That Noble blood is tricky stuff. No matter how you might bend your principles or how much you might try to accommodate the world, you couldn't allow yourself to do that. I suppose it'd take, say, a hundred years before you'd settle into it."

"Why a hundred years?"

"What I mean to say is, if they tried at it hard enough for that long, even a Noble could wind up being agreeable to their situation.

Of course, I'm not sure there'd be any guarantees where you're concerned."

"Why do you think that?"

Granny gazed at D intently. "You're out looking for something." She said this casually enough, but the words were tough as steel. "People are always making a big deal about 'Hunters this' and 'Hunters that,' but if you ask me, they're all just a bunch of muscle-bound social misfits. There's only one thing any of 'em care about—being good at killing. When it comes to the worst of the lot, the killing is the whole point of it. Some have wound up plying their skills on upstanding folks; others have been killed by fellow Hunters. Take a peek into their dreams sometime. They're all either pitch black or blood red. And out of the lot of them, there's only one word you'll never find in their heads. I'm sure you know what that is?"

"I don't know. What?"

"'Tomorrow,'" Granny said with quiet confidence. "But you have it in you. Heck, it doesn't even matter whether you think you do or not. And it doesn't even have to be the word *tomorrow* . . . it could be *dream* or hope or *rainbow* . . . or even *love*. Don't laugh. I tell you, there's a huge difference between those who're looking for something, and those who've never had it. But in your case, I get the feeling it's something altogether different."

"What do you think it is?" D asked.

"I don't know. I can't even imagine what it'd be. But you're searching for something, nonetheless. And I bet you could tell Tae's baby all about it someday, too."

The Hunter said nothing.

"You should do that. Shoot, once I've brought her home, it's no skin off my nose. Run off with her if you like. There's a girl who'd be tough enough for a life of one road trip after another. And if she wanted to settle down when the kid got older, you could go back out on the road alone. After you've seen to it that the little one has a proper 'education,' of course."

"Sorry to say it, but there's someone else far better for the job."

"Huh?" Granny said, knitting her brow as she turned around. Under a lumpy pile of blankets some way off, Lance was staring at them. "Spare me. You think a plain old farmer's cut out to handle a dhampir? I can just imagine him trying to run away in the dead of night if it went after him. Even a dhampir's real parents can't hold back its Noble blood."

While it wasn't immediately clear if he'd caught the crone's remarks of bald-faced contempt, Lance got out of his blankets and lethargically made his way over to the campfire. "I heard your conversation," he said as he gazed at the flames.

"Well, you shouldn't have," Granny said angrily. "D, you knew he was awake and you still let him listen in, didn't you?"

Of course, D kept his silence.

"I don't know about all that stuff," Lance said in a weary tone. "But I've got a feeling I'm up to it."

"Up to what?" Granny asked, her face growing pale.

"Well, you know—making a life with the girl," Lance replied, flushing madly.

"Sonny, you must still be talking in your sleep. You, a lousy little farmer of all things."

"What does the girl's family do?" D asked.

"They're farmers," Granny said, somewhat crestfallen.

"Then it doesn't sound like an odd match at all."

"That's right," Lance agreed. "Leave the baby to me. I'll help the kid find the life that suits him best."

"The world's not as simple as all that," Granny declared. "For the most part, dhampir men and women are gorgeous. As babies or even small children, they're goddamn cherubs. Heck, there's plenty of folks who'll try to get close to someone they know is a dhampir. But sooner or later, when that Noble blood shows itself the ones who buttered them up with all that sweet talk are the first ones to take to their heels. And what the blazes are those they leave behind supposed to do, eh? You'll do the same. I'm sure of it. So, stop trying to be so glib."

"That's telling him, you old hag!" another voice added nastily.

Lance and Granny turned to see Clay coming toward them.

With his hatred-filled eyes fixed on Lance, he added, "She's a lot more than a lousy sodbuster like you deserves. Before this trip's over, you'll be dead anyway. Then anybody who wants to can woo her."

"And you think you can win her heart?" Granny asked, glaring at Clay with her hard gaze until he looked away. "You might want to consult a mirror," she sneered. Granny's eyes then shifted to Clay's hip. "Say, does that weapon of yours have any use besides killing?" she asked.

"You're joking, right?" the warrior snarled back like a beast. His right hand skimmed by his hip, and an elegant note resounded. Apparently, the weapon could also be used precisely as its form suggested. "I got this beauty after killing a Noble," Clay told them. "Found it in his concert hall. Just look at her, would you? The strings are silver and the body's gold. And she plays music like you never heard before—music that's pure heaven."

"Then play something."

"Excuse me?!"

"Don't give us that sour puss," the crone said. "You've gone and got our attention. Now, why don't you play us a tune that'll tug on our heartstrings? If you can't manage that, a lullaby will do."

Clay snorted angrily. "Right. You're flat out of luck. I don't use it for useless crap like that. This little treasure keeps me alive. You think I'd play it for a bunch of scum like you?"

"Sure you wouldn't play it for *her*?" D said.

Everyone turned toward the wagon then, even Clay. A tiny figure was crouched in the driver's seat. The eyes that looked at her held so many various emotions that Tae had to divert her own gaze from them.

"You'd like to hear a tune, wouldn't you?"

The girl's pale face bobbed sharply in reply to Granny's question.

"Well?" D asked. Astonishingly enough, it almost sounded like he was ribbing the warrior.

Clay remained hesitant.

"Oh, is that how it goes? The Frontier's top warrior turns down a young lady's request? You can kill folks just fine, but can't even make one girl happy—I guess men aren't worth spit these days."

"You'll eat them words!" Clay said in response to Granny's insults. He began grinding his teeth together as his whole body trembled with rage. It wouldn't have been strange if he'd unleashed an explosion of ultrasonic waves just then. "It's really more than your grubby little ears deserve, but I'll play you one of my best songs. Just don't get so swept up by my sweet voice you go and jump in the lagoon or anything."

Granny and Lance cried out with surprise and delight and clapped their hands.

Clay's rough fingers took to the strings. It was as if the white darkness gave birth to the sounds. Granny's smirk disappeared.

The song was about a man and a woman who lived on the Frontier. The man traveled, and the woman chased along after him. And then both the man and the woman grew tired and settled down into their own lives without ever meeting each other. Long, peaceful days stretched by, and then one day the woman suddenly recalled her old love and gave up everything to follow after him.

High and low, Clay's voice flowed along the ground and danced across the sky in a way that made Granny bug her eyes. His voice was so rich, his notes so precise. The warrior had undergone a remarkable transformation into a troubadour.

Having laid the weary heroine to rest in the cold earth, Clay intoned a few words of prayer, and then halted his fingers on the harp.

The very first applause came from the farthest away. As the men gazed silently at the pale and dainty hands the girl was clapping together, they realized she was weeping.

"Damn, you're good!" Granny said in a voice perilously close to tears.

"Damn straight I am, hag! See, sodbuster?" Clay said, glaring around at the others with loathing before puffing his powerful chest out in Tae's direction. "How's that? Pretty great, wasn't it? Unlike a certain Hunter, I got more than just looks going for me. Yeah, I reckon anybody with an eye for men could tell in a flash who's the best around here. How about it, missy? Forget about going back home—oh, that's right! As long as the sodbuster's alive, I ain't supposed to woo you. Well, don't take it too hard."

And having said everything he wanted to say, the younger Bullow went right back to his blanket, pulled it up over his head, and went to sleep.

Turning to each other, Granny and Lance grinned wryly. Even Tae was smiling. Some people could prove useful in the most unexpected ways.

For a long time, no one moved or said anything.

"Why don't you get some sleep?" D finally suggested.

"I believe I will," Granny said as she got up. "You get some shut-eye, too," she told Lance. Her tone was amazingly amicable.

Lance didn't move. Though he kept staring at her, Granny said nothing more to him and climbed up to the driver's seat.

"Head inside now," the old woman told Tae.

The girl didn't move.

Granny's brow furrowed. Fine blue veins bulged to the surface. The crone then let out an exasperated sigh. Shooting Lance a look he wouldn't soon forget, she hunched her back and disappeared into the wagon.

Both hands folded neatly in her lap, Tae sat staring straight ahead. Seating himself by the fire, Lance wrapped both hands around his knees as he gazed straight ahead, too. Tae watching Lance. Lance watching Tae. The pile of logs must've collapsed, because the flames danced wildly and released a flurry of sparks.

As Lance closed one of his hands around the other, they were both trembling a bit. "Um, I . . ." he mumbled. He sounded like someone else entirely. What would come next?

The flames blazed, and Tae patiently gazed at the emaciated young man.

"Stupid bastard . . ." a jet-black voice grumbled from under the blankets.

Clay's hand crept to his harp, and then stopped suddenly. Something slim and white had zipped between his hand and the instrument, pinning his blanket to the ground. Even without seeing the finely honed tip, he knew it was a wooden needle. Rattled to his very bones by anger and horror, Clay then heard the steely voice of the one who'd hurled it.

"Human or dhampir, no one knows what's going to happen."

Lance turned to D in astonishment. In the Hunter's words he'd heard the very thing he'd been struggling to say. *I want to spend my life with you.* An almost heartbreaking decisiveness surfaced on his face, and he headed toward the wagon.

D's eyes thrust open and caught a glimpse of ripples on the water's surface. Black as the darkness, the Hunter jumped up. Something whizzed loudly through the air, and whatever it was then spattered black blood all around him.

A cry of pain arose nearby.

When D looked back, Lance was pinned on the ground with what looked like a black spear protruding from his chest. The body of it stretched back to the lagoon, painting a gentle yet disturbing parabola that sank back into the water at one end. There was no mistaking what it was—a tentacle tipped with steel.

Melody of Destruction

CHAPTER 6

I

L ance!" two people called out at once. One was Tae, leaping down from the driver's seat. The other was Clay, who threw off a blanket that'd been run through as well.

Several tentacles that'd been severed by D squirmed away, but new ones shot from the water's surface, stretching for the Hunter, Tae, and Clay.

Forgetting her own fear, Tae raced to Lance's side, but the tentacle that had impaled him instantly wrapped around the girl's body. Assailed by the agony of being bound tight with steel cable, Tae could barely scream, let alone breathe. But the second it jerked her toward the lake, a figure in black blew in like a veritable gale and severed the tentacle.

Zing! Zing! Zing! Tentacles continued to tear through the air to attack the group.

"Get in the wagon," D said, lending Lance his shoulder as he gave Tae a shove.

Lance convulsed. The tentacle piercing his chest thrashed fiercely despite the fact that it'd been cut off. The naked blade flashed out once more, slicing off its tip and putting an end to its movements.

"Cover your ears and hit the dirt!" Clay shouted.

For a moment, there was nothing—and then the most exquisite melody filled the night air.

They watched. All of the fiendish limbs whirring through the air broke apart, reduced to shattered fragments, and then faded before they reached the ground. Not only that, but the rocks of the waterfall, the trees on the opposite shore, and even the now-frothy water disappeared, robbed of their molecular bonds.

Perhaps unable to take any more of this, what remained of the tentacles retreated into the water. There would be no further attacks from them.

Clay's harp was truly something to be feared. If the sonic waves of death were only focused in an extremely narrow kill zone and not capable of being directed with an ease that was itself terrifying, then a monster moving as fast as the wind might be able to avoid them. However, the slightest touch by a single finger of the warrior's hand would send the deadly melody out at anything within listening range. Who could possibly defend themselves from ultrasonic waves that fanned out from the instrument, breaking virtually any material down to its constituent atoms?

"What in blazes is it?!" Granny cried as she flew out of the vehicle. Trusting Tae and Lance to the old woman, D hopped onto his horse. Clay followed after him.

"We're getting out of the woods. Follow me."

Leaving only his words behind, D galloped off. The wind snarled in his wake, but a second later, the strangest thing happened. All around them the light rapidly faded. Even the glowing fungi were under the desert's control.

Abandoning the path they'd come by, D shot straight through the forest. Throwing up a cloud of dust, the wagon and Clay followed close behind.

"D, where are we going?" Granny shouted shrilly from the driver's seat.

But the old woman's query was quickly obscured by Clay as he cried, "Here they come!"

When Granny took a peek in her omni-directional safety mirror, her hair stood on end. Once more the surface of the water had grown rough, and tentacles began to rise from its depths. Beyond numbering, together they looked like a single gigantic tree.

Every detail then vanished from sight for all of them. Darkness had claimed the world.

"Dammit! I can't see anything!" Clay howled.

"Tae," Granny shouted, "break out the glow bugs!"

Scant seconds later, a dazzling circle of light gave a bluish glow to the back window of the wagon and its surroundings—yet the light wasn't strong enough to reach D's back as he rode ahead of them.

Could D tell the way out in the pitch blackness? His super-keen dhampir senses could. D had noticed an imperceptible sound coming from above him. He sensed that it was silently descending. Before the spider person had a chance to bring a blade down on D's head, he sliced its torso in two. The Hunter's steel blade cut through the air in an arc, knocking back a number of would-be attackers on either side. They made not a sound, as their deaths were instantaneous.

"They're coming from above us!"

D's words were replaced by the roar of a gun and its fiery trail, and something heavy seemed to be blown off the wagon. There was a repulsive thud near one of the tires, and then an ear-splitting scream arose from the same area.

Tae had her arm out the rear window of the wagon, holding the light-giving glow bugs out to guide Clay, when suddenly long, insect-like fingers grabbed her hand from above. Despite her screams, the fingers tightened their iron grip. The glow bugs fell.

Thunder shook the vehicle's interior. The bullet of iron that had punched through the roof ripped open the spider man's abdomen and hurled him off into the darkness.

"Lance!" Tae cried. Forgetting the pain of her red and swollen hand, she latched onto the young man, who still held a gun in one hand.

His pale face smiling above a blood-soaked torso, Lance asked, "Are you okay?"

"Yes."

"Don't worry . . . I'll always be here . . . to protect you . . ."

"I know you will," Tae replied, tears spilling from her eyes. Just then, she heard a jubilant cry from Granny that sounded miles away.

"There's the way out!"

A pale gray light enveloped the world. D was in the lead, but the wagon was close behind, seeming to pounce like some gigantic animal as it bounded out into the moonlight. The horses' hooves and wagon wheels sank into sand.

"Yahoo! We're out!" Granny exclaimed, smacking the floor of the driver's seat with one hand. Tightly gripping the reins with the other, she prepared to apply the brakes.

"Keep moving!" a low voice urged her, though she had no idea how it drifted all the way back to her from some twenty feet ahead.

"Bu . . . Bu . . . But . . ." the old woman stammered. Before she could finish asking why, an unbelievable scream arose from inside her wagon. "Tae?!"

The door opened and the girl burst out. Her hands and bosom were bright red with fresh blood.

"What's wrong?" the old woman asked.

"It's the forest—the forest!"

"The forest?!" Granny exclaimed, the earth-shattering news shaping her expression.

The forest wasn't shrinking in the distance. Rather, it was getting closer. The whole expanse of trees headed toward them like a wave of epic proportions.

"D, is this another mirage?"

"No. It's real," D said as he rode beside them.

"You don't say," Granny replied with a grin. "In that case, I should be able to deal with it, too."

Shifting the reins to her left hand, the old woman went for the jar on her hip with her right—the source of the same insane power that'd wiped out the sand people in a heartbeat out in the desert.

What sort of picture would the sand from her jar paint?

Knees far apart, Granny pulled her hand back out of the jar. Beautiful colors poured smoothly from her tightly balled fist before spreading across the floor of the wagon. Granny gave a series of small shakes to her hand. But just what sort of unearthly rite were her five fingers working as they held that sand? Flowing steady and unbroken like a thread, the sand seemed unaffected by the motion of the vehicle, or else it incorporated the jolts into its design. Though somewhat fuzzy, the image that formed at the crone's feet was clearly something that existed in this world. It was, in fact, the very forest that was coming up behind them now.

Granny's hand halted. The picture was complete. Now all she had to do was—

It was at that moment that the door behind her opened.

"Mrs. Viper—" Tae said, her face pale. "Clay's been left back in the woods!"

Granny whipped around. "How the blazes did that happen?"

"I, um . . . I dropped the glow bugs. Then after a while, I couldn't hear him behind us anymore . . ."

"Damnation!" Granny growled, grinding her teeth together.

The edge of the forest was following less than twenty yards behind them.

"That bastard Clay. Do you suppose he's dead?" Granny shouted to D.

"I don't know."

"He's dead. I'm sure of it."

"No," D said with a look over his shoulder.

Following his lead, Granny stopped breathing. Perhaps she caught the faintest of sounds.

A black spot suddenly appeared in the otherwise unbroken wall of tree trunks, and from it bounded a figure on horseback. Wildly kicking up sand, the rider chased along after them.

Now out in the moonlight, Clay was licking his lips. And then suddenly the warrior's body lurched wildly forward. His horse had caught its leg on something! As the beast nosed into the ground with a great cloud of dust, Clay sailed over its head, curling himself up in a ball. Amazingly, he landed on his feet when he hit the ground.

The way he straightened smoothly from the landing was superbly acrobatic. However, instead of lauding his feat, the forest behind him merely continued its silent advance.

There was no time to make a dash for his cyborg horse. Clay's right hand grasped his harp, but no matter how far and wide the deadly sounds could fly from his weapon, the warrior was up against a vast forest that was miles across. The strings twanged. The number of trees that disappeared must've been in the hundreds . . . but that wasn't enough.

Clay watched absentmindedly as the wall of colossal trees loomed over him. But even in the depths of his despair, he managed to hear something running up behind him, as only the greatest of the Frontier's warriors might. Even before he knew for sure it was the low rumble of hoofbeats, he'd launched himself into the air. He had no idea as to the distance or speed of the rider—well-honed instinct was all he had to rely on. But that was enough to put the warrior's massive frame squarely on the back of D's horse after the Hunter's sudden stop and complete change of direction. By the time the shadow of the forest swallowed the spot Clay had previously occupied, the cyborg horse had galloped forty feet ahead.

"Looks like that's another one I owe you," Clay said, baring his teeth. The words had been a groan of pure hatred.

"Save your thanks for Granny."

"How's that?"

"She told me to go save you," said D.

"Sheesh. What an old busybody."

In a matter of seconds, their horse was alongside the wagon.

"The forest is picking up speed," Granny shouted to the two men.

"We can't outrun it," Clay said, gnashing his teeth. A second later, his eyes went wide.

The wagon had engaged its emergency brake. At the same time, D halted as well.

"What the hell do you think you're doing?!" Clay stammered, foam flying from his mouth.

Grinning at him, Granny said, "Just you wait and see. Watch what I can do!"

The weird sand painting at Granny's feet was still completely intact. While it wasn't all that large, Clay could still make it out clearly in the moonlight. Knitting his brow, he looked to the rear—at the vast forest pursuing them. That's what her picture was. The pattern that had emerged on the ground was the moon and a desert and a forest—the very same forest rolling after them to swallow them all.

Clay forgot all about taking flight. No matter how they struggled, victory seemed impossible. In seemingly impossible cases, he'd normally flee without a backward glance. That was the way Clay was. The only way he and his brother had remained alive and famous for so long was by avoiding futile battles. But now Clay was caught in a raging storm of desire to see the old woman work her magic with his own eyes, a desire that suppressed even the strongest of human urges—that of self-preservation.

Without a sound, a mountainous shadow hid the stars. The chain of enormous trees bearing down on them was like some demonic beast. Clay's field of view was far wider than that of an ordinary person, and it now held two spectacles: Granny, and the forest.

The old woman leaned far forward. Her tiny chest swelled to nearly twice its normal size. She'd taken a deep breath. And then, with all the force of a bent fire-dragon bone snapping back into shape, the old woman leaned forward in the driver's seat and violently expelled the breath in her lungs through her pursed lips. Scattering dazzling colors in the moonlight, the sand painting blew away, and a cry of astonishment slipped from Clay's mouth.

Now bending forward from the overwhelming mass of the vast forest behind them, the foremost rank of trees was suddenly touched with a blinding iridescence, and a second later they had utterly vanished, like dust driven before a mighty gale.

All around D and Clay—the latter of whom sat dumbfounded on the back of the Hunter's steed—glittering particles of light drifted down from the sky. While Clay realized they were the grains of sand that Granny had scattered, he didn't even have the strength to hold his hand out to catch some.

The desert lay flat in the moonlight. It all seemed like a dream.

"Oww," Granny moaned, pounding on the small of her back up in the driver's seat. Her voice sounded weary, and her face looked strangely exhausted. "That was a heck of a thing to be doing at my age! Would it be okay if we took a breather, D?"

"Your wagon has an autopilot setting, doesn't it?"

"You're a heartless one, you know that? You want an old lady like me at death's door up here bumping along like no one's business? My wagon's controls aren't really in the best condition, either. Left to its own devices, there's no telling where this thing may end up."

"That forest was just a sample to test our strength. We didn't hurt the desert that badly. It'll attack us again."

Apparently grasping the situation well enough, Granny reluctantly said, "Okay already," and nodded.

Just then, Tae came out of the vehicle. Her eyes were puffy. She looked just like a fairy who'd come bearing ominous tidings.

"What is it?" asked Granny.

"Lance is dead," Tae said in a firm tone.

II

It took less than thirty minutes to make the small mound of sand. As everyone stood in a circle around it, D took a steel pipe that'd been in the wagon and stuck it in the center of the mound.

"Kind of a strange shape for a grave marker, isn't it?" Granny said dubiously.

A little bit above the center, the long metal pole had a shorter piece strapped perpendicularly with cord. No one there noticed the change in D's expression when he took the marker in his hand. Like a shadow of pain, the palm of his hand was seared and bruised in the same shape as the pipes.

"Never seen one like that before," Granny said, her eyes staring off into the distance. "No, that's not entirely true," she added. "A long, long time ago I think I saw one somewhere in a distant land . . . Now, what the blazes was it? A Noble's grave?"

D gave a small but firm shake of his head.

"Well, isn't someone gonna say a prayer for him?" Granny asked with her hands on her hips. "I'm not really good at that myself. Didn't even say one when my husband died. Too gloomy for me. Would somebody else do it?"

"What's it matter?" Clay said, shrugging his shoulders. And then, staring intently at the grave, he added, "The dolt. Went and died before we could have another rematch. You know, five minutes after we leave, no one will even know this is here," he said, spitting in disgust.

Looking at D, Granny said, "I don't suppose there's any chance a dhampir would know a prayer for a funeral either. So, what are we to do?"

"I'll do it," Tae offered.

"Oh, my—I nearly forgot the most important person. That'll be fine. He sure was devoted to you. That'd be the best memorial he could ever hope for," Granny said, and her tone made it clear her heart was in those words.

In truth, they would've been better off sticking to D's earlier plan and leaving immediately. Their first consideration was making it to the edge of the desert as soon as possible, but not one of them mentioned that. D had carried Lance's body from the wagon, and Clay had dug the hole. While they worked, Tae and Granny kept their eyes on the men every second, as if it was the least they could do.

Taking a few steps closer to the grave marker, Tae wrapped her arms around her own shoulders. Her voice was somewhat indistinct.

We hereby commit our beloved
Into the eternal rest of Thy kingdom,
Into the dreams of Thy gentle arms . . .

The verse broke there. Tae squinted her eyes as she tried to remember. Her frail body shook, but no words came out.

"I've forgotten how it goes," Tae said in a hoarse voice. "It's funny. I used to say my prayers every morning without fail when I was back in the Nobles' castle. I wonder why I can't remember it now."

Something glittered on its way down the girl's cheek. Before it had reached her jaw, D's rusty voice continued her prayer.

Neither great nor small are we;
Off into the distance we go, only to be born again,
And thus are we called the far wanderers . . .

Shifting her line of sight, Tae saw the Vampire Hunter through hazy eyes.

No one moved.

The wind and the moonlight alone flowed around them, disturbing the surface of the sandy mound ever so slightly. Sand coursed smoothly down the slopes. Suddenly, the flow of sand became heavier, and various shapes began to rise from the otherwise flat surface.

Though we wander the earth seeking Thee,
No answers are we given,
Naught but shadows do we see in this troubled world . . .

Behind the stationary figures, other forms moved. Like ghosts walking across the bottom of a lake, they swayed to and fro as they approached. Whether the group noticed them or not was unclear. D didn't move. Clay and Granny both kept their positions by the grave. The wind blew a bit of sand from the shoulders of those drawing ever nearer.

D's voice remained as soft as ever.

Yet we know not fear;
The words of silence are known to us,
And as we see the unseen,

We are Thee and Thou art us.
This far wanderer we now commit to Thee.

The moonlight became a blade that danced out. The sand men who challenged D broke apart, each being cleanly bisected, while the others collapsed before a melody strummed beneath the crescent moon.

Silence descended.

"Well, that didn't take them all of thirty seconds!" Granny said as she pushed Tae toward the wagon.

D turned around. Clay did, too.

New figures were being born of the sands.

"This is crazy!" Clay exclaimed in a voice that choked with fear for the first time. The warrior's self-confidence had crumbled; he realized that these new figures were actually just revived versions of the sand men they had just defeated.

Shapes flowed from the sand like water, encircling the party.

"So, the desert is evolving, too," D muttered.

"Time for fun. I'll blast every stinking one of them to smith-ereens!" Clay shouted, all five of his fingers tugging at the instrument's strings.

"D, someone's coming!" Granny called out as she sat in the driver's seat with one arm extended.

"Bro!" Clay shouted, but he seemed surprised by something as he froze.

Following the younger Bullow's lead, the sand men also watched the rider approaching from beyond the dunes. There was no telling where he'd been or what he'd been doing, but the sleeping man that swayed there on the back of his horse was the very same Bingo as always. Perhaps his outlandish appearance frightened the desert, because the sand men froze in their tracks. But soon enough, several of them headed toward this new foe.

"Damn! Get in the wagon!" Clay shouted. "You'll be wiped out!"

Not understanding what that was supposed to mean, but goaded by the urgency with which he'd bellowed it, Granny and Tae dove into the wagon.

"Shit! It's too late now," Clay clucked, waving both hands at his older brother. "Stop, Bingo! It's me!"

Whether or not the older Bullow heard him was unclear, but a second later, spheres that sparkled like foam on the water issued from Bingo's mouth. While they may have resembled soap bubbles, the effect they had was beyond anyone's wildest imaginings. The bubbles shattered right in front of the sand men shambling toward him. For a short time there was no change at all in the sand men, but seconds later their bodies began to look incredibly blurry, and then they were suddenly gone.

At that moment, D had the weirdest sensation. Somehow, it felt like the moment one awakens from a dream.

Once more, the group stood squarely in the middle of silence.

"Hey, bro . . ." Clay said, his tone as muddled as if he'd just woken up.

Not replying to the cry from his younger brother right away, Bingo was swaying back and forth in the saddle, but his face suddenly jerked up. Looking and sounding refreshed, he said, "So, you're still with them?" And as he stared in D's direction, his eyes were once again filled with the lethargy of the bizarre sleeper.

When Bingo asked if his brother was still with them, it was probably just another way of saying, "Why haven't you killed the Hunter yet?" Judging by the way Clay grew pale, his brother was reproaching him.

Turning his vacant gaze to D, Bingo said, "Seems you folks have been looking after my brother."

D was silent. His longsword remained in its sheath. Perhaps he assumed no enemies would be coming because Bingo had destroyed them all.

"Suppose I could join your merry band?" Bingo said, his face aimed at the ground as he gave a light kick to his horse's flanks. It looked like something a drunk would do. The mount staggered over to the group. Even the sleeper's horse had a funny gait.

"Another unwelcome guest," Granny snorted. At some point, she'd poked her head out over the driver's seat. "Haven't lost your food and water, have you? Because we don't have any to spare."

"My brother don't need food or water," Clay said with a smirk. "He gets them someplace else."

"That's just fine, then. At any rate, what do we do now, D?" asked Granny. "It looks to me like this blasted desert is even stronger than before. At this rate, we'll never get of here."

"We'll finish it off," D said succinctly.

"How?"

"Someone tried something like this on me before. I'll beat this the same way I once did."

"And how was that?"

"The day will break soon," D said as he looked to the sky in what seemed to be the east. "Until it does, we'll head back to the southwest."

"Southwest?" Granny asked, her head cocked to one side. But her eyes soon went wide. "You mean toward that cloud of dust . . . that sandstorm? Tell me you're joking because—"

Before the crone could finish saying there was no way in hell she'd be following suit, Bingo stopped her. "Right on the money," he said in a tone as vast as the universe.

"Did you see it?" D asked.

"You bet," the elder Bullow replied. "And we ought to put this thing down real quick."

Straddling his horse, D said, "Let's go."

"You're a lost cause, you know that? Never listen to a thing anyone says," Granny muttered. "Remind me of my husband. In the end, he took off one day and never did come back."

"Did you try to stop him?" asked D.

"Nope," the old woman replied, slowly shaking her head from side to side as she jerked on the reins.

A few glances fell on the sandy grave—from D, Clay, and the old woman. Right before they disappeared beyond the dunes, the pale blossom of a face peered sadly from the back window of the covered wagon. And then a wind from nowhere in particular carried a cloud of sand that covered the tiny cross and made the deceased a permanent resident of the desert.

III

The light of dawn revealed a high wall of sand that extended thousands of feet into the heavens. Back on the ground, D halted his horse when a spray of grains began to strike his cheeks. The sandstorm was less than a mile away.

"Wait here," the Hunter said as he turned his back on the party.

"I wasn't about to go into that thing," Granny said, a gloomy look in her eyes as she sat in the driver's seat. "Don't know what you'll find there, but I'm sure you'll probably be back safe and sound, right?"

"Wait twelve hours. If I don't come back, use one of your sand paintings to erase the sandstorm. You can do that, can't you?"

Granny looked at D for a second with apparent surprise, and then quickly pursed her lips as if angry. "Sure, and wipe you right out with it." No sooner had she spoken than she grew pale and added, "But you'd better come back. Without you, I don't know how we'd ever get out of this place. If you think it's getting too dangerous, remind yourself you have a duty to protect a weak old woman and a girl and turn yourself right around. We're still counting on you."

"They'll protect you," D said, looking back at the warrior brothers.

The sight of the two grown men straddling a single horse surpassed amusing and went right into disturbing. There was nothing else they could do, however, as Granny refused to let Clay sit up front with her—mainly because she didn't want him anywhere near Tae.

"But what's inside the sandstorm?"

"I don't know," D replied.

"You don't know, but you're going there anyway? Guess us mere mortals just can't figure what goes through a dhampir's mind."

"When we were going to cut through it before, Tae led us off to the forest," D said as he turned toward the sandstorm.

"You know, you're right," Granny said.

"Most likely, it didn't want us going in there."

"Why not?" asked the old woman.

"That's what I'm going to find out."

Without any words of parting, D advanced into the wind on his horse. After the Hunter had gone fifteen or twenty feet, Bingo came chasing after him and pulled up on his right side—apparently he'd left Clay behind. Considering which hand D used to wield his weapon, the warrior could've easily been cut down there and he'd have no one to blame but himself. Was it merely carelessness on his part, or was he confident he wouldn't suffer that fate? And just what was that bizarre talent for disintegrating things he'd displayed the night before?

Bingo hadn't mentioned that he'd be accompanying the Hunter, nor did he even look at D. While they rode along with a scant three feet between them, neither of them seemed to take any notice of the other. In no time at all, a golden veil of sand and dust shut them in. The sun vanished. It was impossible to see more than a yard ahead of them with the naked eye. Yet through that storm the pair of riders silently advanced.

"My kid brother told me what happened," Bingo said in a sleepy tone. "Seems you saved his life twice now. I'd like to thank you for that."

D said nothing.

"It was the desert that was out to get us, wasn't it?"

"That's right," D said in a rare response. "How did you know?"

"I saw it in a dream," Bingo replied, his voice clearly audible despite the whipping winds. "In my dreams, I saw the desert's dreams. You know, that's where our true intentions come out."

"How about my dreams?" the Hunter asked.

"I'll have to pass on yours. I don't exactly feel like going crazy at my age."

Just what did the elder Bullow mean by that?

"Doesn't seem like anything's lying in wait for us," Bingo said in a tone that suggested he wasn't bothered by the lack of reaction from D. "And after we took the trouble of riding all this way. I wonder if the desert might've changed its mind? Or does it just know what lies ahead for us?" Bingo said, but the howls of the wind scrubbed away his words.

The two riders then kept silent and let the snarling wind tear at the edges of their clothes as they advanced through the golden dust. And then, before they knew it, a shape darker than the hue of the sands came into view up ahead. Neither of the men seemed bothered by it as they advanced.

The wind sideswiping them seemed to strip away the very same yellow curtain it had raised, as desolate ruins stretched all around the riders. And what a wealth of structures this place boasted—even in the midst of a wicked sandstorm. There were vast streets and intricately carved columns. The scattered remains of mysterious machines—parts of some gigantic mechanism perhaps—stretched on forever, fading into the far reaches of the cloud of dust.

Taking a paved road neither end of which they could see, they crossed a bridge that was on the verge of collapsing. At some point, Bingo let his horse fall a length behind D's. The elder Bullow probably realized which of them knew where he was going.

After traveling down a corridor laced with a spider web of cracks, they suddenly came to a magnificent valley. This land where merciless dust clouds ran wild now opened a gaping maw, and from what appeared to be the bottomless darkness a resilient object that looked like a conglomeration of massive crystals stretched to the heavens. The girth of the various crystals only increased as they stretched higher. The strange disproportion of these objects indelibly stamped both the purpose and consequences of their creation in what could only be described with a single adjective—disturbing.

From the depths of the earth there spilled a pale light. It was alive.

At the edge of the earth, D gazed in silence at the crystalline mountain. Whatever sort of thoughts D had as he looked out at the scene couldn't be read in his elegant features.

"Is that it?" Bingo called out from ten feet behind the Hunter.

"You said you saw it in a dream—was this it?"

"Yep." His reply was gummy with sleep and fatigue. "It had some crazy idea about combining humans and Nobility, of all things. Even after the research center here fell into ruin, the machines kept going, and they let the things they made run loose in the desert. Can't say I blame the thing for wanting to get smarter."

Almost as if in response to Bingo's explanation, the light in the depths of the earth grew stronger.

Long before, forbidden experiments had been conducted in the vast region guarded by the sandstorm. Regardless of what the results might've been, time marched on cruelly, and unbeknownst to anyone the abandoned machinery produced a child beyond anything they could have intended.

What did D think of the desert having a will, or the reason it sought to evolve even further? His gorgeous visage clouded darkly from the incessantly blowing sand and glowed mysteriously with the light rising from deep in the earth.

"What now?" asked Bingo.

Saying nothing, D got off his horse. In his left hand he carried a rolled-up blanket. The wind echoed through the heavens. Taking a knife from his pocket, he bent over and began digging up the ground.

The actions that followed were most likely beyond the comprehension of Bingo, who watched the Hunter from behind. But then, in this condition there was really no telling whether Bingo was awake or asleep, and perhaps the daydreaming warrior never had any intention of watching D at all.

Once he'd dug up enough earth to fill both arms, D opened the blanket. A bundle of thick, twisted branches spilled out—no doubt procured back in the moving forest. Taking two of the logs in hand, D rubbed them together lightly until they produced flames. Throwing them down on the dirt and adding the remaining wood, D then held his left hand up to the flames. The knife in his right hand flashed across the opposite wrist. Fresh blood gushed out like a torrent, falling on the flames and the dark earth so that a strange black smoke billowed from them.

"Is that enough?" D asked.

"I suppose that will do," a hoarse voice somewhere around D's left wrist replied.

That same hand rose high into the air. And as soon as it did, a howling wind twisted all around the young man in black. Sand and dust dancing wildly, the smoke and flames stretched long and thin and perilously close to snapping. Then, finally, they did snap right off. The flames flowed into a single stream of a color that defied description. The palm of D's outstretched left hand swallowed the stream—not only the flames, but the earth that'd tasted his blood, as well.

Earth, wind, fire, and water—all four elements had been assembled. In less than three seconds the strange suction ended. It seemed to have some significance to D, as he then walked over to the rim of the crack in the earth. His horse whinnied and backed away. Arriving at the edge of the precipitous drop, D pulled out a knife with his left hand.

In his mind, something spoke to him and asked: *Are you going to do it?*

The Hunter drew his left hand back behind his head.

A gleaming sphere poked halfway out of Bingo's mouth.

How I've waited for this day so very long. The whole reason I attacked you was because I thought you might put me to rest.

D stopped moving. The prismatic sphere leisurely approached his head.

"Why don't you put yourself at rest?" the Hunter asked.

I tried, but I could not, even though it was what I wished. The temptation to rise again was simply too great. You must tell me, am I the only one who finds it so?

D bent back at the waist. The globe burst without a trace.

Tell me. Everyone wishes to be something else, don't they? Even when they know that it would involve incredible pain and weariness.

D's knife became a flash of light flying through the air.

Don't they?

The flash of light disappeared, swallowed up by part of the crystal forest.

Without pause, D mounted his horse.

"Is that the end of it?" Bingo inquired in a vague tone.

Giving no reply, D began to slowly ride away. After his mount had taken three steps, what sounded like a sigh could be heard from the hole at his back. Seven steps and one part of the crystals gave off a pale glow. Ten steps and the glow became points of light that collapsed into the crystal with a serene sound. After this, nothing more could be heard. Perhaps that's how ruin was. Thousands and then tens of thousands of cracks raced through the glittering mass. Countless fragments formed, and then collapsed.

The two figures slowly riding away didn't flinch. Needless to say, they didn't look back, either.

Two hours after Granny and Clay looked around in amazement at the suddenly abating sandstorm, D and Bingo returned.

"It's finished, isn't it?" Granny asked. "If it's a regular desert now, we should have no problem. Another two days and we'll be across it. It looks like we'll somehow make our arrival date after all. Well, then, let's get a move on!" the old woman cried, pulling on her reins. Her team of four cyborg horses began tearing up the ground.

"Somebody up there must like that guy," Clay grumbled as he climbed on the horse behind his older brother. "Of course, since he had you with him, bro, there was never any question he'd be okay." Only after he'd said it did he seem to realize the contradiction in that logic; he could do no more than don an odd expression.

D rode by the brothers and asked, "Why did you stop what you were doing back there?"

His question dwindled in the distance, but in the end, Bingo never replied.

Three days later, in the early morning, the party entered the town of Barnabas.

"Well, this is where we say our goodbyes. Really, the only reason we made it this far was thanks to all of you. I could thank you a million times. Hey, you come out here, too," the absurdly jubilant Granny called back to Tae from the driver's seat.

D rode on without saying a word. Right behind him was Bingo on his horse, and Clay—who, not surprisingly, had climbed down to the ground.

"What, you boys going already?" asked the old woman. "I was just about to go deliver the girl to her home. Say, before I do, why don't we have ourselves a drink?"

Clay alone looked back at her. When he saw the figure that lingered by Granny's side like a white bloom, his ferocious face was suffused by a wondrous peace.

Perhaps noticing him, Tae lowered her head a bit.

Cupping his hand by his mouth, Clay coarsely shouted, "Hey, missy! I'll be seeing you! It was a fun trip. Oh, and Granny—I'll be sure to pay you back for making him go rescue me that time."

"Okay, but I'm not gonna hold my breath waiting on it," Granny said, both her voice and form dwindling in the distance, as did the form of the girl by her side. No one noticed that the girl watched the back of that black long coat for ages, her eyes hinting that it was the most dazzling thing she'd ever seen.

Wasting no time, D rode down one of the main streets and dismounted in front of a three-story building five blocks away. There was no sign of the Bullow Brothers; the town of Barnabas had a population of twenty-five hundred. As far as the buildings went, most were made of wood. Only after D had disappeared through a doorway did the first hopeless sighs escape from the dazed women who stood paralyzed in various parts of the street.

Just inside the door was a staircase, and to the right of the stairs hung a brass plaque engraved with the names of tenants.

Room 202: Thornton Law Offices. A black-gloved hand rapped on the door in question, and it opened right away. A young lady—apparently the secretary—froze there with her lipstick-rimmed mouth agape.

"Oh, don't mind her—c'mon in!" a voice the Hunter had heard before called from beyond the entryway.

Gently pushing the woman aside, D slipped through the waiting room and opened the door.

The room was of moderate size. Behind the desk by the window sat Thornton, a sullen look on his face. "Welcome. Right on time. But what else should I expect from Vampire Hunter D?" The lawyer offered his hand, but then reconsidered and withdrew it. Many Hunters avoided shaking hands. It was a precaution against being caught off-guard.

"Tell me what I want to hear," D said softly.

Thornton's condition had been that he cross the desert and reach this location by a designated time—which was this morning. Now it was time to collect on the other half of the bargain.

"You aren't going to ask how I was able to get here before you?" asked Thornton.

"No," the Hunter replied, "Although there aren't many who can operate a flyer."

The lawyer nodded, saying, "I happen to be one of them, though. So, how was your trip?"

"Where did you meet him?" asked D.

"You should ask him that yourself."

For the first time a hue of emotion surfaced on D's face. "Where is he?"

"He's in a certain run-down house on the southern edge of town. A long time ago, it was a Noble's mansion. It's all overgrown with weeds, but it seems he chooses his lodging based less on present appearances, and more on past glories. He should be sleeping at this hour."

D turned around.

"Wait. I was merely conveying a message for him. Nobility or not, he is my client, you know. Why did he have you cross the desert?" Thornton asked, but his words merely crumbled as they met D's back.

As the secretary watched him go, her mouth dropped open once more.

Thirty minutes later, the Vampire Hunter showed up at the dilapidated mansion. Across from the entrance, where even the bronze had crumbled with age, lay a hall as vast as the sea.

"Watch yourself," his left hand said. "He's here. I can feel him."

And, almost as if to overshadow that remark, a solemn voice said, *So glad you could make it.*

The source of that comment was clear. Halfway up the grand staircase that curved into the feeble darkness from the far end of the hall there stood a ghostly figure.

Crossing that desert was to be a trial for you. Not one of combat. What you witnessed was the end of something.

There was a flash from D's left hand, and three streaks of white light zipped through the black figure. As the rough wooden needles were swallowed by the darkness behind him, the figure smiled silently.

What did you see? What did you think? What of your own future? Do you still intend to subject yourself to day after merciless day of this? Do you not yearn for a life of peace?

D ran without making a sound. The rotten boards couldn't take the impact of a pebble, but as D dashed across them he didn't leave a single footprint. The Hunter cleared the first twenty stairs in just two bounds. He sprang—then slashed.

As the blade came straight down from above, the figure made no attempt to dodge it, but simply let it come. The blow passed through him without meeting any resistance.

This is your answer, then? Very well. That is what makes you my only success. But so long as you embrace that fate, death will ever cast its shadow over you.

Once again, D's blade shot up from below, slicing the steel banister in two.

"It's no use," the voice in his left hand said. "This is just some residual image from the past. Quit it already."

The shadowy figure leisurely receded up the staircase.

About to follow him, D was suddenly struck by a strange sensation—like he had just awoken from a dream. A single bound took him down the staircase, and the world grew hazy. Now D was in a dream. If the dreamer awoke, it would all disappear. The power to manipulate dreams was truly incredible.

D's left hand stretched out before him. A black line shot out toward the door. Even that rectangular region was distorted, but the instant it burst open to reveal blue sky, the door returned to reality.

Leaping out into the overgrown garden, D looked over his shoulder. The house behind him suddenly vanished, and a few prismatic orbs of light drifted toward him. Dreams. The orbs themselves were purely dreams. Anything they touched turned to dreams and faded away.

The black thread snagged a globe of light in midair. A second later, D drove his blade into the stain spreading across the surface of the globe, and the substance of the dream shattered to pieces.

"Outstanding!" a sleepy voice could be heard to say from the overgrown grass. As the swaying figure got to his feet, his legs wobbled unsteadily.

"Where's your brother?" asked D.

"In a saloon."

"Who put you up to this?"

"Didn't you know already?" Bingo said drowsily.

His body was pierced by a needle that scorched through the air, and then vanished as it still jutted from his flesh.

"When I dream, I am a dream," Bingo told the Hunter, laughing in his sleep.

Being real, D couldn't carve up a dream; at that moment Bingo was essentially immortal.

"I put a hole in your dream," D said softly.

Thin flakes of dark red fell like dust from his opponent's chest. The black lines that had flown from the Hunter's left hand were thin trails of blood.

"Shall we do this another day?" Bingo said calmly. As he slept, his serenity only seemed natural. "You can name the time."

"I'll leave that to you," D replied.

"Okay. Early tomorrow morning, then. Dawn is at four o'clock. So, right here at three-thirty."

"Why don't you make it during the day?" the Hunter inquired.

"Why don't you cut me down right here and now?"

The guard on D's longsword clicked home as the Hunter sheathed his weapon.

Pointing a slowly swaying hand in the direction of town, Bingo said, "I'll be in a bar called El Capitan all day long. Stop by if you like."

Night came. The wind that had been blowing out into the desert changed directions, carrying the grains of sand back to town. As they struck the windows and wooden fences, they made a lonesome hum. It was a melancholy sound both for those it saw off on departure and those it welcomed back on arrival.

It was late that night that Granny Viper called on D as he slept in the overgrown garden of a mansion. He ended up there after the hotel had refused to give him a room.

"Tae didn't come by, did she?"

Those were the very first words out of the old woman's mouth, after she'd called out to D in a shrill voice and followed his voice back to him.

"If she didn't come with you, then she's not here."

Granny sighed dejectedly. "A fine mess this is. Running off the very same day she gets here, the little fool." The old woman took a seat on the ground. Her shoes were white with dust. There was no light save that of the moon.

"What happened?"

According to what Granny told D in answer to his question, when the girl called on her brother and his wife, things didn't go so well. Her sister-in-law heaped abuse on her, determined from the very start to drive her away. *You're the Nobility's plaything,* she'd sneered. *Why couldn't you have just died somewhere along the way? It was my mother-in-law and father-in-law that asked them to look for you, not me. If you hang around, they'll burn our house down.* Tae's older brother said nothing as he simply watched his sister walk away.

"There's no reason to be so upset," D told the crone. "You must've imagined this would happen. Besides, your job is done when you deliver someone."

"That's true," Granny said, shrugging her shoulders. "But, you see, even *I* worry about what becomes of my merchandise from time to time. Why, I even swung by the saloon and asked those boys if they'd seen her. Well, I don't know about the older one, but the younger one ran out like I'd lit a fire under him. He's probably still looking for her now."

"If she comes by, I'll contact you. You're at the hotel?"

Granny mumbled something once again about the girl's stupidity, how she couldn't restrain herself for even a single day. Compared to how tough she'd have it trying to make it on her own with a dhampir baby to look after, a little verbal abuse should be music to her ears. Saying she was heading out to look for the girl again, Granny took off.

"A dhampir baby? Yeah, a dhampir . . ." she muttered, the words growing fainter and fainter until they were like a whisper through the trees.

A short while later, someone called out, "D!"

The pale figure appeared between the trees in the distance. By the time the figure reached the Hunter, he could see that it was Tae.

"Granny told me what happened."

"I . . . I really was going to put up with them," the girl stammered. "No matter what they said about me. But . . . when they called the baby inside me a vampire . . ."

"It's a dhampir."

"It's the same thing to everyone else!" The tracks of tears remained on Tae's cheeks, but no sparkling beads could be seen. She'd run dry. Held captive by the Nobility for eight long years, when she finally returned home she couldn't stay even one day . . .

"What will you do?"

"Let me rest here just for tonight," Tae said, her tone firm for the first time. Her single-minded gaze met D's eyes. "Come tomorrow, I'll manage something on my own. Just until then. Please, just let me stay with you."

"Do as you like."

Tae seated herself by D's side. He dropped a blanket in her lap.

"But this is yours . . ." said the girl.

"It's not for you."

Tae gazed at the blanket and then back up at D. A tear fell from her cheek, splattering against the back of the hand that held the edge of the blanket. Her supply of mournful tears had nearly been exhausted.

"Okay," Tae said as she pulled up the blanket.

"You said you'd manage something on your own, didn't you?" D asked as he gazed straight ahead.

"Yes."

"Well, there'll be two of you soon."

Tae didn't know what to say.

"It seems dhampir children are quite considerate, although there are exceptions."

While the young man seemed as cold as ice, a faint hint of a smile skimmed across his lips. Tae watched with utter disbelief and then sheepishly touched D's chest with her pale hand. D didn't move.

"I . . . I'll try to be brave," Tae mumbled, bringing her cheek to rest next to her hand. "Good," she said after a little while. "I can hear the sound of your heart. When I was a little girl, Papa told me something. He said dhampirs didn't breathe. And so their hearts didn't beat. I honestly believed him. That the Nobility had hearts of gold and veins of crystal, and that dhampirs did, too. Now I know that's not true, though after seeing you, I sort of thought it still might be."

D said nothing.

"But I'm glad it's not. A dhampir's heart beats just like ours. Your blood is warm, too. I'm glad. My baby will be just like you, won't it?" Tae said. She was crying. And she went on crying. Her voice was full of joy. Without knowing why, Tae thought that somehow she'd get by now.

At some point the girl lapsed into the quiet breath of sleep, and D had a puzzling look in his eye as he gazed down at her. A lock of hair had fallen across her forehead. His left hand reached out and stroked it back into place. Then he raised his face and stared off into the darkness before him.

A trio of silhouettes suddenly appeared. It was Granny and the Bullow Brothers.

"I'll look after her tonight," D said.

Granny twisted her lips at that, and Clay snapped in a deep voice, "You've gotta be shitting me! Would anybody leave a girl alone with a sex fiend like you in the dead of night? Behind that iron mask of yours, you're just looking for some fast action, you bastard!"

Her eyes shifting from the girl to D, Granny said, "It just occurred to me—isn't this going to wake her up?"

D's left hand came to rest of the back of Tae's head, and then came away again quickly.

"That won't be a problem now," the Hunter told her.

"I see," Granny said with a nod. But it was unlike the nod she always gave. "I think that rather than having the two of them live in misery, it'd be better for one of them to lead a regular life. You know what the best thing to do would be," Granny said, her right hand going for the jar on her hip. "You know, my sand paintings can even picture the insides of a person. I'm going to do this," the crone said, her voice trembling. But the quavering only served to make the strength of her resolve all the more apparent.

Gently setting Tae down on the ground, the Hunter in black slowly straightened up again. "Leave her alone," he said. Though his tone didn't hold so much as a hint of a threat, it froze not only Granny, but the Frontier's greatest warriors as well. D's eyes were glowing deep red—the color of blood.

"See . . . You see that?" Granny said, the words spilling from her trembling lips. "Would you look at your face now? That's what Tae's kid will be like, too. No matter how handsome he might be born, or how much stronger than a human being, in the end he'll always show that face. And every time he does—mark my words—every time it happens, everything he's managed to build up 'til then is finished. Not just once or twice. *Every time.* How many times have you worn that face so far? How often have you had the face of a Noble?"

"Leave her alone," D repeated.

"No, I won't stop. You may be a dhampir, but you're a man. How could you know the least bit about how a woman feels?"

The bloody hue rapidly left D's eyes. Staring at Granny, his expression was calm as he said, "You're a dhampir, aren't you?"

Time seemed to stop.

Granny was mired in a perplexity she couldn't begin to conceal. "What?" she exclaimed. "What do you mean?"

"Back in the desert, Clay came to lead you and me away. But Lance and Tae he carried off asleep."

"Pure coincidence is what that is."

"There's more. Except for the first glance you caught of the marker I set up on the grave, you wouldn't look at it at all. Because it's a shape you have trouble with. And why is it that when you came here earlier looking for the girl, your shoes were white with dust but you weren't breathing hard?"

D stared at her. The silence following the question was a hundred times more fearsome than any enraged shouting could've been.

Granny shook her head feebly from side to side. "Lies," she said. "You're making this up . . ."

"I have one more piece of evidence I couldn't have made up." D dealt the coup de grace.

"What . . ."

"The hatred you have for dhampirs. Only another dhampir feels that strongly."

"Stop it!" Granny exclaimed. As she shouted, she raised her right hand high in the air. Sand billowed from between her fingers.

A shot rang out.

The crone's right hand was thrust as high as it could go, and the sand in it scattered vainly in the breeze.

As he watched D dash toward the falling crone, Bingo called out, "Clay!" His voice may have been sleepy, but his orders were sharp.

"I'm on it!" Clay replied as his massive form vanished in the direction from which the shot had come.

There was never a second round fired.

D inspected Granny's wound; it went right through her heart. It must've been the work of a firearm of some sort. While it wasn't exactly a wooden stake, surely the only reason she was still alive was because she was a dhampir.

"D—" the old woman rasped.

"Don't speak."

"Don't boss me around." Granny took a shallow breath. "Don't know who the blazes did this or why, but there's no saving me now. That's okay. Let me go. And don't you dare think about waking up the girl. I wanna go out smooth. Say, would you mind holding my hand for a bit?" And as soon as Granny said that, she grabbed hold of D's hand herself. "Come on, it's not like we've got a lot of time. Ah, just as I thought—a cold hand. That's okay. It's a dhampir's hand. There's not much anyone can do about it. Oh, it's been decades."

D looked down at her face, the paleness of which was evident even in the darkness.

"You know . . . I had a child," Granny said with a laugh. "The mother was a dhampir, so her son was bound to be one, too. That's why my man ran out on me. I must've worked ten times as hard as anyone else bringing up my boy. If he had to be a dhampir, I wanted him to at least have a good dhampir life. But in the end there wasn't anything I could do. The night before his wedding . . . he went and sank his fangs into the throat of the girl he loved and was set to marry. Cried tears of blood, I did."

Granny turned her gaze toward Tae.

"Looks pretty while she sleeps, doesn't she?" the old woman remarked. "Tonight may be the last night for that. You know, other people always used to tell me the same thing. They'd say they'd never seen anyone look so hurt and angry in their sleep. It shouldn't be that way. I never wanted her to have to go through what I did. I still don't think what I was about to do was wrong. There are dhampirs who live like you do. Well, maybe I was in the wrong after all . . ."

Suddenly, Granny's complexion became more pallid.

"Oh . . . goodbye . . . Looks like peace is mine at last," the old woman said, her head dropping sharply to one side.

D peered down at her.

"Ah, that's right," Granny said as she opened her eyes. "I forgot to ask you to say some last words to me. Don't worry, I'm not asking you to tell me you love me or anything. Just say something."

"The girl's child won't run off."

"Is that a fact?" Granny said, breaking into a smile. "Great . . . If you can guarantee me that, everything will be fine." The old woman laughed heartily, and her head lolled to one side. After that, she moved no more.

Putting his hand to her temple, D folded her wrinkled hands on her chest.

"Is she dead?" Clay asked. He was standing next to his brother again.

"What about our duel tomorrow?" Bingo asked.

"Push it back to noon," the Hunter replied. "I've got a funeral to attend."

"If we've gotta postpone it, we could make it for the same time the next day instead."

"Think your employer would want that?" D asked, gazing at Bingo. Bingo turned to Clay, but Clay looked away. "Tell him I'll be paying a call on him a little past noon," D said in a bloodcurdling tone, and then he turned to Tae.

Tomorrow the girl would have to start her life all over again. But for now, her breathing was serene as she slumbered.

At noon the next day, a black carriage set out from a funeral parlor on the edge of town. Carrying the coffin, it would typically make its way through the major streets of Barnabas, with those in mourning for the deceased walking along behind it. Relatives, friends, and acquaintances alike had a chance then to bid farewell to the departed. Apparently, the person being buried that day didn't have a peaceful death. The driver of the carriage was still a young lady, and the lone mourner in tow was a gorgeous young man in black raiment.

There were remarkably few people on the streets in the strong light of midday. Those who were there watched the lonely funeral procession suspiciously. Ordinarily, even townsfolk who had nothing to do with the deceased would join the procession—that was simply Frontier courtesy toward those who died without family around. But not a single soul did so today. The previous night, certain facts about the nature of the driver, the deceased, and the lone mourner had blown through town like a hurricane. And the woman who'd whipped up that storm had left town early that morning with her husband.

Out in the white sunlight, there was no sound save the creaking of the wheels on the black carriage as the woman and man went by. The girl had lowered a black veil over her face, and the young man held his wide-brimmed traveler's hat over his heart. An almost imperceptible wind tousled the hair of both.

Before long, the procession passed by a three-story building. In one of the rooms there, three men were looking out the window.

"Perfect timing," the lawyer Thornton said, snapping his pocket watch closed with a crisp sound. Looking back at the men behind him, he said, "The time necessary to report Granny's death, the criminal investigation, and the arrangements for the hearse were all taken into account—there's no better time than high-noon for the dead to make that final journey. Don't you think so?"

There was no reply. Bingo Bullow and Clay Bullow—two of the Frontier's greatest warriors—looked rather displeased as they stared at their employer's back.

"Statistics say that for a dhampir, doing battle in broad daylight means a 40 percent drop in combat effectiveness. Don't look so unhappy," Thornton told the brothers. "It's not like I wanted to have to do this, either. Hell, if she hadn't been the grubby little people-finder she was, I don't think I would've used her like this at all. But to be perfectly frank, this all springs from your failure to get rid of him out in the desert."

As the lawyer needled him in that sore spot, Clay shrugged his shoulders. Bingo was looking down at the floor—though, of course, he was neither deeply impressed nor conscience-stricken.

"Desert crossing or not, this job isn't done until you kill the Hunter. And until then, I don't get my due, either. See to it you kill him today for sure." With these words, Thornton shut his eyes—one had to wonder just what sort of compensation he'd requested. The lascivious and arrogant expression he wore was unique to a certain sort of person, and it spread across his face like an oily film. His plump hands lovingly massaged the back of his own neck.

Clay leaned forward a bit. The creaking of the approaching carriage had reached the second-story window.

"Well, now. This warrants full marks for effectiveness—he certainly looks like he's in pain. It would appear I haven't lost my knack for judging characters. Not only is the Hunter seeing her off at this hour, he's actually got his hat off, too. It only goes to show you can't believe all those rumors you hear about some people being heartless and cold."

The two brothers silently watched the passing carriage.

"You could take him now. Go to it," Thornton said, his voice vested with a strength that would brook no resistance.

Turning their backs on him, the pair walked toward the door.

Coming out of the building's entrance, the Bullow Brothers went right out into the street; the carriage and D continued to move along about forty feet ahead of them. The pair walked quickly. At a point about two yards from D, they slackened their pace. Neither D nor Tae turned around. Both brothers took off their hats. Holding them gently to their hearts, they followed along behind D. Now there were three mourners.

An hour later, the carriage halted at the communal cemetery out behind the same funeral parlor where its journey had begun. The gravedigger and undertaker were waiting by the hole they'd already completed. The group gathered around the grave, the coffin was lowered into the earth, and the undertaker began to recite a prayer. It was a short one. Tae chewed the words over in her mouth.

The ceremony ended, and the gravedigger began shoveling dirt back into the hole.

"Well, then," Clay said in a way that suggested the time had finally come to square accounts. "There's an open spot over that way. Let's settle this there."

"I just don't get it," Bingo said in a sleepy tone. "The night we first met, we were ready to kill you . . . But to be honest I really don't feel much like doing it now."

D started walking straight ahead. He got the feeling he heard Tae's voice.

Leaving the rows of gravestones, the trio squared off in an almost circular section thick with grass. They were ten feet apart.

"I have to thank you," said D.

"What for?" the smirking Clay replied. Making a massive leap away, he went for his harp with his right hand.

D made a dash for Bingo.

As proof that his foe had expected as much, the sleeper spat dream bubbles from his mouth. But spitting was exactly what D's left hand did, too. Strings of black blood attacked the cloud of bubbles with the suppleness of a whip, but slipped between them. The bubbles had skillfully avoided the attack.

"Good work, bro!" Clay howled. As long as Bingo was locked in battle with D, he couldn't let his deadly ultrasonic waves fly, but it looked like his older brother was doing pretty well.

Dodging the bubbles that came at him, D flung strings of blood at Bingo from his left hand. A new dream glittered into being in the sunlight to meet that attack. Every bloody thread broke against the surface of the bubble—blocked off completely. But once that bubble was gone, Bingo's expression showed agitation for the first time—his face filled with a forced vitality. Having spit up all of his dreams, the dreamer had awakened.

Using a melody of unearthly beauty to change the black shape that hung high in the air for a second like a mystic bird to dust, the younger Bullow gave a shout. Dazed, Clay then swayed unsteadily as he saw the naked steel that protruded from his brother's back. It'd dawned on him that what his harp had destroyed had merely been the Hunter's coat, just as D had raced across the ground and impaled his brother. His fingers went for the strings as his warrior training made him prepare a second attack reflexively, but then he stopped dead. D was on the far side of his brother. A split second of indecision—

As Clay stood there, a wooden needle whined through the air and sank into his forehead, dropping him. Due to the time necessary to extricate the Hunter's blade, Bingo didn't hit the ground until after his younger brother.

Two corpses lay in the white sunlight. The battle was done.

The wind blew by. For a time, D gazed at his two foes. Suddenly, he ducked as something hot whizzed over his head, followed by the delayed report of a gun. It came from the direction of the graveyard.

Crouched down and about to sprint into action, D heard a faint melody slip past his ear.

A cry of agony arose in the graveyard.

When D turned and looked down, Clay was lying there smiling. His harp trembled at the end of his outstretched hand.

"So . . . does that even the score?" Clay said, blood spurting from his forehead as he spoke.

"It was more than enough," D replied.

"Was it . . . really? Well, here's some interest on it. The guy that hired us . . . was Thornton. And that character just now . . . was another one of his killers."

"I know."

"In that case . . . let's finish this . . ."

The warrior's harp rose, then swiftly fell again.

"My luck is crap," Clay said, and then he closed his eyes.

D turned around.

Tae was standing there. That was why Clay hadn't used his harp.

The girl's face was pale with fright.

"Scared?" D asked.

"Yeah."

"Don't let your child become a Hunter."

"That'll be up to him or her," the girl replied in a trembling voice that was charged with power. "But even if my baby doesn't grow up to be a Hunter, I'll raise him or her to be like the Vampire Hunter I saw."

"It's almost time for your ride to leave," D said as he took a quick glance at the sun.

"You give me money and buy me a ticket for a coach . . . and there's nothing I can do to repay you?"

"Just see to it that I hear rumors that you're doing well."

Tae's eyes sparkled. "I'm sure you will," she said with a nod. Taking a bundle of white fabric from the bag she carried, she unfolded it. It was a tiny garment to swaddle a tiny life. "This is what I made on the sewing machine," Tae said, as if lost in reflection. "Now I have a feeling I'll be able to get by somehow. And it's all thanks to Granny. She did nothing but help me, and we weren't even kin."

"I still have business here in town," D said as he gazed at the girl's face. "Godspeed."

"You take care, too." Tae watched as he turned his black back to her and went off into the white light. Her womb was filled with the movements of the tiny life within her, and felt warm. Just as they parted, she'd seen a smile rise on D's lips. And for a long, long time after that, through days of intertwining joy and sadness, the girl would recollect how she'd been the one to put it there. She would tell the tale to her only child with a touch of pride. It was just such a smile.

Postscript

How did you enjoy this *D* novel? It's hard to believe we're already up to the sixth book. Actually, 6 is my lucky number, and if you put two more 6's after that, you wind up with *The Omen*. (Laughs) Of course, if it'd get me that kind of power, I wouldn't mind putting those extra 6's on there. (Laughs)

Well, as this is my third new postscript in a row, I thought I might talk about how the *Vampire Hunter D* series came to be. My debut as a novelist, *Demon City (Shinjuku)*, was published in September of 1982, and because it sold fairly well, the publisher asked me to get to work on another novel right away. At the time, something about vampires popped into my head as the prime book candidate—although it would be more accurate to say that I had wanted to do a story about vampires for my first book. The reason I ended up going with something else first was because the theme of vampires seemed to be much too specialized, and, up until that time, there really hadn't been a book intended for a juvenile audience that dealt with such grotesque material. Most likely, a horror tale written to illustrate the terror of the protagonist as he or she is menaced by supernatural forces would've been poorly received by young readers (males in particular). In order to avoid that pitfall, I introduced action into my debut novel. It is an indispensable element in stories for younger readers, and since I'd always liked action myself, it was almost inevitable that I'd wind up writing books like this. What's more, I decided to include more elements of science fiction in my new novel. The reason for this should be obvious: young people seem to prefer sci-fi to horror. (Although the reception horror receives may differ in this respect between Japan and America.) At that time, no one here had written a novel like *Demon City*. It proved to be the birth of what I later termed "horror action." Fortunately, it got results—and because the sales were good, the editorial staff had no complaints when I said I wanted to go with vampires.

Basically, I grew up watching movies about Japanese ghost stories; Hammer Films from England like *Horror of Dracula* and *Curse of Frankenstein*, and Universal offerings from America such as *Dracula* and *Frankenstein*. I had but one complaint about monster movies, and a wish to see it remedied. I always thought, "Instead of having these monsters and ghosts just beating the hell out of everybody non-stop, wouldn't it be great if there was a hero who had even greater strength than they did?" After all, who likes losing all the time? To be perfectly honest, my novels take a lot from the best points of horror movies. The setting of *Demon City*, where Shinjuku has been cut off from the rest of Tokyo by a massive earthquake, is very similar to that of the John Carpenter film *Escape from New York* and the Japanese manga *Violence Jack*. Also, the protagonist of Vampire Hunter D is reminiscent of the titular character of the Hammer Films movie Captain Kronos—Vampire Hunter (though D is about ten thousand times more handsome than the actor who played the lead in that movie (laughs)). And D's also naturally patterned after the leading character of the classic *Horror of Dracula*, who scared the life out of me when I was nine or ten— Count Dracula, as portrayed by Christopher Lee. Despite the fact that I found Count Dracula to be a creature that should obviously be destroyed, and regardless of the fact that at the time I was more enthralled with Peter Cushing's role of Van Helsing than I was with the vampire he kills, the utter coolness of Count Dracula dressed in black and standing at the entrance to some beautiful woman's room was something I couldn't overlook simply because he was the villain—it had a great impact on me. D's hallmarks—being distant, tall, and garbed in black—were all traits borrowed from Lee's Dracula. In other words, you could say D is like *Horror of Dracula* embracing the trappings of *Captain Kronos*.

Having the hero be a man of peerless beauty wasn't actually a matter of my own personal tastes, nor was it a ploy to secure female readers—it was to make his coolness perfect and complete. Furthermore, D is burdened with the fate of being a dhampir—a human/vampire half-breed. Until now, I've always said the reason for this was because a purely human hero would've been boring, and also because having D be both human and vampire—but shunned by both sides—only served to intensify his tragic nature. But the simple truth is that I really wanted to try and give him some of the wonderful vampire characteristics from Lee's excellent portrayal of Dracula. And that's how D was born.

Next time, I'll try to touch on D's world and his partner after a fashion, "the left hand."

Pilgrimage of the Sacred and the Profane is one of the great books in the series as far as the color and development of the cast of characters are concerned. In particular, the two heavies were my favorite characters, and I still regret only using them in this one volume—it seems like such a waste. Incidentally, there's a scene near the end that's borrowed from a certain American movie, and I wonder if my English-speaking readers will know what film that is. No one in Japan ever caught it.

Hideyuki Kikuchi
June 28, 2006
while watching *Billy the Kid versus Dracula*

VAMPIRE HUNTER D

CONTINUES

This omnibus collects volumes 4, 5, and 6 of *Vampire Hunter D*. Here is the full list of *Vampire Hunter D* volumes published by Dark Horse Books to date:

ABOUT THE AUTHOR

Hideyuki Kikuchi was born in Chiba, Japan in 1949. He attended the prestigious Aoyama University and wrote his first novel, *Demon City Shinjuku*, in 1982. Over the past two decades, Kikuchi has written many novels of weird fiction blending elements of horror, science fiction, and fantasy, working in the tradition of occidental writers like Fritz Leiber, Robert Bloch, H. P. Lovecraft, and Stephen King. Many live-action and anime works in 1980s and 1990s Japan were based on Kikuchi's novels.

ABOUT THE ILLUSTRATOR

Yoshitaka Amano was born in Shizuoka, Japan in 1952. Recruited as a character designer by the legendary anime studio Tatsunoko at age 15, he created the look of many notable anime, including *Gatchaman*, *Genesis Climber Mospeada* (which in the US became the third part of *Robotech*), and *The Angel's Egg*, an experimental film by future *Ghost in the Shell* director Mamoru Oshii. An independent commercial illustrator since the 1980s, Amano became world famous through his design of the first ten *Final Fantasy* games. Having entered the fine arts world in the preceding decade, in 1997 Amano had his first exhibition in New York, bringing him into contact with American comics through collaborations with Neil Gaiman (*The Sandman: The Dream Hunters*) and Greg Rucka (*Elektra and Wolverine: The Redeemer*). Dark Horse has published over 40 books illustrated by Amano, including his first original novel *Deva Zan*, as well as the Eisner-nominated *Yoshitaka Amano: Beyond the Fantasy–The Illustrated Biography* by Florent Gorges.

VAMPIRE HUNTER D OMNIBUS BOOK TWO
© Hideyuki Kikuchi, 2022. Originally published in Japan in 1986, 1988 by ASAHI SONORAMA Co.
English translation copyright © 2022 by Dark Horse Books.

Cover art by Yoshitaka Amano
English translation by Kevin Leahy
Book Design by Kathleen Barnett

Published by
Dark Horse Books
A division of Dark Horse Comics LLC
10956 SE Main Street
Milwaukie, OR 97222
DarkHorse.com

First Dark Horse Books edition: August 2022
eBook ISBN 978-1-50673-189-6
ISBN 978-1-50673-187-2
10 9 8 7 6 5 4 3 2 1
Printed in the United States of America